ARCANE ART
and
FAMILIARS

-BOXSET-
MAGGIE SHAW

CONTENTS

FAMILIAR MAGIC

Chapter 1	3
Chapter 2	11
Chapter 3	19
Chapter 4	31
Chapter 5	43
Chapter 6	55
Chapter 7	67
Chapter 8	77
Chapter 9	87
Chapter 10	99
Chapter 11	109
Chapter 12	121
Chapter 13	131

FAMILIAR LOVE

Chapter 1	143
Chapter 2	153
Chapter 3	163
Chapter 4	173
Chapter 5	181
Chapter 6	193
Chapter 7	207
Chapter 8	217
Chapter 9	229
Chapter 10	245
Chapter 11	253
Chapter 12	263
Chapter 13	273

FAMILIAR FATE

Chapter 1   289
Chapter 2   307
Chapter 3   323
Chapter 4   337
Chapter 5   351
Chapter 6   361
Chapter 7   379
Chapter 8   395
Chapter 9   405
Chapter 10   421

FAMILIAR DESTINY

Chapter 1   437
Chapter 2   455
Chapter 3   469
Chapter 4   487
Chapter 5   503
Chapter 6   519
Chapter 7   539
Chapter 8   559
Epilogue   571

FAMILIAR MAGIC

MAGGIE SHAW

FAMILIAR MAGIC

CHAPTER
ONE

Sage.

I shoved a piece of candy into my mouth, a nervous habit that never got old. My gaze dragged up to the sound of my best friend, Evie Black, cackling loudly.

Her laughter was as familiar and comforting as the worn edges of our dorm room, like a cozy blanket made of inside jokes and shared memories. Unable to resist, I chuckled along, the sound spilling into the eclectic space we'd called home for five long years.

"Earth to Sage! Are you lost in the candy dimension again?" Evie teased.

"No, just tangled in my thoughts," I admitted, offering a small, rueful smile.

Shifting in my seat, I flicked a strand of my long, dark hair over my shoulder, the blue highlights catching the dim light and making me feel like a mermaid out of water. I was happy with the outfit I'd chosen for today. A stylish blend of bohemian chic with a witchy twist—a flowy, black blouse adorned with constellations, paired with high-waisted jeans and ankle boots.

"I can't believe graduation is tonight!" Evie squealed. "I'm getting nervous." She put her hand over her belly as though that would help her nerves, then leaned back against her chair. Unlike me, Evie liked to be casual. She was dressed in a graphic tee and ripped jeans. Her jet-black hair stopped above her shoulders in an edgy bob style. "Can you believe it?"

"Hardly." I sighed heavily and glanced around, wanting to imprint these final moments into my mind forever. Our room was a physical interpretation of the lives we'd shared together. The walls were plastered with posters of magical boy bands and photos of us through the years, documenting our transformation from awkward first year students to slightly less awkward fifth years.

Fairy lights were strung across the ceiling, twinkling over the mismatched furniture.

"It feels like just yesterday we were freshmen, scared of our own shadows—or at least I was," I said, remembering the days when I jumped at the sight of my own reflection in the mirror.

Evie had never been like that, though. She'd always had this air about her, a confidence I admired and maybe even envied a little.

"Only because my shadow can turn into a freaking dragon!" She laughed, her humor as potent as her potions.

I took a deep breath, the weight of my decision pressing down on me like a spell gone heavy. "Evie, I've been thinking that I'll go back home after graduation."

Her eyebrows knitted together. "Back? As in... to Emberwick Crossing?"

My childhood home...

"Yep." I chewed on my lower lip. "It's time, you know? Plus, I haven't been home in years and I can't put my finger on it exactly, but there's something calling me there. I can't ignore it."

Her expression softened. "You're brave to make that choice, Sage. And, hey, if you ever need any back-up, I've got a cauldron and you know I'm not afraid to use it."

"Thanks, Evie," I said, my voice thick with emotion. "I just hope I'm doing the right thing. Leaving here is like stepping off the edge of a cliff."

I gulped at the air, trying to regain my composure. Up until this point, I'd been pretending that my life here at the Arcane Arts School would go one forever. But now I had to face the fact that University was coming to an end, and I had a home to return to.

"You'll be fine," Evie said with a grin, digging her hand into my candy bag and finding the purple sweets she'd been looking for. "Seventh-level magic isn't given to just anyone, you know. You're meant for great things."

I shook my head. Everyone, including Evie, had all these expectations of me. How was I ever going to live up to the witch they all thought I could be when I didn't even want to face an empty house in the suburbs alone?

"Or spectacular failures..." I grumped, sagging in my seat.

The truth was, I'd miss everything about this place—the late-night study sessions and the spellwork sessions. The comfort of having Evie just a broomstick ride away, and of course, the High Witch, my mentor.

Evie gave my hand a squeeze. "And no matter where you go, I'll always be a crystal ball phone call away."

"Promise?" I asked, holding her gaze even though I knew from the burning in my eyes, she'd be able to see the tears I couldn't hold back.

"Promise." Evie sat up, changing the subject to lighten the mood. "Now, where did I leave my cap and gown?"

My best friend jumped out of her seat and rummaged around our cluttered dorm room, tossing clothes and spellbooks in the air as she searched for her graduation regalia. I adjusted the moonstone circlet in my hair, trying to ignore the swarm of nerves in my stomach.

Today was the day I'd been dreading all year. Our commencement ceremony. We'd each be assigned a role in the wider magical community. My future was balanced on a dagger's edge. Would I measure up to the expectations placed on a seventh-level witch, or would I fail and dishonor my parents' memory?

"Aha! Found it!" Evie emerged triumphantly from the closet, cap and gown in hand. She haphazardly threw them on. "Let's go see what destiny has in store for us."

"Okay." I nodded, my throat tight. I put on my own ugly cap and gown over my outfit, then we left our room and made our way across the quadrangle where the other graduates were assembling.

The ceremony was held in the Great Hall, its vaulted ceilings draped in gossamer and glowing with ethereal light. The High Witch, Ingrid Nightspire, presided from an onyx throne. She was dressed in regal, embroidered robes that shimmered like the night sky. Her strange violet stare settled on me as I took my place among the other students.

My chest tightened, and there was a shift inside my heart as though my magic knew something was coming, but I couldn't understand what it was.

One by one, Ingrid called each graduate forward and proclaimed their assignment. My stress built until I thought I'd shake apart. What great things did she see in my future? Or had she deemed me unworthy?

"Sage Holland," the High Witch's voice rang out in the Great Hall, beckoning me forward.

I managed to get to my feet and make my way over to her, only to stumble up the dais. My face burst into a hot, embarrassed blush, but I righted myself and lifted my chin.

The High Witch reached out her hand and smiled as I took it. "Your gifts are rare and valuable, Sage. I expect you to use them in service to our world." She then placed a hand on my shoulder. "You will take your place as my new assistant."

I gasped loudly, shock coursing through me as eager whispers broke out among the crowd. Me, the High Witch's right hand? It was an esteemed position and more than I'd ever dreamed possible.

I curtsied deeply, focusing on not falling over. "I am honored, High Witch. I won't fail you."

Ingrid gave a slight nod, shadows flickering across her face. "See that you don't."

As I descended the dais on trembling legs, my elation transitioned into a strange sort of sadness. I wished more than anything that my parents could be here to witness the culmination of all my hard work at university.

Even though they were gone, sometimes I could sense their presence, but maybe that was just wishful thinking. But I wished it wasn't. When I closed my eyes, I could feel their love and pride enveloping me. I silently promised to make them proud, to honor their memory with every spell I cast.

After the ceremony, I found Evie in the crowd. She threw her arms around me and squealed with happiness. "I can't believe it!" she exclaimed. "Assistant to the High Witch. You're moving up in the world."

I returned her hug fiercely. "I'll miss you. Promise you'll visit?"

"Wild hippogriffs couldn't keep me away." Evie laughed.

Arm in arm, we left the hall, heading out into the moonlit grounds. A wave of sadness washed over me, and I had to blink back the hot tears that filled my eyes. This beautiful place had been our home for so long, and everything was changing.

Emotion constricted my throat. Then a small meow pierced the silence. I stopped in my tracks and stared down at the stone path before me. There sat a black cat, its bright yellow eyes glinting with intelligence. The cat's posture was prim and perfect and seemed almost human-level alert.

"Greetings, Sage," the cat said in a raspy female voice. "I am Agatha, your new familiar."

My jaw dropped as I stared at the talking feline. Familiars

were gifted at graduation, but I hadn't expected mine to be so beautiful.

Agatha snickered, a rough purring sound. "Surprised? I haven't always been a cat, you know. Once I was a powerful witch, and I transferred my spirit into this form. But that's a tale for another time."

I gulped down the lump in my throat. Wow. I had been thinking about how much I missed my parents, and now it seemed that I'd inherited a grandmother of sorts.

"It's nice to meet you, Agatha." I smiled and offered the cat my hand to sniff, not quite sure what the protocol was.

Agatha lifted her nose in refusal.

Evie snorted with laughter and said in an old-lady voice, "I expect treats daily, ear scratches, and a live sacrifice on occasion. A rat or small bird will do."

I shot her a mock scowl before scooping up my new cat. Her fur was soft and warm against my skin as I rubbed my cheek against her. Yes, we would be fast friends, I was sure.

With Evie by my side and my new companion perched on my shoulder, I left behind the only home I'd known for the past five years to return to Emberwick Crossing. The place of my birth, and my parents' home.

CHAPTER
TWO

Gliding just above the forest path on my broomstick, I steered my way through the ancient trees that reached toward the sky. Their leaves rustled with the secrets of old, and the crisp, clean air around me filled my lungs.

The suitcase I'd tied securely behind me swayed gently as we passed over a carpet of moss and ferns. The earthy scents of rich soil and pine filled the air, stirring memories of my childhood spent playing hide and seek among these towering trunks, where I was certain fairies and spirits lurked just out of sight.

I grinned as I flew, memories of magical classes flashing

through my mind. In some of the early years we'd learned about creatures of light. Mischievous sprites and mystical fairies, regal creatures of immense magic.

Agatha was perched on the front of the broomstick, her tail flicking contentedly as we moved. I'd spent hours in the forest as a child, gathering herbs and flowers for my mother's potions and remedies. At night, the groves were lit by glow-bugs casting an ethereal shine under the moonlight.

I couldn't believe my classroom learning was done. There had been so much safety in learning within the walls of the Arcane Arts Academy. We'd blown things up, cast the wrong spells, and singed the hair off a classroom's eyebrows.

Learning magic, especially physical magic, had been daunting, but I'd loved it. I was the only one of my friends who'd risen to level seven magic and succeeded. But now I'd be expected to cast my spells without a safety net, and the idea of that made the hairs on my neck prickle with unease.

Agatha nudged my hand, breaking my reverie. "It's good to be back, isn't it?"

I smiled though my heart was aching in the strangest way. "Yes. It feels like I just left, somehow."

We crested a hill, and Emberwick Crossing appeared, nestled amongst the trees. It was a quaint, picturesque town. A hidden gem, known only to the magical community. We flew over Main Street, lined with old-fashioned shops and cafes, their storefronts adorned with colorful awnings and intricately carved wooden signs. The buildings were constructed of honey-colored brick and stone, with ivy and flowering vines climbing their facades. Wide sidewalks and gas-lit streetlamps dotted the landscape. In the center of town, a grand marble fountain depicting mythical creatures stood as a gathering place for locals and a symbol of the community's magical heritage.

Agatha and I landed on the lawn in front of my childhood home, my breath catching at the sight.

It was a modest two-story house with a wraparound porch. My parents had painted the exterior light blue with white trim, and it was topped with a slate-gray roof. The porch was adorned with a swing and hanging ferns that had long given up the ghost. Their dry and brown tendrils made my heart sad and I reached out to put a little magical life back into them.

Mom had landscaped the front yard neatly with colorful flower beds. Inside, the house featured hardwood floors, faded area rugs, and an eclectic mix of vintage and modern furniture. The walls were painted in shades of green and blue, and the windows were framed by sheer curtains. The living room boasted a large stone fireplace and built-in bookshelves filled with magical tomes and family photos.

The rusted iron gate squealed in protest as I pushed it open. With Agatha at my heels, I crossed the overgrown yard. There was a hidden key, but I used my magic to open the front door, the protection spells programmed and linked to my bloodlines.

The door swung open, and I stepped inside, looking around at the home I hadn't seen in too long. Dust motes danced in beams of moonlight. I reached for the light switch and flicked it on with a click.

"Welcome home, Sage," Agatha said softly as we both stared around the well-lit room.

I stepped further into the cottage, memories washing over me. The sitting room was just as I remembered it—two plush armchairs angled towards the fireplace, shelves of leather-bound books I had spent hours reading.

I sighed. "It's like I'm fifteen again."

Agatha padded along beside me, her yellow eyes taking everything in. "It must be strange being back after so long. Are you okay?"

I was so grateful in that moment for my familiar. I couldn't even imagine how I'd be feeling here, alone. Instead, I had someone to chat to who wouldn't judge me.

"I think so." I ran my fingers over the back of an armchair, leaving trails in the dust. "It's funny... I felt so lost and small in this house after my parents died. Now I just feel sad."

Agatha nudged my leg and purred, a sound that was more reassuring than I expected.

I wandered through the rest of the first floor, the groan of the floorboards under my feet an ever-present reminder of how old the cottage was. The kitchen had faded yellow walls and an old-fashioned round wooden table.

The study where my dad would read the newspaper every morning sat too quiet. The formal dining room we only used on holidays was no longer clean or shiny, my mother's magic fading away.

I took a short breath and cast my first spell, a dust collector. I picked up an empty glass jar left on the counter and waved my hand over the opening. In a moment, the glass glowed, and I grinned. No dusting or vacuuming for me.

I lifted the jar in the air and a soft, sucking noise filled the room as the container collected the dirt, dust, and grime from the room. It had been years since anyone had stepped foot into the house, and the air smelled clogged and thick.

Each room unlocked memories I'd tucked away in the deep recesses of my heart. My mother baking snickerdoodles, my father patiently helping me with math homework. I took my dust collector jar into every room I navigated, lifting the blanket of age and dirt from my parents' beloved home.

Upstairs, I paused outside my childhood bedroom. The purple walls still had my favorite band and movie posters taped to them. I took a breath before crossing the threshold. My bed was neatly made, pillows plumped as if I'd never left. The bookshelves were still stuffed with fantasy novels, crystals and geodes I had collected over the years.

I'd had the perfect childhood and a beautiful, safe home in which to grow up.

Tears stung my eyes as I sat on the edge of the bed, the springs squeaking in protest. A cloud of dust rose around me, and once again, I lifted the jar, sucking in the dirt. My mother would be appalled to know her home lay in such filth, but it wouldn't take me long to whip this place into shape.

Speaking of... I stood up and cast a spell to remake the bed with fresh sheets and pillows and blankets. Looking around, I wrinkled my nose at the teen angst purple, but putting that job aside for the moment. I'd design a whole new décor for the house soon, but I wanted to live in it first. To wallow in my memories before I changed anything else.

Agatha jumped up beside me on the bed. "Are you sure you're okay? Being back here, back home after all this time, is surely a lot to deal with."

I scratched her head absently. "I think so. It hurts, but in a good way." I lay back on the pillows and closed my eyes. "I wasn't sure I wanted to come back. I think I was afraid of what would be here, and how I'd feel. But now that I am... I'm just so glad to be home."

The next few hours were spent using the dust collector jar and my physical magic to give the house a proper cleaning. I changed all the beds and mopped the floors.

A lot of the lights needed new globes, so I fixed all that as well. When I finally crawled into my old bed to rest, I was exhausted but happy.

I was home, and the smell of my mother's lavender now lingered in the air. Why had I put off coming here for so long? This was the last place my parents had lived, and even now I could feel their love surrounding me.

There was no way I was going anywhere else now.

CHAPTER

THREE

I was sitting on the old, comfy sofa, tracing the delicate ripples of a new spell on an ancient scroll when Agatha's sharp yowl snapped me back into the present. "Sage, look!" she urged from her place on the window ledge.

"Ugh, not now. I'm onto something with this—" My protests died as I followed her gaze out the front window.

"Something wicked lurks in this town," Agatha said, peering outside.

I walked over to stand beside her, and what I saw made every hair on my arms stand on end. A shadowy figure cut across the sky, its form a miasma of darkness, tendrils of inky blackness snaking behind it.

I pressed my hand to the cold glass panel as I leaned forward even more. "Agatha, what is that?" I whispered, though I wasn't sure I wanted to know.

"Evil," she hissed, flattening her ears against her head. "Pure and simple."

"But why is it here?" We'd never had any problems with evil entities before. Not that I knew of, anyway.

She lashed her tail and answered like a fortune teller. "An ancient evil seeking to feed on fear and despair. We must stop it before it grows stronger."

My skin prickled with an unnatural chill. I had to get closer. Agatha hopped on my shoulder, and together we stepped through the side door and stood outside. I shivered. The air was tinged with a magical charge, and I wasn't surprised, considering what was flying above our heads. The entity swooped low, and a cold wave passed through me, goosebumps erupting across my skin—a sure sign of malevolence nearby.

"Chaos incarnate," Agatha mumbled, watching as the dark force sent newspapers flying and rattled the windows of the sleepy neighborhood.

Screams and shouts filled the air as residents emerged from their homes, expressions wide with fear.

"Agatha, we've got to do something." I was already reaching for my power, the perceptible tingle of magic at my fingertips.

Agatha nodded, her yellow eyes sharp. "Yes. This entity... it must be stopped. But how, Sage? This is no ordinary dark magic."

I swallowed hard, feeling the stress in her words. "We need to investigate further, don't we, Agatha?"

"Be warned," she said, her voice taking on the timbre of ancient knowledge. "These entities feed on negative emotions. Their strength grows with each act of terror they cause."

"Like parasites," I said, a tremor in my voice as my own fear ratcheted up a notch.

"They're old as magic itself," Agatha went on. "Older than any witch or warlock. They slip through the cracks of our world, seeking destruction."

"Let's make sure this one doesn't get what it wants." I squared my shoulders, feeling the need to do something. But what?

Agatha jumped to the ground with ease and stared up at me. "Your magic is rare, Sage. Your spells could be the key to destroying it, but you must consult the High Witch first."

She was right. And although my fingers itched to throw some magic at the entity that I could so clearly see, I had no idea how to destroy it. Forcing myself to take a breath, I tried to remain calm. "Let's contact her right away then. We don't want to waste any more time."

This was about more than just proving myself to the High Witch, this attack on my town was personal. I could feel my resolve solidify within as I made a promise to myself that I would unearth the truth and safeguard the magical world from this encroaching darkness.

I stepped further away from the house and into the cool embrace of nightfall, the cobblestone path leading away from my home. A feeling of purpose propelled me toward town, under a sky painted with bruised purples and oranges as the sun retreated.

"Going somewhere?" The male voice snagged my attention, and I froze.

I turned to find Bradley "Brad" Adams, leaning casually against the white picket fence that bordered his parents' house.

He hadn't changed much, with the same spiky crown of dark brown hair and wide-set blue eyes that seemed to hold entire oceans. His tall frame was clad in a simple plaid shirt that hugged his well-built torso, sleeves rolled up to the elbows revealing forearms etched with veins. A builder's arms, with dark jeans and scuffed boots.

"Brad." My heart lurched.

"Hey, Sage. It's been too long." He smiled, pushing off the fence.

"Way too long." An odd sensation of warmth bloomed within my chest.

Agatha cleared her throat pointedly beside me.

"Ah, right. Brad, this is Agatha, my familiar." I gestured at the sleek black cat, whose yellow stare assessed Brad critically.

Brad tilted his head at the feline. "Nice to meet you, Agatha. Any friend of Sage's is a friend of mine."

"What are you doing here?" I asked, gesturing at the house that shared a fence with mine.

"Well, I've been working as a magical architect and I bought this place from my folks," Brad said, his face shining with pride. "Using my elemental manipulation to create and shape structures. It's been a wild ride, but I love it."

I nodded, impressed by his qualifications. "That sounds

incredible. I always knew you'd do something amazing with your powers."

"Thanks, Sage. That means a lot coming from you." His smile softened, and I felt a flutter in my stomach that I hadn't felt in a very long time. "So, what about you? What have you been up to all these years?"

"I've been at the Institute for the Arcane Arts. Spent the last few years honing my magical talents, especially in interior design magic and crystal ball scrying. I just graduated a few days ago."

"Interior design magic, huh?" Brad raised an eyebrow, a smile lifting his full, sensual lips. "Guess that means you can make any space look enchanting, just like yourself."

Heat rushed to my cheeks. "Flatterer."

"Just calling it like I see it." He winked, and I swear my heart did a backflip.

Agatha rolled her eyes. "Oh, please. If you two are going to keep making googly eyes at each other, I'm going to hack up a hairball."

I shot her a glare, but Brad just laughed. "Feisty one, isn't she?"

Smiling, I shook my head. "You have no idea. But seriously, it's great to see you again, Brad. I've missed you... you know, our friendship."

I tried not to blush further, but I was bumbling over my words like an idiot. Brad and I had always been friends. He was the boy next door, quite literally.

"Me too, Sage." His voice lowered, and he took a step closer. "Maybe we could catch up some more over dinner? I know a place that serves the best pasta in town."

My heart raced at the thought of spending more time with him. "I'd like that."

While we stood there, grinning at each other like two loons, I knew coming home had been the right decision. Everything was going to be okay.

Agatha snorted, her gaze lingering on Brad before turning away. "We need to focus on the evil, Sage. Not dating."

"Actually, I might be able to help with that," Brad said, his expression turning serious. "There have been rumors around town... tales of a powerful warlock acting in the shadows. Someone not just dabbling in dark magic, but fully embodying it."

"Could it be related to what we've seen tonight?" I asked.

"Perhaps." Brad's expression darkened. "I bought this place when my folks retired. Thought I'd stay close to where the magic is, you know? And since then, I've heard things, felt disturbances in the natural balance of the town."

I looked up at the sky, where the last vestige of daylight clung desperately to the horizon, and shivered—not from fear, but from a strange anticipation.

"Brad, if this warlock is behind the evil entity, they might also know what happened to my parents." I whispered the last syllables, almost afraid to put the hope out there, speaking it aloud. The weight of years was in those words.

"Then you're going to need all the help you can get," he said with a nod and the crossing of his arms over his chest. "Count me in."

"Thank you, Brad. That would be great." Unexpected gratitude filled my voice.

A dog barked nervously in the distance, a sound that ricocheted through the uneasiness settling over our small town.

I glanced over at Agatha, who gave me an encouraging nod.

"There's something I should tell you," I began, turning back to Brad. "I'm not just passing through. I've taken a position as assistant to the High Witch herself."

Brad's eyes widened. "No way! That's huge, Sage. You must be something special for her to take you on."

I smiled, warmed by his faith in me. "Let's just say my particular talents intrigued her, and I want to learn as much as I can. I'm hoping she can teach me more advanced magic. Things I'll need to face whatever's coming."

"Well, it sounds like you're on the right path," Brad said. "And for what it's worth, I think I remember an ancient text at the library that may shed some light on dark entities. I can try to track it down for you."

"That would be amazing. Thank you."

I couldn't help but want to show him how much I appreciated his help. Without my parents, I was at a loss for people I trusted, so I stepped forward and awkwardly leaned forward, wrapping my arms around him in a grateful hug. Brad tensed in surprise before relaxing into the embrace. When we pulled apart, the air between us was sizzling with a new sort of magic.

I took a deep breath, trying to steady my stupid hormones. "Right now, I need to speak with Ingrid, see if she knows anything about a rogue warlock in the area. Will you let me know if you find anything?"

"You know I will," Brad promised.

As I turned to leave, his voice stopped me. "Sage, wait."

I glanced back, raising an eyebrow. "What's up?"

He rubbed the back of his neck, a telltale sign of nervousness. "Just... be careful, okay? I know you're a badass witch and all, but this feels different somehow. Dangerous."

A smirk tugged at my lips. "Ha! Where's the fun in being careful?"

Brad rolled his eyes, but a smile played on his face. "I'm serious. Promise me you'll watch your back."

"I promise." I held up my hand in a mock scout's honor. "Or Agatha will watch if for me. Either way, I really need to go. Catch you later, Brad."

I walked away with a smile on my lips, but he was right. This was different. The dark power that was rising all around us made it feel like something big was coming. Something that could destroy everything.

I pushed the thought aside. One problem at a time. First, I needed to talk to Ingrid. See if she had any idea what we were dealing with. Then, I could worry about the impending doom looming over us all.

Agatha and I went back inside the house, where I sat on a sofa in the living room, and Agatha jumped up next to me.

"Any advice?" I asked.

"Young witch, when have I ever not had advice?" Agatha purred from her cushioned spot on the sofa. Her yellow eyes held a depth of wisdom that always comforted me.

"Okay, shoot," I said, trying to keep my tone light even with the churning in my stomach.

"First, Sage, remember that evil feeds off fear and misery. It's like catnip for the malevolent." She flicked her tail, her feline features dead serious. "You mustn't let it be aware of your apprehension because thatwill only make it stronger."

I nodded, absorbing her words. "Got it. Fear is food. Don't be a buffet."

"Exactly." Agatha's whiskers twitched in approval. "Now, about this entity... You felt it before you saw it, didn't you?"

"Goosebumps galore," I confirmed. "Felt like I'd plunged into an ice bath with my clothes on."

"Your senses are sharp, my girl. Trust them. They'll guide you to the heart of this darkness." Agatha's voice was firm, instilling confidence within me.

I could do this with her help.

"Thanks, Agatha. I just wish I knew why this feels personal somehow, like it's linked to my parents or something." The words spilled out before I could stop them, raw and revealing.

"Your parents' passing was tragic," Agatha acknowledged, her tone softer now. "Yet, answers may lie where we least expect them. This evil—perhaps it's a piece of a larger puzzle."

"True... A puzzle with missing edges and a picture of 'Here Be Monsters'," I joked, but worry gnawed at me. "Do you really think it might know something about what happened to them?"

I grabbed a pillow and hugged it in my lap, the scent of age and dust lingering in the air.

"Perhaps," Agatha said, settling onto her pillow even more. "Knowledge is power in our world. If this entity possesses such knowledge, it won't part with it easily."

I sighed. "Well, I'm not backing down. Not when there's a chance for answers." My parents' deaths still haunted me, and if this new thing could help me solve the riddle, I'd do anything to get that information.

"Brave and relentless as ever. Just tread sensibly, Sage. Evil is most dangerous when cornered," Agatha warned.

"I understand. Guess I'll start by seeing what Ingrid thinks."

"Smart girl," she said, curling up into a ball. "And while you do that, I'll meditate on the matter. Perhaps the spirits will be chatty today."

"Let's hope they're more gossip than cryptic," I said with a small smile. "Thanks, Agatha. For everything."

"Always, young witch." Agatha closed her eyes, already slipping into her trance.

I grabbed my jacket from the coat hook in the foyer and opened the front door. When I reached for my broomstick, it was gone. Strange. Instead of seeking the High Witch's counsel in person, I tried to call her on my cell phone but only got her voicemail and left a message. I'd wait until I heard back from her for further instructions.

CHAPTER
FOUR

I nudged the couch a smidge to the left, then stepped back to survey the room. Agatha, perched on the windowsill, followed my gaze.

"My mom would've loved this," I said, staring out at the newly rearranged space. My fingers trailed over a tapestry that shimmered with threads of my memories—birthday parties, scraped knees, and bedtime stories.

"Your folks had taste, young lady." Agatha yawned, her yellow gaze reflecting the afternoon sun. "Though, I bet they never imagined their living room would double as a witch's workshop."

I shrugged, feeling the magic hum in the newly arranged space. Maybe not, although part of me hoped that my mother would approve.

Opening my laptop, I began working on a new website for my magical interior design business specializing in customizing spaces to enhance the magical flow and wellbeing of its occupants. "Mystical Motifs" was now officially in business, and I couldn't wait to start enchanting homes with more than just throw pillows and mood lighting. The skill was passed down to me from my ancestors, who were renowned for their abilities to infuse magic into everyday objects.

"Got your spiel down?" Agatha asked, hopping down to weave between my legs.

"Yes! 'Let Sage Holland revitalize your domicile with charms and chic decor to soothe your soul.' Kinda catchy, don't you think?"

"Sure beats 'Sage will fix your drab pad.'" Agatha yawned.

Before I could laugh at the rather catchy phrase, my phone buzzed with an arcane pulse. A rune glowed on the screen—a sure sign of a secure call. Only one person used that kind of encryption: Ingrid Nightspire, the High Witch herself.

Shit. Breathe.

"Hello?" I answered, trying not to sound like I was nervous, which I was.

"Sage, listen carefully," Ingrid said, her voice crackling with urgency. "I have concerns about Amara Black. I need you to keep an eye on her."

"Amara Black?" I frowned. That was Evie's mom. "Are you sure?" Amara was sweet, cool, and very powerful.

"Very. I suspect that woman might be causing the havoc in the community," she said.

"Havoc?" I repeated, my mind reeling. Amara Black had always seemed like the epitome of a protective mother to me. "What kind of harm are we talking about here?"

Ingrid's sigh hissed through the phone. "I can't divulge all the details yet but trust me when I say it's serious. Keep your eyes peeled for anything suspicious, and report back to me immediately if you notice anything out of the ordinary."

"Got it," I said, my stomach twisting into knots. "I'll do my best to uncover whatever the hell Amara's up to."

"Good. And, Sage?" Ingrid's voice softened a touch. "Be alert. We don't know what she's capable of. And this is top secret, understood? You cannot tell anyone. Not even Evie."

"Understood," I said solemnly. "I have another matter to discuss with you, High Witch."

"Go on," Ingrid prompted, her tone still carrying the weight of authority.

"There's an evil entity at Emberwick Crossing. It's causing trouble, attacking people."

"An evil force...how very interesting." There was a rustle, like Ingrid was taking notes. "I'll look into this matter personally. But, Sage, for now, focus on Amara Black. Do not engage with this entity."

"Okay," I replied, though curiosity gnawed at me. "But—"

"No buts, Sage. Leave it to me and focus on your assignment. Keep a watchful eye on Amara and stay safe."

I sagged, disappointed with her instructions. "Okay, High Witch. Will do."

"Good. I'm counting on you, Sage. Stay vigilant."

The line went dead with an ominous click, leaving me with an impression of foreboding and the lingering stench of ozone from the magical call.

Amara Black, a threat to the community? It seemed impossible, but if Ingrid was concerned, I couldn't ignore it. Plus, it was my job to do what the High Witch instructed.

"Well, shit." I shoved my phone back into my pocket. "Looks like I've got some spying to do."

Agatha leaped onto the counter, her stare narrowed. "Spying on Evie's mom? That's going to cause a rift with you and Evie, Sage."

"No, it won't, because I won't tell her," I said, trying to play it cool despite the unease prickling my scalp. "Orders from the top, Agatha. Can't exactly tell the High Witch no, can I?"

The cat snorted, her tail twitching. "Just don't get caught, or Evie will have your head on a platter."

"I know."

Investigating my best friend's mother felt like a betrayal, but if Amara was up to something nefarious, I had no choice but to find out what was going on. The safety of the magical community came first, even if it meant risking my friendship with Evie.

What could Amara be doing that had Ingrid so worried? And how the hell was I supposed to uncover her secrets without tipping her off?

I stood up and stretched a little. "Time to see what skeletons Amara Black has hidden in her closet."

Agatha meowed. "Crystal ball magic?"

"Yep. Guess my scrying skills are about to get a workout." It was a better idea than going over to their house and looking through her actual closets.

"This sucks," I grumbled, running a hand through my blue highlighted hair. "Evie will be so mad at me if she finds out. She'd flip if she knew her mom was under surveillance by witches."

"Best keep mum about that," Agatha advised with a regal nod of her head. "Revealing the truth could be dangerous for everyone involved."

I reached out and scratched behind her ears gently. "Looks like it's just you and me on this one, Agatha."

So we officially had a plan: watch Amara Black and pretend everything was peachy with Evie. All while an unknown evil lurked in the shadows, and I wasn't allowed to do anything about it. Easy. No pressure.

"So now what?" Agatha asked.

"I get out my crystal ball," I said, then marched into my bedroom to find it. Agatha, my shadow followed, as always.

The crystal ball sat atop an antique stand of my grandmother's, nestled between two stacks of grimoires on my oak desk. I pulled the heavy velvet drapes shut over my window to dim the room, leaving only the soft light from a few candles that I lit with a quick spell. My fingers traced the smooth, cool glass as I settled onto the chair cushion in front of it. Agatha hopped onto the bed to watch me.

I wriggled my fingers and tried to smooth the anxiety from my heart. "Okay, Agatha, let's see what we're dealing with." It didn't feel right to spy on someone like Evie's mom, but what choice did I have?

"Be cautious, Sage. You know how this magic can drain witches," Agatha warned.

"Relax, I've got this." I inhaled deeply and raised my hands. "Show me Amara Black."

I gazed into the crystal ball, my hands hovering above its smooth surface, channeling my seventh-level magical energy into its depths. The mists inside began to swirl, coalescing into a clearer form. Gradually, a vivid image emerged—a glimpse into Amara's living room. She looked animated but intense, conversing with a group of cloaked figures whose faces were obscured. My breath caught in my throat. The figures leaned in closer, their movements deliberate, and their voices a low murmur, hinting at the gravity of their clandestine meeting.

A chill of apprehension crept up my spine. I leaned closer, my eyes narrowing. I tried to discern more details, a feeling of urgency gnawing at me. The secrecy of their meeting, the intensity of their conversation—it all pointed to something ominous brewing.

"Damn, that's weird."

"Slow down, Sage. Remember your training. Don't push so hard," Agatha reminded me, concern lacing her voice.

"Right, right. But look at this, Agatha!" I pointed at the scene in the glass orb. "That's no neighborhood gossip session. They're planning something big."

"Any familiar faces?" Agatha hopped onto the desk.

"Hard to say with those hoods, but wait..." My gaze sharpened as one figure pushed back their hood. "No, I only recognize Evie's mom."

"Seems like you've stumbled upon a secret society. And not the fun kind," Agatha said dryly.

"Shit." My head was starting to pound, the strain of maintaining the scrying spell evident. "I'm going to need more than coffee to keep this up."

"Freya Weissdorn could help with that," Agatha offered. "Her herbal concoctions are perfect for magical stamina."

"Freya. I know her. She's an old friend...yeah, she'd have just the thing. I'll drop by her place tomorrow."

"Now stay focused."

I nodded, taking Agatha's advice to heart. "Okay." I closed my eyes and steadied my breathing, centering myself before attempting to delve deeper into the crystal's vision.

When I reopened my eyes, the image sharpened, the cloaked figures' voices becoming clearer. "...the ceremony must be held on the next blood moon," one of them said.

Amara shook her head adamantly. "That's too soon. We need more time to gather the necessary components."

"Time is a luxury we cannot afford," another figure countered, their voice distorted, almost inhuman. "The stars align perfectly. To delay would be foolish."

My heart pounded in my chest as the implications sank in. A ceremony? On a blood moon? Whatever they were planning, it couldn't be good.

"Shit, this doesn't sound good at all." I pursed my lips, my brow furrowing.

Agatha's tail whipped back and forth nervously. "Don't let your curiosity blind you to the dangers."

Ignoring her warning, I leaned closer, straining to catch every word. Amara's expression hardened, her jaw set in determination. "Very well. We proceed as planned. But if anything goes awry, it will be on your heads. Meeting adjourned. Thank you, Eclipse Society."

The cloaked figures nodded in eerie unison, their movements almost ritualistic. The vision faded, leaving me with more questions than answers. Who and what was the Eclipse Society?

"Dammit, what the hell are they up to?" I grumbled, frustration seeping into my voice. "And why is Evie's mom involved in something so shady? I don't like the looks of this one bit."

Agatha tilted her furry head. "We must proceed with caution."

I nodded, dragging a hand through my hair. I couldn't believe it. Evie's mother was involved in something wicked. In fact, I wouldn't have believed it if I hadn't seen it with my own two eyes. "You're right. We need to figure out what they're planning, and why Evie's mom is involved." I touched my crystal ball, the smooth surface cool against my fingertips.

Agatha snickered. "You are not bad at scrying for such a young witch."

I shot her a sassy glare. "Thanks, I think."

"One day, you'll become a formidable force, Sage. Your parents would be proud."

The mention of my parents sent a pang through my heart, but I pushed the feeling down.

I leaned back in my chair, squeezing my eyes shut for a moment. They were aching from staring unblinking for too long. "Just once, I'd like to have a vision that didn't involve impending doom and gloom. Why couldn't she have been, I don't know... baking cookies or something?"

Agatha chuckled, her whiskers twitching. "Where's the fun in that? A witch's life is never dull."

I turned around and opened my eyes to stare at my familiar.

"I'm curious. Just how old are you, Agatha? You've never really told me."

The cat's stare narrowed, her tail flicking with indignation. "A lady never reveals her age, young witch. Surely, you know that by now."

A lady over the age of fifty, maybe. I'd tell anyone who wanted to know my age.

I laughed and couldn't help but tease her. "Oh, come on, Agatha. You can't be that old. What were you... like, a hundred when you died and possessed this cat?"

Agatha huffed, leaping off the desk and onto the floor. "I'll have you know I was a spry witch when I possessed this feline, who was dying at the time. Now she has nine lives in a literal sense, and so do I. Besides, age is only a number."

"Yeah, a number you're apparently too embarrassed to share," I teased, earning a disgruntled meow from my familiar.

"Enough of this foolishness," Agatha said, her tone turning serious once more. "We have more pressing matters now. We must unravel the mystery of this dark ritual before it's too late."

I nodded, my smile fading. "You're right. Let's get to work and see what we can discover about the Eclipse Society. We've got a coven of creepy cultists to stop and a best friend's mother to save." I couldn't believe that Evie's mom was evil, I just couldn't. There had to be a reason for her participation.

"We should proceed to your father's study. Make haste, young witch."

"Fine," I said, standing up with a stretch. "But let's make it quick. I've got a fresh batch of sage and lavender that won't bundle itself."

We went into my father's former study, which was mine

now, and turned our attention to the towering bookshelves crowded with dusty grimoires and ancient tomes. Agatha leapt onto the highest shelf, her black fur scarcely visible in the dim light.

"Start with 'The Chronicles of Shadowed Societies'," she ordered. "If the Eclipse Society is as old as I suspect, there will be a mention of them there."

"Got it." I reached for the leather-bound volume, its spine squeaking as I opened it. Pages fluttered under my fingers, the musty trace of magic and history filling the air.

"Can you see anything pertinent?" Agatha asked impatiently.

"Patience, oh bossy one," I replied. "These things don't exactly come with an index." I scanned through the archaic handwriting, searching for any reference to the Eclipse Society.

"Here!" I exclaimed, excited to have found something. "It says the Eclipse Society was rumored to convene during lunar events, harnessing the moon's energy for... Huh. It doesn't say for what."

"Typical," Agatha grumbled. "Secret societies love their enigmas."

"Looks like we'll have to do some more digging." I frowned. Every moment we spent researching was another moment Amara or one of her followers could be weaving more sinister plans.

"Let's keep looking. There has to be something more concrete, something actionable," I said.

Agatha lifted a paw and pointed. "Over there. 'Lunar Rites and Rituals'. It might have what we need."

I grabbed the book, flipping through the pages until a partic-

ular passage caught my eye. My heart raced. I read about cere-
monies that sounded eerily similar to what I'd seen through the
crystal orb.

"Agatha, this could be it, They're using the lunar cycles to
amplify their power, but for what purpose?"

"Evil rarely announces its intentions, young witch," Agatha
said solemnly.

"Right." I closed the book with a snap.

Evie's face flashed in my mind, so trusting and unaware of
the danger lurking so close to home.

"Whatever they're planning, we'll stop them," I said, more
to myself than to Agatha. "We have to."

"Now, let's not waste any more time. The next full moon
approaches, and with it, our best chance to uncover their
secrets."

"Okay, I'm on it." I closed the book and picked it up in my
arms, energized by the thought of protecting my friend. "No
dark cult is going to get the better of Sage Holland."

"Nor Agatha," the cat added with a swish of her tail.

"Teamwork makes the dream work," I joked weakly.

"Let's hope so," Agatha replied. "For everyone's sake, let's
hope so. Now rest, Sage. You look like hell."

I rolled my eyes at the ancient cat. "Gee, thanks, Agatha."

After leaving the study, I blew out the candles and
collapsed onto my bed, letting the darkness envelop me. Tomorrow, I'd look into the secret society more. Tonight, I needed
sleep.

CHAPTER
FIVE

After dinner the following day, I was curled up on my soft leather couch in the living room, the one I'd charmed to always feel like a hug, when Agatha sauntered in, her sleek black coat shimmering under the dim glow of the fairy lights.

"Agatha, you ever think the Eclipse Society might be more than just a bunch of dark magic hobbyists?" I twisted a lock of my blue highlighted hair around my finger. "Like, maybe they're tied to that evil warlock we've heard about, or that evil force in town?"

"Considering their penchant for secrecy, it wouldn't

surprise me, young witch," Agatha replied, eyeing me with that wise stare of hers. "The threads of darkness often weave together in bewildering ways."

I huffed, pulling my knees up so I could rest my chin there. "Right? It's just... something feels off. And Amara, she's involved with the society, obviously. But could she be our link to figuring this out?"

"Perhaps." Agatha jumped onto the armrest of my couch. "But we tread precarious paths when we pry into the affairs of any magical society."

"Which is why I was thinking..." My gaze drifted to the dusty Ouija board atop my bookshelf. "Maybe we should try to communicate with the evil spirit."

I retrieved the board, my fingers trembling as I carried it to the round coffee table and sat on the floor.

"Let's hope this doesn't unleash something we can't handle." I placed the spirit board down, and then lightly laid my fingers on the planchette, the cool wood smooth beneath my touch. Agatha watched with keen interest from the armrest but didn't tell me to stop.

"We wish to speak with the malevolent entity causing the recent turmoil in our town. Can you reveal your name?" I asked, my pulse thrumming.

The ground trembled around me, books toppling from shelves, artwork on the walls shifting. I swallowed the squeal that rose in my throat. This was what I'd wanted. I needed to stay calm. Then, everything went unearthly still and eerily silent. I held my breath, waiting, watching.

The planchette moved rapidly across the board, spelling out T-E-N-E-B-R-I-S, a name.

"Whoa, okay. Hi, Tenebris," I said, my voice unsteady. "A name to the nightmare. Somehow, that doesn't make me feel any better." I sighed, running a hand through my hair.

"Such pleasantries are unnecessary," Agatha admonished, though I could tell she was equally unsettled.

I shifted and kept my fingers gently on the planchette. "What do you want, Tenebris? Why are you in Emberwick Crossing?"

Tenebris continued to answer: Y-O-U...W-I-L-L...S-U-F-F-E-R.

"Okay, that's not the friendliest answer." I frowned and repeated, "What do you want?"

The planchette moved forcefully, spelling out a haunting message: T-O...C-O-N-S-U-M-E...Y-O-U-R...F-E-A-R...S-T-U-P-I-D...W-I-T-C-H.

With a gasp, I jerked my hands back as if burned by the board, then thought better of it and shoved the board straight off the table. It hit the carpet with a thud, and I shivered all over. "This is serious, Agatha. Tenebris isn't just some low-level poltergeist."

"I could have told you that!" Her ears flattened against her head. "Darkness like this does not remain idle. It devours. And now it knows who you are, Sage."

"Thanks, I really needed to hear that," I grumbled. The gravity of our situation hung between us, heavy and silent. I knew one thing for certain—we were in way over our heads.

Which the High Witch had warned me. Damn. She'd been right. I should have left well enough alone.

My thoughts were a jumble of words and emotions as the implications of what had just transpired settled within my mind. Tenebris, a malevolent entity of immense power, had taken notice of me. The thought chilled me to the marrow. I couldn't help wondering what it wanted, what dark plans it had next. The responsibility of dealing with such a formidable foe pressed on my shoulders, and I questioned whether I could stop the evil myself.

Yet, amongt the fear and uncertainty, a glimmer of fortitude burned within me. I had come this far in my magical training, and I refused to let Tenebris win without a fight. But I couldn't do it alone, and I was grateful for Agatha's presence, her wisdom, and her unwavering support. Once I told the High Witch what I'd learned, I was sure she would have a solution.

After putting the spirit board away, I sat cross legged on the floor, the crystal ball nestled between my palms. It was time to do the High Witch's bidding and spy on Amara again. My brow furrowed as I concentrated to encourage the visions.

"Show me Amara Black," I urged, seeking answers about the Eclipse Society and its possible connection to Tenebris.

"You are the High Witch's spy, young witch," Agatha meowed from her seat on the windowsill. "But she should not ask this of you. Amara Black has many allies, and the High Witch is endangering your life by asking you to do all this prying...and even worse—my life."

I ignored my cat, peering into the depths of the orb. An image shimmered into focus—a figure shrouded in shadows, recognizably Amara. But around her twirled a barrier like silver smoke, impenetrable and unnervingly serene.

I frowned. "There's a protective spell around Amara now. It won't let me see what's she's up to. Crap!"

Agatha blinked her eyes. "She is a powerful and very clever

witch. This shows that she is hiding something—or hiding from something."

"Or someone."

The idea unsettled me. Before I could probe further, the image in the glass contorted, the protective spell dissolving into shadows. A dark spirit appeared, twisted with malevolence. Tenebris.

"Shit!" I recoiled, my fingers digging in deeper, refusing to let go of the scrying image.

The crystal's view shifted abruptly, settling on the town square. Tenebris was everywhere at once, a furious eruption of dark, whipping shadows. Through the commotion, a woman sprinted desperately for cover. Her foot caught on a cobblestone, and she stumbled, falling hard onto the ground. Her scream rent the air, a bleak, chilling sound that was swiftly swallowed as the shadows attacked. They enveloped her completely, and when they finally receded, all that remained was a lifeless husk.

My heart pounded with adrenaline, and angry tears burned in my eyes. "Dammit, we have to do something!"

Agatha leapt from the windowsill, her eyes glowing like molten gold. "We are not equipped to handle this, Sage," she warned, her voice quivering with concern. "The High Witch explicitly ordered you not to engage with it."

"I don't care!"

With courage fueling my steps, I jumped up and ran out the front door. Agatha followed close behind me, the door swinging shut behind us.

We made our way across the lawn and onto the darkened street. The wind howled, whipping my hair into a frenzied mess and carrying with it the smell of rain and sulfur. A dog barked frantically in the distance, its cries punctuated by the ominous rumble of thunder.

"Stay close," I told Agatha. "We can't let him hurt anyone else."

"Lead the way, young witch," she replied, her form blurring in front of my eyes. She was readying her magic, preparing for whatever we faced next.

As we stepped onto the sidewalk, the first drops of rain splattered against the cobblestones.

Tenebris materialized before us, an eddying mass of gloom and malice. His presence drained the color from the world, leaving only shades of gray and despair.

I gasped in fear, pulling my magic to my fingertips. The evil spirit had spindly limbs that moved with an unnatural, spider-like grace, each jerky motion causing us to back up. Tenebris's form shifted and undulated, a dark mass that seemed to absorb the very light around it.

While I stared into the void, I realized with horror that Tenebris had no discernible features. No eyes, no nose, just a wide, gaping maw filled with jagged, razor-sharp teeth. The stench of sulfur and decay emanated from that mouth, a foul odor that made my stomach churn and my eyes water.

The evil spirit's presence was suffocating. Oppressive, as if the very air had turned to lead in my lungs. I could feel the icy tendrils of its power reaching out, probing, seeking to latch onto my deepest fears and darkest secrets. Tenebris hungered for my misery, yearned to feast upon my terror, and I knew that if I allowed it to take hold, I would be lost forever in its endless abyss.

Tenebris hissed, then lunged at me with an otherworldly speed. Barely having time to react, my body moved on reflex as I dove to the side, narrowly avoiding the creature's grasping, skeletal fingers. The air sizzled with dark energy as Tenebris whirled around, its movements a blur of shadow.

Needing to do something and quickly, I summoned my magic, feeling the power surge through my veins like liquid fire. Unleashing a bolt of searing light, I aimed directly at the heart of the dark entity. The light pierced through its middle section, illuminating the front lawn in a blinding flash. Tenebris screeched, its form blinking and wavering as my magic seared its essence.

The world exploded in a kaleidoscope of light and shadow, the two forces colliding in a cataclysmic burst of power. I was thrown backwards, my body slamming against the lone tree in the yard with a sickening thud. Through the haze of pain and exhaustion, I saw Tenebris falter for a moment, then his form grew bigger and stronger.

Shit!

Obviously, this creature was far from defeated. It lashed out with tendrils of pure shadow, seeking to ensnare me in its grasp. I leapt and weaved, evading each deadly strike by mere inches.

I couldn't keep this up forever. Tenebris was relentless. I needed to find a weakness, a chink in its armor.

With a desperate cry, I summoned the last of my strength and magic. My hands moved, tracing symbols in the air, my voice steady despite the pounding of my heart. "Lumina virtus!"

With a flick of my wrist, I summoned a surge of power that blazed in my fingertips. It rushed forward, lashing out at the dark entity with a blinding flash of light.

Tenebris retaliated. Shadows twisted and looped around my limbs, threatening to choke me.

Agatha's essence blended with mine to help me strengthen my own magic. I called upon the elements surrounding me. Fire frolicked in my palms as I released an inferno upon Tenebris, who shrieked from the scorching flames.

The rain poured down upon us like tears from the heavens, and I mustered every ounce of power within me for one final assault. My voice echoed through the commotion as I channeled my magic.

Light erupted from my fingertips, streaking toward Tenebris like a comet. It struck him, eliciting a roar of anger rather than pain. Fear lanced through me, but Agatha joined in to help me, her incantations adding to the assault, ribbons of mystical energy weaving through the air.

"Keep going, Sage!" Agatha shouted over the howl of the wind around us. "Your magic is strong!"

I nodded, focusing on the raw power coursing through me. "Tenebris," I said firmly, feeling the name vibrate with power, "you will not harm this town!"

Sweat beaded my forehead and trickled down my neck as I pushed back against the malevolent energy.

"Take care, young witch," Agatha warned. "Do not let it inside your mind."

"We've got to banish it!" I cried, my arms and legs shaking under the strain.

"We do." The black cat's tail flicked sharply.

"By the light that guides us, by the earth that grounds us," I chanted, weaving new spells with every word, drawing upon the seventh-level magic that flowed in my veins.

"By the spirits that watch over us," Agatha continued, her own ancient magic resonating with mine. "We banish you!"

With a loud, inhuman groan, Tenebris finally let go of me and retreated into the shadows, leaving behind the chill of its presence and my exhausted body. Agatha and I slumped against the porch railing, our breathing coming in ragged pulls, the strain of battle still tight in our muscles.

I knew that this was far from over. Tenebris had tasted my power, glimpsed the depths of my resolve. It would be back, stronger and more determined than ever to claim my soul.

"Did we—" I started, but the silence was broken by a low, guttural laugh that seemed to come from everywhere at once.

Agatha shook her head. "No, he will return after he gathers his strength."

"Dammit," I cursed, my entire body shaking from exertion until I finally fell onto my knees on the grass. "That was too close."

"Are you hurt?" I reached out and examined Agatha for injuries more severe than the scrapes I sported.

"Nothing that won't heal." Agatha winced when she licked her paw. "You fought bravely today."

I tried to offer a smile, but it probably looked as tired as I felt. "Thanks."

"You're not going to let this go, are you?"

Let it go? Never.

"Can't afford to," I said, gently touching her head. "More people could get hurt. Worse than us."

Agatha nodded "The High Witch will not be pleased, young witch."

At this point, I didn't care. I was just happy to be alive. "I'll worry about that later. First, we better go lie down. Then we need to try and find out who's controlling the spirit."

I dragged myself to my feet once more, when headlights swept across the front lawn. Evie's car pulled into the driveway, and she hopped out, oblivious to the sinister battle that had just happened in the yard.

"Hey, Sage!" Evie said, her cheerful voice making me faintly smile. "You look like you've seen a ghost. Rough training session?"

I grimaced, pain slashing through my back. "Actually, Evie, we were attacked by an evil spirit."

"Attacked? What do you mean?" Worry creased her forehead, and she stepped closer.

"It's a long story, but there's a dangerous entity in town. We're trying to stop it."

"Wow, that's intense. And here I was, coming to invite you to a party on Friday."

Really? "A party?"

"Yeah, it'll be fun. You should come, take your mind off all this...whatever it is."

I shook my head. "I don't know, Evie. It might not be safe with Tenebris in town."

Evie raised an eyebrow. "Tenebris? Sounds like some ancient demonic shit. Come on, Sage. You can't let fear control your life. Besides, we're witches. We can handle anything."

I sighed, running a hand through my tangled hair. Evie had a point, but the memory of Tenebris's twisted form made shudder.

"I don't know. It's not just me. If something happened to you or anyone else because of this thing..."

"Hey, I get it. You're trying to be responsible. But you gotta live a little too, you know?" She nudged my shoulder. "Plus, Brad will be there. Don't you want to see him?"

The mention of Brad made my heart do a little flip. Perhaps Evie was right. One night of normalcy couldn't hurt.

"All right, fine. I'll think about it," I relented, managing a wider smile. "But if anything weird starts happening at the party, we're out of there. Okay?"

"Sure." Evie grinned, her expression radiant. "Now, let's talk about what you're going to wear. You need something that says, 'I'm a badass witch who knows how to have a good time.'"

I laughed, shaking my head. Leave it to Evie to prioritize fashion in the face of impending doom. Her enthusiasm was a balm for me, so I let myself forget about the looming threat and focused on the prospect of a night out with friends.

CHAPTER
SIX

T *he party*

The moment Evie and I stepped into the grand ballroom, a mixture of nervousness and anticipation struck my chest. The centuries-old mansion had towering ceilings and gothic arches right out of a storybook. Shadows flickered on the walls as candles struggled to hold their flames against the draft whistling through the cracks.

"Look at this place, Sage," Evie murmured, her expression wide with wonder beneath her jet-black hair. Her dress, a daring ensemble of leather and lace, hugged her frame, making her hazel eyes pop with excitement. "Can't wait to see every-one's faces when they get a load of this outfit."

I smiled at her enthusiasm. My own attire—a sexy, chic dress adorned with intricate beadwork that shimmered under the candlelight—felt plain compared to hers. With every step, the blue highlights in my long, dark hair caught the glittering light.

"Your dress is killer, Evie," I said, trying to focus on my friend and ignore the prickling premonition creeping up my arms.

We mingled with clusters of chatting witches and warlocks, then my gaze landed on Brad. He stood across the room, his spiky brown hair and welcoming smile warming my insides. My heart leapt but then plummeted as I saw who stood by his side— a girl with long silver hair, her slender arm looped through his.

"Oh, um... who's that girl with Brad?"

"That's Sarah Prestwood," Evie replied, following my stare. "She owns this creepy museum of a house. It's her party."

My heart sank like a lead balloon.

Crap. Looks and money. How am I going to compete with that?

But before I could process the twist in my chest, Brad spotted us and waved us over. His blue eyes, usually like a calm ocean, were turbulent with something I couldn't quite read. When we drew near, Brad introduced us to the girl on his arm with a shyness I hadn't seen before.

"Evie, Sage, meet Sarah Prestwood," Brad said, gesturing to the silver-haired beauty who regarded me with what I could only describe as thinly veiled disdain.

"Nice to meet you both," Sarah said, her voice colder than the draft in the room.

"Likewise," I replied, struggling to keep my tone even. Was this chick Brad's friend? Girlfriend? I couldn't imagine warm, kind Brad dating an ice queen like this.

The fire of jealousy ignited somewhere deep within my belly, fueled by Sarah's haughty gaze.

"Nice place you have here," Evie said, gesturing to the ornate ceilings with a wave of her hand.

"Thank you," Sarah responded, her hard stare not leaving mine. "It takes a discerning eye to appreciate the finer things."

I inwardly flinched. There was a history here that I wasn't part of. I could see it in the curve of Sarah's lips, in the way Brad looked at her.

"Looks like you've got everything, Sarah," Evie trilled. "Fancy house, fancy party, fancy new boyfriend."

"Evie!" I chided, my cheeks blazing with heat. Was that true?

Brad chuckled, a familiar sound I'd heard most of my life. He was happy, and that hurt. Why hadn't anyone told me that Brad was taken?

"Yeah, it's something, all right." His gaze briefly met mine before returning to Sarah.

Sarah glared at Evie and flipped her hair over her shoulder in response.

"It certainly is something," I said, shifting my weight from foot to foot.

We stood there for a long moment in awkward silence. This is fun.

"Well, we should mingle. Nice seeing you, Brad," I said, eager to escape the tension.

"Yeah, you too, Sage," Brad replied. "We'll catch up later."

I nodded and grabbed hold of Evie's arm and steered her away, into the crowd. My heart sank as I caught one last glimpse of Brad and Sarah, heads together in an intimate conversation.

"Can you believe her?" Evie whispered. "What a witch."

"Tell me about it," I muttered.

I scanned the ballroom, searching for a friendly face to distract me. Then I saw her—my childhood friend, Freya, chatting with a small group. Her short brown hair bounced around her happy face as she laughed, a sound that lifted my spirits.

"Freya!" I called out, waving frantically.

She turned around and her face lit up when she recognized me. "Sage!"

I rushed forward, and we embraced. Freya still smelled of lilac, which made me nostalgic for my childhood.

"It's so good to see you!" she cried, still hugging me tightly. "I heard you were back in town."

"Yeah, just finished up magic college," I replied. "What have you been up to?"

"I'm training to be a healer now," she said with a proud smile. "Putting my skills to good use."

"That's amazing. What does your job entail?" I asked.

"Oh, you know, mending broken bones, treating magical maladies, and dealing with the occasional curse or hex," Freya said with a grin. "Never a dull moment in the magical medical field."

I chuckled. "I bet. Sounds like you're kicking ass and taking names."

"You know it, girl. But enough about me. I heard through the grapevine that you're working with the High Witch now. That's a pretty big deal."

I shrugged, trying to play it cool. "Yeah, it's been intense. Ingrid's a tough mentor, but I'm learning a lot."

"No shit. I can't even imagine the kind of magic she's teaching you. Seventh-level stuff, right?"

"Mhmm. What we learned at college was wild, Freya. I never thought I'd be crafting my own spells and rituals."

Her mouth dropped open. "Damn, Sage. You're really making a name for yourself. Your parents would be so proud."

A lump formed in my throat at the mention of my folks. "I hope so. I just want to prove myself, you know? Show everyone what I'm capable of."

"Well, from where I'm standing, you're already doing that and then some. Don't be so hard on yourself, okay?" She reached out and squeezed my arm.

I nodded, blinking back the tears that threatened to spill. "Thanks, Freya. That means a lot."

She pulled me in for another hug. "Anytime, Sage. I'm always here for you, no matter what kind of magical shit storm comes your way."

I laughed, feeling the weight on my shoulders lift just a little.

Evie joined in our conversation, and we reminisced about old times, forgetting the world around us. With Freya, it felt just like it used to—easy, fun, light-hearted.

For a moment, I forgot about Brad and Sarah, about the evil lurking nearby. I was just a girl at a party with her friends, gossiping like the world would never end.

Suddenly, darkness fell over the room, heavy and smothering. A sudden chill clung to my skin.

"What's happening?" Evie asked, her eyes widening with fear.

A window shattered with a violent crash, and through the broken glass, Tenebris burst into the ballroom like a squall of destruction. The air chilled, thick with screams that resonated around us. Evie's hands, cold and trembling, clung to my arm, her fear pulsating through me.

Magic blazed through the air, an electric current of ancient power clashing with the dark forces at play. My heart hammered, each beat of panic resonating deep within my chest.

Before I could formulate a plan, Brad stepped forward. He drew himself up, muscles tensed, his expression, alight with a fiery intensity. Words of ancient power rolled off his tongue, each syllable summoning raw magic that sang in the air.

The battle was a blur of energy and motion. Brad's movements were fluid and precise, each strike weaving a tapestry of force and light against the dark swells of Tenebris. The room trembled with their power, the very foundations groaning under the strain of their duel.

When Brad unleashed a final, desperate thrust of energy, it hit Tenebris with the force of a breaking wave. The dark entity staggered, its form wavering like a shadow in strong light, before it pulled back, disappearing into the night.

Silence fell, viscous and bloated. I rushed over to Brad, my legs unsteady. When I found him still standing, exhausted, his chest heaving with labored breaths, it brought a surge of relief that flooded over me.

"You all right?" I asked, my voice shaky.

He nodded, breathing heavily. "I think so." Brad's eyes met mine, their blue depths whirling with emotion. "But it's not over. That creature will be back."

I trembled, hugging my arms close. Around us, the partygoers were slowly recovering from the shock and terror of the attack.

"What was that thing?" Evie trembled and kept looking about as if the creature might return at any second. "Where did it come from?"

"I don't know." Brad's expression was grim. "But it's strong. Stronger than anything I've ever faced before."

He wiped a hand across his brow, smearing dust and sweat. I could see the toll the battle had taken. His shoulders sagged with exhaustion and his hands trembled ever so slightly. But there was also a simmering anger in his expression that I knew well.

"I should have been able to stop it," he said bitterly. "If I were stronger..."

"Hey." I put a hand on his arm. "You did everything you could. None of us were prepared for this."

He sighed, the fight going out of him. "You're right. I just wish I knew what it was after. It came here tonight for a reason."

I glanced around the ruined ballroom, taking in the shaken partygoers. A cold feeling settled in my gut.

"It came for us," I said quietly. "For the magic users here tonight. Its name is Tenebris."

Brad's expression darkened. He didn't ask how I knew, rather he took me at my word.

"Then it's up to us to be ready for when Tenebris returns,"

he said. There was an edge to his voice. "And next time, I'll be prepared."

I glanced over at Evie, standing off to the side, her face pale and mouth wide open. She hadn't moved since the pandemonium erupted, frozen in shock.

"I need to get Evie home."

"Of course." He nodded. "She okay?"

"Shell shocked, I think." I managed a weak smile, though my lips felt like they might crack from the strain. "Come on, Evie," I called softly, reaching out for her.

She stumbled closer, her movements jerky and disjointed, as if there were invisible strings tugging on her like she was a marionette. Her hazel eyes met mine, searching for some semblance of normalcy in the madness.

"Let's go home, okay, Evie?" I said, gently squeezing her hand.

"Be on your guard," Brad said, his voice low. "That thing is still out there."

"I know." The words tasted like ash in my mouth. "We'll be ready the next time it attacks."

"Damn straight," Evie said, finding her voice. Her usual spark was dimmed but not extinguished. I admired her for trying hard to fake courage even if she was terrified.

Sarah came running towards Brad, throwing herself into his arms with a sob.

My heart squeezed tightly at the sight, but I tried to focus on Evie as the rest of the party began to disperse.

"Take care, Brad." I led Evie away from the remnants of the party and towards the door.

The night air hit us like an arctic blow as we slipped out of the mansion. The stars overhead were shrouded by ominous clouds, making the night feel oppressive rather than merely dark. We hurried across the lawn, our footfalls muffled by the damp earth until we reached my car.

My heart was pounding like a hammer against an anvil.

"Get in," I urged, unlocking the doors with a trembling hand.

Evie climbed into the passenger seat, her body still shaking from the ordeal. I raced around to the driver's side and slid into the seat. The engine roared to life, slicing through the silence of the evening.

"Hey, you're safe now," I reassured her, pulling her into an awkward side hug.

"I'm glad you were there, Sage. It was so s-scary." Evie's voice was small, vulnerable.

"I know," I said, thanking the universe for a reliable car as I drove away from the mansion, a massive amount of guilt bearing down on me. I hadn't told Evie that the High Witch had ordered me to spy on her mother. How could I betray her trust like this?

"Evie," I said, my throat tightening. "There's something I need to tell you—"

"Later," she cut me off, staring out the window at the passing houses. "Right now, let's just focus on getting home."

I wasn't sure how being silent would keep us safer, but did as she asked.

"Okay." I nodded, though the guilt I carried continued to feel like a thorn in my side.

Tenebris had marked us for a feast of misery, and it would return. The familiar streets rolled by, and I made a silent vow to protect my friends. I would stop the evil plaguing our town. And somehow, confront Evie's mother without losing the one person who meant the world to me.

Evie.

"Home sweet home," Evie murmured when I pulled into her driveway, still shivering.

"Go get some rest," I said, smiling the best I could.

"You too, bestie," she replied, mustering a tired smile before stepping out of the car and running for the front door.

Watching Evie disappear into her house, a sudden revelation came to me. I had to confront Amara Black.

CHAPTER
SEVEN

I killed the engine, the soft purr of my car fading into the silence of the evening. The pale glow of porch lights illuminated Evie's home. I sat in the car, gripping the steering wheel tightly, my mind replaying the pandemonium of Tenebris' attack at the party—screams fusing with the hiss of dark magic.

Taking a deep breath, I unfolded myself from the front seat, the fabric of my trendy jacket whispering against the leather car seats. My boots squeaked on the path leading up to the porch, each step trying to still my shaking hands before they betrayed me. I got out of the car and walked up the path to the front porch. The wooden steps shuddered their distinguishable greeting as I stepped onto them, the perfume of freshly bloomed roses surrounding me.

One look back at my car, and there was no backing out. I rapped my knuckles against the door once, twice, three times, each sound making my heart rate shoot up again.

The door swung open abruptly, and Amara Black's sharp green stare met mine. Her face was a canvas of surprise painted with a stroke of suspicion, her mouth a thin line.

"Mrs. Black," I greeted, my voice steadier than I felt.

"Sage? What are you doing here so late? Is everything okay?" She arched an eyebrow, her straight black hair framing her face perfectly, untouched by the evening's humidity. Her clothing, as always, was impeccable—a dark blue blouse that complemented her slender form, rayon trousers, and heels.

"Can we talk?" I asked, hating how small my voice sounded.

The night was cool, a gentle breeze, rustling the leaves around us. A cat, sleek and black as midnight, watched us from a distance, yellow eyes unblinking. Agatha?

"Of course, come in," she said, stepping aside, though her body language remained cautious. "But make it quick. I have a book club meeting soon."

"Thanks," I said, and followed her inside, leaving the scent of roses behind.

Amara's living room was an array of earthy tones, the furniture aged but well cared for. I settled into an armchair, its fabric soft under my fingertips. Bookshelves lined one wall, teeming with leather-bound spines and curious knick-knacks.

"Mrs. Black," I said, gathering my courage. "I think you're hiding something. Something about the Eclipse Society and a cloaking spell."

Her posture stiffened. "And why would you think that?"

"Because...um, well..." I hesitated, my voice hoarse. "The High Witch asked me to spy on you."

A laugh, high and startling, burst from Amara's lips. "Oh, is that so? Well then, Sage, that explains the cloaking spell."

My heart hammered in my chest. "You admit it?"

"Of course, I do." She leaned back, crossing her arms with a smirk playing at the edge of her mouth. "How else do you think we keep our book club selections a secret?"

I stared at her, dumbfounded. "Book club?"

"Yes, dear. The Eclipse Society. It's just a fancy name I came up with for our monthly gatherings."

"Then why the secrecy?" I asked, my confusion mounting.

"Have you met Ingrid Nightspire? That woman has ears like a bat and a curiosity that could rival any cat's. We needed some way to surprise her."

"What? I don't understand." I frowned, trying to connect the dots.

"Never mind that now." Amara waved a dismissive hand, her expression luminous. "Tell me, Sage, how did you stumble upon our little secret?"

"Oh, uhm..." I faltered, my cheeks heating up. "Crystal ball spying. I saw... I thought I saw..."

"Something sinister?" Amara smiled, raising an eyebrow. "Young witch, your talents are wasted on espionage."

"I don't understand," I said, feeling like I was missing a vital piece of the conversation. "What's going on here, Mrs. Black?"

She smiled at me, a glint of amusement in her gaze. "Let me explain to you what the Eclipse Society really is." Amara's expression softened. "We are planning a surprise birthday party for Ingrid," she said, her lips curving into a tender smile.

Relief flooded through me like a soothing balm, the tension that had coiled within me unraveling with each passing second. I felt a twinge of embarrassment for having let my imagination run wild, conjuring up dark conspiracies where there were none. It was a sharp reminder of the lessons I had learned at magic college—to seek the truth, to look beyond appearances, and to trust in the goodness of others.

I processed Amara's words and felt a flash of excitement ignite within me. A surprise birthday party for my mentor! The thought of celebrating the High Witch's birthday made me happy. She had been a constant source of support, and she deserved a party.

I marveled at the lengths Amara and the others had gone to keep their plans hidden, the intricate cloaking spells and secret meetings suddenly making sense.

"Wait. Seriously? A party?" The tangle of thoughts in my head began to unravel. "So, no secret sinister plots or... or dark magic?"

The High Witch was going to be so surprised! She was the one who'd asked me to spy on Amara. She'd known something was up, but this was the last thing she would expect.

She chuckled. "No, nothing of that sort. Just a bit of harmless fun. We've been cloaking our plans to keep it a surprise."

"Holy hell." I rubbed the back of my neck. "I've really confused everything, haven't I?"

"Let's just say you've taken quite the detour." Amara's green eyes crinkled as she considered the mix-up.

"I'm really sorry, Amara. I thought..." My voice trailed off as I shook my head, feeling like an absolute fool.

Her expression softened. "Look, Sage. It's okay. You're trying to do your part for the community. But sometimes things aren't always what they seem."

Her words struck a chord within me, a gentle reminder of the wisdom I had yet to fully embrace. It was true—in my eagerness to protect and serve, I had allowed my suspicions to cloud my judgment, to paint shadows where there was only light. It was a humbling realization, one that I knew would shape my actions and decisions in the days to come.

"Guess I learned that the hard way," I replied, offering a sheepish grin.

Although I sat there relishing the kindness of Amara's understanding, my thoughts drifted to the darker corners of my mind. The memory of Tenebris lurked like a malevolent specter. It was a nightmare given flesh, a manifestation of the darkest depths of the arcane.

And yet, even as fear rose within me, what was stronger was the burning desire to unravel the mysteries that surrounded this evil entity. I couldn't face this threat alone. I would need the support and wisdom of those around me to even stand a chance against the encroaching darkness.

I hesitated for a moment, choosing my words wisely. "Do you know anything about the evil entity named Tenebris? The creature attacking our town?"

Amara's demeanor shifted, the light in her eyes dimming. "Tenebris," she repeated quietly.

"Yeah, it attacked the partygoers tonight. And I can't help worrying..." My voice wavered. "You've heard of the creature?"

The conversation turned more serious, heavier somehow.

"Unfortunately, I have." Her tone was serious, measured. "There are rumors of a malevolent force stirring in the shadows."

"Shit. This is bad." I chewed on my bottom lip, the weight of the situation settling over me like a thick cloak.

Amara leaned forward, her eyes narrowing. "I believe Tenebris is an ancient evil, a spirit that feeds on agony and grief. It's been dormant for centuries, but something or someone awakened it."

I swallowed hard, my heart pounding in my chest. "Damn. Any idea who or what could've stirred it up?"

She shook her head, a grim expression on her face. "Hard to say. Could be a powerful ritual gone wrong, or perhaps someone deliberately summoned the creature for their own twisted purposes."

I tsked in disgust. "Just what we need—some power-hungry asshole messing with forces they can't control." I ran a hand through my hair, frustration seething inside me.

"I agree, dear. Whoever's behind this is playing a dangerous game. Tenebris is not to be trifled with." Amara's voice was low, almost a sigh.

I bit my lip. "Tenebris is scary..."

"Listen, Sage." Amara reached out, placing a pacifying hand on my arm. "We'll get to the bottom of this. You don't need to be scared. We'll figure out who's responsible and put a stop to Tenebris before it's too late."

I managed a weak smile, grateful for her words. "Thanks,

Mrs. Black. I just hope we can do it before anyone else gets hurt. Rumors are there is also a dangerous warlock in town. He could be behind all this."

"Rumors are a dangerous thing, Sage," Amara said, her expression filled with knowledge that stretched far beyond the comfy confines of her living room. "But in this case, they might just bear a kernel of truth."

I leaned in closer, my heart sprinting with each word she uttered. "What kind of truth?"

"Corbin Grimm." She let the name hang between us like a dark omen. "Some believe he's involved with Tenebris."

"Corbin Grimm? I've never heard of him."

Amara nodded solemnly. "He's a warlock with necromancy powers whose ambitions stretch into unsavory realms. If Tenebris is his doing..." She trailed off, leaving the implications hanging thick in the room.

My hand instinctively fidgeted with the hem of my shirt, a habit when nerves kicked in. "What if Tenebris targets the High Witch? At her own birthday party?"

"That's a possibility," Amara admitted. "If he can breach our defenses—"

"Then no one is safe," I finished for her, feeling the somberness of the situation press down on me. "What do we do?"

Amara leaned back, the shadows from the subdued lighting stretching across her face.

"We stay vigilant, and we protect our own," Amara said firmly. "And perhaps, we should all be a little less quick to judge and jump to conclusions, hmm?"

"Point taken." I nodded, a rueful smile jerking at my mouth. Technically, it had been my job to investigate her, but I was so glad I'd come here and asked her straight out what was going on.

"Good." Amara stood, signaling the end of our discussion. "Now, let's try to keep this party a surprise, shall we?"

"Absolutely," I agreed, standing as well. "And thanks for being so understanding, Mrs. Black."

"Anytime, Sage." Her smile returned, genuine and kind. "And next time, maybe join our book club instead of spying on it, dear."

"Thank you, Mrs. Black. Really. For everything." There was a newfound resolve in my voice, a steel spine forged by necessity.

"Of course, dear. Be on your guard out there." Her tone was laced with genuine concern, maternal almost.

I nodded, my mind wandering to the unexpected turn the evening had taken. It was funny how quickly suspicion could give way to understanding. Or how a simple conversation could shift the entire narrative. I had affection in my heart for Mrs. Black and the others, for the attention and care they had poured into planning Ingrid's surprise birthday party.

It was a reminder of the beauty that could be found in people, the light that could shine through even the most ominous of shadows. And wasn't that what magic was all about? Finding the extraordinary in the ordinary, hope in the face of despair?

I smiled at the thought. Yes, Tenebris was a threat that needed to be reckoned with. But in that moment, I realized that the true magic lay in the bonds we shared, in the compassion and friendship that tied us together.

I walked towards my car parked under the watchful eye of a

crescent moon. Then I felt it—the weight of what had to be done. The night was quiet, but my purpose was clear. Protect the High Witch, protect the community, put an end to Tenebris' attacks. Whatever it took.

With one last deep breath of the rose-infused air, I opened my car door and slid inside. It was time to get to work, but I would need help from my friends.

I clacked my fingernails against the aged wood of my coffee table, the surface scattered with open grimoires and half melted candles. Brad and Evie slumped beside each other on my couch, their faces drawn in concentration. We were a trio united by a purpose.

I was staring into a crystal ball that hummed with latent energy. "We've got to be cunning. Make the creature think it's winning until the very last second."

Brad nodded, his blue eyes sharp beneath furrowed brows. "And timing is crucial. We can't let it near the High Witch's celebration. That'd be...well, catastrophic."

It certainly would be. Not just for my future job prospects, but for our whole town.

Evie's hazel stare flicked from me to Brad. She leaned forward, her elbows on her knees. "That's the understatement of the century. Let's weave an illusion over the trap to disguise it, and we need something irresistible to lure that shadowy fiend."

A tingling of anticipation spiraled in my stomach. Something that creature couldn't resist? That would be me. "Yeah, and everything will need to be perfect. No room for error on this one." My voice was steady, but inside, my pulse sped up and doubt crept in. Did we really have a chance against such dark, ancient magic? I liked to think so, but were we deluding ourselves here?

"Evie," said Brad, turning to her with a set to his jaw, "you're on diversions. Sage, you and your spell craft are the linchpin. And I'll—" He paused, his gaze meeting mine. "I'll take care of the containment since that is my specialty magic."

"Got it." I nodded and went back to my task.

Hours later, the smell of ancient parchment filled the air as Evie and I hunched over even more dusty tomes, our fingers tracing lines of forgotten languages. These books hadn't been opened in years, but I was grateful we had access to them now.

"Here," said Evie, pointing to a passage in front of her and moving the book closer so I could see. "This incantation is unbreakable—if combined with dragon's bane and phoenix feather."

"Rare ingredients for a rare spell," I said, feeling the rush of seventh-level magic surge at the prospect. "But we don't have to time to locate those items." And I wouldn't even know who to ask.

Brad stood in the corner of my living room, where runes glowed beneath his hands on a set of chains. "I'm reinforcing these with elemental wards. Earth, fire, air, water—Tenebris won't be able to break free once he's stuck... at least I hope not."

I glanced over, my gaze roaming over Brad's strong arms and body as I watched his masterful work. The intricacy of the elemental wards was a testament to his skill and dedication, a reminder of the incredible talents possessed by those I called my friends. But even as I marveled at his handiwork, worry roiled in the pit of my stomach.

Our plan was bold, daring even, but it was also fraught with danger. Tenebris was no ordinary foe. No mere creature of darkness to be easily vanquished. It was a manifestation of pure malevolence, a being that fed on despair and reveled in the suffering of others. The thought of facing such an entity, of willingly placing myself in its path... well, it only strengthened my resolve to kill it.

Beneath my fear though was also a glimmer of hope, a burning desire to put an end to Tenebris, once and for all.

I'd made the decision to act as bait, of course. It was the only way to draw the creature into our painstakingly crafted trap. It was a role that filled me with equal parts fear and resolve.

"Evie, can you whip up one of your illusions? Something to keep Tenebris distracted?" I asked, trying to sound more confident than I felt.

"Of course," she replied with a smirk. "I'm thinking a spectral parade—phantoms, wraiths, the whole eerie ensemble."

"Make it convincing," I urged, picturing the ghastly figures that Evie could conjure, her talent for illusions almost as renowned as my own for spell crafting.

She nodded, her fingers weaving through the air as she began the incantation. Wisps of silver light materialized, coalescing into shapes both graceful and grotesque. A spectral procession formed before us, hauntingly beautiful and unsettlingly real.

As I considered my decision to act as bait, a cold, prickling sensation crept along my skin, raising goosebumps in its wake. My heart thrummed against my ribcage, a frantic, erratic beat. Proof of the turbulent emotions churning within me.

I could feel the tremors starting in my fingers, a subtle quivering that gradually spread through my hands and up my arms. It was as if my body were physically revolting against the idea of confronting Tenebris again. I'd barely made it out alive the first time. Every fiber of my being was screaming out in primal fear and self-preservation.

But even as the icy tendrils of dread twisted around my heart, I refused to let them take root. I clenched my fists, willing the trembling to subside, and focused on my breathing. In and out, in and out, each breath a silent mantra.

"Damn, Evie, even knowing it's fake..." My voice trailed off as a cold sensation tingled at the base of my neck. A reaction not just to the illusionary magic, but also to the gravity of what we were about to do.

"Will it work?" Brad asked, his voice steady but his brow furrowed with worry.

"It has to," I said, catching his eye. Beads of sweat gathered at my temples, a clammy sheen that spoke of the intense inner struggle raging beneath the surface.

"Then let's get ready," Evie said.

Once we stepped out of my home and into the chilly air, a brisk wind whipped through my hair. The sky above was a canvas of mottled grays and deep blues, the fading light of dusk emitting long shadows across the ground. Brad and Evie walked beside me as we made our way towards the secluded location we had chosen for our trap.

The hike through the woods was somber. The crunch of leaves and twigs beneath our feet sounding too loud amongst the lack of chatter. The air held the aroma of damp earth and decaying foliage, a musky perfume that teased my nostrils with each breath.

Brad, Evie, and I walked deeper into the forest, the canopy above us growing denser, the interwoven branches filtering the remaining daylight into a soft glow. The occasional skittering of small animals made me jump. A squirrel darting up a tree trunk, a bird fluttering from branch to branch. They all added to the heightened awareness that stoked up my fear.

Every fiber of my being seemed to vibrate with a barely contained energy. It was as if my body was attuning itself to the magic that would soon be unleashed, preparing for the battle ahead.

I turned to Brad and Evie with a smile. "You know, if this whole battling evil thing doesn't work out, we could always start a band. What do you think?"

Brad chuckled, shaking his head. "Sage, only you could find humor in a situation like this."

My grin widened. "Hey, laughter is the best medicine. And if we can't find laughter in the little things, what's the point?"

Evie skipped ahead. "I call dibs on lead vocals!"

I couldn't laugh, even though I wanted to, so I just grinned and followed my friend deeper into the forest.

Once we reached the clearing and began setting up the trap, I took a moment to place a hand on each of their shoulders. "I know I don't say it enough, but I'm so grateful for you both. Your friendship means the world to me, and I couldn't imagine facing this without you by my side."

Brad, his expression dark with emotion, pulled me into a tight hug. "I'll always be here for you, Sage. Always."

Evie joined the embrace. "We've got this, and we've got each other."

We separated, and I took a deep breath, my heart enlarging with love and gratitude. "All right, let's do this. For the High Witch, and for our community."

We set to work with focused intensity. Brad and Evie moved with practiced efficiency, conscientiously laying out the components of the trap—the enchanted chains, the intricate runes, the sacred herbs and crystals. Each element was placed with meticulous precision, forming a complex web of power that would, if all went according to plan, ensnare Tenebris and bind the creature within the trap's confines.

While I watched my friends work, a speck of doubt flared within me, a nagging that questioned whether I was truly ready for what was to come. But I pushed the thoughts aside, focusing instead on the magic. I liked to listen to my inner voice, my intuition a nudge from the universe. But sometimes it was hard to distinguish between that knowledge and my own fear.

It was time. I stepped into the trap's center while Brad and Evie hid among the foliage to wait.

My chest rose and fell too fast with my exaggerated breathing. We had a plan. I just had to wait, but that didn't stop my skin from prickling into goosebumps under the stress. I didn't have to wait long.

Too soon, Tenebris emerged from the trees, the creature's form a writhing mass of darkness and spidery limbs. The stench of sulfur choked the air, and I coughed, the acrid tang burning the back of my throat. My heart thumped hard against my ribs, adrenaline surging through my veins.

Oh, crap.

I wanted to run, wanted to fight. But that wasn't the plan. I had to stand there and wait like some sacrificial lamb taken to slaughter.

Tenebris lunged towards the trap, the evil spirit's twisted limbs propelling it forward with a speed that defied comprehension. The entity's hunger for suffering was intense, a tangible force that pressed against my skin like a physical weight.

"Now!" I shouted.

I leaped clear of the trap just as Tenebris crossed the threshold.

Evie and Brad's magic flared to life, brilliant beams of light illuminating the gloom. Their combined magic struck Tenebris' form and held him in place.

I could taste the metallic tang of magic on my tongue, a supernatural energy that set my nerves ablaze. My own power surged within me, a thundering inferno that threatened to consume me from the inside out.

The containment spell snapped into place with an audible crack, the enchanted chains materializing out of thin air to wrap around the entity's form. Tenebris screeched, a sound that tore at my eardrums and sent icy daggers of pain lancing through my skull. The spirit thrashed against its bonds, his rage a tangible force that buffeted against my skin like a physical blow.

But the trap held fast, the chains glowing with an otherworldly illumination as they strained against the entity's fury. I could feel the magic thrumming through the air, a pulsing vibration that resonated in my bones.

"Sage, now!" Brad yelled, his face contorted with the effort of maintaining his part of the spell.

I nodded, steeling myself. Drawing in a deep breath, I began to chant the words of the binding incantation, my voice ringing out with the authority of the arcane.

Each syllable was a struggle, a battle against the overwhelming power that threatened to consume me. I could feel the magic surging through my veins, a searing heat that burned away all traces of doubt and fear.

Brad and Evie added their own power to the mix, their magic intertwining with mine in a brilliant surge of supernatural energy. The air around us buzzed with electricity, the hair on my arms standing on end as the spell reached a crescendo.

I poured every ounce of my will into the incantation, my voice rising to a fevered pitch as the final words left my lips. The world around me seemed to fade away, narrowing down to the single point that was Tenebris.

The moment the final word left my lips, a deafening explosion of energy rocked the forest. The ground shook beneath our feet as Tenebris' form compressed and contorted, writhing in agony.

"Damn," I whispered, my focus locked on the creature as it finally succumbed to the binding spell. "We did it."

Tenebris was destroyed, its dark essence evaporating into

the air like a sinister vapor. I could feel the relief crashing over me.

"We really did it!" Evie jumped up and down, clapping like a child.

"Damn straight we did!" Brad said, grinning hard

The three of us collapsed onto the forest floor, our bodies drained from the effort we had expended. My heart swelled with triumph, knowing that we had succeeded in ending Tenebris forever.

"Thank you," I said, puffing now. "I couldn't have done any of that without you."

"I love you, Sage," Evie replied, reaching out to squeeze my hand. "You're like my sister."

Brad nodded, a tired but genuine smile on his face.

As we sat there, recovering from the battle, I knew that nothing could ever break the bonds of friendship I had with these two. I was truly blessed.

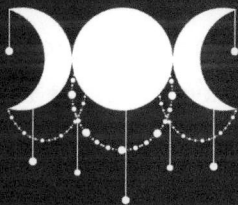

The sun had dipped low in the sky, casting an amber hue over Evie's house. The air was thick with the fragrance of roses, their perfume weaving through the trees that stood like ancient guardians around the home. The mystical symbols etched on the door and windows lent the place an otherworldly charm.

I stood and stared, taking it all in. "Wow, Evie, your mom really went all out."

Brad led the way towards the house, his broad shoulders cutting a sharp silhouette against the soft glow of twilight. He'd swapped his usual casual attire for a dark blue suit that complemented his spiky brown hair and blue eyes. The jacket hugged his well-built frame, making him look even more dashing than usual, if that were possible.

"Only the best for the High Witch," Evie said, her expression gleaming with excitement. Her shoulder-length hair framed her face in soft waves, and her fitted emerald gown had subtle accents of gold that caught the light as she moved.

She looked beautiful, but Brad... he looked amazing.

"Brad, you clean up pretty well," I said, nudging him with my elbow and trying to play it as casually as possible.

"Thanks, Sage." He winked and grinned. "Not looking too shabby yourself."

I smoothed down my own dress, a midnight blue fabric with silver filigree along the hem. It was trendy but had a classic feel, much like my taste in décor. And it made my long, dark hair with blue highlights really stand out.

The door swung open before we could knock, revealing Evie's mom in a sleek, tailored black dress that underscored her no-nonsense demeanor. She arched an eyebrow at us.

"Sorry we're late, Mrs. Black," I said quickly, grabbing hold of Evie's arm. "We ran into a bit of... trouble on the way here."

"Magical mishaps?" she asked dryly.

I tried not to laugh. If only she knew!

"Something like that," Evie replied, sharing a conspiratorial glance with me.

"Come in, then. Ingrid is already holding court." Mrs. Black pushed open the door and stepped aside to let us pass.

The moment we entered the once silent house, the

atmosphere shifted as though a spell had been lifted. What we couldn't hear before, we suddenly could. The happy chatter of the party carrying snippets of conversation, laughter, and gossip.

The High Witch, Ingrid Nightspire, stood in the heart of the room, commanding everyone's attention without uttering a word. She was an ethereal figure, her long silver hair rippling in soft waves down her back. Her gown was a masterpiece of dark silk, flowing around her like liquid starlight. Ancient spells and symbols were embroidered along the fabric, each stitch glinting with power.

"Isn't she magnificent?" I said, unable to tear my gaze away from my mentor.

"Yes," Brad agreed, his admiration clear.

I felt a recurring pang of longing in my chest. Ingrid was everything I aspired to be—powerful, confident, and revered. But as I watched her, I wondered if I'd ever truly fit into this world of high magic and higher stakes. Even after everything we'd done, there was so much more to prove—to her, to myself, and to the memory of my parents.

"Let's go say hello," Evie suggested, breaking my reverie.

"Right behind you," I said. We wove around the groups of witches and warlocks, their robes a spectrum of sunset hues. Tables adorned with crystals and candles glimmered with enchanted flames, hurling shadows that played along the walls inscribed with protective runes. A melody of harps and flutes, charmed to play by themselves, created a haunting tune resonated inside of me.

"Can you believe we did it?" I murmured to my friends, my gaze lingering on the symbols of power and unity around us. "We trapped and killed Tenebris."

"Believe it? I'm still waiting for someone to tell me it was all a dream." Brad chuckled, though his expression held the weight of what we'd been through.

Evie wore a sly grin, plucking a mini hors d'oeuvre from a passing platter levitated by magic. "This food is too good to be a dream."

I smiled, allowing myself a brief, blissful moment to savor our victory. But a tinge of apprehension hit me hard. We had stopped Tenebris, but the warlock or witch who had summoned the creature was still out there somewhere. That thought alone was enough to temper my joy.

"Hey," Brad said, touching my arm gently. "You okay?"

I nodded. "Yeah, just thinking about what's next. We stopped Tenebris, but—"

"Whoever is the mastermind behind this magical uprising is still a mystery," Evie finished for me, her smile sharp. "But tonight, we celebrate. Tomorrow, we worry."

"You're right. We should celebrate," I agreed, forcing the worry away. "Tonight's for Ingrid... and for us. We did something amazing tonight."

"Let's wish her a happy birthday." Brad led the way to the High Witch herself.

"Happy birthday, Ingrid," I said, brightly, then sidled up next to her with a conspiratorial whisper. "I guess Mrs. Black wasn't up to anything sinister. Unless you consider her planning this surprise party in your honor?"

"Thank you for all your hard work, Sage," Ingrid replied, her violet stare meeting mine with an intensity that made me feel scrutinized, and not in a great way. "Enjoy the party."

She moved on, and we focused on the fun, laughter and

music weaving a spell of their own. But the enjoyment of the celebration did little to stave off the chill that came with not knowing who'd conjured the dark entity.

"Corbin Grimm... could he be the necromancer that was controlling the evil spirit?" I overheard a member of the Eclipse Society asking not far from where I stood.

I edged closer, straining to hear what they were saying. The woman's companion, a tall, severe-looking witch with a tight bun, shook her head. "Grimm's a slippery bastard. If he's involved, we're in deep shit."

"But why would he want to control that that monstrous thing?" the first woman asked, her voice trembling.

"Power, why else? He's always been hungry for it. Probably thinks he can use the creature to stage some sort of coup."

I felt a chill shudder through me. Corbin Grimm. The name sounded familiar. Mrs. Black had mentioned him once. Her tone had been laced with suspicion, painting him as a potential mastermind behind the magical uprising.

"We need to tell the High Witch," the first woman insisted. "She has to know."

"And risk her wrath? No way in Hades. We keep this to ourselves until we have proof. Solid proof."

Their voices faded as they moved away.

Risk her wrath? Was the High Witch so exacting?

I had no idea who Corbin Grimm was, but I had to find out. Could he be here tonight? I looked about. How could I find him in this crowded party?

Each face I studied brought a gleam of hope, followed swiftly by doubt. None carried the mark of a known necromancer, or at least what I imagined one would bear.

I made my way through the crowd and my gaze fell on a small group gathered around the High Witch.

Warily, I edged closer, catching snippets of their conversation about the latest magical theories. No one seemed particularly sinister, but then again, the best deceivers never did. Just as I was about to turn away, a man approached the group, his confidence unmistakable as he greeted the High Witch with a casual familiarity that spoke of deep connections.

His appearance was unremarkable, yet there was an intensity in his gaze that seemed to pull the shadows closer around him. I lingered nearby, pretending to adjust the decoration on a nearby table while tuning in to their exchange.

"You're as punctual as ever, Corbin," the High Witch remarked with a shrewd smile.

My heart galloped. Corbin. This had to be him. Corbin Grimm. I stole a glance at his hands, half expecting to see them shimmer with dark magic, but they were normal, betraying nothing of his alleged necromantic skills.

He laughed, a sound that seemed too cheerful for someone reputed to be so evil. "I try, Ingrid. But tonight, I'm more interested in discussing your thoughts on the new elemental alignments proposed last meeting."

Elemental alignments? It seemed like a normal enough topic for a gathering of witches and warlocks, yet there was an edge to his voice. A subtle hint of menace lurking beneath the surface. Was this a cover for his true intentions? I had to speak to him. And if I didn't go up to him now, I might never get the chance again.

I wasn't sure where I got the guts to do it, but I began to

panic about missing my chance. So, I jumped into the unknown with both feet.

I took a deep breath and bolstered by my earlier success, I walked up to Corbin Grimm after he'd left the High Witch and wandered over to the refreshments table.

He was standing alone, his dark eyes surveying the room from beneath a hood that seemed to swallow any light that dared approach. He was dressed in a suit that screamed gothic elegance, the silver embroidery catching the candlelight with an almost mocking gleam.

"Excuse me, Mr. Grimm?" I said, extending a hand that he regarded but didn't take. "I'm Sage Holland."

Grimm's gaze shifted to me, sharp and assessing. "Hello, there," he replied, his voice smooth as silk. "What can I do for you, Miss Holland?"

Caught in Grimm's scrutinizing look, my mind raced. My heart thudded. The silence awkwardly lingered, and every second stretched longer as I wondered if I had just exposed myself to a major threat.

"Did you summon Tenebris?" I asked bluntly, unable to skirt around the question that burned inside me.

Corbin's lips curled into a tight smile. "Summon? Such a harsh word. I prefer to think of it as... negotiating."

"Negotiating?" I repeated, incredulous. "With a creature that could've torn our world apart?"

He leaned closer, and I fought the urge to step back. "Many things in this world are misunderstood, young witch."

"Tenebris is dead," I said firmly, trying to gauge his reaction.

Grimm's face momentarily darkened, a brief flare of anger

or perhaps frustration flashing in his expression. Almost as quickly as it appeared, he composed himself, his features settling back into a calm, unreadable mask. "Dead, you say? How tragic."

"Whoever summoned the spirit...they'll know that they failed." I slanted my head, watching him closely.

Corbin's response was a subtle narrowing of his eyes, a glimmer of intrigue—or was it defiance—playing briefly across his features. "That's an interesting assumption."

"Interesting?" I repeated, taking a moment to choose my words carefully. "But it's clear that Tenebris was just a tool for someone's agenda. Someone who wanted to create a magical uprising."

Corbin sneered, his voice low. "You seem to have a vivid imagination."

"But why did you do it? I know it was you, Corbin." My voice sounded calm, even though I was shaking.

Corbin shook his head with mock disappointment. "Assumptions again. I've always found direct action to be more effective than rumor and speculation."

"Then let's be direct. What's the gain?"

Corbin rubbed his chin, his expression tightening. "You are treading into dangerous territory, young lady."

"I'm aware," I responded. "But someone's playing a very high stakes game with us as the pawns."

He paused, a calculated silence stretching between us. Finally, he leaned closer, his voice dropping to a conspiratorial whisper. "Let's just say, not everyone at this gathering is acting of their own volition. Sometimes, those with the power to command also have the ambition to manipulate the board." His expression glimmered with a hint of something deeper, perhaps a reluctant respect or a veiled warning.

"Who?" I asked, the question slipping from me before I could consider its weight. "You have to tell me!"

"Ah, silly girl, a word of advice." Corbin sighed, a thin smile playing on his lips. "Stop being such a nosey young witch."

Frustration rose up within me, hot and insistent. "Seriously? Tell me."

He rolled his eyes as if I bored him now. "Now if you'll excuse me, Miss Holland."

The warlock slipped away before I could think of something to stop him. But I continued to stand there, feeling the weight of his words, understanding that this was far from over. Whoever was pulling Corbin Grimm's strings, they were still out there, and I couldn't let it go. Not now. Not when we were so close to the truth.

"Damn it."

The party buzzed around me with laughter and conversation, but I barely heard it. A determination settled in my bones, a resolve to peel back the layers of deception. Whoever was behind Corbin and thought they could use us as chess pieces didn't know who they were dealing with.

"Hey, Sage, are you okay?" Brad's voice broke through my thoughts.

"Yeah," I replied automatically, though my clenched fists said otherwise. "Just thinking about who ordered this magical uprising."

"Anything we can help with?" Evie asked, her bright eyes searching mine.

"Possibly," I said, brushing a stray lock of blue highlighted hair behind my ear. "But first, I need to talk to Ingrid."

I made my way through the crowd, weaving past witches and warlocks lost in merriment, their laughter a discordant melody against the thrumming urgency in my veins. The High Witch stood near the fireplace, her silver hair glinting in the firelight like strands of moonbeam.

"Ingrid, I need to speak with you, please."

"What is it, Sage?"

I could hardly contain the tremor in my voice. "I spoke with Corbin just now."

Her eyebrows arched ever so slightly as though I'd commented on the weather outside. "And?"

"I think he was the one who summoned and used Tenebris to terrorize the magical community."

Her gaze sharpened, a flare of concern betraying her composed exterior before it was swiftly masked by indifference. "Sage, you're a talented witch, but this is above your paygrade."

My heart clenched. "But—"

"Listen to me," Ingrid cut in, her tone firm yet not unkind. "You are young, and while your courage is admirable, there are matters that require... let's say, a more experienced hand. I will look into this matter."

"But this affects all of us," I persisted, feeling the sting of her dismissal. "I can't just stand by and watch."

Ingrid sighed, her gaze moving over the partygoers. "It's not your responsibility, Sage. Enjoy the celebration. Leave these concerns to those of us who have been dealing with such threats for decades."

"Even if that means more danger could be looming?" I pressed, unable to quell the passion rising within me.

"Especially then," Ingrid replied, her voice softening. "Sometimes, we must trust in the strengths of others."

She turned away to join her guests while I stood there, grappling with a whirlwind of emotions. She cared, I could tell, but her dismissal felt too harsh.

No matter what Ingrid said, I couldn't just stand by and do nothing. This was my fight, too.

TEN

I smoothed the velvety throw rug over the back of the couch for what must have been the tenth time and glanced at the clock. Brad would be here any minute, and I wanted the house to look nice.

With Tenebris defeated and the immediate threat to our community gone, I found myself longing for the comfort and closeness of Brad's presence.

Meeting Brad's girlfriend had stirred something up inside me. Jealousy. And I couldn't shake it off.

I didn't want to come between them or anything. My feelings were more a sense of longing for what could have been if I'd stayed in town.

The boy next door and I had a history that ran deeper than mere friendship. There was a time when I'd thought we might have a future together, but that was before my parents had died. Before I'd gone off to one of the most prestigious magic colleges around.

It seemed that life had different plans for us. But now that he'd found someone else, and I hadn't... well, it kinda sucked. To compensate, I'd decided to just throw myself into my work. I would hone my craft and help Ingrid with her duties as High Witch.

Inviting him over today when he was committed to someone else was probably selfish of me, but the truth was, Brad was more than just a friend to me. The bond we shared was special, built on shared experiences and history.

And so, I'd asked him to hang out.

"Agatha, do you think I've overdone it with the candles?" I asked, igniting one last wick.

The black cat moved a muscle from her curled up position in front of the fireplace.

"Less worrying, young witch. More trusting in your friendship," Agatha mumbled without opening her eyes, her words laced with drowsy sarcasm.

With a sigh, I retreated to my bedroom to change my shirt. There, atop my dresser lay a small locket, slightly tarnished but cherished all the same. I opened it to reveal a photo of Brad and me as teenagers, our smiles wide and joyful. We'd been inseparable once upon a time. Before life got complicated, and I missed that.

The locket's weight in my palm felt like a talisman of hope for a future with Brad by my side once more. Even if it was just as friends.

Friendship was powerful all on its own. I tucked the locket into the pocket of my skirt. Dark hair with blue highlights fell across my face as I leaned forward, catching my reflection in the mirror.

A knock at the door made me grin, and I rushed through the house to open the front door.

"Hey, Sage," Brad greeted me, stepping into the living room with his easy smile. In his hands, he held a beautifully wrapped box, the kind that promised something far too indulgent inside.

"Brad!" My voice came out breathier than I intended as I took in the sight of him—those intense blue eyes, the casual tilt of his head.

He extended the box toward me, and my fingers brushed his. "For you."

I lifted the lid to find a collection of decadent chocolates nestled within, the very ones we'd once shared on an afternoon by the lake. My pulse quickened, memories flooding back with every sniff of yummy cocoa and caramel.

"Chocolate, Brad? You do know the way to a witch's heart," I teased, the corners of my lips quirking up.

"Only the best for you, Sage," he said, his voice low and tender.

"Thank you. It's very sweet."

Why bring me such a thoughtful gift? I wondered if it was simply friendly affection, or perhaps... did he feel the way I did?

"Come sit down." I gestured toward the couch, the soft cushions promising a comfort I hoped would ease the fluttering in my stomach. "We've hardly had a chance to catch up, what with everything that's gone on since I got back."

"I know." Brad took a seat on the couch, and I sat beside him, close enough to feel his body heat radiating. Our thighs nearly touched.

Brad's gaze roamed around the living room, taking in the artfully arranged furniture and flickering candles. "Damn, Sage. Your place always has this magical touch."

A pleased grin quirked my lips. I tucked some stray strands of hair behind my ear, hyperaware of his stare on me. "Thanks. Guess it comes with the territory of being an interior design witch."

"Nah, it's all you. You've got a gift." Brad's deep voice sent a delicious tingle down my spine.

Once our gazes locked, electricity sizzled between us. My breath caught in my throat, but I pushed on to keep talking. "Well, if you ever need a magical makeover at your place, you know who to call." I nudged him with my elbow playfully. "I could even throw in a special discount for my favorite next-door neighbor."

Brad chuckled. "I like the sound of that. Though I'm not sure my mom would appreciate me hiring another witch to redecorate her former home."

"Oh, I'm sure she'd love it," I dismissed easily. Brad's mom had always liked me, as far as I could tell. "Who wouldn't want a touch of enchantment in their decor?"

"True, but I think the real enchantment is sitting right next to me." His voice lowered to a husky whisper.

I felt my cheeks flush, a giddy smile emerging. "Oh, Brad. Keep flirting with me, and I might just put a spell on you."

He leaned in closer, his breath tickling my cheek. "I wouldn't mind being under your spell, Sage."

My heart leapt as his tone changed to pure flirting. I knew we were treading on thin ice here, breaking the boundaries of our current friendship. But at that moment, I couldn't bring myself to care.

"Well, in that case, maybe I should show you some of my more... enchanting designs sometime."

His mouth opened, then he chuckled. "Sage, are you trying to seduce me with interior design?"

I threw my head back and laughed. "Maybe I am. Is it working?"

He grinned, shaking his head and looking away for the first time. "You're impossible, you know that? But I have to admit, it's part of your cuteness factor."

I swallowed hard. "In all serious... how are things with Sarah?"

Brad stilled, a shadow passing over his handsome face. "Actually, we broke up a few days ago."

"Shit. I'm sorry." The words felt hollow even as I said them. I wasn't sorry, not at all. My pulse kicked up a notch as I realized that the breakup meant he was available.

"Don't be." He shrugged, but I caught the slight tremble in his hands before he laced his fingers together. "It's for the best."

I nodded slowly, fighting the shameful thrill that shot through me at this news. A shameful part of me wanted to believe that he'd ended things because of me. Because of us.

I bit my lip, my body hyperaware of every breath he took, every flex of his muscles beneath that tight shirt. Hell, I needed to get a grip. This was Brad. I'd just gotten him back in my life. I couldn't risk ruining everything just because my foolish heart raced every time he walked into a room.

"Sage." His low murmur snapped me out of my spiraling thoughts. "You okay?"

"Yeah. Yeah, I'm good." I forced a smile, but I could tell he saw right through it. He always could.

Brad shifted closer, his knee bumping mine and sending fire shooting up my leg. "Hey. It's okay. You can talk to me."

I met his soft blue gaze, and the genuine concern I saw there made my heart clench. I couldn't have him the way I craved, but having Brad in my life in any capacity was a gift. One I wouldn't throw away.

"I'm fine, really. Just processing." I laid my hand over his, marveling at the perfect way our fingers intertwined. "I'm here for you, Brad. Always. You know that, right?"

His expression softened, and he squeezed my hand. "I know. Me too, Sage. Me too."

And there it was again. That bone-deep connection that kept drawing us back together. Dangerous and exhilarating and so very right.

One day possibly, I'd find the courage to tell him how I really felt. To risk it all for a chance at something real. But for now, this was enough. More than enough.

I patted his thigh. "If you need to talk about it..."

"Thanks, Sage." He offered me a grateful smile. "But no. I don't want to talk about Sarah. It's over, plain and simple. For good."

I hesitated, the words lodged in my throat like a spell gone awry. I needed a friend today, someone I could talk to and trust. Opening up to Brad about my innermost fears was akin to casting a circle—vulnerable, yet necessary for any true magic to happen.

My weighty thoughts were pressing down on me like a physical force. I realized that I couldn't keep these fears bottled up any longer. Brad was one of my closest friends. The loss of my parents had left a gaping hole in my heart, a void that no amount of magic or success could truly fill. I had thrown myself into my work, stopping Tenebris and stepping into my role as Ingrid's assistant. Desperately trying to prove myself worthy of my parents' memory, to make them proud even in death. But it had been a lot. Returning home after all these years wasn't easy.

So, with a trembling breath and a heart laid bare, I decided to let the walls come down and reveal the broken pieces of myself that I had kept hidden for so long.

"Brad," I said, leaning back. "I'm scared."

"Of what?" he asked. "Tell me."

I bit my lip, already struggling with hot tears. "Of being alone and failing as a witch. But mostly..." A shudder ran through me. "I'm terrified that one day all the spells and charms won't be enough to hide how broken I've fe since my parents died."

He turned towards me and leaned in, his forehead pressing lightly against mine, his breath's minty scent on my lips. "Sage, we're all a little broken. It's what makes us... us."

He pulled back and used his thumb to brush away an errant tear that had escaped down my cheek. "And you? You're the most incredible person I've ever met, witch or not."

"Brad," I breathed, heart fluttering madly. "You don't have to say things like that."

"Of course, I do," he said, his eyes searching mine. "You

need to hear the truth. Your past isn't what defines you, Sage. It's your heart."

"Sometimes, I think my heart is the most fractured part of me."

The confession hung between us, heavy and raw.

He let out a shaky laugh. "But it's also the strongest. Believe me, I know. My fears? They're about not measuring up. About losing people I care about. Losing you."

"Brad—" The rest of my words were lost when he dropped his head and his lips met mine.

His hands cradled my face, thumbs caressing my cheeks as if I were something precious, something to be cherished. The whiff of the scented candles converged with the taste of him—a flavor more intoxicating than any elixir.

I froze for a moment, gasping against his lips, then gave up fighting whatever was holding me back. I kissed him with everything I had, pouring into that single, searing contact all the attraction and desire I'd kept bottled up inside. Our breaths mingled, and our hearts beat in sync as if they too had been waiting for this moment.

For once, my mind was silent, no thoughts of spells or consequences. Just the overwhelming sensation of Brad's lips on mine. We existed in a world apart, where only we could go—a place where magic wasn't just about power, but about connection.

This kiss would be a turning point, a marker etched into the timeline of our relationship. There would be no going back from this, no simple friendship to return to. And as terrifying as that thought was, it was also exhilarating.

"Brad," I murmured against his lips. "I—"

"Shh, don't talk, please," he whispered, pulling back just enough to rest his forehead against mine again. "We have all the time in the world, Sage. For now, let's just be here. Together."

"Okay." I smiled, my voice steadier than I felt. And for the first time in a long while, I allowed myself to believe that everything just might turn out all right.

CHAPTER
ELEVEN

M y crystal ball was cool and substantial in my hands, its smooth surface reflecting the dim candlelight of my quiet room. I sat cross-legged on the floor, the woven rug beneath me. I centered myself for the scrying ritual. The world outside quieted to a hush, and all that existed was the deep thrum of magic coursing through my veins, connecting me to the divine.

I exhaled, my breath fogging briefly over the crystal's clarity. "Show me Corbin Grimm. Show me the puppet master pulling his strings."

"The High Witch told you not to interfere," Agatha said from atop the bookshelf.

"The High Witch just doesn't want me or my friends to get hurt," I replied. Which was virtuous of her, but not what I needed.

My fingertips traced the orb's surface, and it began to glow with an inner light, hues of indigo eddying within its depths. It was like diving into a deep, dark ocean.

"Then why are you doing this? If she finds out there will be hell to pay," Agatha said.

I tore my gaze away from the spiraling depths of the crystal, fixing Agatha with a determined stare. "Because I can't just sit by and watch as Corbin Grimm keeps attacking our town. If there's someone else behind this, someone pulling his strings, I need to know who it is."

Agatha's tail flicked back and forth, her eyes narrowing. "And what do you plan to do with this information, little witch? Confront them on your own? You're powerful, but you're young. You have your limits."

I sighed, running a hand through my hair. "I know, Agatha. But I can't just do nothing. If there's a way to stop this, to protect the people I care about, I have to try."

The cat leaped down from the bookshelf, landing gracefully on the floor. She padded over to me, her voice taking on a softer tone. "I understand your need to help, Sage. It's one of the things I admire most about you. But please, be careful. Don't let your desire to do good blind you to the dangers."

With a smile, I reached out, scratching Agatha behind the ears. "I'll be cautious, I promise."

Agatha leaned into my touch, purring softly. "I know, young witch. Just remember, you're not alone in this. You have friends who care about you, who would be devastated if anything happened to you."

I nodded, feeling a warmth spread through my chest at the thought of my friends and the unwavering support they had always shown me since I returned. "I won't forget that, Agatha. And I won't take any unnecessary risks. But I have to see this through for the sake of everyone in our town."

The cat sighed. "Very well. But know that I'll be watching over you, ready to intervene if things get out of hand."

I gave Agatha one last scratch before turning my attention back to the crystal ball. "I wouldn't have it any other way, my feline friend. Now, let's see what mysteries this orb can unveil."

I focused my energy on the roiling images in the crystal, Agatha's comforting presence beside me.

The visions started as mere flickers, shadows darting just beyond my grasp. A hooded figure here, a glimpse of a twisted smile there, all shrouded in an ethereal mist. I squinted, trying to pierce through the veil that separated me from the answers I so desperately sought. The crystal's energy pulsed against my skin, a silent beat that quickened with my own heart.

"Something's there, Agatha," I said, my voice tinged with frustration. "A ritual, dark and foreboding. There are figures, but their faces are obscured by—"

"By their own wickedness, no doubt." She licked a paw. "Can you see him? Our adversary, Mr. Grimm?"

"Only his silhouette. He's there, among them, his aura black as night—" I paused, my gaze never leaving the crystal's enigmatic scene. "But the one behind it all—the ringleader—remains a shadow within shadows."

"Patience, Sage. Your power grows, but some secrets are well kept. Perhaps they are meant to be unraveled in time, not forced."

Agatha was the voice of reason, but that didn't help my frustration.

"Yeah, yeah." I sighed, feeling the burden of our situation grow.

Then again, she was probably right. Mysteries such as these didn't just show themselves.

I released a slow breath, my focus unwavering as the images continued to play like a silent film only I could see. The crystal's glow ebbed and flowed, throwing ghostly patterns upon the walls. My link to the magical realm intensified, a pressure at the back of my skull that was starting to hurt.

"Agatha, I see something else," I said. "A symbol, repeated throughout the visions. It's important, I can feel it, but it's meaning eludes me."

"Describe it," she prompted, her whiskers twitching with interest.

I closed my eyes, stretching out with my supernatural senses.

"An ouroboros, but not quite. The serpent devours not its tail but a star... or maybe it's protecting it?"

"Protection or possession," Agatha said. "Such symbols are often dual natured. Keep it in mind, the cosmos has a way of illuminating the obscure when least expected."

The crystal's power waned, and my headache exploded

behind my eyes. I pulled back from the vision and grabbed onto my head, the room returning to its mundane state.

"Ow, that hurt."

The knock at the door jolted me from my trance-like state and forced me to take a breath. Whoever was at the door, they were a welcomed interruption to clear the lingering fog in my mind. Agatha leapt off the table, her black form slinking through the house.

I got to my feet, blinking rapidly as my eyes refocused and my headache slowly receded. I crossed the room and opened the front door to reveal Evie.

"Hey," she greeted with a half-smile, stepping inside without waiting for an invitation. She was like that—casual, direct, and always carrying the essence of wild herbs and potions on her. That's what made her Evie.

"Any luck?" she asked, her eyes searching mine for clues.

"Bits and pieces," I admitted, leading her to the living room, where Agatha had already reclaimed her seat. "Shadows, rituals, but nothing concrete. It's like chasing mist."

I conjured myself a cup of tea with a painkiller potion, feeling the need to quell the pain after such an intense experience. "Do you want one?" I asked her, gesturing to the cup.

She shook her head. "No thanks. Go for it."

I took a sip and sighed as the potion spread through my body. "That's better. My head was killing me."

Evie flopped onto the couch decorated with plush cushions and pastel throw blankets. "We'll figure it out," she said with more certainty than I felt.

"I hope so," I said, allowing myself to be momentarily comforted by her confidence.

"Spill it, Sage," Agatha said, her whiskers twitching and tail flickering. "There's more troubling you than elusive visions."

I hesitated, my gaze wandering to the bright flames of the fireplace. The weight of my secret pressed heavily on my chest, a burden I'd carried for the last few days. I knew I could trust Agatha and Evie, but the words seemed to stick in my throat, as if speaking them aloud would make them all too real. The memory of Brad's lips on mine, the electric thrill of our kiss made me smile.

I took a steadying breath then said the words I needed to say, my heart fluttering at the memory. "Brad kissed me."

Evie shot upright, her eyes wide. "Holy hell, Sage! When? How?"

"A few nights ago." I fidgeted with the hem of my sweater. "We were hanging out for some downtime. It just happened."

"Well, thank the goddess!" Evie exclaimed, throwing her hands up in the air. "I thought you two would dodge your feelings forever."

Agatha sniffed disdainfully. "Young witch, you allowed yourself to be distracted by fleeting passions when darkness looms."

I ignored my familiar, who was probably centuries older than me, and focused on my friend who understood my age better. "But, Evie, what if he doesn't feel the same? What if I've ruined everything by giving in to my feelings?"

"Hey, hey. Stop that." Evie reached over and placed her hand over mine to squeeze my hand. "Brad's a good guy. He's been your friend forever. He was your high school sweetheart. This could be wonderful, you know?"

"Or catastrophic." I sagged onto the sofa. The fear of rejection, of altering our friendship beyond repair, gnawed at me. When we were kids, it was easy to walk away and not ruin everything, but now...

Agatha leapt onto the coffee table, her tail swishing. "Do not be daft, young witch. That warlock has fawned over you since you were mere fledglings."

"She's right," Evie chimed in. "Remember when we were sixteen and he brought you those enchanted roses that never wilted? Or when he learned advanced transmutation just to craft you that moonstone bracelet for your birthday?"

Heat crept up my neck. "Those were just friendly gestures."

"Friendly gestures?" Agatha scoffed. "The boy is utterly besotted. Why, I've caught him staring at you with those dopey eyes more times than I can count. He's ridiculous."

I fidgeted, recalling the way Brad's blue eyes had lingered on me lately, full of passionate longing. "Holy hell, what if you're right?"

"Of course, we're right." Evie squeezed my hand. "Just ask him, Sage. I bet he's been waiting for this as long as you have."

Nodding slowly, I took a deep breath. Maybe it was time to stop hiding from my feelings and take a leap of faith.

Evie smiled big and wide. "And listen, Sage. Regardless of what happens with Brad, we're here for you."

"Thanks, guys," I murmured, feeling a surge of gratitude for their unwavering support. "I don't know what I'd do without you."

"Die alone and friendless, most likely," my familiar said dryly, but the amused gleam in her eye softened the joke.

"Probably," I agreed, a small laugh escaping.

Evie pulled out her notepad, the edges worn from constant

use. "All right, enough talk of boys. Now we need to focus. How do we uncover who's behind this? We're still thinking there's a magical uprising going on, yeah?"

I nodded, agreeing with her that something else was definitely going on. "Scrying hasn't revealed much."

"Maybe we're looking at this the wrong way," Agatha suggested. "Instead of seeking answers directly, let's trace the magic. Every spell leaves an echo, a signature. Something that could lead us to the one who cast the spell."

Evie tapped her pen against her lips. "Like a magical residue, you're right. If we could isolate those echoes—"

"Then we might pinpoint where they're coming from." I took another big sip of tea for fortitude and got to my feet.

Evie stood up next to me. "I'll start gathering components for a location spell. We can amplify the resonance of their magic and track them down."

I nodded at her. "Good idea, but this isn't like any other dark magic we've faced."

"Since when has danger stopped us?" Evie grinned, her expression alight with the thrill of the challenge.

I laughed. "Never."

"Before we get started on this new challenge, I have to ask you something, Sage." Agatha's gaze was sharp on me now. "How are you holding up? You've been rather pensive lately."

"Is it that obvious?" I asked with a sigh, realizing that Agatha was going to see things others wouldn't. She did live with me, after all. "It's just... sometimes I wonder if I'm really cut out for this path. The High Witch—Ingrid—she trusts me to assist her, and I keep worrying that I'll mess things up for her. That I'll disappoint everyone."

"Your powers are extraordinary, Sage. Unlike anyone else's I know." Evie patted my shoulder. "You were chosen for this because the High Witch knows you can do it. You've gotta have more faith in yourself."

I inhaled sharply, feeling a wash of coldness move over me. "Does she, though? Or is she just waiting for me to prove myself?"

Evie scoffed gently. "Are you kidding? You've done more for the magical community than most witches twice your age. You've got nothing to prove. You killed an evil creature and confronted a wicked necromancer!"

Agatha stretched her legs. "Validation from others—even the High Witch—is fleeting. What matters is that you fulfill your duty with conviction."

I was touched by their faith in me, but it would take me a while to catch up with their level of faith. "I won't let fear hold me back. Not when there's so much at stake."

"Damn straight," Evie agreed, her voice firm. "We've got your back, Sage."

I pressed my hands together in a prayer-type gesture. "I guess I just worry too much." I nodded, appreciating their reassurance. "Thanks, you two. I really needed to hear that."

I sat back on the couch, relieved to hear the boosting words. Agatha hopped onto my lap, and I stroked her soft fur.

"Don't sell yourself short, young witch." She purred. "Your talents are unparalleled. Ingrid recognizes your potential. That's why she entrusted you with such a crucial role."

Evie grinned. "Yeah, and let's not forget how you kicked that necromancer's bony ass back to the underworld." She mimed a few mock punches. "That was some serious badassery."

I couldn't help but laugh. "Okay, okay. I get it. No more self-doubt. I'll try to do better. I promise."

Agatha purred approvingly. "That's the spirit. Now, let's get to work."

CHAPTER
TWELVE

T he sun rose high in the bright azure sky, bathing
Evernight Meadow in a golden haze that made the
wildflowers shimmer like scattered jewels. It was the
perfect day.

Brad and I sat on a patch of lush grass, our tartan blanket a
small island amidst a sea of green. He unpacked the basket,
revealing an array of treats that smelled of enchantment and
would taste delicious.

"Try the pixieberry tarts," he said, pointing to the latest
thing he pulled out of the basket. "They're supposed to bring
good luck."

I bit into the tart's flaky crust, and a burst of sweetness filled my mouth—berries mingled with a hint of magic that fizzed on my tongue. "Holy hell, these are amazing," I said, licking my lips.

"I'm glad you like them." Brad stretched out beside me, looking every bit the part of a relaxed, sexy man. He certainly made my heart sing.

The afternoon breeze blew through the meadow, carrying the fragrance of jasmine and moonflowers. I stared out at the distance and really took it all in. There was a peace here with Brad that I rarely felt. I was always moving, always yearning. Here... now... this was peace.

Brad took my hand, pulling me back to reality. I stared down at our hands. A faint glow emanated from our touch, a soft luminescence that shimmered upon our skin.

"Your beauty outshines even the magic of this place, Sage." His voice was light, teasing.

A laugh escaped me before I could stop it, and a hot flush spread across my cheeks. "And your charm, Brad Adams, is as potent as any spell you could cast."

"Is it now?" His thumb stroked the back of my hand, sending tingles up my arm. "Even more potent than my taste in movies?"

"Definitely not!" I squeezed his hand. "Remember that horror flick you made me watch? I couldn't sleep for days."

He smiled. "Because it was terrifyingly good."

"Or just plain terrifying. My music playlist, however, is pure magic."

"Ah, but can it compete with my book collection? Full of

ancient lore and forbidden spells?" His gaze was feisty but proud. Knowledge was his treasure.

I poked him gently in the ribs. "Depends. Does your bookshelf have space for interior design magic? Because that's where the real creativity lies."

"Of course, right next to my treatise on elemental manipulation. Fire, earth, air, water—I've mastered them all."

"Except when it comes to beating me at Elemental Conquest," I teased, knowing full well how our last game night had ended.

"Cheater," he murmured affectionately, pulling me closer.

"Hey!" I feigned indignation, a grin lifting the corners of my mouth. "I'll have you know, my victory on board game night was as legitimate as any spell in your precious tomes."

"Sure," he drawled, his blue stare glinting with impishness. "Just like that time you claimed you'd 'forgotten' to use your most powerful cards until the end."

"Strategy, Brad," I corrected him, laughing. "It's all about strategy."

"Or convenient forgetfulness."

I rolled my eyes at Brad's teasing, a small smile touching my lips. Our light-hearted banter was as natural as breathing, and always had been. Regardless of his accusations of cheating, I knew he didn't really mind that I made sure I won sometimes. It was all part of our game.

Once our laughter subsided, my thoughts drifted to my fledgling business, Mystical Motifs. The idea of enchanting entire homes had been simmering in my mind for weeks, a tantalizing prospect that could take my interior design magic to new heights. "You know," I began, meeting Brad's gaze. "I'm serious about expanding the business. Imagine being able to rearrange your entire living space with a simple incantation. No more heavy lifting or rearranging furniture manually."

Brad's brows lifted, intrigued. "That's ambitious, even for you. But if anyone can pull it off, it's the spell-crafting extraordinaire herself." A hint of pride colored his words, and I felt a warmth bloom in my chest. His unwavering belief in my abilities never failed to bolster my confidence.

"You're right. It's a huge undertaking." I chewed my lip, considering the challenges. "But holy hell, the potential is mind-blowing. Can you imagine the convenience? The possibilities for interior design would be limitless!"

"Sounds like seventh-level magic to me," Brad said, admiration lacing his tone once more. "You never cease to amaze me, Sage. Your parents would be proud of you, you know."

My heart swelled at the mention of my parents. "They always encouraged me to think outside the spellbook."

"Which is why you're the best at what you do," he said earnestly. "Your designs don't just change spaces, they change lives."

"Wow, laying it on a bit thick, aren't you?" I teased, but inside, his words bolstered me more than any incantation could. "Maybe you should write my marketing copy. You do it better than I do."

"Only stating facts." He grasped one of the pixieberry tarts and lifted it into the air. "Here's to changing lives and winning at board games," he toasted before taking a large bite. Brad's lips curved into a sexy smile as he swallowed the last bite of the sweet treat.

I laughed at his playful antics. "You're such a dork," I said, shaking my head in amusement. My gaze lingered on his lips, still glistening from the sweet treat's glaze.

"Hey, don't hate the player," he retorted with a wink, leaning back on his elbow. "Appreciate the game instead."

I rolled my eyes, but the corners of my mouth tugged upward. "Speaking of games..." I clicked my fingers and conjured up a pack of cards from my study at home. "I believe it's my turn to deal the cards." I shuffled the deck with a practiced hand and made some space between us on the blanket.

"Prepare to be dazzled, Mr. Adams." As I dealt the cards, I had a sinister thought. I made a magic move with a tiny movement of my wrist, and Brad's cards rearranged into a less-than-ideal hand.

I batted my eyelids and lifted my hand up so he couldn't see what I held. "May the best witch win."

Brad grinned wickedly. "You're playing with fire, Holland." He studied his cards, a crease forming between his brows. "Holy hell, did you rig this?"

"Who, me?" I feigned innocence, struggling to suppress a grin. "I would never stoop so low."

"Uh, huh, sure you wouldn't." Brad smirked, his expression vibrant with amusement. He sat up and held his cards in one hand. "I've known long enough to recognize your tells, Sage. You're not as innocent as you'd like me to believe."

I gasped in mock offense, placing a hand over my heart. "Brad Adams, are you accusing me of cheating? I'm wounded by your lack of faith in my integrity."

"Oh, I have faith in your integrity," he countered, his voice dropping to a low, teasing murmur. "Just not when it comes to card games."

The air between us buzzed with a delicious blend of joking banter and fiery desires. I found myself drawn to the intensity of his gaze, the way his lips curved into that infuriatingly attractive smirk.

"Well, then," I said, my voice taking on a sultry edge, "I guess I'll just have to prove my innocence through my superior skills."

Brad chuckled. "Bring it on, witch. Let's see what you've got."

As we delved into the game, our hands brushed against each other, lingering a moment too long. The casual touches ignited a fire within me, a longing I'd tried to suppress for years. Being around Brad was both exhilarating and frustrating, a constant push and pull of emotions that left me breathless.

"Crap," I grumbled.

Brad played a particularly clever move, his expression glinting with triumph.

"What's the matter, Sage? Losing your touch?" he taunted, his voice laced with a challenge.

I narrowed my eyes at him, determination coursing through my veins. "You wish, Adams. I'm just getting started."

The game continued, our teasing and laughter becoming more animated. The air hummed with a different kind of magic. One that had nothing to do with spells or enchantments. It was the magic of two hearts forever entwined by a bond that defied explanation.

Brad's gaze locked onto mine, the intensity in his blue gaze causing my breath to catch. He reached out, his fingers grazing my cheek with a tenderness that made my heart flutter wildly in my chest.

"Sage," he murmured, his deep voice husky with emotion. A hint of a smile played at the corners of his mouth. "I've wanted to do this for so long."

Before I could form a coherent response, he leaned in and captured my lips with his own. Desire, hot and dizzying, ignited inside me as he kissed me deeply, passionately. Our magic blazed around us, vibrant colors painting the air.

I melted against him, the hard planes of his body molding perfectly against my curves. His strong arms wrapped around my waist, pulling me flush against him. A breathy moan escaped me as his tongue teased the seam of my lips, seeking entrance. I parted them for him, the kiss turning hungry, desperate.

Holy hell, the man could kiss. My spine turned to jelly, and my mind went blissfully blank, lost to the feel of his lips moving over mine, his fingers tangling in my hair. Kissing Brad was like coming home, a fleeting sense of rightness settling deep in my bones.

When we finally broke apart, both of us were breathing hard. Brad rested his forehead against mine, his eyes dark and heated as they bored into me. His voice lowered, hoarse and deep with desire. "I care about you, Sage. I always have."

Tears pricked at the back of my eyes. Those were the exact words I'd been hoping to hear. I cupped his face in my hands, my heart so full it felt ready to burst. "I care about you too, Brad. So much."

His answering grin was blinding before he swooped in to kiss me again.

When we parted once more for air, Brad whispered, "Sage, I want more than just friendship between us." His voice was low, husky with longing.

My breath caught. I wanted that too, so badly it hurt. "What about our friendship if this doesn't work out?" I bit my lip, searching his face for an answer to the fears I'd just put out there. The thought of losing Brad completely terrified me.

Part of me had dreamed of this moment, yearned for the sweet moments we'd shared as high school sweethearts to evolve into a more adult relationship. But another part couldn't help but worry. What if this kiss, as magical as it felt, was nothing more than a fleeting moment of weakness?

And if things didn't work out, would our breakup leave us both with shattered hearts and a void where our friendship once thrived? The thought of losing Brad, not just as a potential lover but as one of my closest friend, overwhelmed me.

He brushed a strand of hair from my face, tucking it behind my ear. "Hey. Nothing could ever ruin what we have. You're my oldest friend, Sage. That's never going to change."

I swallowed past the lump in my throat. "Promise?"

"Cross my heart." His lips twitched. "And hope to fly."

A surprised laugh burst out of me. It was an old joke between us, a twist on the usual "hope to die" that referenced Brad's air elemental powers.

I shook my head, fighting a smile. "You're such a dork."

"Takes one to know one," he shot back with a grin.

I rolled my eyes. "Wow. Real mature."

"I'll show you mature." His voice dropped an octave as he leaned in, his nose brushing mine. My pulse jumped.

"Is that a threat or a promise?" I said, my breath caressing his lips he was so close to me. Desire coiled low in my belly.

"Definitely a promise." And then his mouth was on mine

again, hot and hungry, chasing all rational thought from my mind. Holy hell, the man could kiss.

THIRTEEN

The town square was alive with a vibrancy that defied the recent shadows cast upon our small, magical community. The air was imbued with laughter and conversation for the first time since I'd been home.

"Heroes of Emberwick Crossing," boomed Ingrid Nightspire's voice, her presence as commanding as the bright banners fluttering in the breeze. "We gather today to honor Sage Holland, Evie Black, and Brad Adams."

I stood slightly awkwardly under the gaze of so many, feeling Brad's reassuring hand on my lower back. Ingrid's gaze found mine, the violet in them reflective like twilight skies.

With her head held high, she continued, "For their courage, for their strength, and most importantly, for their resourcefulness in defeating evil, we owe these three our deepest gratitude."

Warmth spread through my entire body as applause erupted around us.

An elder warlock, whose beard seemed to be a nest for chipmunks, stepped forward. "Sage, Brad, and Evie, your spell crafting was nothing short of miraculous."

His compliment left me flushed with pride, yet I could only offer a faint smile and a glance towards my friends, sharing the moment with them.

"Thank you," I said.

Evie leaned in close, her dark hair tickling my cheek. "Sage, can you believe this shit? We're heroes now."

I couldn't help smiling. "Don't let it go to your head."

"Too late for that," Brad joked, his laughter filling the air.

Evie shot him a playful glare. "Watch it, Adams, or I'll hex your balls off."

Their teasing provided me with a slice of normalcy in the midst of the grandeur of the ceremony. It was a reminder that we were still just us—three best friends who had faced the darkness together.

Ingrid's voice cut through the chatter. "Now, I believe our heroes deserve a feast befitting their triumph. To the Great Hall!"

Once the crowd began to disperse, I caught Ingrid's gaze once more. There was pride in those violet depths, but also something else. A secret that was just out of reach.

"You did well, Sage," she said, her tone softer than before. "Your parents would be proud."

The mention of my parents sent a pang through my heart. I wished they could have been here to see this moment.

"Thank you, Ingrid," I managed, my voice thick with emotion. "I couldn't have done it without your teaching and guidance."

She placed a hand on my shoulder, the weight of it both calming and heavy with expectation. "You have a great destiny ahead of you, Sage Holland. Don't forget that."

The gathering's elation ebbed into a gentle murmur of celebration, and Brad and I found ourselves alone in the middle of the revelry. The morning sun cast long shadows across the cobblestones of the square, dappling the ground with patterns that shifted with the movements of people and animals alike. A couple of iridescent hummingbirds flitted about a nearby blossoming bush, their wings beating softly.

"Listen, Sage, I've been thinking... With everything that's happened, it's made me realize how much you mean to me."

My heart stuttered in my chest. OMG, was this really happening? "Brad, I..."

"I know we've got a history, and I don't want to mess anything up. But I can't ignore this anymore." He took a step closer, his gaze intense. "What do you say we give this thing between us a shot? Take it slow, see where it goes?"

Butterflies erupted in my stomach as I stared up at him, barely daring to breathe. "I'd like that."

A slow grin spread across his face. "Yeah? Well, that's a relief. I was worried I'd just made a complete ass of myself."

I laughed, shaking my head as relief flooded me. "Oh, please. We both know you've got no shortage of confidence."

"True, but even I can get nervous sometimes." He reached out, tucking a strand of my hair behind my ear. "Especially when it comes to you."

My skin tingled where his fingers brushed against it. Crap. How was it possible that such a simple touch made me feel like this? "I guess we'll have to see how it goes then. No pressure, right?"

"No pressure, okay?" Then he laughed loudly. "But I've got a good feeling about this, Sage. You and me, we've always had something special."

I couldn't argue with that. Brad and I we went way back. He knew me better than anyone, even Ingrid. But this? This was uncharted territory for us. "Just don't go getting any crazy ideas, okay? We take this one step at a time."

"I wouldn't dream of it." He held up his hands in mock surrender. "Scout's honor."

I snorted. "You were never a Boy Scout."

"Details." He waved a dismissive hand. "Point is, I'm in this for the long haul. Whatever pace you want to set, I'm game."

My heart swelled at his words. Brad Adams, ever the gentleman. Who would've thought? "All right then, let's do this. But if you break my heart, I'll hex your ass into next week."

He threw his head back and laughed. "Duly noted, witch. Duly noted."

Moving slowly, giving me time to pull away, Brad leaned in and brushed his lips against mine. In public! For the first time.

This kiss was soft, sweet, filled with promise. We drew

apart, and I couldn't stop the giddy smile that spread across my face.

"Come with me, Sage." Ingrid's voice cut through the tenderness of the moment, and I jerked my head around to look at her. Her tone was carrying an undercurrent of urgency that pricked at my senses.

The High Witch was standing a few paces away, her hard stare fixed on me with an intensity that made me step away from Brad.

"Of course, Ingrid," I replied.

Brad's eyebrows knitted together, then he nodded in respect to the High Witch, understanding the need for privacy between mentor and mentee.

Ingrid led me away from the crowd, her silver hair shimmering like a stream of moonlight. We found a spot beneath the shade of an ancient willow, its leaves concealing us.

It was obvious that she wasn't happy, and I wasn't sure why. Tonight was meant to be a celebration. When she didn't speak, I had to ask, "What's wrong?"

The lines on Ingrid's face seemed to deepen as she regarded me solemnly. "There is a disturbance, Sage. A ripple in the fabric of our mystical dominion. A sign of a darkness that threatens to undo the peace we have worked to secure."

My brain screeched to a halt. What? I was trying to make sense of what she was saying. We'd managed to stop Tenebris from wreaking havoc, but it wasn't like we'd come out of it unscathed. And now, hearing about some new bad guy waiting in the wings? It was almost too much to process.

"Like what? What have you heard, seen?"

Her gaze drifted toward the sky, as if seeking answers in the sunlight through the leaves. "Visions are often an enigma, Sage, fragments of possible futures. But this much is clear... the balance has been disturbed."

Her warning hit me hard, and I could feel the weight of it all pressing down on me. My mind was spinning. There was no way I was going to let our little slice of paradise crumble into chaos, not after all the crap we'd been through already.

I took a breath and said as calmly as I could, "Thank you for trusting me with this."

Ingrid and I had a connection that kept growing stronger. It was more than just the whole mentor and mentee thing. She was like the family I never had, or at least the family I didn't have anymore. Knowing that she believed in me, that she trusted me? That meant the world to me, more than any trophy or prize ever could.

"Trust is earned, Sage, and you have shown yourself worthy. More than that, you have shown yourself to be essential." Ingrid's hand came to rest on my shoulder, her touch gentle. "And remember, you are not alone in this. We stand together— as a coven, as a community."

I nodded, swallowing hard against the knot in my throat. "I know, Ingrid. It's just...this is a lot. The balance, the visions, all of it." I let out a shaky breath, my fingers curling into fists at my sides. I'd hoped we were done. That everything would be okay now, but it obviously wasn't. "But I'm not backing down. I'll do whatever it takes to protect our world, our magic."

Ingrid's violet expression gleamed with pride, a hint of a smile on her lips. "That's the spirit, Sage. Embrace the challenge, for it is through adversity that we grow strongest."

I smirked. "Damn, Ingrid, you should write fortune cookies."

She arched a perfectly sculpted eyebrow. "Perhaps in another life, my dear. But for now, we have work to do."

As we walked back towards the heart of the town to rejoin the celebration, I realized that everything was about to change. My intuition was sparking, telling me that the world was shifting beneath my feet.

"So, what's our next move?" I asked, glancing over at Ingrid as we walked. "Please tell me it involves kicking some serious ass."

Ingrid chuckled, a rare sound that made me feel like I'd just won the lottery. "All in good time, Sage. First, we must gather information, then strengthen our defenses. Then, when the moment is right, we strike."

Tenebris, the evil spirit that had threatened to tear our community apart, was gone, but it was just the beginning of a larger threat. Ingrid's warning echoed in my mind, a reminder that there would always be new dangers lurking around the corner. Change could be scary as hell, but it could also be exhilarating. It was a chance to grow, to learn, to become stronger than I ever thought possible.

The sounds of laughter and music grew louder as we got closer to the celebrations. I found myself smiling in spite of a new impending danger. Whatever the future held, I knew I wouldn't be facing it alone.

I had my friends, my mentor, and my sassy black cat.

What else could a young witch like me need?

FAMILIAR LOVE

MAGGIE SHAW

FAMILIAR LOVE

CHAPTER
ONE

With a flick of my wrist, I infused Council member Alden Voss' study with a fresh wave of magic, the air shimmering around us as the magic took effect. The once drab walls bloomed like a time-lapse garden into an array of muted pastels, tailored to the specifications of Emberwick Crossing's most discerning warlock.

With my design magic tingling in my fingertips, I turned around and focused on the armchairs in the room. I reupholstered each piece of furniture in velvety textures, then stepped back to admire my handiwork.

"Looking good, Sage," My familiar purred from her seat

atop a mountain of dust covers and drop cloths. "But when are you going to finish? I'm hungry."

"Patience, Agatha," I said, stepping back to admire the transformation. "Creating magic takes time." I tucked my hair behind my ear then swept it up into a high ponytail so I could focus on my work.

My cat scoffed, "Patience be damned. My stomach hurts."

"You can always hunt for mice in the meantime," I teased, scanning the opulent room for more design options.

"Just hurry, young witch." Her yellow eyes flashed with exasperation.

She looked so pretty in this room. Agatha's black coat was sleek and shiny, her fur reflecting the light from the crystal chandelier above.

Rolling up the sleeves on my new bohemian dress, I advanced to the east wall where layers of wallpaper clung stubbornly to a bookshelf. With a chant under my breath, glowing glyphs appeared on my hands, and I pressed them against the wood. The shelves vibrated beneath my fingertips, but instead of doing as I'd commanded with my spell, the wallpaper peeled back, revealing a passage obscured by darkness.

"Holy hell!" I exclaimed, jumping back a little. That was not what I'd been expecting.

I peered into the dim space and felt a strange tingle of excitement at the discovery. The thrill of uncovering secrets never got old, even if those secrets might be better left buried.

"What on earth have you found?" Agatha asked as she leapt down from the desk gracefully and joined me at the threshold of the hidden chamber.

The entrance was very narrow and as we stood frozen,

staring into the darkness, a cold draft swept the room and ruffled my long hair. I shivered, and not just from the chill. The chamber was etched with mysterious runes that crawled up the walls like sinister ivy. The symbolss thrummed with archaic power; the air thick with the stench of dark sorcery.

"Whoa, look at these..." I reached out and traced a symbol with my finger. My skin prickled with fear the longer I stared at the rune. My gut told me we were in way over our heads here. But when had that ever stopped me? If anything, I was even more curious than before.

"Careful, Sage," Agatha said, her voice taking on a solemn tone. "These were crafted by someone who didn't want to be found. Someone bending the fabric of malice into an invisibility cloak."

"But who and why?" My heart hammered against my ribs. A dozen prospects came to mind, each more troubling than the last. What had we stumbled into?

Agatha examined the markings with a narrowed stare. "I'm not sure. But if they're here, concealed in Councilman Voss' study... then we must assume he's the one who cast the spell. The real question is, what did he use this place for? What was he hiding?"

"Or what is he still hiding?" I swallowed hard.

I reached out, my fingers barely grazing the symbols before the room pulsed with an ominous threat that seemed to radiate from the very walls. A violent burst of power erupted, and I stumbled backward, a scream caught in my throat.

Oh, crap. Oh, crap. Definitely shouldn't have touched that...

"Agatha!" The name was a strangled cry in my throat as shadows snaked around me, tightening like a noose around my neck. I fought against an invisible force, my breath coming in short, panicked gasps.

The shadowy tendrils twisted and writhed, tightening their grip around my wrists and ankles. I could feel their cold, inky presence seeping into my skin, dragging me down into the dark abyss that had formed beneath me. Every movement was a struggle, every breath a desperate gasp. I'd once joked that my curiosity would be the death of me someday. I really hoped today wasn't that day.

"Focus, Sage!" Agatha's tone was sharp. "Remember your training!"

Right, my training. The countless hours spent honing my craft, pushing myself to the brink of exhaustion. All those lessons, all those late nights poring over ancient tomes—they had to be good for something. I just prayed it would be enough to get us out of this mess I'd gotten us into.

I forced myself to remember the spells, to recall the teachings that had been drilled into me. With a fierce strength of mind, I began to chant, the verses tumbling from my lips in a rush. My hands glowed with a soft, blue light as I drew upon my inner power, forcing it to the surface.

The shadowy creatures recoiled a little at the touch of my magic, but they didn't release their grip. I pushed harder, feeling the need to survive surge through me. The room seemed to vibrate with the intensity of the clash between light and dark, the chandelier above our heads swinging wildly.

"Agatha, I need your help!" I shouted; my voice strained beneath the grip of the dark magic.

The black cat leapt from her perch, landing gracefully beside me, her yellow eyes burning with her powers. With a powerful swipe of her paw, she tore through the nearest shadow, the force of her attack causing it to dissipate into wisps of smoke.

"Focus, young witch! Your magic!" Agatha's voice broke through the confusion, her sleek form untouched by the maelstrom.

Desperation lent strength to my trembling limbs, and I summoned every ounce of willpower. I envisioned a sphere in my mind, clear and pure, and stretched out my hands. Magic surged through me, a torrent of light battling the encroaching blackness. A glowing orb materialized between my palms, encapsulating the malevolent sorcery.

"Keep going, Sage! You're almost there!" Agatha urged, her voice now a deep growl.

Drawing strength from Agatha's presence, I focused on the spell. The orb solidified, a prison for the murky shadows that tried to escape its confines. Panting, I lowered my arms, the orb floating beside me, my heart thumping loudly in my chest.

"Okay, I wasn't expecting that." I managed a shaky laugh, trying to brush off the fear that lingered.

"Nor I. Something is deeply wrong here."

Voss... what have you entwined yourself with? My thoughts were a whirlwind of questions and possibilities, but a resolve settled within me. We had to uncover the truth.

"Let's keep poking around," I said, my voice steadier than I felt. "This... whatever it is. We can't just leave it be."

Agatha nodded, though I could sense that she was as shaken as I. "We'll figure this out, Sage. You're not alone in this."

"I appreciate that, Agatha," I said, shivering due to the chill in the chamber. "I don't know what I'd do without you."

"Probably get eaten by a grue," she deadpanned.

I burst out laughing, I couldn't help it. She was probably right.

"Come on, let's see if there are any more clues on these runes," I suggested, moving closer to inspect them.

Agatha hopped up onto my shoulder. "Nothing good ever came from secrets like these."

I totally agreed with her. "Ain't that the truth?"

I started with the desk. Checking for clues, I opened each drawer. There was nothing there except the normal stationery and paraphernalia. But I didn't give up. There had to be something more here.

I slid my hand down and felt the underneath of the desk with my fingers. I searched around until I found an oddity. With a gentle prod, the wooden panel on the top of the desk slid aside. I caught my breath. There, nestled in a velvet-lined nook, lay a communication crystal, its facets barely glinting in the low light of the Councilman's study. My fingers trembled as I reached for it.

"Agatha, look at this." I held the crystal up to the light, then moved it beneath the lamp on Councilman Voss's mahogany desk to get a better look.

"Sweet Circe, Sage, what have you found?" Agatha's eyes were wide as she jumped onto the desk, her black fur bristling.

I closed my hand around the cool surface of the crystal, feeling an odd sensation of foreboding. "Let's find out."

Once the crystal warmed to my touch, a holographic message sputtered to life, throwing eerie shadows across the walls. The image of Alden Voss materialized, his silver-streaked hair and blue eyes unnervingly lifelike. Beside him stood Corbin Grimm, a warlock we were certain was evil. His onyx cloak billowed around him, his presence exuding an ominous power.

I exchanged a tense glance with Agatha. *Well, this can't be good.* Whenever holograms pop up unexpectedly, it's never to share a cookie recipe.

The hologram revealed a dimly lit chamber where Councilman Voss and Corbin stood in hushed conversation.

"Voss," Corbin's voice was a low growl, dripping with malice. "The Council is growing suspicious. We must act swiftly."

Councilman Voss glanced around nervously before responding. "I understand, Corbin. But we must be careful. If they discover our alliance, it will be the end of us both. The balance of power is delicate, and any misstep could be disastrous."

I rolled my eyes. Why did power-hungry men always worry about nothing more than saving their own skin? You'd think that being on the Council would come with a complimentary backbone.

Corbin's stare narrowed, a sinister grin spreading across his face. "You've secured the spell?"

Councilman Voss handed over a scroll, his hand shaking as he did. "This contains the incantation you need to breach the Council's defenses. Use it wisely."

Oh, sure, I'm certain he'll use an illicit spell "wisely". And I'm the Easter Bunny.

I shot Agatha a look that said *can you believe this guy?*

Corbin's eyes glowed an unearthly green, and he took the

scroll. "With this, nothing will stand in our way. The Council will fall, and we will start a new era."

My heart pounded as I watched the exchange, the implications of this conversation sinking in. "Councilman Voss has been aiding Corbin?" I gasped. "But why?"

Agatha's claws flexed against the wood of the desk. "Power, control... the usual. This is bad, Sage. If they succeed, our world is doomed."

I swallowed hard. *No pressure or anything. Just the fate of the entire magical world resting on my shoulders.* I really should've read the fine print before taking this job.

The hologram wavered, showing Councilman Voss and Corbin shaking hands, their alliance sealed.

"We must act soon," Councilman Voss said. "Before we are caught."

Corbin nodded. "I know, asshole. And once the Council falls, nothing will stop the supernatural uprising."

"You require further protection from the Council's prying eyes. I'll ensure that their suspicions are redirected."

"Oh, brilliant. A corrupt councilman AND a foul-mouthed necromancer. It's like the universe decided to hand deliver my worst nightmares." I pinched the bridge of my nose, feeling a headache coming on.

The message ended abruptly, the crystal dimming as the room fell into heavy silence. I could hardly process what I had just seen.

"Bloody hell. Agatha, we need to act. If the Council is compromised, we have to find a way to stop them."

"Damnation," Agatha spat. "That weasel has been using his position to shield that necromancer from discovery. You must tell the high witch."

I nodded grimly, squaring my shoulders. My main role was assistant to the high witch, and she definitely needed to know about this. I clenched my fists, thinking of the innocent lives twisted by such greed. "Dark sorcery, Agatha... necromancy. You know the devastation it can wreak."

"Of course, I do," Agatha said somberly. "Remember the Blackthorn Blight? A whole village turned to wraiths."

"Six months of rumors about the Council," I said, tapping my fingernails against the desk. "And now we have proof of corruption."

"Proof that could get us killed if we're not careful," Agatha warned. "Councilman Voss is cunning, and he'll not take kindly to being exposed."

"Then we won't let him know we're onto him," I said, my resolve hardening. "Not until we can use this to stop him and Corbin for good."

"Careful, Sage." Agatha's gaze was narrowed. "This will be much more dangerous than redecorating homes."

I inhaled sharply through my nose. After everything that

happened with the entity, I'd sworn off saving the world and instead focused all my energy on my new career.

But it seemed that my interior design skills had brought me straight down the path of corruption once more. I tucked the communication crystal back into its hiding place. "I know, Agatha. But I'm still going to do it."

Agatha's ears perked up suddenly, and the cat hopped down from the desk. "Someone's coming."

Panic shot through me. I had to hide all the evidence quickly. I waved my hand to seal the chamber behind the bookcase once more. Agatha and I took up our work positions as footfalls stomped down the hall.

"Miss Holland?" A servant appeared in the doorway. "Councilman Voss has returned home early. He requests your presence downstairs."

My pulse quickened. "Of course. Please let him know I'll be right down." I kept my tone light even with the anxious butterflies causing havoc inside me.

What was Councilman Voss doing home so soon? And why did he want to speak to me?

After the servant departed, I turned to Agatha. "We need to act natural." And not get killed.

"Be careful, Sage. He's dangerous." Her expression was clouded with worry as she hopped down on the carpet beside me.

"I know." I steeled myself as together we headed for the grand staircase.

Councilman Voss stood at the bottom landing, imposing in his somber robes. His sharp gaze settled on me. I had to fight my own instincts to not look away.

"Miss Holland. How goes the renovations?" His voice was like silk wrapped around steel.

I met his stare evenly. "Splendidly, Councilman. I'm finished for today. I'll send my invoice by tomorrow. Good day, sir."

"Good night," he said, then turned away to continue up the stairs.

Agatha and I scurried toward the front door, a wave of relief passing over me.

Stepping out from the grandeur of Councilman Alden Voss's mansion, Agatha and I were greeted by a cool evening breeze that carried the earthy perfume of damp foliage and blooming roses. The setting sun colored the sky in shades of dusky pink and burnt orange, while fireflies began their nightly ballet among the hedgerows.

"Chilly this evening, isn't it?" I remarked, pulling my sweater tighter as we walked down the cement path.

Agatha's feline form brushed against my ankles. "Better than scorching heat. And the cold never bothered me."

"I know, you're tough." I smiled, though my thoughts were a tempest of worry.

What we'd found in Councilman Voss's study had shaken me. How could someone overseeing the protection of our magical world be conspiring to be a part of its potential undoing?

"Let's make a call and let Ingrid know what we found," Agatha suggested.

"Good idea," I said. "But let's get home before we do. I don't want anyone overhearing us."

I'd brought my broomstick with me, as the Councilman's

house was only one town over from my parents' place. I climbed aboard and cast a spell, making the broom levitate in the air. Agatha hopped aboard in front of me, and we flew into the air.

We made our way home, over the fields and through the forest until finally, the cobblestone streets of Emberwick Crossing came into view.

The colors of the sky had deepened by the time we reached my childhood home. The exterior was still painted blue and white, just as it always had been. The porch light threw a mellow brilliance across the wraparound deck, where the swing swayed gently in the breeze.

"It's good to be home," I murmured, stepping onto the porch with a sense of relief.

"It certainly is, young witch," Agatha said.

"Right." I plucked out a small, opalescent stone from my pocket—my own communication crystal linking me to the High Witch. "No time like the present." With a gentle rub, the crystal glowed warmly, projecting Ingrid's image into the air before us.

"Yes, Sage. How may I help you?" Ingrid said without preamble, her violet eyes sharp even through the ether.

"We found something troubling, and we thought it best to share with you as soon as possible. Councilman Voss has been conspiring with Corbin Grimm," I said, my voice laden with trepidation and urgency.

"Is that so?" Ingrid asked, then sighed heavily. "We have graver concerns with the Council I'm afraid. But your report is noted."

"Um, sorry? Graver concerns? With all due respect, High Witch, this is serious."

"Follow your instructions, Sage. For now, I require you to

proceed with the renovation on Councilman Voss's residence. But from now on, you'll need to weave surveillance spells into your designs as well. We'll monitor him and the other two we have on our radar, very closely."

I frowned. "Isn't that a breach of trust?" And was definitely not part of the contract I'd originally agreed to.

"Trust is a luxury we can no longer afford. Do it discreetly. I rely on your talents, Sage," Ingrid said before the connection ended.

I was left with a hollow feeling right in the pit of my stomach.

"Are you comfortable with this?" Agatha asked.

I sighed. "No, but what choice do I have? If Ingrid believes it's necessary..."

"Sometimes, what is necessary is not always right." Agatha grunted.

"Maybe so, but I need to prove I'm more than just a designer. I need to show Ingrid that I'm someone she car rely on." It shouldn't have been such a difficult decision to make. This Councilman was part of a conspiracy to bring down our community. I should want to help the High Witch gather intel on him. And yet, inside, I was wrestling with the conflict between loyalty and conscience.

"Even if it means spying on those you're meant to serve?"

Agatha's question poked at me. "Especially then," I answered. "I have to believe Ingrid knows best."

She was the High Witch. Surely, she knew the right course for us all?

"Faith in our leaders is noble but remember to keep faith in yourself too. You're no puppet, Sage. Your magic means they are your choices—and yours alone."

I sighed. "Yeah... I guess." It was finally time to go inside. I pulled the key out of my pocket and unlocked my front door. I pushed it open, but unease twisted my insides.

Before I could ponder the issues further, Evie walked down the path. "Hi, Sage. Hi, Agatha!" Her shoulder-length black hair framed her face in waves, and she wore a leather jacket over a pink dress, her style effortlessly edgy as always.

"Hi, Evie," I said, ushering her inside. My living room was already cozy, but I started a fire in the hearth just to make things more welcoming.

So, with the fireplace crackling softly, I sat down on the couch and readied myself to confide in my best friend. "I'm glad you stopped by. There's so much happening."

"Tell me everything." Evie sat on the sofa opposite me and kicked off her shoes.

I recounted the discovery of the hidden chamber, the runes, and the crystal's message about Councilman Alden Voss. My voice trembled despite my attempts at staying calm.

"Dark sorcery at Councilman Voss' house? That's... unnerving," Evie said when I'd finally finished.

"That is one word for it," Agatha replied.

I tucked a strand of blue hair behind my ear. "But there's more. Ingrid has asked me to weave surveillance spells into my designs."

"Sage, that's serious stuff. Are you sure—" Evie started to say, then Agatha cut in.

"Of course, she's not sure. It reeks of ethical muck," my familiar said from her spot curled up on the windowsill.

I shrugged. "Well, I kinda have to, Evie. I mean... this guy is bad! And we need to prevent something terrible from happening. What if..."

Evie reached out and squeezed my hand. "I know you're trying to do the right thing but be careful. Once you start walking the line of ethically gray areas, it's hard to go back."

"I know, Evie," I said, feeling a fission of anxiety. "I just hope I'm making the right choice."

"Also, Sage, you know that keeping an eye on someone can be done without blinders on your own conscience," Agatha said.

"Agatha's got a point," Evie agreed. "Keeping a close eye on Councilman Voss will probably reveal more than just his secrets."

"Let's hope it's enough to stop whatever terrible plan they're hatching," I said, staring into the fire.

Because the last thing I wanted was to become a part of a magical community that justified using their powers for evil.

THREE

T he moment I stepped into Councilman Alden Voss' mansion again, I tensed up under the weight of what had been asked of me. My fingers trailed over the oak banister, leaving a trail of glimmering glyphs in their wake. The surveillance spells had taken me all night to master.

Agatha's voice cut through my focus. "Careful, young witch. These walls have ears and egos... and staff lurking about."

I couldn't suppress a grin at her dry tone. "Then let's not give them anything to eavesdrop on." My hands moved deftly, weaving magic into the tapestries and under the rugs as I walked through the house.

"That should do it." I said as I sensed the enchantments take hold.

"Your optimism is adorable but misplaced," Agatha said. "You're playing a dangerous game here."

"Isn't danger a bit exciting though?" I whispered back, feeling the thrill of using my own magic pumping through my veins.

The chandeliers above us blinked off and on as if in agreement, and I knew we were set. Every muffled voice within these walls would find its way to me now.

"Excitement is for fools rushing toward their demise," my cat scoffed, her tail flicking with each sassy syllable.

"Maybe, but some mysteries are worth solving. And we make a pretty good team, don't you think?"

"Flattery will get you nowhere." Agatha shook her head, but I caught the hint of a purr in her voice.

I moved on to the living room, where Councilman Voss had requested a more "inviting" atmosphere. I could see what he meant. The place felt like an opulent mausoleum. A few swipes of my hand, and the walls shimmered, transforming from cold marble to warm oak paneling. While I arranged cushions and drapes, memories of my childhood home flooded back.

Our homey living room, with its mismatched furniture and faded photographs, had always felt more alive than this sterile showpiece. What they would have thought about me using my magical talents to redecorate for a shady politician. They probably would've gotten a good chuckle out of it.

"What's got you all misty-eyed?" Agatha hopped onto a newly upholstered armchair.

"Just thinking about Mom and Dad," I murmured, more to

myself than her. "I think they'd be happy that I followed my dream of becoming an interior designer."

Even if that dream had taken a few unforeseen detours along the way. Life sure had a twisted sense of humor sometimes.

"Well, I think you have a flair for the dramatic," Agatha said.

My parents' deaths were still a puzzle with too many missing pieces. Their demise was still considered an unfortunate car accident. But nothing in this magical world was simple. My heart ached, not just for their loss, but for the truth that seemed so elusive.

Call it intuition, or possibly just stubborn denial, but I wouldn't rest until I had answers. Even if it meant stirring up secrets this town wanted buried.

"All right, that's enough moping around," Agatha said, nudging my leg with her head. "You've got a job to finish."

I sighed, shaking off the melancholy. "Yeah, you're right. Let's make this place look like it belongs to someone who isn't plotting the end of the world."

By the time I'd finished, the mansion looked like a completely different place. Updated and refreshed. Light and bright and fabulous. And despite its makeover, I knew the truth. This mansion was hiding secrets in every shadowed corner, just like its owner.

In my experience, the prettier the façade, the uglier the truth lurking beneath. But hey, I wasn't here to judge. Just to make sure Voss's shady dealings never came to light.

"Time to head home," I told Agatha, stretching my arms above my head. "I want to search the attic and see if we can find anything on my parents' death. I think my grandma had started to look into it before she passed away. Think we'll find any answers tonight?"

"Only one way to find out," Agatha replied, her tail flicking excitedly from side to side.

Knowing my luck, we'd probably just unearth more questions. But I had to try. For my parents, and for that little girl inside me who never really got to say goodbye. Time to crack open Pandora's box and see what secrets came spilling out.

We decided to walk back to Emberwick Crossing, and the gas-lit streetlamps created long shadows on the walkways. The town was quiet, save for the occasional rustle of leaves and distant hooting of owls. The walk gave me time to reflect. My parents' faces formed in my mind, and I tried to remember the sound of their laughter.

Why did they have to leave me so soon, and all alone too? And why did it feel like their deaths were more than just a random car crash?

"You're brooding again," Agatha remarked.

I paused and looked down at her as we reached our front porch. "Can't help it. It's like there's this... this gap in my life that nothing can fill."

"Except maybe the truth," she said softly, surprising me with her gentleness.

"Yeah," I said. "The truth."

We entered our house, and I went straight to the bathroom to wash up. Once settled, we pulled down the ladder and climbed the narrow stairs up to the attic. Each step groaned under our weight. The air grew cooler the higher we went, and the odor of old paper and dust tickled my nose. The attic held a lot of my family history, with stacks of mystical tomes, photo albums, and journals sprinkled across two worn wooden desks. Cobwebs hung like delicate lace from the rafters, and the single window let in a soft, diffused light.

"Well, this is snug," Agatha said, jumping up onto a pile of hardbacks, then sneezing rather loudly.

I chuckled a little then started casting spells, cleaning the attic of all the dust and creating two floor lamps to give us better light to work under. Once the place was clean, I grasped a dusty ledger from off the desk, then sat in a squeaky chair with wheels. "Let's get to work. What secrets do you hold?"

"Hopefully something that won't bore me to death," Agatha snapped, her tail flicking impatiently.

"Always eager for drama, aren't you?" I teased, flipping through the pages.

"Among other things." The cat was eyeing a moth fluttering near the window.

I resumed sifting through the journals and ledgers. My fingers trailed across yellowed pages filled with delicate hand-writing. Memories of my childhood flashed in my mind—my parents' laughter ringing in our living room, their tender, loving embraces. And how everything had changed the year I started at the Institute for the Arcane Arts. The car accident, the sudden silence that replaced their voices.

"How much longer shall we up here?" Agatha complained, knocking over a small trinket box with one of her paws. The lid clattered open, revealing an old locket and some aged photographs. "I'm starving."

"Not now, Agatha," I snapped, more harshly than I'd intended.

I took a deep breath, trying to calm myself down. The frustration was boiling up, making my hands shake. I searched through the pages at a frantic pace. My gaze scanned line after line, seeking, yearning for any clue that could piece together the puzzle of their deaths.

"Young witch, you're about to tear those pages apart."

"Huh? Oh, yes... my bad," I murmured, loosening my grip. "It's just... they died right when I started magic college. It feels like there's something I'm missing, something they never got to tell me."

"Well, it could be in here somewhere," Agatha said, her tone uncharacteristically soft. "This place is full of memories and journals."

I sighed, rubbing my temples. "Yeah, I think so too."

I lifted another journal from the pile, its leather cover worn and faded. My heart missed a beat when I saw the recognizable scrawl on the first page—Grandma Lianne's handwriting. She had always been the secretive type, but this was unexpected. I would never have thought we'd have something so personal of hers in our house.

I read through the diary, my pulse quickening with each entry.

"What's that?" Agatha asked.

"Grandma Lianne's journal. Looks like she was investigating Mom and Dad's deaths too."

Each page lifted the veil on a clandestine world of secret meetings and covert transactions. One entry caught my eye, hinting at the possibility that dark sorcerers had orchestrated my parents' deaths.

"Well, holy hell," I whispered, feeling a chill rush over my skin. "I'd considered that. But to see it written down in black and white..."

I could barely believe it. Tears welled in my eyes, and the text I'd been reading became blurred. Grandma had found something she considered important enough that she continued to dig, heedless of the danger.

"Are you okay?" Agatha hopped up onto my lap and purred loudly. Her furry body grounded me, and I ran my hand along her back.

"Not really," I said, wiping away a tear. "If this is true, then this changes everything. It means that they didn't just die in an accident. Someone wanted them dead and gone."

"Shady dealings? Sounds like we've got some investigating to do," Agatha said, her fur bristling beneath my palm.

"Yeah, I suppose so," I said, anger hardening my resolve.

This wasn't just about uncovering the truth anymore. No, it was about justice for my parents.

"I will do what I can to help, young witch."

"I appreciate that, Agatha," I said, feeling a bit of comfort in her words.

I stood up, setting Grandma Lianne's journal aside on the desk. "I should talk to Brad. He's someone I can trust, and I need someone I can share this with."

"Lead the way," my feline companion said. She leapt down from the armchair and padded toward the attic stairs.

Agatha and I descended into the heart of the house once more. The wooden stairs sagged underfoot, each creaky step rumbling in the stillness. My thoughts were racing nonstop, piecing together everything I had just learned. If dark sorcery was involved, then Corbin Grimm might be responsible for my parents' death.

"Do you think Brad will believe us?"

We reached the bottom of the stairs.

"That goes without saying," Agatha replied, flouncing ahead with her tail held high. "He's always believed in you."

"You're right." I said it more to reassure myself than anything else.

Agatha and I moved through the house quickly, passing by the eclectic assembly of antiquated and modern furniture that decorated my living room. Outside, the sunlight was fading, emitting a golden hue on the wrap-around porch.

I pushed open the front door. The moment we took a step outside, a chilling sight stopped us in our tracks on the porch. Five undead minions, their flesh rotting and eyes hollow, lumbered toward the house. Their appearance was grotesque—patches of decaying skin clung to their bones, and a foul stench coated the air. They moved with unnerving purpose; their ghastly forms illuminated by the dying light of day.

My body trembled. The creatures shambled toward Agatha and me on the porch. The rotting flesh clung to their bones, emitting a foul stench that choked the air. Panic gripped me as I stumbled backward, my voice trembling with fear.

"Faaar out!" I exclaimed, my brain trying to find a way out of this terrifying situation.

Agatha hissed, her fur standing on end as she prepared for battle.

From the corner of my eye, I caught sight of Brad sprinting out of his house next door. His face flushed with the heat of battle, his blue stare blazing with an unyielding resolve. "Sage! I'm here!" he called out, jumping the short picket fence and sprinting toward me.

Relief swept over me as Brad joined us on the porch. With a wave of his hand, the earth beneath the approaching minions trembled and shook. Rocks and dirt surged upwards, forming barriers that slowed their advance.

"Okay, okay. We got this," I said, summoning my own magic to protect us. A glowing circle of protection formed around Brad, Agatha, and me, pulsing with ethereal fire.

Brad glanced at me, a small smile playing on his lips. "Ready when you are."

"Let's give them hell," I shot back and moved into a battle stance.

A surge of supernatural power coursed through my veins as I faced the undead minions. Our spells swirled and intertwined in the air, creating a mesmerizing display of light and magic.

With a flick of my wrist, I unleashed a barrage of magical projectiles at the minions. The air hissed with magic as my spells plowed into decaying flesh and bone. I moved with precision now, my actions fluid and calculated.

Brad's magic complemented mine perfectly. He conjured golems made of earth and stone, their massive forms striking down the minions with powerful blows. The ground shook beneath our feet as Brad's golems fought alongside us.

"Take that!" I yelled, a fierce joy bubbling up inside me with every new spell.

"Nice moves!" Brad called out, sweat dripping off his forehead.

Agatha darted between us, tripping up the minions.

"Thanks a million, but don't get distracted," I replied, dodging a swipe from a particularly persistent minion.

"Wouldn't dream of it," he said, sending another burst of flames toward our enemies.

Agatha darted between the minions, her shadowy form becoming a blur as she attacked with razor-sharp claws. Her magic swirled around her, enveloping the minions in a shadowy fog and disorienting them.

Tears welled up in my eyes as I fought hard. I couldn't help but think about my parents, of the injustice that had been done to them. I channeled my anger into my magic forces and kept fighting.

Magic erupted from my hands, forming dazzling arcs of light that struck the undead minions. Each strike and spell imbued with raw emotion and supernatural intensity. I could feel my heart thumping hard in my chest, adrenaline coursing through my veins. We refused to back down, refusing to let Corbin's minions defeat us.

"Hold your ground, we've got this," Brad reassured me, his voice even.

"Right," I said, steeling myself.

As one, we stood firm, pushing back against the tide of darkness. The bond between us felt almost tangible, a shared strength that bolstered our efforts.

"Look out!" Brad yelled, wrenching me out of the way just as a minion lunged.

"Close one," I said breathlessly, gratitude and something deeper swelling within me.

"Always got your back," he replied, his gaze fastening onto mine for a brief, electrifying moment.

"Same here," I whispered, focusing on the fight but unable to ignore the affection spreading through me.

"Let's finish this," Brad urged with renewed vigor.

We unleashed our combined power.

I stood tall, feeling our magic intertwine, unstoppable and unyielding.

Finally, the creatures were piles of bones and ash, scattered across the lawn. Sweat beaded my forehead. I caught my breath, my body trembling with exhaustion and triumph.

Brad's expression shone with pride and concern. "Are you okay?" he asked, his voice gentle.

I nodded, wiping away a trickle of sweat on my brow. "I'm fine. You?"

"I'm good," he said.

Agatha purred nearby, rubbing against my leg. The adrenaline began to subside. Brad's hand landed on my shoulder, his touch both comforting and electric. I turned to face him, my heart racing even faster, not just from the battle, but from his proximity.

"Sage, that was incredible. You never cease to amaze me," Brad said, his voice low and sincere.

Heat crept into my cheeks. "You weren't so bad yourself, mister," I teased, butterflies flapping in my stomach.

Brad chuckled, his laughter warming me from the inside out. "Well, I had a pretty great partner."

"Oh, stop," I said, friskily swatting his arm. "You're going to make me blush."

Too late, but anyway...

"I think it's cute when you blush," Brad said, stepping closer.

I bit my lip, suddenly shy under his gaze. "Brad, I..." The next words caught in my throat.

He took a step even closer, his hand reaching up to tuck a stray lock of hair behind my ear. "Sage, I've been wanting to tell you something for a while now."

My breath hitched, my skin tingling where his fingers had brushed against it. "What is it?" I whispered.

"I care about you, Sage. So much," Brad confessed, his voice raw with emotion. "You're not just my best friend... you're the one I want to be with. Through thick and thin, magic and mayhem."

Tears pricked at the corners of my eyes. "I feel the same way. I care about you, too. I just didn't know how to tell you."

A grin spread across his face, his expression shining with happiness. "Well, I'm glad we finally figured it out."

Cupping my face in his hands, he kissed me, his lips soft and warm, molding perfectly against mine. I melted into his embrace, my arms winding around his neck as I deepened the kiss.

Now that I finally had him, I was determined not to let him go.

CHAPTER
FIVE

I flopped onto the mismatched throw pillows that had been tossed over my green couch, the heart of my comfy living room. Sunlight filtered in through the sheer curtains, dappling light across the hardwood floors and rugs. I'd always loved this room, with its blues and greens, reminiscent of a tranquil sea cove, bookshelves stuffed to the brim with magical lore and family memories.

"Agatha, not on the table," I chided as my familiar made herself comfortable amid a scattering of papers. She shot me an unbothered look before curling up on a nearby cushion, her yellow eyes slipping shut. That cat's sass never failed to amuse me.

Evie lounged in the armchair, her hazel stare sharp under jet-black bangs. Brad leaned against the stone fireplace, his casual poise belying the tension in his broad shoulders. I studied him, appreciating how he filled out that green shirt.

Down girl, I scolded myself, forcing my thoughts back to the present.

"Okay, so... I talked to the high witch the other day," I said, twisting a blue-highlighted lock around my finger. "I'm only to keep tabs on Councilman Voss, no digging deeper into whatever else is going on."

The words tasted like ash in my mouth, because I yearned to do more than just watch him. That man was shadier than a weeping willow on the solstice. If something big was brewing, I wanted to get ahead of it, not wait for the world to come tumbling down around my ears.

Brad frowned. "Seriously? That's like asking a storm not to break."

I smiled. "I know, right?" Brad had always known how to voice my feelings, even when I couldn't. He read me so well. Which was probably why we clicked so well, even after all these years apart.

Evie sighed. "Sounds about as fun as watching paint dry."

"I agree," Agatha murmured from her spot, her voice dripping with sarcasm without even opening her eyes. "All the excitement is making me tired."

I stared at Agatha in wonder.

That cat could out-snark a bridge troll.

"Look, we've got to do something," I said, slamming my fist

onto my open palm. My parents didn't raise me to stand idly by while the world went to hell. If I could stop a disaster before it began, their spirits would rest peacefully.

Brad's expression looked serious and resolved. "Secret investigation, then?"

"Under the radar. But if we get caught..." Evie sat back and crossed her legs.

"You'll end up in jail," Agatha drawled, "and what a pity that would be, because napping through a Council meeting while doing surveillance is precisely how I envisioned my day."

Brad paced the room. "We can't let anyone else find out what we're doing. If Corbin, Ingrid, or even Councilman Voss catches wind of our investigation, we could all be in real danger." I watched Brad pace, his protective streak showing. He'd always looked after the people he cared about, even when we were just kids playing hide and seek.

"Which means we have to be extra careful," I replied, resolve firming my voice. "I didn't learn seventh-level magic for nothing. I'm ready to fight."

"All right. I'm in," Evie said, standing up and brushing off her jeans. "But now I need to head to work before my boss turns me into a toad for being late again."

I couldn't help but laugh. "Have a good day, Evie." I gave her a quick hug, and she returned it with a squeeze.

"Stay safe, you two," she said, giving me a faint smile before heading out the door.

"I'm in need of a long nap." Agatha yawned, stretching her limbs. "I'll be in your bedroom if anyone needs me. But please, try not to need me." With that, she sauntered off, leaving Brad and me alone in the living room.

"Don't worry about me, Mr. Protective," I said in a teasing tone, because Brad's concern was endearing. "I can handle myself."

While I appreciated Brad, I didn't want him to see me as some weak damsel in distress. After everything we'd been through, he knew I could take care of myself.

Still, it was nice to know he cared.

Brad sat down beside me. "Oh, I have no doubt about that," he said with a smile. "But it doesn't hurt to have someone looking out for you."

Heat bloomed in my cheeks. "Is that your way of saying you want to be my knight in shining armor?" I teased, raising an eyebrow.

"More like your partner in crime," he shot back, grinning. That smile could light up a room.

Brad had always known how to make me laugh, even in serious situations. It was one of the best things I liked about him.

"Better watch out, or I'll start calling you Robin Hood."

He chuckled, the sound sexy and deep. "Hey, someone's got to keep an eye on the merry band of witches."

Could he be any more charming? I mentally rolled my eyes at myself.

Get it together, Sage.

"Especially when the leader has a penchant for getting into trouble," I admitted, feeling a warmth in my chest at his concern. It reminded me of old times.

"Exactly," he said, his voice softer now. "I care about you, Sage."

His hand found mine, and the touch was gentle yet electrifying. Butterflies erupted in my stomach as my heart fluttered.

Was he saying what I thought he was saying? A smile jerked at my lips, unbidden.

"You're not alone in this, Sage," he whispered earnestly, giving my hand a gentle squeeze.

Alone.

The word resonated deeply within me, stirring up memories of everything I'd lost. My family. My happy home. But with Brad here, that ache didn't feel quite as sharp.

"Well, it's nice to know that I'm not flying solo," I replied, squeezing back.

My thumb grazed his skin, heat vibrating in the air between us.

Brad's eyes lit up suddenly. "Remember that time we tried to create an invisibility spell in high school?"

"How could I forget? We ended up turning Mrs. Thornton's cat invisible instead!" I laughed, flooded with nostalgia. "Jeez-zus, that was a mess."

Those carefree days seemed so far away now, but reminiscing with Brad made my life brighter. We really had been two troublemaking kids back then.

"Yeah, but we got through it together," he said, tracing circles on my hand. "Just like we'll get through this."

We'd always made a great team, even when we messed up. With Brad as my friend and supporter, I could handle anything.

"And while we're on the subject of getting through things," Brad said, his expression thoughtful, "do you remember our first date?"

"Please don't remind me." I groaned in exaggeration, then laughed. "The one where you accidentally reconstructed the table and chairs in that cafe?"

"Hey, I was trying to impress you with my magical skills," he defended, laughing along with me.

I shook my head, amused by the memory. Only Brad could turn a romantic dinner into a construction zone. That night had shown me his heart was in the right place, even if his magic was a bit unpredictable back then.

"Well, you certainly left an impression," I joked.

"At least it wasn't as bad as that time I took you to the haunted house, and you screamed so loudly you scared the ghosts away."

I shook my head. "We've had our fair share of awkward moments, haven't we?"

"Yeah, and they're all part of what makes us... us," Brad said, his expression softening. "And I wouldn't trade any of those memories for anything."

I felt a pang of something in my chest. Our shared history ran deep. Full of magic, friendship, and mistakes. And through everything, we'd always been there for each other.

"Neither would I," I said. "You know, Brad, you're a pretty amazing guy."

"Right back at you, Ms. Holland," he replied, leaning in a little. "For a girl who scares ghosts, you're pretty incredible yourself."

My pulse quickened with him so close. There was a connection between us that time and distance couldn't sever. Still, was going down that road again wise?

"That's so sweet, Brad," I said softly, my emotions a jumbled mess.

"Did you date much after...us?" he asked.

"A bit. And you?"

"Yeah, and it was a disaster." Brad chuckled, shaking his head. "Oh, man. I dated this one girl during my sophomore year who had this pet ferret and was obsessed with interpretive dance. Well, on our third date, she decided it would be romantic to bring her ferret along to the restaurant. Long story short, the little weasel escaped and caused absolute chaos. I spent half the night chasing it through the kitchen while she sobbed into her spaghetti."

I couldn't help but laugh at their misfortune. "Okay, that's pretty bad. But have I ever told you about the guy I went out with who collected taxidermy?"

Brad's eyes widened. "No way. This I gotta hear."

While launching into the story, I marveled at how comfortable I was sharing my dating disasters with Brad. He always managed to find the humor in even my most cringeworthy moments.

"He invited me over to his place for dinner, and I kid you not, every inch of his apartment was covered in stuffed animals. And not the cute, cuddly kind. I'm talking full on mounted deer heads and glass-eyed squirrels. I've never been so creeped out in my life."

"Yikes. That's a whole new level of weird." Brad shuddered. "I guess we both have a talent for attracting the eccentric types, huh?"

"Seems that way," I said, grinning. Bonding with Brad over our shared history of romantic misadventures filled me with a pleasant warmth, like sipping hot cocoa on a chilly day. "But you know, even with all the craziness, I wouldn't trade those experiences either. They taught me what I want and don't want in a relationship."

Brad nodded, his expression turning thoughtful. "Same here. Every mistake, every awkward moment... all lessons learned, I hope."

His easygoing wisdom never failed to soothe my soul.

"You're right," I said softly. "And I'm glad we can share these stories with each other. It's nice to have someone who understands, you know?"

Having Brad back in my life, being able to bare my true self to him without fear of judgment, felt like rediscovering a missing piece of myself.

A piece I hadn't even realized I'd lost.

"Definitely." Brad's gaze met mine. "There's no one else I'd rather reminisce with, Sage. No one gets me quite like you do."

My heart galloped like a racehorse. The friendship between us was as strong as ever, but I was hoping for more.

"I'm glad you moved back home," Brad said, his voice low and husky. His blue eyes locked onto mine, and for a moment, the world outside my living room ceased to exist.

"Brad..." I whispered.

"Yeah?" he asked, inching closer.

I couldn't help noticing how his gaze flicked down to my lips. My breath stalled, and an electric current ran through me.

"Nothing," I whispered, my voice barely audible now.

His smirk returned. "You sure about that?"

"Maybe not," I admitted, feeling my cheeks warm.

Our faces were mere inches apart now. "Every time I'm near you, all I want to do is kiss you, Sage," he murmured, his breath merging with mine.

I inhaled sharply, my pulse quickening. Brad's confession confirmed my own hidden desires, feelings I'd barely admitted to myself until now. After so many years apart, so many missed chances, were we finally on the verge of something more? Trembling, I met his intense gaze, my pulse thrumming in anticipation of what might come next.

Slowly, deliberately, Brad closed the gap. His lips touched mine, tentatively at first, then more insistently. It was as if a dam had burst, releasing a flood of pent-up emotions and desires. The kiss became fiery and all consuming, overflowing with a passion that had been simmering between us for too long. All doubts and worries melted away. There was no Councilman Voss to worry about here. No High Witch's warning, no looming danger. Just Brad and me, lost in each other.

My body reeled, drunk on the taste of his lips, the heat of his touch. How long had I yearned for this closeness? And now that it was happening, it exceeded every fantasy.

When we finally pulled apart, breathing hard, I searched his face for any sign of regret. Instead, I found only affection.

"Wow," was all I could manage, still dazed from the intensity of our kiss. My lips tingled; my heart pounded. I wanted nothing more than to kiss him again and again.

"Yeah, wow," he said, his grin widening. "You're a really good kisser."

I smiled, still reeling from the intensity of our kiss. "You too..." An understatement, really. Kissing Brad left me electrified in the best possible way.

"Glad you think so," he replied, sitting back. "So, tell me about your latest design project. Anything exciting?"

His casual tone surprised me. Could we really go back to chatting normally after a kiss like that? I took a steadying breath, trying to gather my scattered thoughts.

"Actually, yeah," I said, letting my emotions settle. "I just got hired to work on an interior for the new library annex. Enchanted bookshelves, self-lighting reading nooks—the works."

"Sounds incredible," he said, genuine admiration in his voice. "Your creativity never ceases to amaze me."

I couldn't help but be warmed by his praise. "What about you? Any new architectural marvels in the making?" I asked, falling back into our friendly rapport.

"Funny you should ask. I've been experimenting with creating golems for construction work. They can handle heavy lifting and intricate details, which frees me up to focus on the finer aspects of design."

"That's brilliant," I said, genuinely impressed. "You've always had a knack for blending magic and architecture."

Brad grinned. "Coming from you, that means a lot. You know, we've both come a long way since high school."

"Yeah," I said, smiling as memories flooded through me. "We really have." Though how he made me feel hadn't changed at all.

His eyes searched mine, and in them I saw a future I'd only allowed myself to imagine in my most vulnerable moments. A future by his side.

The brick-paved walkways of the Institute for the Arcane Arts resonated beneath my boots as I made my way to Ingrid's office. The castle-like structure loomed ahead, its gray stone walls softened by climbing ivy and vibrant bursts of flowering vines. Students bustled around me, their robes whispering against the ground as they passed.

It was a strange feeling really, to be back on the grounds of my university that for so long was home for me. Now, I was a graduate and the High Witch's assistant. I used to look up to the graduating class as wise and old witches. Now, I was even older than those seniors I used to look up to.

I reached the grand oak door of Ingrid's office and stopped. The brass nameplate gleamed and "Ingrid Nightspire, High Witch," was inscribed. My hand trembled as I knocked.

"Come in," her voice commanded from within.

I entered the room, immediately struck by its opulence. The air smelled faintly of incense and old books. A crystal chandelier radiated shimmering light across the room. Ingrid sat behind a massive desk, her high-back chair giving her an almost regal persona.

"Hello, High Witch," I greeted her, trying to keep my voice steady.

Ingrid looked up, her violet stare boring into me. Her long silver hair flowed down her back, complimenting her elegant gown that was adorned with delicate silvery embroidery.

"Ah, Sage," she said with a small smile on her lips. "Do sit."

I took a seat across from her desk in a hard and uncomfortable chair. Perhaps she didn't want any of her guests to stay for any length of time?

Ingrid's office had always felt otherworldly, like stepping into another realm. It was both intimidating and awe-inspiring. Perhaps that was the point? Was the décor designed to intimidate visitors on purpose, or did Ingrid just have peculiar taste?

Volumes of arcane knowledge lined the bookshelves of one wall. I pondered, not for the first time, what it would be like to possess even a fraction of Ingrid's power and wisdom. To command that kind of respect, to shape the very fabric of the magical world...

But who was I kidding? I would never be like her. I was just Sage, fumbling my way through this witchy business with no one to guide me except the teachers who were responsible for providing education and guidance.

"Thank you for coming," Ingrid said. "I wanted to express my gratitude for installing the surveillance enchantments at Councilman Voss' house. It's given us invaluable insights."

Discomfort prickled at my conscience like a persistent thorn. Sure, I wanted to prove myself to Ingrid, to show her that I was a valuable asset. But at what cost? Invading someone's privacy, even if he was a shady Councilman, felt wrong on a fundamental level. I bit my lip, trying to summon the courage to voice my concerns more firmly.

"Uh, you're welcome," I replied hesitantly, shifting in my seat. "But I'm not entirely comfortable with spying on him."

I hoped voicing my unease might make Ingrid reconsider, but I knew better than to hold my breath.

"Your discomfort is noted, but it is necessary for my work." Ingrid waved a hand dismissively, as if clearing away an annoying fly.

I hesitated a moment, then blurted out, "Um, I know you're busy High Witch, but I wonder if Corbin Grimm or Councilman Voss might be linked to my parents' deaths."

The words tumbled out before I could think of a better way to phrase them. They were, in fact, a desperate plea for answers to the questions that had haunted me for years. Deep down, I knew this was a long shot. But I still clung to the hope that Ingrid, with all her power and influence, might be able to uncover something I'd missed. Some clue that would finally bring me closure, allow me to make peace with the gaping hole my parents' absence had left in my life.

Ingrid's expression didn't change. "I doubt it, Sage. They

were tragic accidents. Furthermore, I have more pressing Council matters to attend to."

Her indifference stung, but I tried not to show it.

"Like what? What's so urgent?"

Curiosity burned in my veins along with a touch of indignation. How could anything be more pressing than getting to the bottom of my parents' deaths? They may have been mere humans, but they were my world. Didn't that count for something?

"High-level Council decisions. Negotiations," Ingrid said, her tone turning distant. "Matters too complex to delve into now."

"Uh huh," I murmured, feeling my stomach twist with anger and a healthy dose of disappointment.

Of course. I was just a lowly apprentice, not privy to the inner workings of the Council. Still, a part of me bristled at being brushed off so easily. I may not have Ingrid's experience or power, but I wasn't a child. I had a right to know what was going on, especially if it could impact the people I cared about.

"Focus on your work, Sage." Ingrid's voice was sharp and authoritative now. "Leave the bigger picture to those of us equipped to handle it."

My jaw tightened at her being so dismissive of me. Wasn't I the one that had dealt with an evil entity terrorizing my town only weeks ago?

But I managed to force a smile to my face and said, "Sure thing."

As much as I respected Ingrid, moments like these made me question her priorities. Was maintaining the status quo more important than seeking justice for those who had been wronged? Than protecting the innocent from harm?

"Is there anything else?" she asked, already turning her attention to a stack of parchments on her desk.

"No, that's all," I said, standing up. *So glad I made the trip.* "I'll see myself out."

"Farewell, Sage," she said without looking up.

"Goodbye, High Witch," I replied, closing the door behind me.

I walked back through the winding corridors of the academy, my thoughts a whirl of unanswered questions and nagging doubts. Ingrid may have dismissed my concerns, but I knew in my gut that there was more to the story. One way or another, I'd get to the bottom of the mystery surrounding my parents' untimely deaths, even if I had to do it on my own.

I stepped out into the courtyard and tilted my face up, sunlight warm against my skin. Ingrid's dismissal really troubled me, a persistent itch that wouldn't go away.

"Focus on your work," the high witch had said, as if surveillance enchantments were the be-all and end-all of our world's problems. I needed answers, not more bureaucracy.

I paused under the sprawling branches of a towering oak tree and took out my cell phone. Brad would be more supportive. He always was. I dialed his number, tapping my foot impatiently as I waited for him to pick up.

"Hey, Sage," Brad answered, his voice crackling through the connection. "What's up?"

"Can you meet me at the college? I need your insight into something."

"Sure thing. Be there in ten."

DURING MY YEARS at the Arcane Arts Institute, my friends had become my family. Now? Well, I wasn't sure how I felt about any of those memories anymore. Could I trust myself to remember the full extent of comradery and help I'd received from my professors and my friends?

Or was it all a lie wrapped up in the emotional torment surrounding my grief?

"Hey, there you are," Brad called out to me, jerking me back to reality. He approached with a casual stride, his jelled, spiky hair catching the light. "What's going on?"

"Thanks for coming." I stood up, brushing off imaginary dust from my skirt. "I want to talk to Professor Rowan Elderwood. I think he might have some answers."

"Never heard of him," Brad said, raising an eyebrow in question.

"Well, he's an expert in necromance symbols and obscure runes. We need someone who knows about that sort of stuff."

Brad shrugged. "All right. Let's go see him."

We walked through the campus side by side, memories flooded my mind – late-night study sessions, the thrill of mastering a new spell, the support of fellow students through those hard times. Yet now those memories felt distant, overshadowed by the looming questions about my parents' deaths and Councilman Voss' potential involvement.

When we reached Professor Elderwood's classroom, the door was ajar. I knocked gently before pushing it open. The professor sat alone at his desk, surrounded by stacks of magical books and flickering candles. His short auburn hair was neatly combed, and he wore a tailored suit.

"Professor Elderwood?" I asked gently, trying not to startle him as I stepped inside. "I'm Sage Holland, and this is Brad Adams. Could we talk to you if you have a moment, please?"

"Nice to meet you, Miss Holland, Mr. Adams," Rowan greeted us, not getting up from his desk. His gray eyes were sharp and inquisitive. "How can I be of service today?"

The classroom was as incredible as I'd imagined, full of magical artifacts and dusty scrolls. The air hummed with latent, unharnessed power, a verification of the magic contained within the walls.

My belly twisted with nerves as I stepped further into Professor Elderwood's domain. The amount of magical knowledge surrounding me was both exhilarating and intimidating.

"Professor Elderwood," I started, choosing my words carefully, "I've come across some necromancy symbols and malevolent runes in a client's house. I need to understand them better."

"Necromantic symbols, you say?" Rowan's face lit up with interest. "Quite the complex subject. You see, necromancy has been both revered and reviled throughout history, often misunderstood by those who lack the proper context. These symbols, if they are necromantic in nature, could signify any number of things."

I fought the urge to roll my eyes. Leave it to Professor Elderwood to turn a simple question into a long-winded lecture. I appreciated his knowledge, but sometimes a girl just needed the cliff notes version.

"Professor," I interrupted gently, "can we chat specifically about the practical applications? What do these symbols mean in today's context?"

"Ah, yes," Rowan said, adjusting his glasses. "In today's context, such symbols could indicate a binding spell, a summoning ritual, or even a protective ward, depending on their arrangement and the intent behind their placement."

Well, that narrowed it down to... pretty much *everything*. I suppressed a sigh. This was going to be a long day.

"I'm so thankful for your assistance," I said, trying to keep my impatience in check. "That's helpful. What else can you tell us?"

Professor Elderwood leaned back in his chair, steepling his fingers. "The necromantic arts are not to be trifled with, Miss Holland. In the wrong hands, they can unleash unspeakable horrors upon the world."

I tried not to let the grimace behind my smile show. I knew that, of course, but hearing the professor voice my fears made it all the more real. The thought of facing down a horde of the undead was not exactly how I'd planned to spend my weekend. But hey, at least it would make for a great story.

"Is there any way to counter these symbols? To neutralize their power?" Brad asked.

"Countering necromancy requires a delicate touch and a deep understanding of the forces at play." Professor Elderwood finally stood up and came around from his desk. I thought he might come over to where we were, near the students' desks, but instead, he began pacing the room, his robes swishing around his ankles. "One must fight darkness with light, death with life.

It's a precarious balance, and not one for the young or inexperienced to attempt."

I nodded, trying to absorb his vague advice. Why did warlocks always have to be so damn cryptic? Would it kill them to give me a straight answer for once?

I tilted my head. "I don't suppose you could give me a crash course in anti-necromancy spells?"

Professor Elderwood chuckled dryly. "If only it were that simple, Miss Holland. Anti-necromancy, you see, is not just a branch of magic, but an entire discipline on its own, steeped in ancient lore and fraught with peril at every turn. The roots of necromancy stretch back to the dawn of magic itself, entwined with the very essence of life and death. To counter it, one must understand not just the spells, but the very nature of the magic that animates the dead, the rituals that bind spirits to the corporeal plane, and the malevolent energies that sustain such abhorrent practices."

Well, that was a mouthful. I tried to absorb the professor's info, but my thoughts kept wandering. Necromancy, archaic lore, peril at every turn—it sounded like a recipe for disaster. Or at least a really bad hangover.

Was I in over my head?

"Oh?" Brad said dryly. "You don't say."

The professor paused, his expression gleaming with a blend of wisdom and nostalgia. "The ancient texts speak of long-forgotten wards and sigils, incantations uttered in the Old Tongue, and potions brewed under the light of a waning moon. Each element, each symbol, carries a credence of significance, a resonance with the forces we seek to repel. It is not merely a matter of casting a spell. Oh, no, it is a delicate balancing act between light and shadow, life and death."

The professor droned on, and I kept nodding along, pretending to understand every word, but I was barely keeping up. Wards, sigils, Old Tongue? It sounded like a foreign language to me. I glanced at Brad, but he seemed just as lost as I was. So much for that crash course.

"Okay, Professor Elderwood," I said, cutting through his monologue. "I appreciate the confidence boost, but could you possibly point me to a beginner's guide or something? I'm going to need some serious handholding here."

Professor Elderwood wandered back to his desk then leaned back in his chair, his fingers steepled thoughtfully. "To embark on this path, you must first immerse yourself in the study of necromantic principles—understand the workings of the soul, the binding of spirit to flesh, the forbidden rites that draw power from the nether realms. Only then can you hope to unravel the intricacies of countering such dark arts. It requires patience, diligence, and a stanch will. But above all, it demands an unyielding sense of purpose. A clarity of intent that can pierce through the gloom of necromantic corruption." He sighed deeply, his expression softening. "I have faith in you, Miss Holland. You are a resourceful young witch, with a mind both sharp and inquisitive. Though I cannot walk this path for you, I can offer you guidance and the wisdom of those who have walked it before. Trust in your abilities, seek knowledge with an open heart, and remember that the true strength of a witch or warlock lies not in the power of the spells, but in the purity of intent and the resilience of spirit."

Great. Thanks.

A pep talk was the last thing I needed right now. I had a client waiting and a potential undead uprising to prevent. But I couldn't deny the small flutter of something akin to... pride, in my chest. It was nice to know someone believed in me, even if that someone was a long-winded, cryptic warlock.

"Thanks for the vote of confidence, Professor. Is there anything you can give me to take home... or...." I let my voice drift, hoping he'd get the hint.

The professor's brow furrowed, then he pulled open the drawer on his desk, pulled out a large book and held it up. "Take this. I can't loan you anything belonging to the school, but this is one of my own books. It might help to nudge you in the right direction."

I hurried over to take the book from him, "Thank you so much." I took the book and slid into my satchel, which I'd cast a spell upon to hold a mountain of things. Not unsimilar to a Mary Poppins type bag.

I walked back over to Brad and grinned at him. At least this trip hadn't been fruitless. "Shall we go?"

Brad nodded. "Yeah, let's do it."

"Be careful, kids. The forces you're dealing with are not to be underestimated. If you find yourself in over your head, don't hesitate to ask for help," Professor Elderwood called out.

I paused at the door, my hand on the knob. "I'll keep that in mind."

"Always happy to assist young minds eager to learn," the professor replied with a nod. "But remember, knowledge is a double-edged sword. Use it wisely."

"Of course, Professor," I said, smiling back at him.

"Now, if there's nothing else..." the professor trailed off, already turning back to his books.

"That's all for now," I said, exchanging a glance with Brad. "I'm indebted to you, Professor."

"Anytime," he replied, his attention already on his studies.

Brad and I stepped out into the hallway.

"That was... something," Brad said, shaking his head as though he was as perplexed as I was.

CHAPTER
SEVEN

We walked away from Professor Elderwood's classroom, a laugh bubbling in my throat.

"Yeah, tell me about it. He's got a lot of knowledge, but seriously... he sure loves to hear himself talk."

"Guess it's part of the package deal with being a professor," Brad joked, "They have to talk all day to students who barely respond. It would be hard to teach if you didn't like the sound of your own voice."

"True," I said, grinning at him.

Brad nudged my shoulder gently as we continued to walk

through the campus. "So, what do you think about Corbin Grimm? Think he's really involved in some sort of supernatural uprising?"

"Honestly, I'm not sure if he's the mastermind or just a lackey," I said, frowning. "It feels like every bit of information we find just leads to more questions and more information. It's a veritable maze, and I'm not sure which way to turn to be honest. But if there's a chance he's involved, we need to find out."

He was a bad guy. Every instinct I possessed told me it was true. We just had to prove it.

"I agree," Brad said, his tone serious for once.

I smiled at him, grateful for his support. We'd stepped out of the buildings on campus and began heading towards town. We walked in silence, the midafternoon sun filtering through the trees and forming dappled shadows on the path. It was peaceful, almost like old times when we were kids, before magic and tragedy complicated everything.

I had to go home and get to work, and yet I was loathe to interrupt what was happening between us.

"Remember when we used to race each other home from high school?" Brad asked suddenly, breaking the silence.

I laughed, remembering it well. "You always cheated by using your magic to trip me up." Not that he'd ever let me get hurt, but it had certainly slowed me down.

"Hey, I prefer to call it a 'strategic use of resources,' Sage," he said, grinning.

I shoved his arm. "Strategic, my ass! You were just scared I'd beat you fair and square."

"Maybe."

Brad took my hand in his. The heat of his touch sent a tingle of heat down my spine, and I squeezed his hand back.

"But seriously, Sage, I missed this. Us. Just hanging out together."

"Me, too," I said softly, glancing up at him.

"Yeah," he said, squeezing my hand again. "I've been thinking about us a lot. And I think maybe...we should try dating. Take things slow."

I couldn't help the grin that tilted my lips, eagerness and nerves flooding through me. "Okay."

He stopped in his tracks and turned to look at me. "I care about you, Sage. And I always have, always will."

He leaned in slowly and I lifted my chin to meet him half-way. He pressed his lips to mine in a kiss that was soft at first, tentative. But quickly the feelings between us grew more passionate as we lost ourselves in the sensation. I dropped his hand and stepped closer, wrapping my arms around his neck so that I could feel the heat between us intensify. When we finally broke apart, we were both breathless.

"Guess we should get going," I said reluctantly, glancing at the afternoon sun. "You've got work, right?"

"Yeah," he said, sighing. "Duty calls. But we'll pick this up later, okay?"

I couldn't help but grin and nod, then went up on my toes to give him one last quick kiss. "Yep."

We were still a few hours walk from home, or an hour's drive/broomstick ride, so Brad gathered me close. "Hold on. I'll transport us home."

I wasn't as good at these types of spells, so I tucked my head in under his chin and closed my eyes as a tingle of magic coursed over my body.

"So, I'll see you later?" He repeated, stepping back.

I swayed toward him as I opened my eyes and reoriented myself. "Oh... yeah. Thanks for that."

He gave me a wink before heading off toward his house. I watched him go, a jumble of emotions twisting inside me. Part of me wanted to follow him, to curl up in his lap on the couch and pretend the rest of the world didn't exist.

But it did, and I had a shit-ton of responsibilities to deal with. I sighed heavily, then walked up the path and into my own house. The feel of his warm kiss still lingered on my lips, and I pressed them together, memorizing the taste.

My living room was dim, which was unusual, and the curtains were drawn. I flicked on the light and jumped. "High Witch. What are you doing here?"

Ingrid Nightspire, the High Witch herself, was seated on my couch like a queen in exile.

"Good evening, Sage. Something has come to my attention, and we need to talk." Her tone carried the burden of authority and an unsettling amount of calm.

Oh, boy, this can't be good. When the High Witch herself makes a house call, you know it's serious business.

I braced myself for whatever bombshell she was about to drop. "About what? My parents? The supernatural uprising?" I walked into my living room and sat down on the large armchair, grabbing the plush purple pillow for comfort.

"About Bradley Adams," she answered.

The air had thickened around us. Brad? Why would she want to talk about him? Last I checked, dating wasn't a crime in the magical world. The High Witch must've seen Brad and me on campus earlier together, and just now making out in front of the house. A hot flush burned my neck and face.

I frowned at her, ready to ask her what she meant, but I didn't get a chance.

She continued, "You cannot see him any longer. There's a primeval rule—the Covenant of Veiled Boundaries—that strictly forbids any romantic entanglements between members of the Council's inner circle, like yourself, and civilians, like Brad. This rule is not just a mere guideline, it is a binding mandate that prevents conflicts of interest and ensures the integrity of our duties."

Well, smack me with a broomstick.

Apparently, falling for a cute warlock was against some musty old covenant I'd never even heard of. Talk about a buzzkill.

"I've never heard of the Covenant of Veiled Boundaries." I frowned, feeling a twinge of rebellion rise within me. She couldn't possibly think that me dating Brad Adams was going to be a problem. "Brad is a good man. And we're not children, Ingrid. We don't need babysitting."

Ingrid's stare bored into mine; her expression unyielding. "The Covenant of Veiled Boundaries was established centuries ago, after a disastrous incident where personal relationships compromised the Council's ability to make impartial decisions. The consequences were catastrophic, endangering not only the Council but the entire magical community. To prevent such a calamity from ever occurring again, this rule was put in place."

I slumped in the armchair. "So, because of some stupid rule, I have to choose between my duty and my heart?"

Well, wasn't this just a regular old Shakespearean tragedy? Torn between love and loyalty, with no easy answers in sight. I half-expected a droll voice to say "To be or not to be" in the background.

Ingrid didn't show any signs of empathy. Instead, she stuck her nose further in the air. "I understand this is difficult for you, Sage. But as a member of the Council's inner circle, your responsibilities extend beyond personal desires. Your actions must reflect the greater good, the protection and balance of our world. Any personal attachments to civilians could cloud your judgment, lead to divided loyalties, and ultimately put everyone at risk."

"Is there really no other way?" I asked, my voice tinged with desperation this time.

"Rules are not about what we need, they are about order." Ingrid's expression remained impassive, but there was an edge to her voice now. "The Council cannot risk distractions or divided loyalties. It is for the greater good."

I huffed. "Seems more like control to me. Why does it matter who I date?"

Seriously, since when did my love life become Council business? What's next, a magical chastity belt? I couldn't believe Ingrid was pulling the *greater good* card on me.

"Because emotions cloud judgment," she countered with a dismissive wave of her hand. "The Covenant of Veiled Boundaries is a necessary safeguard, ensuring that our work remains untainted by personal biases. I trust you understand the gravity of this situation and will make the right choice. Is a fling worth that risk?"

Was she serious right now? Brad was the only guy I'd ever wanted. The only guy I'd ever felt this way about.

"It's not just a fling!" My frustration was boiling over. "And since when do you care so much about rules? You bend them when it suits you."

Hypocrite much? I'd seen Ingrid play fast and loose with the rules plenty of times before. But apparently, my budding romance was where she drew the line.

"Watch your tone, Sage. I am still your superior." Her voice was as sharp as glass, and it cut. "This isn't about me. It's about maintaining the balance we've worked for centuries to uphold."

"Balance that stifles us, you mean." My hands formed fists at my sides. "Look, I respect you, Ingrid, more than anyone. But I refuse to let archaic rules dictate my personal life."

Especially when they were ridiculous. Brad had been an integral key in me defeating Tenebris, and Ingrid knew that. Who would I go to for help if not Brad?

"Your refusal is noted. But disobedience has consequences," she said as stood from the couch, her height and poise exuding dominance. "Consider this a warning."

"Are you seriously threatening me?" I asked, also jumping to my feet.

Ingrid's gaze narrowed. "Merely stating facts. For your sake, I hope you make the right choice."

With that, she swept out of the room, leaving me standing alone. A tornado of thoughts whirling through my head, I sank onto the sofa. How could something that felt so right be against the rules? This made no sense at all.

Agatha walked into the room and jumped up onto my lap in a rare show of affection.

"There you are," I said, scratching behind her ears and swallowing hard, a lump forming in my throat. "I'd wondered where you were hiding."

Agatha shuddered, her fur prickling over her back. "The High Witch dismissed me from the lower level. I had no choice, but I did manage to hear most of what was said. I'm sorry, young witch."

Her tone and care made hot tears spring to my eyes.

"Damn it, Agatha," I mumbled. "Why does it always have to be so complicated?"

I closed the front door of my client's home behind me, a sense of accomplishment gripping my insides. I'd done a good job, and he was happy.

Then I caught sight of him—Corbin Grimm—and my breath stuck in my throat.

His presence, like a shadow at high noon, had no place here in Emberwick Crossing. He leaned against a gas-lit lamppost, his shoulder-length dark hair framing a cold face that looked as though it were chiseled from stone. Corbin wore a black trench coat that fell to his knees, its collar turned up against the wind, and beneath it, layers of black clothing that seemed to absorb the light around him.

"Ms. Holland!" he called out, his voice tinged with malice.

I suppressed a shudder. Fantastic. Just what I needed. A chat with tall, dark, and necromantic.

"Corbin. What brings you out from under your rock?" I tried to keep my voice steady as I glanced around, but we were alone. The street was eerily quiet, the usual resident noises strangely absent.

His lips twisted into a semblance of a smile, but it was more a sneer. "Your meddling, actually. Cease your interference, or you'll find yourself in a grave of your own making."

Oh, goody. Death threats before dinner. And here I thought my social calendar was empty.

"Seriously, Corbin? I'm not afraid of you." I was lying, of course. My heart stuttered in my chest, blood rushing around my body at a frantic pace.

The air around us grew colder, a chill seeping into my bones. Note to self: invest in a thicker jacket. Preferably one enchanted against creepy warlocks.

"Perhaps you should be." His voice was like ice. He pushed off the lamppost and took a step toward me, his movements smooth and predatory. "You've been sticking your nose where it doesn't belong, Sage. Playing with forces you barely understand."

I swallowed hard, trying to keep my composure. He wasn't the one trying to juggle a magical uprising and a coffee addiction.

"I'm just doing my job, Corbin. Protecting people from monsters like you."

His laugh was a low, sinister chuckle that sent a fresh wave of fear through me. "You think you know what monsters are, little witch? You have no idea." He raised a hand, and the darkness around him seemed to coalesce, shadowy tendrils curling through the air like smoke. "You see, Sage, I'm not just any monster. I'm a force of nature. I can bend death to my will, command the spirits of the damned. And you...you're just a girl with a few parlor tricks."

Well, excuse me for not having a PhD in Creepy Magic 101. Some of us had lives. Or at least, attempted to.

"Back off, Corbin," I said, my voice trembling despite my best efforts to sound brave. "I'm warning you."

"Oh, I'm shaking in my size twelve boots," he mocked, his eyes glowing green with malevolent glee. "Do you really think you can stand against me? I've toppled covens, brought entire cities to their knees. What makes you think you can stop me?"

Before I could respond, a sudden voice cut through the tension. "Holy hell, Corbin, do you ever shut up?" Agatha's voice had a sharp, sardonic tone.

Corbin's gaze flicked to the black cat balanced on a nearby fence. "Ah, the familiar. How quaint. Tell me, Sage, do you truly believe that a talking cat can protect you?"

Agatha's fur bristled, and she hissed. "I've seen more in my nine lives than you'll ever know, necromancer. Try anything, and you'll regret it."

Corbin's smile widened, his white teeth flashing in the artificially fading light. He took a step back, the shadows following him like a cloak. "We'll see about that. Cross me again, and the next time we meet, it won't be a warning."

The necromancer turned on his heel and melted into the darkness.

The sunshine returned as though someone had flipped on a switch, but my limbs shook as though cold. Well, wasn't that just a delightful interlude? I made a mental note to add *Avoid Creepy Warlocks* to my to-do list. Right after *Buy More Coffee* and *Save the World*.

Agatha jumped down from the fence and rubbed against my leg. "You okay, young witch?"

"Yeah, Agatha. Thanks for the help." I took a shuddering breath and aimed for humor. "Just another day in the life, right?"

She let out a hiss. "Right. Just another day with death threats from a creepy necromancer."

I managed a weak smile. "Let's get out of here."

Agatha's tail flicked with irritation as we started our walk home. The afternoon air was crisp, carrying the fragrance of pine and earth after the light rain.

We took a detour to Councilman Voss' house. I still had the kitchen remodel to finish. We let ourselves into the house, and Agatha waited while I did the magical redesign. I traced a spell over the granite countertops and made them look as good as new again. When I'd finished, I glanced about to check no one else had arrived home.

"Let's check out the office before we go," I said, my breath hitching in my throat, belying my unease.

The room was dimly lit by a single lamp shining on the mahogany furnishings. The scent of wood and lemon polish tickled my senses. In the corner stood a large filing cabinet with metal drawers. I carefully yanked open one of the lower drawers and began rifling through the files. My brow furrowed in concentration. After a few moments, I spotted a thick manila folder and opened it to find incriminating evidence against Councilman Voss, including photos and documents linking him to Corbin's necromancy. Agatha leaned in close, her whiskers twitching.

Jackpot.

This was just the break in the case I needed. *Mom and Dad, if you're watching, I hope I'm making you proud. Your little girl's turning into a regular Nancy Drew meets Hermione Granger.*

"Freaking hell, it looks like Corbin has been blackmailing Councilman Voss to help him," I said.

My fingers lingered over the papers inside, revealing the undeniable truth.

"Damn it, Voss," I murmured, scanning the documents. "What have you done?"

I shook my head. And here I thought politicians were supposed to be the ones doing the blackmailing, not the other way around. Guess power and corruption go hand-in-hand, whether you're casting votes or casting spells.

"Complicated things, that's what," Agatha said, her voice low and tense.

"Is someone there?" A maid's voice floated toward us, timid yet inquisitive.

Uh oh. Busted by the cleaning crew.

I'd rather tangle with a demon than try to explain this compromising position. *Think fast, Sage!*

"Shadow Manipulation, now," I whispered to Agatha.

She blended us both into the dimness with her magic. I

froze, holding my breath as the maid peered in, then moved on, none the wiser.

Whew. Nothing like a familiar who can pull off a disappearing act.

"Close call," Agatha said, materializing beside me. "Let's get out before we push our luck too far."

"Right behind you," I replied, slipping the incriminating file into my bag.

Time to skedaddle with the evidence before someone else stumbled onto our midday office raid.

Leaving Voss' house in the early afternoon, I felt a heaviness settle on my shoulders. The sun shone brightly overhead in a cloudless blue sky. Agatha trotted beside me, her fur gleaming like midnight.

"Corbin blackmailing Councilman Voss... this uprising is much bigger than we thought." I mused aloud. "This isn't just about stopping Corbin, Agatha. It's about the entire magical community."

"Seems that way," Agatha replied.

"If Corbin's got Councilman Voss under his thumb, who else is involved?"

"Half the Council, probably," Agatha said, not missing a beat. "Power attracts corruption like flies to honey."

"Or cats to food," I muttered with a weak smile.

"Hmm, tuna sounds delicious, young witch," Agatha said, her yellow eyes flashing.

The town seemed oblivious to the malicious undercurrents running beneath its picturesque surface. The smell of blooming flowers wafted through the air. Every cheerful note, every burst of color, felt like a mockery of the danger we now faced.

"Agatha, this could destroy us all..."

She cut me off, "Yes, we're in deeper trouble than you thought."

Agatha and I finally reached our home, an old, ivy-covered cottage at the edge of town. Brad was there, and from the looks of things, he was reinforcing protection spells around the perimeter. His tall, well-built frame moved with practiced ease, and his spiky brown hair shone in the bright sunlight. He looked up and smiled when he saw us.

"Hey, Sage. Everything all right?" he asked, his expression clouded with concern.

"Not exactly," I admitted. "Agatha, grab a bite inside. I'll fill Brad in."

"Don't have to tell me twice," Agatha said, darting through an open window.

I walked up to the boy next door, dread tugging at my heart. "Brad, we found something big."

He stepped closer, his eyebrows drawn together, "Tell me."

"Corbin confronted me today and threatened me." Brad's eyes bulged at the news, but I pushed forward, as there was more. "Then we found evidence that he's blackmailing Councilman Voss. And it turns out that Voss has been covering up Corbin's necromancy."

Holy hell, saying it out loud made it feel even more real. And terrifying.

Necromancy, blackmail, corrupt politicians... It was like a supernatural soap opera, except I was an unwilling star.

"Whoa, slow down," Brad said, his expression turning serious. "Corbin threatened you?"

"Yes, in person this time. No scary minions," I said, feeling a lump form in my throat. "It's huge, Brad. This could tear apart everything we know."

The magical world was unraveling faster than a kitten playing with yarn. Part of me wished I could crawl under a blanket and pretend none of this was happening. But I knew I couldn't hide from the truth, no matter how ugly it was.

"Come here," Brad said gently, drawing me into a tender embrace. His heat enveloped me, and I closed my eyes. For a moment, the world outside seemed less terrifying.

I melted into him, soaking up his strength like a sponge. Brad's hugs were like a magical elixir, capable of chasing away even my darkest fears. Well, temporarily, at least. If only he could bottle and sell them, we'd make a fortune.

I rested my head on his shoulder. "I don't know what I'd do without you."

Probably spiral into a vortex of anxiety and drown my sorrows in pints of cookie dough ice cream. Thank the goddess for Brad and his uncanny ability to keep me somewhat sane.

"You're strong, Sage. You'll get through this," he murmured against my hair. "I'm always here for you."

I wished we could stay like this forever. Or at least until the whole Corbin situation magically resolved itself. A girl could dream, right? Ugh, adulting was the worst sometimes.

"Just be careful," he added, leaning back to look into my eyes. "Corbin's dangerous. But we'll find a way to stop him."

"Promise?" I asked, my voice barely audible.

"Promise," he said, leaning in to press a gentle kiss to my forehead.

My heart raced at his nearness, making it even harder to focus on the dire situation.

Traitorous heart. Now was not the time for inconvenient feelings to rear their complicated head. I needed to focus on the supernatural crisis threatening to implode my world, not the way Brad's arms felt against my skin. Curse my horrible timing.

"Let's sit on the porch," Brad said, releasing me reluctantly. "We need to plan our next moves."

Next moves. Right. Because apparently, I was now in charge of preventing a magical apocalypse or whatever. No pressure. I took a deep breath, trying to center myself.

One thing at a time, Sage.

We moved to the porch steps, the cool air wrapping around us. I glanced at Brad's profile, his jaw set and firm.

Oh, boy, here we go. Dropping supernatural truth bombs on cute warlocks was not in my weekend plans. But secrets between almost-lovers? A recipe for disaster. Time to rip off the Band-Aid.

"Brad," I said, my voice wavering. "There's something else we need to talk about."

"What's up?" He turned to me; concern etched into his features.

I took a deep breath. *Relax, Sage.* It's not like you're confessing to a crime. Well, unless falling for your best friend is illegal in witch world. Oh, wait...

"The High Witch came to visit me a few days ago and..." I paused, searching for the right words. "She said there's this rule. The Covenant of Veiled Boundaries."

His brows knitted together. "Okay, what's that?"

Ugh, why did witch laws have to sound like a bad fantasy movie? I braced myself for the impending doom.

"It's this old law, and it prohibits any romantic involvement between members of the Council's inner circle—like me—and civilians like you."

"What? Are you serious?" Brad's eyes widened, shock coloring his voice. "That's freaking ridiculous!"

Yep, welcome to my world, where ridiculous is the norm.

I grimaced, my heart sinking low. "I know, but I can't go against the High Witch. I'm so sorry."

"There has to be a way around this rule." His voice was edged with hurt.

Oh, if only it were that simple. Loopholes in outdated witch contracts? Not likely. My chest ached seeing his pain. "I said the same thing, but the High Witch was adamant. And I don't want to lose you. You're my best friend, Brad. I can't lose that."

He was quiet a long time. "So that's all we'll ever be? Friends, now?"

Tears lined my eyes, and I sniffed. My heart was breaking. Fan-freaking-tastic. Ugly crying in front of the guy I was crazy about.

Way to keep it together, Sage.

"Yes. But it doesn't mean I don't care about you. I just—"

He scooted away from me. "Just what? You want me to pretend there's nothing more between us? That I don't care about you anymore? I'm not sure I can do that."

"Brad, please." Fresh tears dripped down my cheeks. "I can't break the Covenant. If I do, there'll be consequences. For both of us."

He scoffed, running a hand through his spiky hair. "You always were a rule-follower, Sage."

Oh, hell no. He did not just go there. My sadness morphed into frustration.

"Not by choice!" I snapped back, more forcefully than I intended. "I have responsibilities. To the Council. To this town. You think I wanted this shit?"

"Maybe not," he said, softer now. "But we deserve to be happy too, don't we?"

Damn straight we do. But apparently, the universe missed that memo.

I sighed. "Of course we do." My voice broke. "But we can still be friends."

He looked at me, his expression full of conflicted emotions. "How am I supposed to just pretend you're not everything to me?"

We sat there, hands intertwined and hearts heavy. Things would never be the same now. Freaking witchy politics, ruining my love life. But I'd rather have Brad in my world as a friend than not at all. Even if my heart didn't quite agree.

CHAPTER
NINE

T he moon hung low, creating a spine-chilling glow over the graveyard. The air was thick with fog, slithering around the tombstones like ghostly figures. Bats swooped and darted above us, making me swallow my shrieks of surprise.

I shivered and tugged my jacket tighter around me, wishing the fabric could protect me from my creeping anxiety.

"Are we sure this is the place?" Brad's voice cut through the silence, his flashlight illuminating the dilapidated funeral parlor ahead of us.

"Yes. I got this location from a reliable source," Evie said, in the lead. Her flashlight lit the way, showing us the cracked wooden front door.

Brad, Evie, and I stepped inside, our flashlight beams slicing through the gloom. Dust motes danced in the air, disturbed by our presence. The funeral parlor was a relic of decay, its wilted wallpaper peeling away from the walls in long, ragged strips, revealing patches of mold that bloomed like dark, sinister flowers. The wooden floor beneath our feet groaned with each step as if protesting our intrusion.

The air smelled thick with the stench of mildew and something else. It clung to the back of my throat, making me want to gag. Cobwebs draped from the corners of the ceiling, their delicate threads shimmering in the moonlight that shone through the windows.

Evie shuddered. "This place gives me the creeps."

Brad nodded, his face pale. "Yeah, let's find what we need and get out of here."

We moved deeper into the parlor, passing rows of empty coffins, their lids askew and interiors lined with tattered satin. I heard the scuttling of tiny feet as rodents darted for cover. A once-grand chandelier hung precariously above our heads, its crystals coated in dust, swaying as if stirred by a ghostly breath.

"This place is charming," Brad grumbled, nudging a broken chair aside with his foot.

"Looks like Corbin's taste in real estate is freaky old morgues," I said, swallowing against the rising panic.

An old, velvet curtain hung limply to one side, partially concealing a door that led to the embalming room. The heavy, oppressive atmosphere made it difficult to breathe, as if the very walls were absorbing the life from us.

Maybe they were? I shook myself. What a horrible thought.

"Check this out!" Evie called from a corner, where her flashlight glinted off something metallic.

Brad and I hurried over, peering at the demonic artifacts Evie had uncovered. The scene was chilling. Skulls and bones were arranged in intricate, ritualistic patterns, forming a macabre circle on the floor. Each bone was meticulously placed, their yellowed surfaces gleaming dully in the flashlight beams. Candles, long since melted into grotesque shapes, stood at the cardinal points of the circle, their wax pooling around them like crimson tears.

In the center of the circle lay a book, its cover bound in what looked disturbingly like human skin, the texture rough and sickeningly organic. The binding was stitched together with blood-red thread, and the edges of the cover were frayed and cracked, as if from frequent, unholy use. Evie lifted the book and opened it. The pages inside looked brittle and yellow, covered with cramped, spidery handwriting and gruesome illustrations of necromantic rituals and infernal incantations.

"Definitely Corbin's handiwork," Brad said, his voice grim.

"Why can't he just stick to a normal hobby... like knitting?" I tried to joke, but the sight before me turned my stomach.

"Because necromancers aren't known for their cozy hobbies," Evie replied dryly, scanning the macabre scene.

"Well, I think it's time he did," I returned, looking away to settle myself.

Evie knelt beside the circle. "These are necromantic rites. Look at the way the bones are arranged. This isn't just for show.

Whoever did this was summoning, or at the very least, trying to commune with the dead." She pointed to the candles. "The wax is mixed with blood, probably human. It's used to bind spirits to this plane, to keep them anchored here." Her finger traced the outline of the circle. "And this pattern... it was a containment field. To trap whatever Corbin summoned."

Well, isn't this just a delightful little arts and crafts project from Hell? Leave it to Corbin to take his goth phase to the next level.

Brad swallowed hard, his expression showing horror. "And the book?"

Evie sighed. "It's a grimoire, and these spells are meant to control the dead, to raise and command spirits. This is some seriously powerful and dangerous, necromancy."

I felt a chill touch my spine. "So, this wasn't just amateur hour."

More like *I majored in raising the dead with a minor in bad decisions.* Whoever said college prepares you for the real world clearly never met Corbin.

Evie grimaced. "No, this is advanced stuff. Corbin knew exactly what he was doing."

Brad looked around nervously. "We need to get out of here. If Corbin comes back..."

I glanced towards the door, "We need to take this book with us. If Corbin is involved, we need to understand exactly what we're dealing with."

Because apparently, my life wasn't complicated enough without adding a dash of necromancy to the mix. Thanks, universe. You really know how to keep things interesting.

Evie closed the book, shuddering as she touched the creepy

book cover. "Let's go, then. The sooner we get out of this place, the better."

I longed to reach out, to let my fingers brush against Brad's, to reassure him and myself that everything was going to be okay. But I couldn't. Not with Ingrid's orders hanging over us like a curse.

Forbidden love. It sounded so dramatic, like something out of a cheesy romance novel. But here I was, living it. I guess I should be flattered that my life had become so literary. Too bad the genre was less "happily ever after" and more "impending doom and gloom."

Focus, Sage. We have a job to do.

"Wait. There's more over here." Evie held up a vial filled with a dark, viscous liquid. "This looks like blood magic."

"Great." I sighed. "Just what we needed."

Another complication, as if my day wasn't already chock-full of delightful surprises. I mean, really, who doesn't love stumbling upon a vial of blood magic on a Tuesday afternoon? In an abandoned morgue, no less. Totally normal.

"Brad, can you use your powers to check if there's anything hidden in the walls?" Evie asked, turning to him.

"On it." Brad nodded, placing his hand against the wall and closing his eyes. His face tightened in concentration. As he worked, I admired his focus and dedication. He was so strong, so capable—everything I admired, especially in moments like these.

I appreciated the way Brad's brow furrowed as he channeled his magic. It was like watching a master artist at work, except instead of a paintbrush, he wielded supernatural powers.

"Found something," he announced, breaking my reverie. A

section of the wall shimmered and then dissolved, revealing a hidden compartment. Inside were more artifacts, each more sinister than the last.

"Corbin really went all out," Evie said, her voice low, raspy.

"We need to report this to Ingrid. She needs to know just how far Corbin's gone, but she forbade me from investigating. Do what if we leave an anonymous tip?"

Or more like a one-way ticket to the magical doghouse. I could already picture Ingrid's disapproving glare, her eyebrow arched so high it practically merged with her hairline. But what choice did we have? It's not like I could waltz up to her and say, "Hey, remember when you explicitly told me not to investigate? Well, surprise! I did it anyway."

"We can try," Brad said, his voice firm. Yet, when he looked at me, there was softness there, a tenderness that made my heart ache.

Evie moved towards the exit. "Let's get out of here. I've seen enough."

"Right behind you," Brad said, giving me one last lingering look.

I forced myself to turn away, following Evie out of the funeral parlor.

We stepped out into the graveyard, the breeze odiferous with decay. The moon barely penetrated the overcast sky.

"Do you smell that?" Evie wrinkled her nose, taking out her flashlight and scanning the area.

Brad froze. "Yeah. It's getting worse."

"Stay sharp," I warned. "Corbin might have booby traps in place or worse..."

Ah, the glamorous life of a witch—traipsing through graveyards and battling the forces of evil. I really should've become an accountant like Mom wanted. At least their biggest occupational hazard was paper cuts.

Suddenly, there was movement from the gloom. A dozen undead creatures staggered towards us, their eyes lifeless, their mouths hanging open with drool. Their clothes hung in tatters, revealing mold-covered skin and exposed bones.

"Zombies!" Evie shouted, reaching for her utility belt.

Oh, goody. Brain-munchers. And me without my industrial-sized bottle of hand sanitizer. *Note to self: invest in a flamethrower for these delightful encounters.*

"Get behind me!" Brad commanded.

He was raising his hands to conjure a magical shield around us. The translucent barrier shimmered, but I could see the strain on his face.

My knight in shining armor. Well, minus the armor. And the horse. But that chiseled jaw and dogged bravery? Classic fairytale material.

Focus, Sage! Time to kick some zombie butt.

"Time to light things up." I started summoning my magic.

Energy surged through my veins, and I released it in a dazzling display of light and force. Bolts of power shot from my hands, striking the zombies with precision. They staggered back, disoriented.

Ha! Take that, you walking corpses! Sage: 1, Zombies: 0. If only the High Witch could see me now.

"Nice one, Sage!" Brad called; his voice tight with effort.

Every spell took a piece of me, but I couldn't stop now. I had to protect my friends. Plus, I had a reputation to uphold. "Sage the Zombie Slayer" had a nice ring to it.

"Take this!" Evie yelled, throwing a potion at the nearest zombie. It exploded on impact, sending bits of decayed flesh flying. The creature transformed into a harmless rabbit, hopping away in confusion.

I couldn't help grinning. Leave it to Evie to bring some whimsy to a life-or-death battle. That girl had style.

"Keep those potions coming, Evie!" I urged, launching another magical blast at a group of the undead. They convulsed as though they were about to drop, their connection to Corbin severed by my magic.

"Watch out, Sage!" Brad shouted as a particularly grotesque zombie lunged at me. Its breath was a rancid cloud of death.

"Got it!" Brad's voice rang out, and he used his powers to erect a wall between me and the creature, crushing it under the force.

"Close call," I said, wiping sweat from my brow. "Thanks, Brad."

His stare met mine for a brief moment.

"Focus, guys!" Evie was hurling another potion that erupted in a blaze of green fire, scattering more zombies.

"Let's finish this." My spells flowed more smoothly now, each strike weakening the undead further. For a moment, I was lost in the progression of battle, every action proof of our teamwork.

"Behind you!" Brad's warning snapped me back.

I spun around, unleashing a burst of light that vaporized the creature sneaking up on me. My body trembled, fear melding with adrenaline.

Evie tossed her last potion, transforming another cluster of zombies into harmless hamsters.

"Keep it up!" Brad encouraged, reinforcing his shield to give us a moment's respite.

"Just a few more," I said, focusing on a final, powerful spell. Lightning crackled from my fingertips, arcing towards the remaining zombies. They convulsed, their forms disintegrating under the raw power.

"That's the last of them," Evie confirmed, breathing heavily. "For now, at least."

"Terrific job, everyone," Brad said, lowering his shield and looking around. "But we need to stay vigilant. Corbin won't stop here."

My body ached, but I knew we'd have to keep pushing forward. There was too much at stake.

"That was intense," I said, trying to catch my breath. "I've never battled zombies before."

"Nor do I want to ever again." Brad grunted, wiping grime off his face with his sleeve.

"I need to gather my potion bottles," Evie said, already scouring the ground for her containers.

"Be careful," Brad called after her.

"Always am, Bradley." She disappeared behind a crumbling crypt.

"Well, that went better than expected," I said, glancing at Brad.

Zombies, necromancers, magical artifacts—just another weeknight.

"Yeah. You, okay?"

"Just feeling the rush." My heart was pounding, but not just from the fight.

Brad's presence seemed to have that effect on me lately. It

was like my body couldn't decide whether it wanted to run a marathon or melt into a puddle of goo whenever he was near.

Get it together, Sage. Focus on the mission, not the man.

Easier said than done.

Brad moved closer, his voice softening. "You were incredible tonight, Sage."

"You weren't so bad yourself."

Okay, that was the understatement of the century. Watching Brad unleash his warlock powers was awesome. The way his eyes flashed with arcane sorcery, the fluid grace of his movements as he cast spells—it was enough to make a witch weak in the knees.

"Is that a compliment?" He grinned, his usual teasing timbre returning.

"It could be." I smiled back, feeling the tension ease.

"Damn the rules," he muttered, closing the distance between us.

Our lips met in a tumultuous kiss, a fiery blend of passion and longing. The intensity of our emotions spilled over as we pressed our bodies closer in a desperate embrace. It felt like a collision of two hearts, bound by lust and desire, exploding in sensation.

Woah.... the man could kiss.

If this was breaking the rules, then sign me up for a life of crime. I'd gladly face a hundred zombies if it meant I got to experience this rush again. Brad's lips were like a magic spell all their own, turning my brain to mush and my body to jelly.

"Guys!" Evie's voice shattered the moment.

We broke apart, breathless and wide-eyed.

Well, that was awkward. Nothing like getting caught making out in a graveyard by your best friend.

Evie placed her items back into her belt and dropped eye contact. "Found all the bottles. Ready to talk necromancy?"

"Um, sure. Y-yeah," I stammered, tugging on my sweater and brushing my hair back off my face, trying to cool the heat from my blood.

Smooth, Sage. Real smooth.

You'd think after years of magical training, I'd be better at thinking on my feet. But apparently, all it took was one knee-weakening kiss from Brad to turn me into a tongue-tied mess. Some badass witch I was.

Brad looked equally flustered but managed a nod.

"Great," Evie said, glancing around as though checking for more zombies.

I began to fidget. "How about we get out of here before we get attacked again?"

Evie snorted. "Sure, okay... but I need to think out loud so I'm gonna talk."

I nodded. "Go for it."

We started walking back through the cemetery, and Evie began to chatter, "So, here's what I've found out. Necromancy isn't just about raising the dead. It's about controlling them, bending their will to the necromancer's commands."

And now the zombies made sense.

"Like Corbin's doing," Brad interjected, stealing glances at me.

"Exactly," Evie said. "But it requires immense power and a deep connection to the underworld. The artifacts we've seen are likely conduits, amplifying his control."

"Why would he need such control?" I asked. And why would he need such power?

I was trying really hard to focus on the conversation and not on the lingering taste of Brad's lips or the way his hand kept brushing against mine, sending little jolts of electricity up my arm.

Priorities, Sage. World-ending necromancer now, tonsil hockey later.

"Power. Influence. Chaos," Evie replied. "Necromancers like Corbin thrive on disrupting the natural order. If he succeeds, he could unleash an army of the undead on Emberwick Crossing, and the supernatural uprising will officially begin."

Oh, joy. An undead apocalypse. Just what this town needs to liven things up. I suppressed an eye roll. Necromancers and their obsessions with death and decay— some witches and warlocks had the worst hobbies, I swear.

"Which means we need to stop him," Brad said, his voice emotional.

Thank you, Captain Obvious.

I bit my tongue before the quip could escape. Now was not the time for my offbeat commentary, even if it would alleviate the dire mood. Brad looked genuinely worried. His furrowed brow was kind of adorable though.

Stop it, Sage!

We finally reached the huge iron gates, and I staggered through them, my feet touching the pavement. I sighed, feeling exhausted. "It's so good to be out of there."

Evie shot me an amused glance, no doubt reading my mind. Perceptive as always, that one. She knew I was about two seconds away from suggesting we grab a pint of mint chocolate chip and put this whole necromancer business on ice for the night. My bed was calling to me like a siren song.

"What are you thinking, Sage?" Evie turned to look at me with a curious expression.

"Just thinking about what you said. If Corbin's control over the undead is that strong, how do we weaken it?"

"Excellent question," Brad added, his tone serious now.

"From my research," Evie said, "there are a few ways to disrupt a necromancer's connection to the undead. Destroying the artifacts he's using to amplify his magic would be a start. But there are also some very old spells and unholy rituals designed specifically for this purpose. I might find something we can use in his book."

"Like a counter-ritual?" I asked, my brain already whirling with possibilities.

"Exactly," Evie confirmed. "But they're complex and require precise execution."

"Which means we need to find those spells and learn them fast," Brad said, determination etched into his features. "Corbin won't be working alone. He's got followers. People who believe in his cause."

"Great," I grumbled. "More problems."

"Which means we need to be careful," Brad said, his voice softening as he looked at me. "Especially you, Sage."

"Me? Why?" I asked, taken aback.

"Because you're special," he said, his eyes locking onto mine. "Your magic, your creativity... You're a threat to him. And to others who don't understand you."

A sudden thought slammed into me. What if Brad and I

were seen kissing? Crap on a cracker. If I did have enemies, they'd know where to strike to hurt me the worst.

Brad.

Not to mention that the High Witch would have my head on a platter if she found out. I really needed to get my priorities straight, right after I got some sleep.

CHAPTER

TEN

D ays after our zombie showdown in the cemetery, I
found a note resting on my kitchen table.

*Meet me in the woods at sundown. Make sure no
one sees you.*

Brad's scrawl was unmistakable. I threw the paper into the
fireplace and watched it burn. Ingrid would be furious if she
knew, but I couldn't fight my need to be with Brad. She just
didn't understand.

I took a step towards my front door, then froze. What was I
thinking? This was a terrible idea. Sneaking off to meet Brad,

risking everything—my position, Ingrid's trust, the Council's wrath. Yet here I was, powerless against my own desires.

"I should stay home and not go."

The words sounded hollow, even to my own ears. Who was I kidding? Obviously, I was going. Forbidden love waits for no witch.

Still, the Covenant of Veiled Boundaries strictly forbade romance between members of the Council's inner circle and private citizens, like Brad. As if legislating love had ever worked out well.

Romeo and Juliet...

But hey, I was sure this would end much better for Brad and me. At least I hoped so, anyway.

The sun sank lower in the sky, and I walked over to the window. I waited until the world outside fell silent and Tabatha was asleep on my bed, then I slipped out the back door and walked across town until I reached the woods.

I moved through the grove, the path darkening as dusk approached. The woods were alive with sound—rustling leaves, distant bird calls, the faint howl of the wind through the trees. Each noise sent a spike of adrenaline through me.

"Don't get caught." I told myself as I stepped carefully over a fallen branch. The last thing I needed was someone hearing me who shouldn't. My blood pounded louder than my footsteps. "Just keep moving."

Shadows shifted, creating phantom figures that made me jump. The woods seemed to close in around me, each tree a potential witness.

Why am I doing this?

But I knew why. Brad. His smile, his laugh, the way his

expression lit up when he talked about something he loved. I couldn't stay away, no matter what Ingrid said.

Apparently, I had a weakness for pretty boys with nice smiles. Who knew? Oh, right. Everyone.

I ducked under a low-hanging branch. The clearing wasn't far now. The thought of seeing Brad kept me going, in spite of the gnawing fear that we'd get caught. My steps quickened, the anticipation building with each passing second.

My breathing sped up, and I started pushing through the final thicket. The clearing opened before me, bathed in the faint glow of the setting sun. I took a deep breath, the tension in my chest loosening just a bit. I sighed, looking around for any sign of Brad. The swish of branches behind me made me spin around, my heart hammering hard and quick.

"Hey," Brad's voice came softly from the darkness.

I exhaled a breath I didn't realize I'd been holding. He stepped into view, his form bringing a wave of relief and excitement.

"You're here," I said, my voice trembling.

He smiled that same boyish grin that always made my insides melt. "Of course, I am."

My heart swelled. Every fiber of my being warned that this was wrong, dangerous even. Except standing there with Brad, nothing else mattered.

Forbidden love: 1. Common sense: 0.

"Come here," Brad said, opening his arms.

I didn't hesitate. I hurried over to him. He drew me into his arms, and I breathed him in—he smelled like pine and musk. In his embrace, the world seemed to pause as he held me tight.

"Missed you," he murmured into my hair.

"Missed you too." My voice caught, thick with longing.

I pulled back, taking him in. Artfully tousled hair, blue eyes bright in the candlelight. That gray t-shirt hugging his muscular frame and a pair of worn jeans that somehow looked stylish on him.

"What's all this?" I gestured to the blankets, the wine, the lit candles transforming the forest clearing into something magical. A bottle of wine and two plastic cups sat off to one side.

A crooked smile. "Thought we could use a little 'us' time. Wine?"

"Ever the charmer." I tried for coy, but my face betrayed me, breaking into a full grin.

"Only for you." His voice was earnest and soft.

My heart swelled at his sincerity. Classic Brad, always knowing just what to say to turn my insides to mush. I wanted to believe him, to get swept up in the romance of it all. But the sensible part of my brain kept throwing up warning signs. The inner circle and civilians weren't supposed to intermingle. Not like this.

Reality crashed back, cold and sobering. "This is risky, Brad. If Ingrid finds out..."

He pressed a kiss to my forehead, gentle and sweet. "Tonight's ours, okay? Let's make it count."

I swallowed, not wanting to tell him no. Not while he was being so lovely. "Okay."

He poured the wine, handing me a cup. We clinked our cups against each other.

"To us," he said, holding my gaze.

"To us," I said. The sentiment felt loaded. Dangerous yet thrilling.

I took a sip. The wine tasted bitter and a bit yuck. We settled onto the blankets, knees touching. I savored the forbidden thrill of it, the delicious wrongness. Two magical beings, flouting the rules, daring to imagine a future together when we'd been told it *wasn't permitted*.

It was like playing with fire—exhilarating and liable to burn me. But with Brad beside me, I couldn't bring myself to care.

"How's work been?" he asked.

"Busy. Lots of new design clients," I said, sitting beside him. "But it's good, you know? Keeps my mind occupied, busy."

I told him about my design clients, the way the projects consumed my thoughts. Left less room for brooding about impossible futures.

He lifted an eyebrow at me. "Keeping busy to stop from thinking about us, you mean."

Perceptive as always. It was unnerving sometimes, how easily he could read me. Like he had a direct line to my thoughts. I wondered, not for the first time, if warlocks could do that—read minds. It would explain a lot. Then again, maybe he just knew me that well.

I sighed, leaning into his solid frame. "Wishing for something doesn't make it possible."

"Doesn't make it impossible either." He tipped my chin up with his fingers, his expression blazing with intensity. "I'm not giving up on us, Sage. No matter what the Council says."

My pulse thrummed, his proximity sending tingles across my skin. "You really are too stubborn for your own good."

"Persistent," he corrected with a roguish wink. Then he sobered. "I mean it though. I can't stay away from you."

I rolled my eyes, fighting back a smile. Leave it to Brad to reframe stubbornness as a virtue. His optimism was infectious. It made me want to believe in the impossible, in a world where we could be a couple without fear or consequence. A girl could dream...

"I don't want you to stay away," I admitted, desire and dread knotting in my stomach. "Just promise that we'll be careful not to be found out?"

"I promise," he said, sounding sincere. Then he sealed our deal with the softest brush of his lips against mine, a mere whisper of a kiss. "Now, enough serious talk. Tonight's for us, remember?"

I smiled against his mouth. "Mmm. Remind me again what that entails?"

I was torn between the affection I felt for him and the fear of what could happen if we were discovered. But in that moment, all I wanted was him. The rest of the world could wait. He was right. Tonight, it was only me, Brad, and the starry sky above.

"Well," he said, reaching for the wine bottle, "it involves this." He poured the dark red liquid into plastic cups, the sound almost musical in the stillness of the woods. Handing me a cup, he added with a grin, "And maybe a little more of this."

The wine was sweet on my tongue now, and I moaned.

"Remember when we tried to build a treehouse in your backyard?" Brad reminisced, leaning against the tree behind us.

I laughed, the memory resurfacing. "How could I forget? We spent weeks planning it, gathering materials and convincing our parents to let us do it. You were an architect even way back then."

"And then, when we finally got it built, it was so crooked

and unstable that we were afraid to go inside!" He laughed aloud and shook his head.

I smiled fondly. "It was still our little hideout. We had so many great adventures in that lopsided tree house."

"Those were the days." Brad sighed wistfully. "Back when our biggest worry was making it home before the streetlights came on."

I nodded, taking a sip of my drink. "Yeah, life was so much simpler then. Before these stupid rules complicated everything."

Brad leaned closer, his voice dropping to a whisper. "I found this old spell book in my house. Must've belonged to my parents, but they forgot it in a drawer somehow."

He was changing the subject. Typical Brad, always trying to distract me with some new magical discovery when things got too serious. It was equal parts endearing and exasperating.

"What kind of spells?" I asked, unable to ignore the carrot.

"Mostly basic stuff, but there was one about creating more powerful protective barriers. Thought it might come in handy."

"You're always thinking ahead," I said, touched by his thoughtfulness. "I really appreciate it."

"Anything for you, Sage."

We sat in comfortable silence for a while, just enjoying each other's presence. The moonlight filtered through the canopy above our heads, radiating a soft silver glow on the ferns and trees around us. It felt like we were the only two people in the world, wrapped in a cocoon of secrecy and stolen moments.

CHAPTER

ELEVEN

I leaned back against Brad's chest and savored this precious pocket of time with him, away from the prying eyes of the Council. If only we could stay like this forever, unburdened by expectations and outdated traditions. But reality had a pesky way of intruding even the most perfect moments.

"Look at the moon," Brad said, pointing up. "Isn't it beautiful?"

"Hmmm," I murmured, but my stare was fixed on him. The way the moonlight highlighted the angles of his face, the gold flecks in his eyes was breathtaking. "Beautiful."

He caught me staring and smiled. "What are you thinking about?"

"Just... how lucky I am to have you in my life." And how terrified I was of losing him if our secret got out.

"The feeling is mutual," he said with a smile. "You know, we don't have to keep this secret forever."

"Brad, we've talked about this. We can't get caught until we find a work around the rule—"

"Stop worrying so much," he interrupted.

I frowned at him, then looked away. Could we really defy the High Witch and come out unscathed? Part of me yearned to throw caution to the wind and proclaim my love for Brad from the rooftops. But the rational side knew we were treading on thin ice. One wrong move and everything could come crashing down around us.

Would I be banished from the magical community if we got caught? Or worse, forced to scrub cauldrons for the next century as punishment? Not exactly how I wanted to make my parents proud.

But somehow, when I was with Brad, none of that seemed real. When we were together, it was like nothing could touch us. There were no rules, no responsibilities, no judging eyes watching our every move. It was just me and him and the thrill of the forbidden.

"Hey." Brad's voice had softened now, hauling me from my thoughts. "We'll be okay. Trust me."

"I do," I said quickly, surprised he didn't think I did. "It's everyone else that I'm worried about." Especially Ingrid. She already had her suspicions about us. If she found concrete proof that I was doing exactly what she'd told me not to, there's no telling what she might do.

"Trust me. We only have to sneak around for a little while," he said, squeezing my hand.

I leaned my head on his shoulder. "So, tell me more about this spell book." Now I was the one changing the topic.

"Okay, but first—" He paused dramatically. "You have to promise not to laugh."

I arched an eyebrow, grateful for the temporary distraction. "Uh oh. This should be good."

He rolled his eyes. "Apparently, one of my parents had a thing for love potions. There's an entire chapter dedicated to them."

I smirked. "Thinking of brewing one up for someone special?"

He playfully bumped my shoulder. "I've already got the girl of my dreams right here."

My cheeks heated up. "Very smooth." I giggled, and my heart soared.

We continued talking, sharing stories and secrets. Here, under the moonlit sky, we were free. Free to be ourselves. Free to be in a relationship.

But as the night wore on, reality began to creep back in like a spider building a web. It started out small but grew and grew. My loyalty to Ingrid was strong, and the risks we were taking were huge. It all weighed heavily on my thoughts.

Could I really balance my desires with my duties? And what would happen if I couldn't?

"Brad," I said softly, breaking the peaceful silence. "Promise me something."

"Anything."

"Promise me we'll find a way to make this work, no matter what it takes."

"Promise," he said without hesitation. And in that moment, I believed him.

Hope lingered like a fragile thread binding us as one. I wanted to believe it with every fiber of my being.

"Sage," he whispered, leaning closer.

I could feel the warmth radiating from his body, the scent of earth and his sandalwood cologne. He turned towards me, his blue eyes catching the silver light filtering through the trees.

"Yes?" My voice was soft, almost hesitant.

"Let's not waste any more time."

We moved towards each other with urgency. Our lips met in a sudden, electric kiss. Sparks ignited in my veins, and my skin tingled with a blend of anticipation and raw desire. His hands found their way to my waist, pulling me closer as if trying to merge our bodies into one. I responded with equal fervor, my fingers threading through his thick hair.

The kiss deepened, and I could taste the wine on his lips, sweet and beguiling. Every touch, every caress seemed to set my senses ablaze.

"Goddess, Sage..." Brad groaned against my mouth, his breathing fast and ragged. "I love kissing you."

The truth of it hit me like a tidal wave—how much I cared about him, how much I craved this connection, forbidden or not. His hands roamed over my back, and I pressed closer into his body. I felt a surge of heat between us, and the world narrowed down to just the two of us in this moonlit clearing. We tumbled onto the blanket, limbs tangled, kisses growing more frantic.

"You're so beautiful." His lips were caressing my neck.

My skin burned where he touched, a trail of fire left in his wake. I arched into him, wanting more, needing more. I moaned softly, unable to form coherent thoughts. His hands were everywhere—my hips, my thighs—tracing the curve of my body as if memorizing every inch.

Goodbye rational thinking, hello hormones! Who needed magic when you had Brad's hands working their own special brand of sorcery?

His mouth captured mine again. I was overwhelmed with passion and hunger, a desperate attempt to make up for lost time. His fingers slipped under my shirt, grazing my bare skin, and I gasped at the sensation.

"Do you know how much I've thought about you?" he murmured; his voice rough with emotion. "Every single day."

I sighed. The heart wanted what the heart wanted, even if it was completely off-limits, according to witch protocol.

But even as I gave in to the sizzling heat of our embrace, a part of me couldn't ignore the shadow of guilt being cast over us. Ingrid's disapproval loomed in the back of my mind, reminding me of the risks. This wasn't just a simple romance. It was a rebellion against everything I had been taught to value.

Damn it. Ingrid and her rules could wait. Right now, all I wanted was to lose myself in Brad's arms and pretend the world outside didn't exist. But I suppose a little restraint wouldn't kill me. Much.

I moved away, my breathing shallow. He looked at me, worry etched across his handsome face. He lowered his hands and blew out along breath.

"What's wrong?"

"Nothing. Just... let's take it slow."

"No problem," he said quickly, his gaze searching mine as though verifying I was telling the truth. "Whatever you need."

We lay there, bodies entwined, the night wrapping around us like a cocoon.

What did the future hold for us? Could we really defy the odds? Or were we destined for heartbreak?

"Promise me," I whispered again. "Promise me we'll figure this out."

"I promise," he replied without hesitation, his lips grazing my forehead.

The night felt like it belonged to us alone, but reality snapped back when I heard the unmistakable crunch of footsteps on the nearby trail. My heart leaped into my throat. Great, just when things were getting interesting.

"Did you hear that?" I pulled away from Brad.

"Yes. We need to be quiet," he said, his voice low and tense.

A person appeared from nowhere. It was a Council member, cloaked in royal blue robes, walking along the trail with a large black dog. Her brown hair bounced on her shoulders, and the dog's ears were perked, alert to every sound. Being a Council member, this woman would report our illicit meeting without hesitation to the high witch.

She hadn't seen us yet, but she would. Or the dog would point out our presence, that was almost certain at this point.

"Shit." Adrenaline surged through my veins. "We can't get caught." Not after all the trouble I went through to sneak out tonight.

After all, I was Ingrid's ever-loyal apprentice, and I was sneaking around after nightfall with my next-door neighbor like we were a couple of teenagers. What would the High Witch think when she learned I was willing to risk it all—my position, her trust, everything I'd worked for—for a few stolen moments with Brad.

Brad's grip on my hand tightened. "Stay still. Don't make a sound."

Every rustle of leaves was deafening now, each snap of a twig amplifying my fear. The Council member paused, looking around. The dog sniffed the air, its sharp senses making my pulse sprint even faster.

Please, please keep walking. I clutched Brad's hand as if it were a lifeline. What would Ingrid do if she found out? My loyalty to her would be questioned, my place in the magical community threatened. And worse, Brad could face severe consequences too. All because we wanted one night to ourselves. Was that too much to ask?

"Why did we think this was a good idea again?" My voice was quivering.

"Because sometimes, breaking the rules is worth it," Brad said, his breath warm against my ear. "But let's just not get caught doing it." He gave me that roguish smile that made my insides flutter.

The Council member seemed to hesitate for an eternity before finally continuing down the path, the dog trotting beside her. We stayed motionless, barely daring to breathe until they were well out of earshot.

"That was too close." I exhaled a shaky breath. Way too close for comfort.

"But we're okay. For now."

We stood up, brushing off the leaves and dirt. We made our

way back through the woods. The thrill of our secret affair warred with the ever-present danger, each step reminding me of the precarious line we walked, balancing desire and duty. Yet, despite the risks, I couldn't deny the attraction I had for Brad, or the exhilaration of defying the forbidden.

"Next time," Brad said with a wry smile, "let's find a safer place."

"Next time?" I grinned. "Are you always this optimistic?"

"Only when I'm with you. Now, let's get out of here before our luck runs out."

I pondered how long we could keep this secret. The stakes were high, but so was the allure of the forbidden. And for now, that was enough to keep me coming back for more.

CHAPTER
TWELVE

"Sage! Come outside, now!" Brad's voice was urgent and sharp from my porch.

Without hesitation, I bolted through the doorway, the heavy slamming of the door behind me reverberating like a warning.

His eyes—wide with panic—met mine. "Corbin's here," he gasped, "with an army."

My heart pounded in my chest as the gravity of the situation sunk in. "What?"

He panted hard as though he'd been running. "Corbin, an

army... attacking... Emberwick Crossing! An army of the dead, and he's raising more."

I barely had time to process Brad's words before we were hauling ass towards the heart of the town. We sprinted through the streets, Brad's long strides matching mine. Our movements resonated off the cobblestone streets, matching the pounding of fear and adrenaline in my veins.

The sound of battle engulfed us before we even turned the corner. Fear knotted in my stomach, but a fierce protective instinct burned hotter. We skidded into the town square.

The area came into view, transformed into a battleground by Corbin Grimm's fiendish presence. His maniacal laughter cut through the air as skeletal figures swarmed the townspeople, their bones clacking ominously. Evie and Freya stood at the center of it all, surrounded by foes yet steadfast in their resolve.

Bloody hell, this wasn't in my job description.

Emberwick Crossing, my home, was under siege. Corbin Grimm, the necromancer, was cackling like a madman near the fountain's edge. An army of zombies, their bones creaking as they swarmed the townspeople. Evie and Freya were surrounded, fighting with everything they had. I could see the terror in their expressions. Their magic, usually a vision of grace, was now scattered and frenzied.

Emberwick Crossing's very existence at stake as we faced off against Corbin and his horde of death. This wasn't just a battle, it was a fight for our home, our lives intertwined in a desperate struggle against malevolent forces.

I clenched my fists. "We've got your back!"

Channeling my magic into my hands, I formed a protective

shield around them—a fragile barrier against the encroaching darkness. A temporary reprieve.

"We must stop them!" Brad shouted to our friends.

Well, this was just peachy. Emberwick under attack, my friends in danger, and a necromancer who clearly missed the memo on not being a total jerk. Another day in my life. I mean, who needs normal hobbies when you could raise an army of the undead?

Brad's voice blazed with power as he issued commands with stanch authority. "Form a barrier! Now!"

As one, the townsfolk rallied together and raised their hands, their combined efforts creating a shimmering dome that enveloped us—allies united in defense against a common enemy.

"Sage, focus on defending the civilians!" Brad barked. "I'll engage Corbin!"

I didn't agree with his choice and wanted to yell at him to stop, but he'd made the right call. Brad, always the hero. I wanted to argue, to insist on facing Corbin united, but I knew better. The people needed me. And someone had to keep an eye on Mr. Tall, Devilish, and Necromantic. I just hoped Brad's architectural mojo was up to snuff against a guy who could literally raise the roof with an army of zombies.

The air hissed with dark malice as Corbin stepped forward, green eyes glowing. Behind him, skeletal figures emerged, their clattering bones a grotesque concerto. He was unleashing hell upon us.

"Evie, shields!" I shouted over the noise.

"Got it!" she replied, her hands weaving an intricate pattern, conjuring shimmering barriers.

Evie was the best, and always ready with a magical assist. If we survived this, I owed her a girls' night out. Preferably somewhere without zombies and megalo-maniacal warlocks.

"Freya, hold the line!"

Her nod was resolute as she summoned vines from the ground, ensnaring advancing zombies.

Brad's hands moved, earth rising to form golems that marched towards the fray. I could feel his intentions pulsing, his spells a pledge of protection.

I launched my own magic, spells I'd crafted in secret, hitting the dead with bursts of light and color. Each impact was a defiance, each incantation a hope to save our home. Fear clawed at me, but I forced it down. I had to be strong—for Emberwick, for my friends.

Corbin's laughter rang out, his green eyes gleaming with hellish power. "Die, bitch!" he snarled, sending a ripple of necrotic enchantment my way.

Oh, hell no. This jerk did not just try to blast me with his creepy death magic. Time to show him what a real witch could do. I may not have had an army of the undead at my beck and call, but I had something better: friends, tenacity, and a serious knack for kicking supernatural butt.

I dodged his brush of death magic with lightning-fast reflexes, my heart pounding in my chest. The raw power of the necromancer was unlike anything I'd ever faced. But I couldn't let doubt seep in as fear rose inside of me, not now.

"Never!" I spat at him, countering with a blast of my own, a collision of forces that sent shockwaves through the square.

Bone shattered against stone, the sound coalescing with the cries of combat. The stench of decay clogged the air, a visceral reminder of the stakes for which we battled. Corbin's zombie army was relentless, a tide of death that refused to ebb.

Freya stood firm, helping those injured by the zombies. Spells blasted all around us. Weapons clashed in a frenzy of magic and steel.

Freya's voice rang out amidst the madness. "Push them back!"

"I got this!" Brad's voice rang through the air, even as a zombie's blade grazed his arm. He didn't falter, his face set in fierce concentration as he repaired the damaged buildings around us, using them as a fortress of protection.

The clash of metal against bone met my ears. I unleashed bursts of magic—each spell a defiant outcry against the encroaching darkness that sought to engulf us all.

"Stay strong!" I called out, feeling the strain of my magic buckling.

Corbin's gaze met mine, a sinister smile on his lips. A deadly promise of destruction that fueled my resolve even further. Emberwick Crossing depended on us, on this stand. And I wouldn't let it fall—not to Corbin, not to anyone.

Brad, Evie, and Freya fought side by side against Corbin and his army of zombies. The cobblestone streets splattered red with blood as the townspeople valiantly defended their home.

Corbin's unholy spell craft slithered around us, an oppressive force that seemed to sap the very life from the air. Sweat dripped down my face, each beat of my heart a reminder of what was at stake. I glanced over and saw Evie hurling a potion into the fray, and it exploded in a burst of lavender smoke, transforming two skeletal warriors into harmless critters.

"Nice one, Evie!" I shouted, dodging another zombie's

swipe. My hand shot up, releasing a stream of azure flames that incinerated the creature instantly.

"Thanks a bunch, Sage! Watch your right!" Evie yelled back.

I spun just in time to deflect a blow with a hastily conjured shield, the impact sending vibrations through my arm. Pain flared, but I pushed it aside, focusing on survival. On winning.

I unleashed bursts of light and color, each impact a defiance against the darkness, adrenaline fueling my every move.

"Sage, cover me!" Brad's voice cut through the bedlam, the command clear and precise.

I responded by summoning my power. A blast of magic struck a group of zombies and shattered their bones with crushing force.

"Keep pushing forward!" Brad urged, his magic shaping barriers and traps that slowed the undead onslaught.

His face was etched with fierce concentration as he repaired damaged buildings, turning them into fortresses for our defense. Stones shifted and melded all together under his command, creating sturdy walls that deflected the relentless attacks.

Evie's hands worked in a blur, weaving intricate patterns in the air as she threw potion bottles to protect us from Corbin's attacks. "We can do this!" she shouted. Each bottle shattered on impact, releasing bursts of flames—ice, or acid that dissolved the zombies' bones with sickening sizzles.

The scene was anarchy—an orchestra of clashing weapons, sizzling magic, and shouted commands. The odor of burning bones and earth plugged my nostrils, and the metallic tang of blood. Every sense was heightened, every moment a fight for survival. Limbs and shards of bone flew through the air, each strike of our weapons accompanied by the nauseating crunch of breaking zombies.

"Brad, we need to take Corbin down!" I shouted over the din, my voice cracking under the tension. Easier said than done.

"Working on it!" Brad replied, his voice strained as he summoned a massive earthen spike that impaled a cluster of zombies, sending shattered bones in every direction.

Stay focused, Sage. I was channeling energy into a new spell. No pressure, just the fate of Emberwick Crossing in my hands. Sweat poured down my face, my muscles trembling with the effort of maintaining my concentration.

"You're good, but not good enough," Corbin sneered, his stare glowing green as he sent another wave of demonic spell craft towards us. The ground where the magic hit erupted in opaque flames, consuming everything in its path.

"Think again," I countered, discharging a reflective barrier that bounced his attack back at him. The sinister magic collided with his own shield, exploding in a shower of sparks, embers, and smoke.

The shock on his face was fleeting, quickly replaced by rage. Guess he didn't see that coming. Point for Team Sage! I allowed myself a brief, grim smile before focusing back on the fight.

A resident, one of my neighbors I think, swung his sword. The blade flashed as he decapitated a zombie, its skull rolling away.

"Freya, Evie, cover Sage!" Brad commanded.

"On it!" They both chorused. They were moving to flank me, their abilities a protective shield. I couldn't ask for better back-up.

The fate of Emberwick Crossing rested in our hands, and

failure wasn't an option. We fought with everything we had, pushing through the exhaustion and pain. Each strike was met with a counterattack, each spell, a demonstration of our combined resilience. Blood and dirt beneath our feet, and breeze teeming with the constant, haunting clatter of skeletal remains tumbling to the ground.

A zombie lunged at me, its bony fingers reaching for my throat. I blasted it apart with a burst of raw power, the bones disintegrating into dust. But there were always more. An endless tide of undead soldiers driven by Corbin's malevolent will.

"Watch out!" Evie screamed, hurling a potion that exploded into a wall of fire just in time to incinerate a group of zombies that had been closing in on Brad.

"I owe you one!" Brad yelled back, using the brief respite to unleash a wave of earthen spikes, skewering more of the undead.

Corbin's laughter thundered through the battlefield, chilling and mocking. "You think you can defeat me? Pathetic!" He raised his hands, summoning a horde of new zombies from the earth, their eyes radiant with unholy hellfire.

"Don't give up!" I shouted, the power of my spells building to a crescendo.

With a final, focused effort, I released the spell. A wave of pure, red-hot sorcery erupted from my hands, sweeping across the battlefield. Five zombies disintegrated upon contact, their bones turning to ash. Corbin's green shield buckled under the assault, and for the first time, I saw fear in his expression.

Brad sent a massive boulder hurtling towards a group of zombies attacking three witches.

"Here goes nothing," I said.

Famous last words, Sage. Let's hope they're not actually my last.

I started summoning my power into a new, more formidable spell. I could feel the power building within me, ready to be unleashed. With a war cry, I released the spell—a burst of pure, unadulterated magic aimed straight at Corbin.

This better work.

"You can't stop me, you stupid bitch!" Corbin roared, his own spell meeting mine in a cataclysmic clash.

The world seemed to hold its breath as our magic thundered, the air vibrating with raw power. It was now or never. Time to show this jerk who's boss. And then take a long vacation when this was all over.

CHAPTER
THIRTEEN

"Hold the line!" Brad commanded.

I barely had time to register his command before diving to dodge a skeletal warrior's blade. The creature's empty eye sockets seemed to mock me as it swung again.

Seriously, Corbin? How cliché can you get?

I rolled to my feet. For an evil mastermind, his minion game was weak. You'd think a power-hungry warlock could conjure up something more original than the Zombie Crew.

"Evie, a little help here?" My voice was hoarse, my breath coming in short gasps.

"On it!" Evie shouted back. She threw a potion vial, shattering it against the zombie's chest. Green flames erupted, turning the undead monstrosity into a squirrel. "Sage, you need to be more careful!"

"Yeah, tell that to them." I glanced around at the swarming horde.

The zombies kept coming, an endless sea of clattering bones. Mom and Dad always said I was destined for great things. Somehow, I didn't think this was what they had in mind. Battling an undead army wasn't exactly in the "How to be a Kickass Witch" handbook.

Freya was tending to the wounded and healing the townsfolk from gashes and injuries. Bless her heart. Even in the midst of battle, she never stopped caring for others. Me? I was just trying not to become a chew toy for the Zombie Army.

"Incoming!" Brad yelled. He summoned a wall of earth, blocking another wave of zombies. His magic was strong, but even he was starting to show signs of fatigue.

There wasn't time to feel tired or scared. I had to keep fighting, keep pushing forward. For my friends, for the innocent people caught in the crossfire, and for the memory of my parents. They had believed in me, and I wouldn't let them down. Even if it meant facing an army of the undead with nothing but my wits and a killer pair of boots.

Suddenly, Councilman Voss appeared beside me, his robes billowing. "Sage, together we might stand a chance."

"Councilman Voss? What are you doing here?" My mouth popped open, then I slammed it shut. I had lots of questions, but I knew there was no time for answers.

I'd never thought I'd be fighting side-by-side with a Council member. Life was full of surprises, I guess.

"Later," he replied curtly. His magic flared, sending a dozen zombies flying.

"Fine by me," I grunted, focusing back on the fight. I couldn't afford distractions. Not when the fate of the world hung in the balance. Time to show these boneheads what a witch with a mission can do.

"Brad, Freya, cover the left flank!" I called out, trying to keep our formation tight. Evie, you're with me."

"Got it!" Brad replied, his voice resolute.

I hoped Brad's earth magic could shore up our defenses. His boulders had turned many enemies into piles of rubble and dust. Though right now I'd settle for a nice earthen wall to duck behind.

"Let's take down some bony foes." Evie smirked and she tossed another combustible potion into the fray. The explosion sent a shower of bone fragments into the air, the sound of shattering zombies echoing across the battlefield.

We moved as one, a coordinated squad of magic. Bones shattered, spells hummed, and the air was thick with the disgusting odor of burning flesh and ozone. Each moment stretched into eternity, every heartbeat a fragile promise of survival. Brad's earthen spikes erupted from the ground, impaling zombies and turning them into heaps of dust. Freya moved with precision, her healing spells mending wounds in the blink of an eye, allowing the fighters to keep pushing forward.

"Stay sharp, everyone," I warned, my gaze scanning the battlefield for Corbin.

The necromancer was nowhere to be seen, but his influence

was everywhere. The zombies fought with relentless precision, driven by his malicious will.

The ground was littered with fragments of bone and the smoldering remains of zombies. Brad's boulders smashed through the skeletal ranks, their impact resonating with the crunch of pulverized bone. His earth manipulation was relentless, creating barriers and traps that slowed the enemy's advance. He gritted his teeth, sweat glistening on his brow as he summoned yet another stone barrier to protect us.

Brad was really in his element, his magic shaping the battlefield to our advantage. Hopefully, he wasn't tiring himself out too much. I made a mental note to check on him when this was over.

Freya darted between the fighters, her hands glowing with healing magic. She knelt beside a fallen ally, her touch mending wounds and staunching the flow of blood. "Hold on," she murmured. With a wave of her hand, she sent a wave of healing power that revitalized the nearby fighters, giving them the strength to keep battling.

Bless Freya and her healing gifts. She was grace under pressure, never losing her cool even when the fighting got intense. I hoped she knew how much we all appreciated her.

"Watch your six!" Brad shouted, a boulder smashing into a group of advancing zombies, sending them flying in a cascade of shattered bones.

"Thanks!" I replied, releasing a quick shield spell to protect him from an incoming attack. An inhuman bolt of sorcery struck the shield and dissipated, the force of it causing a ripple through the magical barrier.

I gave Brad a quick thumbs up. We made a great team out

here, watching each other's backs. With my shields and his earth magic, we could hold this line. And with Evie and Freya supporting us, I felt like we could take on anything, even Corbin's creepy zombie army. As long as we stuck together, we just might make it through this.

"Don't mention it," he said, panting. "Just stay alive."

"That's the plan," I shot back, though my muscles screamed in protest. Every spell drained more of my energy, but there was no time to rest.

Councilman Alden Voss appeared beside us, his presence commanding and his eyes gleaming with a fierce intensity. "I've got your right flank," he said, raising his hands. Flames burst from his fingertips, incinerating a line of zombies that had broken through our defenses. The fire roared and crackled, the heat intense enough to singe the air around us.

"Voss, good timing!" I shouted.

"Let's make this quick," he replied, an edge to his voice. He unleashed another wave of fire, turning zombies to ash in a heartbeat.

"Need more protection here," Freya said, placing gauze on a man seeping blood from a leg wound. Her healing magic flowed into him, closing the wound and easing his pain.

Councilman Voss stepped forward. Fireballs rained down on the attackers, giving us a momentary respite. The zombies disintegrated in the fiery onslaught, their bones turning to ash.

Suddenly, a burst of flame shot through the battlefield, incinerating a line of zombies. Councilman Voss walked through the middle of the battle, his expression alight with the fury of his fire elemental spells, and his hands glowed with a fierce, orange light.

Evie tossed another potion, this one exploding into a thick, noxious cloud that caused zombies to crumble as they passed through it.

The battlefield was a maelstrom of destruction and death. Zombies swarmed us from all sides, their bony hands clawing and scraping. Brad summoned walls of earth to block their path, while Voss' firestorms created barriers of flame. Evie and I moved in tandem, her potions and my spells weaving together to create devastating effects.

Councilman Voss smirked, then he thrust his hands forward, sending a torrent of fire that swept across the battle-field, reducing the zombies to charred heaps.

"Behind you, Sage!" Freya shouted.

I spun around just in time to see a zombie swinging a rusted sword at my head. I ducked, feeling the blade whistle past my ear, and blasted the creature apart with a bolt of raw magic.

"You're a lifesaver, Freya!" I called out, my heart pounding.

A skeletal warrior lunged at me; its blade aimed for my heart. I sidestepped and unleashed a burst of power, shattering it into dust. The ground beneath our feet was slick with blood and ash, and the air was congested with the metallic tang of battle. Evie threw more potions, creating zones of safety and destruction, while Freya's healing magic kept our wounded in the fight.

Corbin's sinister laugh echoed across the street. "You think you can stop me? You're merely delaying the inevitable!"

"We're almost there!" Brad's voice was a rallying cry. He launched another boulder, smashing through a group of zombies that had been trying to flank us.

"Voss, cover me!" I shouted, preparing a powerful spell.

The Councilman nodded, and a wall of fire sprang up around me, protecting me from the encroaching horde.

The ground trembled. Brad summoned a massive wave of earth to surge forward, crushing zombies under its mass. Bones crunched and snapped, the force of the spell obliterating the undead forces in its path.

Corbin's influence was still palpable, his unholy magic empowering the remaining zombies. They moved with unnatural speed and coordination, their empty eye sockets glowing with a malevolent light. Freya continued her work, her healing spells keeping our fighters in the battle.

"We need to find Corbin and end this!" I shouted; my voice hoarse.

Voss stepped forward. "We'll find him, Sage. And when we do, we'll make sure he pays for this." His voice was cold, with a promise of retribution.

The clash of weapons, the roar of spells, and the cries of the wounded floated on the wind.

"Look!" Brad pointed skyward.

A figure descended from the heavens, riding on gusts of wind.

"Professor Elderwood?" I couldn't hide my disbelief, and I had no idea which side he was on.

"Let's turn the tide," Elderwood said, his voice deep and authoritative. He raised his arms, summoning a cyclone that tore through the zombie ranks, scattering bones like leaves.

There would be time to question alliances later. Right now, I was just grateful for the assistance. Elderwood's wind magic was a breath of fresh air. Literally. Perhaps we stood a chance after all.

"Impressive," Voss said, nodding appreciatively at Elder-wood's display.

I rolled my eyes. Men and their egos, even in the heat of undead battle.

"Focus!" I barked. "We're not out of this yet."

"Right," Brad said, launching another volley of rocks. "Stay vigilant."

Easy for him to say. He wasn't the one internally mono-loguing and questioning everyone's motives. But hey, I guess that was just the burden of being the plucky heroine.

"Voss, behind you!" I shouted, spotting two zombies converging on him.

He turned too late. Bone claws ripped into his chest. Blood poured out, staining his immaculate robes. The skeletal fiends cackled in eerie unison.

"NO!" I screamed, sprinting toward him. Magic buzzed at my fingertips as I cast a barrier spell to push the zombies back. But it was too late. Voss collapsed, groaning in shock and pain.

Well, this day just kept getting better and better. First undead armies, now fallen allies. I was starting to think I should've stayed in bed this morning.

"Stay with me!" I knelt beside him; hands glowing as I tried to heal his wounds. The magic sputtered, ineffective.

Come on, powers, don't fail me now. I was a witch, not a miracle worker, but throw me a bone here. Pun definitely intended, given our skeletal party crashers.

"Save your strength," Voss mumbled, voice barely audible. "It's...too late."

"Dammit, no!" Tears blurred my vision. There had to be

something I could do. I couldn't lose another person. Not like this.

"Freya!" I called desperately.

She appeared beside me. "He's gone, Sage." Her voice was gentle but firm.

I stood, heart heavy, fingers trembling. For a moment, despair threatened to overwhelm me. Then anger took its place. This wasn't over.

Oh, it was on now. Corbin picked the wrong witch to mess with. He wanted a fight? I'd give him a war. And I wouldn't be taking any prisoners—not that these zombies would make good ones anyway. They were a bit too bare bones for my taste.

"Corbin must pay for this," I said through gritted teeth.

"He will," Elderwood replied, summoning a powerful gust that knocked several zombies off their feet.

Brad rallied the townspeople. With renewed fury, we fought on. My spells became sharper, more precise. Fireballs incinerated bone, bolts of lightning shattered skulls. Elderwood's wind tore through the enemy ranks, creating openings for us to exploit.

"Freya, over here!" Evie called, dragging a wounded witch to the healer's side. Freya's hands glowed with healing light, sweat dripping down her brow from the effort.

"Keep them safe," I said, my gaze darting around for any sign of Corbin.

Our combined efforts pushed the zombie army back. Their numbers dwindled, and for the first time, hope flickered within me.

I panted, casting another spell. My body waned, but I

refused to stop. Not until every last one of those abominations was dust.

I paused, glancing at the professor. His face was a mask of concentration, but I saw the grief behind his eyes. We lost so much today.

Finally, the last of the zombies fell. Silence descended, broken only by the groans of the injured and the crackle of lingering magic.

"Is it...over?" Evie asked, voice wobbly.

"Not until we kill Corbin Grimm," I said.

"Then let's find the cowardly bastard and be done with it." Elderwood's voice was gruff but steady.

I spotted Corbin near the marble fountain, his eyes feverish with an unnatural green. He was muttering incantations, trying to summon more of his undead minions. Fury surged through me.

"Corbin!" I shouted, my voice booming across Emberwick Crossing.

He turned, a sinister smile spreading across his face. "Ah, Sage Holland. Come to meet your end?"

"Not today." My hands were already forming intricate patterns in the air. My power pulsed, raw and untamed. I could feel the anger, the grief, the need for justice fueling my magic.

"Let's see how strong you've become." The necromancer sneered, launching a bolt of necrotic sorcery towards me.

I countered with a gust of pure, luminescent magic. It hit him square in the chest, knocking him back. He recovered quickly, retaliating with infernal tendrils that sought to ensnare me.

"You're going to pay for everything you've done," I growled, deflecting his attack with a shield spell. I poured every ounce of my strength into the next incantation, feeling the magic coalesce around me. "By the power of the seventh level, by the light within me, I banish you, Corbin Grimm!" I bellowed, releasing the spell.

A blinding light erupted from my hands, engulfing Corbin. He cried out, his form disintegrating under the force of the spell. When the light faded, he lay on the ground, barely alive.

"Y-you've grown stronger," Grimm wheezed, blood trickling from his mouth.

"Why? Why did you do all this?" I demanded, standing over him.

"Questions. Answers... But your parents... they were part of a secret resistance," he choked out, each word a struggle. "Against the supernatural uprising. They... they were brave, but foolish."

I crouched beside him. "What are you talking about?"

"Here." Corbin reached into his inside jacket pocket with trembling fingers. He withdrew a ledger and handed it to me. "All the records...meetings, transactions. Including... their elimination orders."

"You mean it wasn't an accident?" My voice quivered with shock.

"Payment... made to a dark magic practitioner, a sorcerer hitman. Discreet elimination..." His voice trailed off as life left his body.

I stared at the ledger, my hands shaking. The truth about my parents' deaths was laid bare before me. They hadn't died in a random car accident. They had been murdered. Tears blurred my vision.

Oh, Goddess, had I just killed the wrong man? "Damn it... No...."

"Mom, Dad, I promise I'll find out who did this to you." I stood, clutching the ledger tightly. Resolve burned within me. This battle was over, but my fight for justice and truth had just begun.

FAMILIAR FATE

MAGGIE SHAW

FAMILIAR FATE

CHAPTER
ONE

I bolted upright, soaked through my tank top as if I'd been caught in a downpour. My sheets clung to me, clammy and twisted. The memory of Corbin Grimm's face—twisted in the final agony of my making—flashed behind my eyelids like some grotesque afterimage.

Holly hell. Another fun-filled night in the Sage Holland horror show. My subconscious really needed to find a new hobby. Maybe knitting? At least then I'd wake up with a scarf instead of cold sweat.

"Third time this week, Sage." Agatha's voice cut through the night, dry as the desert sand. "You're gonna run out of clean pajamas at this rate."

"Feels like I'll run out of sanity first." The honesty burst from me, combined with the remnants of spectral screams and incantations that had become my nightly torment.

My heart hammered against my ribs like it was trying to escape. *Join the club, buddy.* I'd love to bolt too, but apparently saving the world came with a side of PTSD. Who knew?

"Nightmares are just your brain's way of taking out the trash. Doesn't mean anything."

There was a rustle of fur against fabric. The cat jumped onto the bed, her yellow eyes two slits of concern—or maybe it was just hunger.

"Easy for you to say, you don't have to sleep." I scrubbed at my face, trying to erase the memory of power surging through my veins, the decision that had ended one life to save countless others.

The irony wasn't lost on me. I could redesign entire rooms with a flick of my wrist, but I couldn't redecorate the inside of my own head. Maybe I should look into magical brain bleach.

"True. But I remember enough about being human to know guilt gnaws at you," she said, then added, "almost as much as my empty stomach."

"Right. Breakfast." A hollow laugh escaped me. I swung my legs over the side of the bed.

My bare feet hit the cold floor, and I suppressed a shiver. Nothing like the icy grip of reality to wake you up. Who needed coffee when you had recurring nightmares and a sassy cat?

"First, though, shower. You smell like a bog witch after a

mud bath." Agatha leapt down, her tail flicking with impatience.

"Thanks for the imagery," I mumbled, standing.

The cool air of the room wrapped around my damp skin, causing my body to tremble.

I made a mental note to work on my personal aromatherapy spell. *Eau de Bog Witch* wasn't exactly the signature scent I was going for.

"Keep in mind, today's meeting is important, Sage. You can't afford to be distracted by dreams, no matter how...disturbing." Her tone sharpened, slicing through my fog of unease.

"Right. The uprising. Can't have any more men like Corbin start climbing from the muck."

My stomach twisted at the thought. Just another day in the life of a witch—nightmares, rebellions, and cats with attitude. Maybe I should've gone into accounting instead.

"Precisely. So, get moving. You've got responsibilities, and I've got an insatiable appetite." She padded toward the door, throwing a glance back to ensure I followed.

"Responsibilities and appetites," I said, finding a wry smile even with the turmoil churning inside me. "Guess we've both got our crosses to bear."

"Or in my case, kibble to devour. Now hop to it, witch." Agatha's command was softened by the twitch of her whiskers, a feline grin that reminded me I wasn't alone in all this madness.

"All right, all right," I said, shaking off the last vestiges of nocturnal dread. "Shower, breakfast, then face the Council. In that order."

"See? You're getting the hang of this 'responsible adult' thing already." Agatha's purr was almost smug.

I headed for the bathroom with a loud yawn. Then I stepped into the steaming gush of the shower, letting the hot water sluice over my skin, attempting to wash away the remnants of the night's terror that clung like cobwebs. As droplets pattered against the tile, I traced the eddying steam with a fingertip, drawing absent sigils that dissipated as quickly as they formed.

After toweling off, I stood in front of the mirror. My reflection stared back: long, dark hair streaked with rebellious strands of teal-blue, brown eyes that held secrets and sorrow, and womanly curves that seemed out of place in a world of straight lines and sharp angles. I chose an outfit that felt like armor—a cute black dress with white collar and thigh-high tights, accented with silver jewelry that jangled softly with each movement. On my feet, I wore practical, black ankle boots.

A witch ready for battle, or at least for town hall politics.

Agatha lounged on my bed, her sleek black fur absorbing the morning light. Her yellow gaze followed my every move, keen and judging. "You're not wearing that to impress the High Witch, are you?"

"Would it work if I was?" I shrugged, slipping into my boots.

"Unlikely. But it does accentuate your—"

"Let's leave my assets out of this." I cut her off with a grin, grabbing my satchel.

"Your loss," Agatha retorted, hopping gracefully from the bed. "Now feed me!"

I trudged to the kitchen; my bare feet cold against the worn floorboards. The fridge squeaked open, revealing a pitiful array of ingredients. A sigh escaped my lips as I reached for the eggs and a wilted bunch of spinach.

The pan sizzled as I cracked the eggs, their yolks a vibrant orange against the iron. I tossed in the spinach, watching it wilt further under the heat. My stomach growled impatiently.

"Patience is a virtue, you know," Agatha said, her tail swishing as she perched on the counter. "But I don't have any!" she cackled.

I rolled my eyes. "Says the cat who just demanded to be fed."

As the eggs cooked, I fumbled through the cupboard for Agatha's special food. The premium cat kibble clinked against her ceramic bowl, and I swear I saw her eyes light up.

"Your gourmet meal, madame," I said with a mock bow, placing the bowl on the floor.

Agatha sniffed it delicately before digging in. "At least one of us is eating well this morning."

I slid my overcooked eggs onto a chipped plate and grabbed a vial of murky green liquid from the windowsill. The potion smelled of moss and morning dew, a concoction I'd brewed last night for extra magical oomph.

Settling at the rickety kitchen table, I took a swig of the concoction, grimacing as it burned its way down my throat. My fingers tingled, a sign the magic was already taking effect.

"So, what's the plan for impressing the High Witch?" Agatha asked between bites. "Other than your questionable fashion choices, of course."

I stabbed at my eggs, buying time. "I was thinking of show-casing my latest spell. The one that turns pebbles into butterflies."

Agatha's whiskers twitched. "Ah, yes. Because nothing says 'powerful witch' like pretty insects."

"Got any better ideas, furball?"

The clock on the wall ticked ominously, reminding me of the impending meeting. I stood to wash the dishes, and my hands shook. The cool water did little to calm the buzzing beneath my skin—a melding of the potion's effects and my own jangling nerves.

I scrubbed the plates, my thoughts sifting through possible scenarios. The High Witch's steely gaze, her reputation for weeding out the weak...

My stomach churned, and it wasn't just from the questionable eggs.

"You'll do fine," Agatha said softly, surprising me with the gentleness in her tone. "Just don't trip over your own feet. Or your words. Or that hideous scarf you insist on wearing."

I flicked water at her, grateful for the distraction. "Thanks for the vote of confidence, you furry oracle."

As I dried the last dish, I took a deep breath. The potion hummed through my veins, my magic simmering just beneath my skin.

My fingers tingled, a reminder of the power coursing through me. Part of me wanted to test it out right there in the kitchen, maybe turn the faucet into a fountain of glitter. *But no, concentrate, Sage. We've got bigger cauldrons to stir today.*

The cool morning air greeted us as we stepped outside. Emberwick Crossing unfurled before us, an aura of old-world charm and hidden power. The main street teemed with life, shopkeepers sweeping sidewalks, their storefronts a rainbow-hued collection of awnings and signs etched with runes.

"Seems like everyone's up early today," I noted, taking in the scene.

"Or they never slept," Agatha said, keeping pace beside me. "Tensions are high after what happened with Corbin."

A knot formed in my stomach. Leave it to Agatha to remind me of the looming disaster into which we were walking. Sometimes I wished she'd sugar-coat things, but then she wouldn't be Agatha.

"Can't blame them. Feels like the calm before a storm."

"Let's just hope we're the thunder, not the lightning," she replied, her tail flicking sharply.

"Always the optimist," I said, then sighed heavily.

My chest tightened. Thunder or lightning. Either way, we were in for one hell of a magical storm. And here I was, armed with nothing but some half-baked spells and a cat with an attitude. Mom and Dad would be so proud.

As we neared the town hall, the building loomed, stately and imposing. Its stone facade bore the marks of time and magic. Gargoyles perched on ledges, watching over us with stony eyeballs. The door, a grand affair of brown wood, stood closed, yet it might as well have been a portal to another world, one brimming with political intrigue and dangerous secrets.

My palms grew clammy. Those gargoyles looked like they were judging me, probably thinking, "This scrawny witch is going to save us? We're doomed."

Well, joke's on them. I'm tougher than I look. I hope.

"Ready for the circus?" I asked.

"Only if there are snacks. Preferably fish-flavored."

"Figures you'd think with your stomach at a time like this."

"Thinking with one's stomach is vastly underrated. Now, let's see what pandemonium awaits inside."

I rolled my eyes but secretly envied Agatha's ability to stay focused on the important things. Like snacks. Maybe I should've packed some courage-boosting cookies.

After taking a steadying breath, I pushed open the doors, Agatha at my heels.

Inside, the town hall was a maelstrom of emotions. Voices clashed in a cacophony that echoed off the high, vaulted ceilings, each timber and stone seeming to absorb the tension and amplify it back onto the crowd. The air buzzed with spells—wards and shields flickering like erratic fireflies as they bumped against each other, conjured by residents who felt safer surrounded by their own magic.

Council members stood on the stage, animated and gesturing wildly, their voices lost in the uproar. Among them, Ingrid Nightspire's presence was like a calm within the tempest. Her long, silvery hair flowed down her slender frame, bright against the deep emerald of her robe. A circlet of moonstones crowned her head, catching the light with an ethereal glow. She was every inch the High Witch, commanding attention without a word.

The battle's aftermath hung over us all, a shadow that groaned out our vulnerabilities. Accusations flew like arrows, suspicion hung heavy in the air, and trust...

Well, trust was as rare as a sunny day in Emberwick Crossing lately.

Agatha's yellow stare was scanning the room with a predatory sharpness. "Such utter bedlam. Humans have reality TV, we have Council meetings."

"Same thing, really, just with more sparks flying," I replied, watching a little hex fizzle out against someone's hastily raised barrier.

The cat shook her head. "Wait until they start voting. That's when the real fun begins."

"Fun" wasn't the word I'd use. More like impending doom. Could we please band together for once without it turning into a magical brawl?

"Order! I demand order!" Ingrid's voice slashed through the noise, authoritative and firm. Silence fell like a guillotine. "We are here to discuss matters of grave importance, not indulge in petty squabbles!"

Grave was putting it mildly. The supernatural uprising was knocking on our door, and all we did was argue about who'd left it unlocked.

"High Witch Nightspire, what assurance do we have against another attack?" someone called out, his expression one of fear and defiance.

Ingrid's gaze swept the room, a hint of frustration flashing in her violet gaze. "We will take all necessary precautions. Our defenses will hold."

"Will they?" I started thinking of how Corbin Grimm had nearly torn through our protections.

"Empty words without action," Agatha said, reaffirming my doubt.

"Yeah," I agreed, feeling the burden of responsibility sitting on my shoulders like one of those heavy velvet curtains framing the stage.

"Be assured," Ingrid said, her tone measured but cryptic, "steps are being taken to fortify our town against further unrest. Trust in your Council."

"Trust?" a witch scoffed from the back. "After what happened?"

"Enough!" Ingrid's command reverberated, her precognition likely giving her a glimpse of where this would lead—a road paved with good intentions and lined with explosive runes.

"Look around," Agatha whispered. "Emberwick Crossing might be quaint, but there's power here. Tradition. History."

"And a whole lot of paranoia, too." I took in the wary faces of my fellow witches and warlocks.

"Paranoia can be useful, young witch. Keeps you alive."

"Or it turns neighbor against neighbor."

"Sometimes, they're one and the same."

I sighed. She wasn't wrong, but that didn't make the pill any easier to swallow. This town, with its gas-lit streetlamps and ivy-covered buildings, was steeped in as much magic as it was fear. And unless we found a way to unite, that fear would consume us faster than any evil spell ever could.

"Let's hope Ingrid's got a hell of a card up her sleeve," I said, meeting Agatha's gaze.

"Let's hope it's not a joker."

As the meeting descended into a harshness of raised voices and wild gesticulations, High Witch Nightspire made her way through the crowd, a serene force amid the turbulence. Her stare burned onto mine, and I felt that familiar jerk in my gut—the reticent command that persistently seemed to find me no matter where I stood.

"Sage," Ingrid greeted me, her voice lost amidst the anarchy but for my keen ears. "A moment, please."

My stomach did a little flip. Ingrid's "moments" usually meant trouble with a capital T. Still, I plastered on my best *everything's cool* smile.

"Of course, High Witch." I maneuvered towards her, Agatha's shadow slipping along beside me.

"Your talents are unique, Sage. Not just your magic, but your...other skills." She glanced around before continuing, "I need you to inspect Council Member Voss's residence again. Discreetly. We suspect there may still be remnants of malevolent enchantments linked to Corbin Grimm's nefarious plans."

Oh, joy. Another exciting adventure in the land of magical espionage. My palms started to sweat, and I resisted the urge to wipe them on my jeans.

"Interior design as espionage?" I raised my eyebrow, but inside, a twist of unease tightened. "I can't do that. Not again."

"Why not?" Her gaze sharpened, drilling into me. "Do not underestimate the importance of this order."

I fought the impulse to squirm under her intense stare. Ingrid had a way of making me feel like a naughty schoolgirl caught passing notes in class.

"Voss is a slimy, conniving bastard," I grumbled. "But he's also a powerful warlock from an ancient bloodline. If he catches me snooping around his mansion again..."

"He won't." Ingrid's tone was steel. "You're the best at what you do, Sage. Your unique magic is precisely what we need right now."

I sighed, running a hand through my hair. The stress of responsibility rested on my shoulders like a lead cape. Why couldn't I just design cute apartments and leave the cloak-and-dagger stuff to someone else?

"Fine. But I'm bringing Agatha this time. Her shadow magic might come in handy if things go sideways."

Ingrid nodded. "Agreed. But remember, discretion is paramount. We cannot afford to tip our hand too soon."

"Yes, High Witch." I gave a mock salute. "One clandestine interior design mission, coming right up."

My attempt at levity felt hollow, even to me. A knot formed in my gut, a premonition of trouble ahead.

"Sage? Be careful. There's more at stake here than you realize."

"Isn't there always?"

Before she could respond, a Council aide summoned her away with urgent matters. Ingrid gave me a curt nod and merged back into the fray.

Why did I constantly end up in these situations?

Agatha was licking her paw. "She knows how to pull your strings, doesn't she?"

"Seems like it." I watched Ingrid disappear into the crowd, a sinking feeling in my stomach. "But you heard her. It's important."

Important. Right. Because nothing says *important* like potentially getting caught and barbecued by a fire-wielding warlock with anger issues. I took a deep breath, steeling myself for the assignment.

Time to channel my inner super-spy... or at least fake it till I made it.

"Important or not," Agatha said, her yellow stare narrowing, "I don't trust her."

"Join the club." I clenched my jaw.

"Let's get out of here," Agatha suggested, leading the way with her tail high.

~

By the time we reached our home—a cozy cottage that bore the marks of my magical touch—morning had fully bloomed, pitching a golden glow on Emberwick Crossing. I watched Agatha slip through the cat flap before turning my attention next door.

Brad's house was almost identical to mine, but I knew every detail he'd changed since we were kids. Taking a deep breath, I crossed the short distance and knocked.

The door opened, and Brad appeared, his spiky brown hair catching the light, his well-built frame outlined against the hallway. His blue eyes darted nervously around like a frightened bird before landing on me.

"Hey, Sage," he said, stepping outside onto his porch. He wore a simple gray tee that hugged his muscles and denim jeans that did nothing to hide his casual grace.

"Hi, Brad." My heart jumped, a fluttering bird trapped in a cage of ribs, and my thoughts swirled with a dangerous jumble of desire and guilt.

"Everything okay?" He frowned.

"Could be better. Could be worse," I replied with a shrug, trying to ignore the electric current that sparked between us.

"Sounds like you." A half smile touched his lips. "Listen, meet me in the woods? Ten minutes."

"Sure. Yeah, okay."

He closed the door behind him with a soft click.

I set off toward the forest, the crunch of leaves underfoot grounding me. I tried to reconcile the tenderness of Brad's smile with the chill of duty. My emotions were a tangled mess—guilt for what I'd done, fear for what was to come, and desire for the man who was off-limits by orders I didn't want to obey.

"Get it together, Sage. You've got bigger spells to cast than love."

The forest surrounding Emberwick Crossing was a cathedral of ancient trees, their branches interlocking high above to create a dappled canopy of light and shadow. Sunbeams pierced through the verdure, creating a medley of gold and green on the forest floor. It felt like stepping into another world—a world where magic breathed in every leaf and whispered in every rustling bough.

I found a fallen log near our usual spot and sat down, waiting. My fingers traced the patterns of the moss, the softness at odds with the turmoil churning inside me. Brad always had this effect on me, even when we were kids. He'd show up with a grin and a plan, and I'd follow him anywhere.

Brad's timbre sliced through the silence like a hot knife. "Hey there, troublemaker."

I looked up to see his tall figure emerging from the foliage. He wore a smile that made my insides melt like butter on a summer day, and my stomach did a somersault. I fought to keep my composure.

"Hey."

We crashed into a hug, his strong arms enveloping me. I breathed in his familiar scent, sawdust and mint, and for a moment, the world faded away.

Brad pulled back, his eyes searching mine. "You've got that 'I'm-about-to-do-something-stupid' look."

I exhaled, releasing a breath I didn't realize I'd been holding. "Ingrid wants me to do some more recon work. You know, at Alden Voss' place. More snooping."

His eyebrows knitted together. "Again? That doesn't sit well with you."

"Feels like I'm crossing a line I can't uncross."

"Sometimes lines are meant to be crossed." He cupped my face, his touch sending tingles across my skin. "Hey, you've got this. You're the most badass witch I know."

The fire in his touch made my body relax. Our faces were inches apart now.

His voice dropped to a huskier tone. "All I see is the incredible Sage Holland, who's always been braver than anyone gives her credit for."

"Even if it means breaking every rule in the book?"

"Rules are more like guidelines anyway," he murmured, leaning in close. "Besides, you look cute when you're being rebellious."

My breath caught in my throat. We were toe-to-toe now, the air between us electric. "Careful, Adams. Keep talking like that, and I might do something really stupid."

His expression glinted mischievously. "Promise?"

I bit my lip, fighting the urge to close the gap between us. "You're impossible."

"And you're incredible," he whispered, his thumb tracing my cheek. "Don't ever forget that."

And with those words, he closed the distance between us, his lips capturing mine in a kiss that was both a question and an answer.

It was passionate, steamy, a blending of breath and longing that made the rest of the world fall away. In that moment, there was no High Witch, no forbidden edicts. Just Brad and me, and the fiery attraction that had always existed between us. My hands tangled in his hair as the kiss deepened, a release from all the pent-up fear and guilt that I carried.

We broke apart, breathless, foreheads pressed together. "We shouldn't..." I started, but the protest died on my lips.

"Probably not," he agreed, yet neither of us moved away.

"Brad..." I trailed off, caught in the gravity of his gaze.

"Whatever happens, Sage, I'm here." His sincerity wrapped around me like a spellbinding oath—one I desperately wanted to believe.

My throat was tight. "Thank you."

"Come on," he said, taking my hand and yanking me to my feet. "Let's walk back. You've got spying to do, and I've got structures to build."

His hand in mine felt more like home than any enchantment I could conjure. We walked back toward the edge of the woods, and for now, we were just two hearts beating in the quiet of the forest.

CHAPTER
TWO

I crept through Councilman Alden Voss's home, the
coolness of the polished marble beneath my feet in oppo-
sition to the warmth of the crystal ball cradled in my
palms. My heartbeat sped up. I chanted under my breath,
invoking the scrying magic that ran in my blood. The room
around me fell away. Then my vision tunneled into the orb's
depths.

Great. Now I was basically playing magical hide-and-seek
in a warlock's lair. Mom and Dad would be so proud. Or horri-
fied. Probably both.

"Reveal what is hidden, show what lies beneath," I whispered, the incantation passed down from a lineage of seers before me.

The crystal began to glow with an ethereal light, shining on the study's bookcases crammed with ancient tomes and artifacts of power.

I leaned in closer, my senses heightened to every minute detail. The patterns within the orb shifted, revealing not just the room as it was, but layers of concealed truths. A faint outline shimmered into existence. Ah, there! A hidden compartment materialized behind a seemingly innocuous section of the bookshelf.

My fingers twitched with anticipation. Secret compartments in a warlock's study? Either I'd stumbled onto the mother lode of magical gossip, or I was about to trigger some nasty curse. Knowing my luck, probably both.

Trembling, I shuffled quietly toward the bookcase and the revealed secret. Pressing on the ornate spine of a leather-bound grimoire, I heard a soft click. A panel slid open with a hiss. Inside, nestled in velvet lining, sat a small crystal, pulsating with an inner light.

"Hello, beautiful." I stepped closer, inching my fingers toward the crystal. It resembled the communication device I'd found earlier, one capable of nefarious communications. The urge to grasp it surged through me. I hesitated, sensing the thrum of malicious magic pulsing within its core.

As if compelled by the moment's gravity, I extended my hand. The moment my skin touched against the icy gem, a vibration of magic lurched, sending ripples up my arm. A warning or a welcome, I couldn't tell.

"Damn it," I cursed softly, wincing at the unexpected sting.

Before I could ponder further, the sound of footfalls ricocheted ominously down the corridor. Instinctively, I withdrew my hand and tucked myself into the room's shadowed corner, scarcely daring to breathe.

Oh, fantastic. Just what I needed – an unexpected visitor. Because apparently, my night wasn't already exciting enough. I pressed myself against the wall, praying to whatever deity looked out for nosy witches in over their heads.

The footsteps grew louder, each step heralding potential discovery or worse. Sweat beaded at my brow, and my breath stalled in my lungs. If I got caught, my uninvited exploration would end disastrously.

I swallowed back the fear, my ears fine-tuning to the sound of Councilman Voss' voice, a grim rumble that carried power and danger with every syllable.

"Listen carefully," he spoke into the phone, his tone a blend of silk and steel. "The movements have begun earlier than anticipated. No mistakes can be afforded."

I leaned closer, the shadows enveloping me like a cloak. I strained to hear more. The stranger's reply was muffled, distorted by the crackle of distance.

"Ensure it's done. We cannot have any...disruptions," Councilman Voss grumbled.

"Understood," came the curt answer. Two words laden with implication.

My brows scrunched. Disruptions to what? And who was on the other side of that line?

A bead of sweat traced a path down my temple. What had I stumbled upon? Perhaps this was bigger than I'd originally thought. Bigger and much more dangerous.

"Everything will proceed at the gathering. Be ready," Councilman Voss said, his command like a final stroke painting a picture of death and doom.

I needed to leave, to report this. Now.

I whirled toward the open window. My foot caught against something—a tiny statuette placed carelessly close to the edge of a shelf. It teetered precariously before succumbing to gravity with a betrayal of a clatter that shattered the silence.

"Who's there?" Voss barked, his head turning in my direction.

"Oh, shit!" I was frozen for a split second before instinct kicked in. I couldn't let him find me here. Not now, not when I was so close to uncovering whatever heinous scheme was on the horizon.

"Show yourself!" The Councilman's demand sliced through the quiet room. The door swung open, revealing the imposing figure of Alden Voss. His hard blue stare scanned the room, eventually landing on me.

Well, crap. Of all the studies in all the mansions in all the world, I had to walk into his. My limbs convulsed, itching to cast a quick invisibility spell. But no, that'd only make things worse.

"Ms. Holland, what an unexpected surprise. What are you doing here?" His voice sliced through the air like a blade, his tone hardened with accusation and an undercurrent of menace.

"Uh, I got lost—" I stammered, trying to keep my tone even. I wiped the sweat from my brow. "Councilman Voss! Fancy meeting you here." I flashed him my most disarming smile, trying to ignore the way my heart threatened to leap out of my chest. "In your own home, no less. What are the odds?"

His eyes narrowed; suspicion etched into every line of his

face. "Spare me the quips, Ms. Holland. Your presence in my private study is highly irregular. One might even say suspicious. You must think I'm a fool."

Oh, if only he knew how much of a fool I thought he was. But now wasn't the time for honesty. I needed a distraction, fast. Maybe I could conjure up a swarm of butterflies? No, too whimsical. A flock of angry crows? Too Edgar Allan Poe.

"Wouldn't dream of it, sir," I shot back, my heart thundering in my chest. My gaze didn't waver from his.

The corner of his mouth twitched, not quite a smile. He took a step closer, his tall frame looming over me. "So, I'll ask again. What are you doing here?"

"Would you believe me if I said I was sleepwalking?"

"No, I would not." His expression was severe, dangerous. A warning.

Um, okay. Plan B, it is. I straightened my spine, channeling every ounce of faux confidence I could muster. *Fake it 'til you make it.*

Councilman Voss' lips twist into a sneer. "I don't believe you for a second."

"Right. Well, then..." I edged towards the door, keeping my eyes fastened on his. "I suppose I should be going. Lots of important witchy business to attend to. You know how it is."

"Not so fast." He blocked my path, his arm barring the way. "You're not leaving until I get some answers."

I laughed nervously. "Answers? I'm an open book, Councilman. But maybe we could discuss this over a nice cup of tea? I make a mean Earl Grey."

His jaw clenched, unamused. "Enough games, Ms.

Holland. I know you heard something. Something you shouldn't have."

"Me? Eavesdropping? Never." I feigned innocence but my heart was pounding so loudly I was sure he could hear it. "I was just admiring your taste in decor. Love what you've done with the place, by the way. Very...ominous."

"You're treading on thin ice." He leaned in close, his breath hot against my cheek. "I won't ask again. What did you hear?"

"Nothing worthwhile," I said, the lie slipping out smoother than I expected. "Just a lot of political jargon and posturing. Honestly, it was like listening to one of those sleep aid podcasts."

Councilman Voss' gaze narrowed. "Clever words for someone in such a precarious position." Damn, he wasn't buying my act.

"Look, Councilman," I tried to keep my voice steady, "I don't want any trouble. I came here on official interior design business. That's all."

"Official business," he said with a sneer.

As his skepticism grew, the room's temperature seemed to rise with his anger. A prickling sensation crept along my skin. I took a step back. Voss raised his hand, palm open.

"Let's not do anything rash," I cautioned.

My warning was swallowed by the sudden sizzle of fire igniting in mid-air.

The flames frolicked in his palm, throwing lurid shadows across the walls. My breath caught in my throat at the sight, both mesmerizing and terrifying. The fiery embers reflected in his eyes, turning them into pools of molten blue. He was showing off, using his fire elemental powers as a direct threat.

"Rash?" he said, his tone punctuated by the pop and hiss of the flame. "No, this is just a demonstration. A glimpse of what could happen if you're lying to me."

"Fire play in a room full of antiques? Seems risky." I stepped back again, trying to mask the fear that was gnawing at my insides. My frenzied mind seeking an escape route or a spell that might save me.

"Risk is part of the game. And right now, Ms. Holland, you're the one at risk."

"Putting on quite the show, aren't we? We both know you won't use your powers against me. Not without answering to Ingrid."

"Perhaps," he conceded, though the fire in his hand did not wane. "But accidents happen, especially to nosy witches who find themselves in the wrong place at the wrong time."

I thought of every defensive spell I knew. None of them seemed strong enough to counter a direct attack from a warlock of his caliber.

"Why are you really here?" Voss' tone was a surly growl, and he edged closer, the fire forming long, sinister shadows behind him.

My mouth went dry. This guy oozed danger like a leaky faucet. But I'd come too far to back down now.

I lifted my chin defiantly. "I know you're hiding something. Something that could put everyone in Emberwick Crossing in danger."

"A bold claim," he sneered. "But baseless. Now, leave before I decide to make an example out of you."

I clenched my fists. No way was I letting this creep intimidate me.

"Not without answers," I shot back, but even as I said it, I knew it was time to go.

The hostility in the room was too thick, suffocating.

Councilman Voss took another step forward, his flaming hand reaching out toward me. Instinctively, I turned on my heel and bolted for the door. His laughter followed me, obnoxious and mocking.

"Run, little witch. Run while you still can!"

Crap, crap, crap. This was not how I'd planned this to go. Maybe next time, bring back-up. Or at least a fire extinguisher.

My legs pumped frantically as I tore through the opulent corridors, my heart thundering in my chest. Footfalls pounded behind me—he was giving chase.

"You're only making this worse for yourself, Sage!" his voice boomed, bolstered with a chilling amusement.

I burst out the front door and down the steps, the cool night air hitting me like a splash of water. I didn't dare look back. My feet hit the pavement hard, each step a desperate attempt to put distance between myself and the nightmare inside. I pushed harder, my breaths coming in ragged gasps.

Suddenly, the ground beneath me shifted, a trapdoor hidden in the cobblestones snapping open. I stumbled, barely catching myself before tumbling into the pit below.

What the holy hell? A hidden escape route or a trap. But which?

"I said run, you little bitch!" Voss yelled, gaining on me.

Desperation fueled me. I veered left, sprinting towards the dense cover of trees bordering his property. He roared, and I felt a searing heat at my back, a fireball, narrowly missing me and smashing into a tree, igniting it instantly.

"Don't underestimate me!" I screamed over my shoulder, diving into the underbrush. Branches whipped against my face and arms, but I didn't stop. Couldn't stop.

Eventually, Voss' shouts faded, replaced by the eerie quiet of the woods at night. I didn't slow until I reached the edge of the magical gardens, lungs burning and legs trembling.

Safe, for now.

The garden had magical lanterns that created a soft brilliance over the vibrant flora, their petals shimmering with ethereal light. The air was heavy with the perfume of night-blooming jasmine and damp earth. This place had always felt like stepping into another world.

"Brad," I called out weakly, collapsing onto a stone bench near the center of the garden. "Brad, where are you?"

"Here, beautiful." He emerged from the shadows, concern etched across his features. "Sage, what happened?"

"Voss—" I panted, struggling to catch my breath. "He...he knows something. He tried to—" Tears stung my eyes. "It was so close, Brad."

"Hey, hey," he said softly. He sat beside me and wrapped an arm around my shoulders. "It's okay. You're safe now."

"Safe?" I laughed bitterly. "For how long? He's dangerous, Brad. More than I realized."

"Tell me everything." He held me gently, his blue stare meeting mine with devotional focus.

"He's hiding something big. I found a communication crystal just like the one before, but he caught me. Used his fire powers to threaten me." I trembled, recalling the flames blazing in Councilman Voss' eyes. "I barely got away."

"That bastard," Brad said, his jaw clenched.

"Yeah, he's a part of the supernatural uprising," I whispered, leaning into him. "I think that's why the High Witch wanted me to spy on him again. I'm glad you're here."

"Sage, we need to be careful. Voss isn't someone we can take on lightly."

"I know! He's crazy. and scary." I sighed. "We need to find out who he's working with, what they're planning."

"One step at a time," Brad said, squeezing my hand reassuringly. "I'm just glad that you're okay."

"Thanks, Brad." I looked up at him, feeling a surge of warmth in spite of the cold reality of our situation. "I don't know what I'd do without you."

"Probably get into more trouble," he teased, his expression softening.

"Probably." I chuckled, tension easing for a moment.

Brad shifted closer on the bench and our eyes met and held. My breathing sped up. My heart swelled as I took in his features —the curve of his jaw, the intensity in his gaze. An electric friction sizzled between us, making my skin tingle. I felt drawn to him like a magnet, even as my head told me to pull away. His cologne tickled my senses, woodsy and intoxicating. His proximity was overwhelming, clouding my thoughts. I knew I should move away, but remained frozen, caught in his orbit.

"Brad," I whispered, searching his face, "we can't keep doing this."

"And yet," he murmured, leaning in, "we do."

His lips met mine, and it was like everything else vanished. The danger, the enigmas, the forbidden nature of our love— none of it mattered in that instant. His kiss was greedy, desperate, as if he needed me as much as I needed him. I tangled my fingers in his spiky hair, tugging him closer, wanting to lose myself in the sensation.

"God, Sage," he breathed against my lips, "I've missed you."

"Me, too," I whispered, my bottom lip trembling with emotion. "So much."

We kissed again, deeper this time, and I felt like I was drowning in him. Every touch, every breath, made the world outside disappear. For those fleeting moments, we were just Brad and Sage, two souls entwined in a forbidden love affair.

But then, a sudden chill coursed through my body, snapping me back to reality. I pulled away, my breath hitching. Then I saw her. Freya Weissdorn stood at a distance, her expression clouded with confusion.

"Freya?" I gasped, my heart sinking.

"Hi, Sage. I didn't know you two were dating," Freya said. "This is great. For how long?"

I glanced uneasily at Brad, unsure what to say. Freya didn't know that we were forbidden from dating, and I wasn't sure what to say, considering her loyalty to the High Witch.

Brad cleared his throat, breaking the awkward silence. "Freya, hey! What brings you here?"

I forced a smile, my palms sweating. "We're not—"

"Oh, just passing through," Freya interrupted, her eyes darting between us. "Thought I'd grab a coffee. Didn't mean to interrupt your... date?"

My stomach twisted. I needed to set things straight, but how? The truth could put us all in danger.

"It's not what it looks like," I blurted out. *Smooth, Sage. Real smooth.*

Brad shot me a look, then turned to Freya. "We were just catching up. Old friends, you know?"

Freya's brow furrowed. "Right. Of course. I usually catch up with old friends by making out with them."

I fidgeted with my bracelet, frantically searching for words. "Freya, listen—"

"No need to explain," she said, her voice tight. "I should go. Patients waiting and all that."

As she turned to leave, I caught a glimpse of hurt in her expression. My chest constricted. I'd screwed up, big time.

"Wait!" I called out. "Let me explain. Please?"

Freya hesitated, then nodded. "All right. But explain what?"

I took a deep breath, acutely aware of Brad's presence beside me. This was going to be tricky.

"Freya, please," I pleaded, stepping forward. "It's not what it looks like. Okay, well, it is, but Brad and I really care for each other, and um..."

Freya frowned. "I don't understand."

I squirmed under Freya's confused gaze. My palms were sweaty, and I could feel my heart pounding in my chest.

"It's complicated," I said, fumbling for words. "Brad and I have feelings for each other, but we're not supposed to act on them. The High Witch forbade it."

Freya's eyebrows shot up. "Forbidden? Why?"

Brad cleared his throat. "It's a long story."

"I've got time," Freya said, crossing her arms.

I glanced at Brad, silently pleading for help. He shrugged, leaving me to explain.

"The High Witch thinks our relationship would be a

318

distraction," I said. "She wants us focused on our duties, not each other."

Freya's frown deepened. "That's ridiculous. Since when does Ingrid dictate who can be with whom?"

"Since always, apparently," I muttered.

Brad stepped forward. "We're trying to respect her wishes, but it's not easy."

"Clearly," Freya said.

I felt a twinge of guilt. "We didn't mean to hurt you, Freya. We should have told you sooner."

"Yeah, you should have," she said, her tone sharp. "Friends don't keep secrets like this."

Her finger pointing stung, and I flinched. "You're right. We messed up."

Brad nodded. "We're sorry, truly."

Freya sighed, her shoulders slumping. "I get it, I guess. But I don't like it."

"Join the club," I said, attempting a weak smile.

"Freya, listen," Brad interjected, trying to calm her down. "This isn't something we planned. It just... happened."

Freya's expression tightened, teeming with frustration. "Do you have any idea what kind of trouble you're in? If Ingrid finds out—"

"She won't," I said quickly, desperation creeping into my voice. "Please, Freya. Don't tell her. We'll handle it ourselves."

Freya shook her head, her expression torn. "Sage, I don't like lying and my loyalty lies with the High Witch."

"Freya," I begged, reaching out to her. "You're my friend. Please."

She hesitated. Finally, she let out a sigh and turned away. "I need to think," she said.

"Freya!" I called after her, but she kept walking, disappearing into the shadows.

"Dammit." Brad grunted, running a hand through his hair. "What now?"

"We wait," I said, my voice hollow. "And hope she doesn't go straight to Ingrid."

"Hope?" He looked at me incredulously. "That's all we have?"

"For now, it's all we can do."

CHAPTER
THREE

The summons came as a jolt, like a lightning strike, leaving my nerves sizzling. Ingrid's office wasn't just any room, it was the pulsing heart of the Council's power. Ancient tapestries depicting battles between mythical beasts and witches clung to the walls like sentinels, while shelves groaned under the weight of mystical artifacts that hummed with their own contained storms.

Our steps slowed as we approached the imposing oak door.

"Brad," I whispered, "this feels like walking into the dragon's den."

My palms were slick with sweat. Ingrid's wrath wasn't

something to be taken lightly, and here we were, marching straight into it. I wanted to bolt, but I couldn't leave Brad to face this alone. We were in this mess together, after all.

"More like the basilisk's lair." His voice carried a tremor that mirrored the quiver in my gut.

I felt his hand graze mine briefly, seeking reassurance or perhaps offering it.

As the door heaved open, a chill greeted us, wrapping around our skin like an unwelcome caress. It was Ingrid's power. A cold front that forewarned of her tempestuous mood.

My stomach churned. This was it. Time to fess up and face the music. Why did I feel like a kid caught with her hand in the cookie jar around Ingrid?

"Enter!" boomed Ingrid's voice, laden with a fury that needed no visual confirmation.

Oh damn, here goes nothing. My heart hammered against my ribs, threatening to break free. Brad's presence beside me was the only thing keeping my legs from buckling.

Ingrid sat behind her desk, a sculpture of ice, her hard stare sharp enough to cut through the antagonism that strangled the air. "I should've known better than to trust you two to follow simple instructions," she said, her words a scalpel slicing open the façade of calm I tried so hard to maintain.

My throat constricted, choking back a flood of excuses. How could I explain that what Brad and I had wasn't just some rebellious fling? That it was worth risking everything for? But one look at Ingrid's steely gaze, and I knew she wouldn't understand. Or worse, she wouldn't care.

"High Witch Nightspire, we—"

"Silence, Sage." Her gaze cut to me, then flicked to Brad.

"Freya has seen fit to inform me of your... dalliances. After I expressly forbade it."

My throat tightened at the mention of Freya's betrayal. Trust was a currency in our world, and Freya had just bankrupted herself in my eyes. The sting of her treachery was a fresh wound, raw and bleeding.

"Freya?" I managed to choke out, disbelief spiking my tone. The woman who'd shared life stories over moonlit concoctions with me as children now the knife in our backs?

"Did you think your sneaking around would go unnoticed? That your caresses would go unseen?" Ingrid's pitch rising with each question. "You jeopardize not only yourselves but also the balance of all Emberwick Crossing."

"High Witch, please understand. We didn't want to break the rules, but...but we can't help what we feel." Brad's plea was earnest, his blue eyes alight with a fervor that spoke volumes of his feelings for me.

"Such insolence!" Ingrid leaned forward, her silvery hair spilling over her shoulders like a waterfall of moonlight. "What I understand is that you, Brad Adams, have put your magical builder's license at risk, and you, Sage Holland, stand to lose much more."

Her threat hung heavy in the room, a guillotine poised above our heads. I tasted the metallic tang of fear, and for a moment, I saw my dreams of designing homes for our kind dissolve into nothingness.

"Your choices have consequences," Ingrid said, her mood now a scary snarl. "And consequences must be faced."

The room spun. I clutched at the reality unraveling before me. Whatever repercussions awaited us, it was clear that Ingrid's wrath would not be easily quelled. And yet, standing there, feeling the influence of her gaze and the gravity of her contention, I knew that no decree could sever what Brad and I shared—not truly.

My fingers spasmed at my sides as if they could weave a spell to undo this mess.

"You two were very foolish," Ingrid said, her eyes narrowing into slits of disapproval. "The Covenant is clear. It forbids romantic entanglements between the Council's inner circle and civilians to protect our confidences and maintain the sanctity of our decisions." She let the truth float in the room before adding, "It's a safeguard against corruption and conflict of interest, ensuring that emotion does not cloud anyone's judgment."

My stomach twisted into knots. Ingrid's argument felt like a slap across the face. I'd known the rules, sure, but hearing them laid out so coldly made my skin crawl. Was love really such a threat to their precious order?

"Isn't there another way? Some sort of exception?" Brad's voice cracked with desperation.

I admired his tenacity. I braced for Ingrid's response.

"An exception." Ingrid scoffed. "You would have me rewrite ancient laws for your adolescent infatuation?"

My blood boiled at her dismissive tone. *Adolescent infatuation?* As if our feelings were some passing fancy, a childish whim to be outgrown. I clenched my fists, nails digging into my palms.

"What?" I found my blood pressure rising in defense, my heart pounding against my ribcage. "Our connection runs deeper than—"

"Silence!" The single word from Ingrid cut through the

room like a shard of ice. "You will end this relationship immediately, or you both will face the full extent of the Council's wrath."

Brad stepped closer to me, his arm grazing mine before he withdrew it as if burned. "Ingrid, please," he implored. "We meant no harm."

The brief contact launched a pulsation through me, a bittersweet reminder of what we stood to lose. I wanted to grab his hand, to hold on and never let go. And yet Ingrid's icy stare froze me in place.

"Intention is irrelevant," she replied coldly. "You have breached the Covenant of Veiled Boundaries. As such, you leave me no choice."

"Choice seems to be a luxury we don't have," I said, feeling the sting of tears that threatened to fall. I blinked them back, refusing to let Ingrid see me crumble.

A lump formed in my throat, choking back the words I longed to scream. How dare they dictate who we could love? The injustice of it all made me want to unleash every spell I knew, consequences be damned.

"Correct," she said sharply. "Sage, should you fail to comply, you will be stripped of your position. And Brad, your license will be revoked. You know the gravity of these penalties."

Her threats were like a physical blow, knocking the wind out of me. To lose everything over something as natural as love felt like the cruelest of fates. A fate I wanted to change, bend to my will. And yet I felt so helpless. Ingrid stood resolute, an immovable force upholding centuries-old traditions.

"Understood, High Witch," I managed to say, my throat tight with emotions I dared not show.

"Then it is done," Ingrid declared, her tone leaving no room for further argument.

With a final, shrewd look, she dismissed Brad with a wave of her hand. I sensed rather than saw Brad stiffen beside me.

As Brad turned to leave, he threw one last glance at Ingrid, the woman who was both my mentor and my tormentor. Our fates now lay in her hands, and as Brad exited her office, the door closing behind him with ominous finality, my heart ached.

His departure left an oppressive silence in the room. I turned to face Ingrid, the silver strands of her hair practically glowing with an ethereal light that seemed at odds with the gravity of our conversation.

"Ingrid," I said, my thoughts wavering in spite of my best efforts to keep myself steady. "Before you pass final judgment on me there's, um... something else you should know."

The High Witch's violet stare bolted onto mine, and I felt as though she could see straight through to my soul. "Speak," she commanded tersely.

Great. One-word responses. Never a good sign. I swallowed hard, my throat suddenly dry as sandpaper.

"Last night, Councilman Voss...he caught me. As you ordered, I was in his house—"

"You were seen?" Ingrid's accusation pierced the air like a shard of ice. "This is not good. Not good at all. You did not mention me, did you?"

I shook my head. "No, never. I'd never betray you..." I grimaced at that because I had betrayed her by sneaking around with Brad. "You were right, he was hiding something, and I overheard him on the phone with someone talking about the supernatural uprising," I said quickly, my anxiety spiking at the memory. "But he caught me and threatened me with fire magic. He chased me off his property."

I shuddered. Councilman Voss' threats ricocheted in my head, the phantom heat of his fire magic prickling my skin.

There was a flicker of something across Ingrid's normally impassive face. Disbelief? Concern? I couldn't be sure. "You realize the gravity of this blunder, do you not? He will come after you now. And I cannot be implicated."

Okay, odd response. Where was the "Are you okay, Sage?" or "That must have been terrifying." But no, it was all about her.

"He knows that I am onto him, and he wasn't afraid to use his power against me. I thought you should know."

Ingrid stood motionless for a long moment, her gaze penetrating. Finally, she spoke, "This is a serious matter, Sage. If Voss is involved with the uprising, we must act cautiously."

"Then you'll investigate?" I asked tentatively, hope pulsating in my chest.

"Of course. But let us not forget your own transgression here today," she added sternly, reminding me that no matter the outcome, I wasn't absolved of breaking the Covenant. "Your actions have repercussions That cannot be ignored."

"I understand, Ingrid."

"Go now," she instructed, her tone softening a touch. "And, Sage, be careful."

With one last nod, I turned and left her office. I stepped into the corridor, the chatter and bustle of the Council's headquarters seeming distant, as if I were moving through a dream—or perhaps a nightmare that had only just begun.

I escaped down the hallway, the echo of my own steps too loud. Making my way to the workspace assigned for the Council's architectural projects, I slid into the chair and let out a heavy sigh. The blueprints that Brad had created lay sprawled before me, their lines and measurements a welcome distraction from the disaster of my personal life.

I started tracing a finger along the outline of the public meeting hall. My thoughts whirled around Brad's involvement in the project, his genius captured in the meticulous detail of the plans. A pang of regret hit me. Our relationship—more than physical, a merging of hearts—was now another casualty of duty.

"Okay, let's make some magic happen," I said, summoning my power.

My fingers tingled with anticipation as I felt the magic surge through me. This was my chance to prove myself. To show the Council I was more than just the orphaned witch they pitied. Maybe then I could shake off the emphasis of my parents' legacy that clung to me like an old blanket.

With each spell I spoke, the designs began to shimmer, lifting a little off the page as if they were eager to become reality. I envisioned a space where secrets couldn't fester in murky corners, where light would shine on truth.

"Transparency, unity, resolution," I chanted softly, my design magic weaving into the very fabric of the blueprint.

The incantation tasted bittersweet on my tongue. If only I could cast a spell to bring transparency to my own muddled thoughts, unity to my fractured heart, and resolution to the apprehension roiling around me, within me. But some things even magic couldn't fix.

The grandeur of the future hall revealed itself to me: sweeping arches inviting open discourse, wide spaces encouraging collaboration, and an ambiance that promised peace. Even as my heart ached with loss, my craft, my essence, took over, and for a moment, I was whole again.

"Quite the visionary, aren't you?" said a shrill-sounding female from behind me.

I TURNED AND LOOKED UP. It was Eden, the Council's scribe, her expression shining with appreciation. Then she peered over my shoulder.

"Trying to be," I replied, offering her a wry smile. "The Council needs a place where all voices can be heard."

Including mine, I hoped. Maybe if I impressed them enough, they'd finally see me as more than just a charity case or a potential threat.

"Then you are the perfect witch for the job." Eden gave a quick squeeze to my shoulder before she left.

As I continued to work, infusing the plans with enhancements for harmony and clarity, I couldn't stop this gnawing feeling in the pit of my stomach. Voss, the uprising, Brad—my world was upended and my fate uncertain. What if Voss came after me? Threatened me again? Or worse, tried to kill me?

My hands shook as I tried to focus on the blueprint. The irony wasn't lost on me. Here I was, designing a space for peace and unity while my own life was falling apart at the seams. But maybe if I could create something beautiful and meaningful, it would be enough to appeal the rule and then Brad and I could be together. At least for a little while.

My concentration finally caved, and I withdrew my hands from the blueprints. The lines had started to blur, and the colors were too bright against the parchment, echoing the turmoil inside my head. I needed air.

Pushing back from the desk, I stood up and stretched, my muscles protesting after hours of meticulous work. Stepping out into the courtyard was like crossing into another world. The vibrant greens and soft floral hues offered a sharp contrast to the bleak office where ancient tapestries seemed to absorb light rather than reflect it.

I inhaled deeply, the aroma of jasmine and lilac wrapping around me like a calming shawl. The gentle rustle of leaves was a soothing sound, coaxing my thoughts away from my worries. Amidst the beauty of nature nurtured by magic, I could almost forget the burdens pressing down on me.

"Remember who you are. Sage Holland, daughter of non-magicals, creative force to be reckoned with." Girl with a broken heart...

As I strolled along the cobblestone path, I let the serenity of the garden seep into my bones. Except peace was a fleeting thing in Emberwick Crossing, especially for those tangled up in Council affairs.

A hushed whisper drew my attention, and I paused near a secluded alcove. Hidden by a cascade of wisteria, two junior Council aides were deep in conversation. One was Eden, her voice distinctive even in a soft voice.

"...not sure if it's safe anymore," said a man I didn't recognize, flecked with anxiety.

"Shh," Eden hissed. "Not here. Walls have ears, and some have eyes too."

"Right," the other person agreed, his tone dropping even lower.

I edged closer, careful to keep to the shadows. Eden was usually so composed, hearing her sound shaken was disconcerting.

"Did you deliver the message?" the unfamiliar aide asked, his tone urgent.

"Of course, but—" Eden cut herself off and sighed.

I held my breath, praying they hadn't spotted me. As their footfalls faded, I let out a slow exhale, my body stiff.

Eavesdropping wasn't my style, but this was too juicy to pass up. Plus, a little recon never hurt anyone, right? Agatha would be proud.

"Have you heard of The Echoing Locket?" Eden asked, her expression faltering. "It's said to grant the wielder the ability to hear the thoughts of anyone they choose. Can you imagine the power that would give someone?"

"That's unsettling," the other aide replied, a shudder in his tone. "Why would anyone want something like that?"

Eden let out a humorless chuckle. "Power, of course. It's frequently about power with these types. But this...this feels different. More urgent, more secretive. It scares me."

I leaned in closer, trying hard to catch every word. The hairs on the back of my neck stood on end. A mind-reading locket? Great. Because what this town needed was more ways for people to invade each other's privacy. My stomach churned at the thought.

"What do you mean?" the aide asked.

"I don't know," Eden admitted. "But I have a bad feeling about this. The way my boss has been acting, the people he's been meeting with... I think there's more to this locket than just mind-reading, you know?"

An artifact that could grant someone access to the thoughts of others? In the wrong hands, that kind of power could be devastating. And if Eden's boss was after it...

Was Eden's boss Councilman Voss? My palms grew clammy. I pressed against the cool stone wall. Voss with mind-reading abilities? The thought made my jaws clench. That man's ego was big enough without supernatural validation.

"We need to move quickly," the male aide whispered. "Before others catch wind of its location."

Eden sneezed. "Damn flowers. Listen, I don't like this. The locket's power is not meant for mortals."

"Since when do you have a conscience?"

"Since I realized what's at stake. This isn't just about magical supremacy anymore."

I inched closer. My foot caught on a loose stone, sending it skittering across the ground. I froze.

Stupid, clumsy feet. I held my breath, praying to every deity I could think of that they hadn't heard me. If I got caught now, I'd never hear the end of it from Agatha.

"Who's there?" Eden demanded.

My heart pounded in my ears. I pressed my back against the wall, willing myself to melt into the shadows. Footsteps approached, slow and deliberate.

"Probably just a rat," the aide said. "This place is crawling with them."

Eden scoffed. "Right."

I held my breath, muscles strung tightly. One wrong move and I'd be caught. And I needed to know more about this locket.

About Voss' plans. I shifted my weight, and a twig snapped beneath my foot. I froze, holding my breath.

"Did you hear that?" the aide said, panic rising in his voice.

"We can't talk here," Eden said, her tone clipped. "Meet me at the usual spot tonight. And don't tell anyone about this. And for the love of magic, be discreet."

They hurried away. I had stumbled onto something big, something dangerous. And I had a sinking feeling that I was about to get dragged into the middle of it, whether I liked it or not. Whatever this Echoing Locket was, it spelled trouble. Big trouble.

CHAPTER
FOUR

I was reclining on the edge of my velvet chaise, my fingers depicting the intricate patterns on the ancient rug below. Agatha lounged lazily across the sun-drenched windowsill. Her yellow eyes flared with interest. I'd confided in her about the secretive murmurings I'd caught between two Council aides.

"The Echoing Locket, you say?" Agatha yawned. "Sounds like a delightful bore, young witch."

I sighed, dragging a hand through my blue highlighted hair. "I know it's more than it seems. And I'm certain whoever wants it is up to something shady."

"Pfft, shady is an understatement, Sage. More like nefarious, malicious, downright dastardly! Trust those instincts. They've served you well so far." Agatha stretched languidly, claws catching on the sill.

I rolled my eyes at Agatha's dramatic outburst. "Okay, okay, I get it. But what could they possibly want with some old locket? It's not like it's the key to ultimate power or anything."

"Oh, you naive little witch," Agatha purred, her tail swishing cheekily. "Never underestimate the allure of a mysterious artifact. It's like catnip for power-hungry warlocks."

I chuckled at her analogy. "So what? We just sit back and let them get their grubby hands on it?"

"Absolutely not!" Agatha leaped down from the windowsill, her expression gleaming with insolence. "We investigate, we snoop, we uncover their dastardly plans!"

I quirked an eyebrow at her. "And how exactly do you propose we do that, oh wise feline?"

"Simple. We infiltrate their inner circle, charm our way into their good graces, and then BAM! We expose their nefarious schemes to the entire magical community."

I shook my head, a wry smile on my lips. "You make it sound so easy. But I doubt they'll just welcome us with open arms."

My limbs shook at the thought of confronting such powerful figures. Councilman Voss and Professor Elderwood weren't exactly known for their cheery hospitality. And here I was, plotting to outsmart them with nothing but my wits and a snarky cat. Mom and Dad would've had a field day with this one.

"Pfft, have a little faith in your own abilities, Sage. You're a seventh-level witch, for crying out loud! Use that interior design magic of yours to dazzle them into submission!"

I laughed at the absurdity of it all. "Right, because a well-placed throw pillow is the key to unraveling a sinister plot."

The image of Councilman Voss tripping over an artfully arranged ottoman flashed through my mind. If only it were that simple. My fingers were itching to grab my crystal ball and scry for answers. Except even magic had its limits when it came to untangling the web of danger we'd stumbled into.

"Hey, don't knock the power of a perfectly coordinated color scheme," Agatha said, her whiskers twitching with amusement.

Before I could reply, a sharp knock at the door cut through our conversation. I rose to answer, finding Evie Blackthorn on my porch, her face etched with urgency.

"Magical disturbances are wreaking havoc across town again," she blurted out.

A knot formed in my stomach. Just when I'd thought things couldn't get more complicated. I fought the urge to slam the door and hide under my bed like I used to as a kid. I wasn't that scared little girl anymore. I was a witch with a job to do, even if it meant magical adulting.

"Great, just what we need." I frowned, rubbing my temples. "Do you think it's connected to the Echoing Locket?"

"What is that?" Evie replied, sweeping a lock of jet-black hair behind her ear.

Agatha crept up from behind me, slinking gracefully to my side.

"What do you know of this locket, Agatha?" Evie asked.

"Only rumors. I heard it can replay past spells, like a mystical recorder. If someone had their hands on it..."

"Then they could unravel secrets or even frame someone for dark magic they didn't commit," I finished her thought, feeling a chill even with the sunlight streaming in through the windows.

With that kind of power, someone could rewrite magical history itself. And knowing our luck, it'd probably end up in the hands of the magical equivalent of a toddler with a flamethrower... like Councilman Voss, my newest enemy.

"Maybe." Evie nodded gravely. "Who would want such a dangerous artifact, and why now?"

Agatha's tails swished. "Power. Control. Revenge. Pick your poison. But whatever their motive, we must tread carefully."

I glanced between my familiar and best friend. "We'll need to investigate without drawing attention to ourselves."

Easier said than done. Subtlety wasn't exactly my strong suit. I'd once turned my entire dorm room back in college neon green during a failed attempt at a camouflage spell. Yet with the fate of the magical world potentially hanging in the balance, I'd have to channel my inner ninja. Or at least try not to trip over my own feet.

"Leave the shadow work to me," Agatha purred with a smirk. "I'll find out what those aides are hiding. And, Sage, curiosity didn't kill the cat—it made her cleverer. But for witches, the stakes are always higher."

"Then we'll just have to be smarter than a cat." I looked at my feline companion. "Do you know the Echoing Locket's origins?"

Agatha yawned. "The Echoing Locket, my dear witches, is

said to have been forged by the infamous Archmage Zephyria during the Great Magical Schism."

Zephyria was practically a boogeyman in magical circles. The kind of witch you'd use to scare apprentices into behaving. And now her legacy was about to bite us all in the ass. Just perfect.

My jaw dropped. "Zephyria? But she vanished centuries ago!"

"Precisely." Agatha's tail swished. "Legend has it she crafted the locket to preserve her most powerful spells before her mysterious disappearance."

Evie leaned forward, her brow furrowed. "If that's true, whoever possesses it could wield magic beyond our comprehension."

I paced the room, my fingers drumming against my thigh. "But why resurface now? And who's pulling the strings?"

Was Zephyria herself behind this? Had she been hiding in plain sight all along, biding her time? Or was someone else trying to claim her power for themselves? Either way, we were in way over our heads.

"My money's on Councilman Voss," Evie said. "I heard he's been sniffing around restricted archives lately."

I scoffed. "Typical. Always chasing power he can't control."

Voss. The name alone made my skin crawl. I'd never trusted that smug, fire-wielding jerk. If he got his hands on the locket, we'd all be burnt toast—literally.

Agatha stretched lazily. "Don't forget Professor Rowan Elderwood. That windbag's obsessed with historical magic."

My stomach roiled at the thought. Both were formidable opponents, each with their own brand of cunning.

"Both are as shady as a grove of midnight oaks," I groused, my thoughts racing faster than the fluttering wings of a hummingbird.

Evie nodded in agreement; her lips pressed into a thin line.

The air buzzed with an electric charge, and the odor of ozone permeated the room. A shimmering glyph appeared before me, pulsating with a message that bore the unmistakable seal of Councilman Voss.

"Holy hell, what does Voss want now?" I exclaimed, reading the message demanding my presence at his office. "To kill me?" The half-joke slipped out, but it wasn't entirely beyond the realm of possibility with the stakes so high.

"Don't go, Sage," Evie said, her expression grave. "Voss is unpredictable."

"I know, but I'm curious," I replied, though my bravado didn't quite reach my heart.

"About what? How he's going to kill you?" Evie spat. "Just ignore him, girl. Don't go into the lion's den unprepared."

"And Evie's right," Agatha said, leaping onto the windowsill, her yellow eyes glinting. "But so is stupidity."

I rolled my eyes. "Guys, I appreciate the concern, but I'm not a kid anymore. I can handle Voss."

Evie crossed her arms. "You sure about that? Last time you faced him, you ran screaming."

"That was because he lost his temper," I murmured, heat rising to my cheeks.

Agatha snorted. "And that's an excuse to chase you and throw ball of fire at you?"

"Look," I said, pacing the room. My hands convulsed,

tingling to cast a protection spell. "I know it's risky, but what if he has information about the supernatural uprising?"

Evie's mouth dropped open. "You think he'd just hand that over?"

"No, but he might let something slip." I grabbed my bag, shoving a few crystals inside. Just in case.

"Sage," Evie grabbed my arm. "At least let me whip up a quick potion. Something to give you an edge."

I hesitated. The clock ticked loudly, reminding me of Councilman Voss' impatience. "Fine. But make it fast."

Evie rushed into my kitchen. We could hear opening cabinets and banging around in there.

Agatha leaped down, tail swishing. "I'll come too. Someone needs to keep an eye on you."

"Great," I muttered. "A cat for back-up."

"Hey," Agatha hissed. "This cat can kick some serious ass."

I couldn't argue with that. As Evie mixed her potion, I tried to steady my breathing. Councilman Voss was dangerous, sure. But so was I. And I had friends watching my back.

Let him try something. I was ready.

Evie thrust a vial into my hand. "Drink this. It'll sharpen your senses."

I eyed the swirling purple liquid. "What's in it?"

"Trust me, you don't want to know." Evie winked.

I knocked it back, grimacing at the taste. A tingling sensation spread through my body, my skin prickling with heightened awareness.

"Wow," I blinked, the room suddenly in sharper focus. "This is intense."

Agatha sniffed the air. "Smells like trouble to me."

"Says the cat who's coming along," I quipped.

"Someone's gotta watch your back," Agatha retorted. "Merlin knows you need it."

I rolled my eyes. "Thanks for the vote of confidence."

"Anytime, young witch."

Evie grabbed my shoulders. "Voss is slippery. Don't let him get in your head."

My stomach clenched. "Got it."

"And if he tries anything..." Evie's expression frowned with worry.

"I'll turn him into a toad?" I suggested.

"I was thinking more along the lines of a dung beetle, but sure."

We shared a grim laugh, then I slung my bag over my shoulder.

"Ready?" I asked Agatha.

She stretched lazily. "Born ready, young witch."

I took a deep breath, squaring my shoulders. "Let's go."

We stepped out onto the porch, Agatha weaving between my legs. I locked the front door. Evie wished us luck, then got into her car parked at the curb. The cool evening breeze kissed my skin as we made our way towards Councilman Voss' imposing abode.

Agatha trotted beside me, her black fur blending seamlessly with the shadows. Her yellow eyes glowed in the dim street-light, catching every trace of movement in the quiet town.

"You know," I said, "most familiars don't insist on accompanying their witches everywhere."

Agatha's whiskers twitched. "Most familiars aren't as clever as I am. And don't forget, I was assigned to you, and someone needs to keep you out of trouble...and alive."

We crossed Moonstone Bridge, its ancient stones thrumming with residual magic beneath our feet. The cobblestone streets gave way to narrower alleys, buildings leaning in overhead like gossiping neighbors. The fragrance of herbs and incense wafted from hidden gardens and open windows, a reminder of the magical undercurrent that ran through Emberwick Crossing.

As we neared the heart of the old town, Councilman Voss' mansion loomed ahead, an opaque silhouette against the star-studded sky. My steps faltered for a moment, my legs trembling.

Agatha pressed against my leg. "Sage, you're more capable than you think. Just try not to turn him into a butterfly."

I snorted, grateful for her irreverent humor. "No promises," I said, squaring my shoulders.

We drew near the wrought-iron gates of Voss' estate. We entered his house and went straight to his study, which was as dimly lit as the future I was trying to predict. Dust motes floated in the scant beams of light that escaped heavy velvet drapes, while the walls were lined with shelves crammed full of books bound in leather and spells sealed in jars. Each object seemed to hum with hidden intent, setting my nerves on a razor's edge.

"Ms. Holland," Voss greeted, rising from behind his mahogany desk, his disingenuous smile making me uneasy. "And..."

"Agatha," I supplied curtly, not missing a beat. "My familiar."

"Ah, yes. How quaint." Councilman Voss cleared his throat.

"I must apologize for my uncouth behavior during our last encounter. I was caught off guard."

My jaw clenched. Yeah, right. The memory of flames licking at my heels as I fled his property flashed through my mind.

Uncouth behavior? That's putting it mildly. I really wanted to cast a silencing spell on this snake.

"Caught off guard?" I shifted my weight, arching an eyebrow. "Is that what we're calling attempted arson these days?"

Agatha's tail swished against my leg. "Careful, young witch," she hissed. "Don't poke the snake."

Councilman Voss' smile tightened. "I assure you, Ms. Holland, it was a misunderstanding. I merely reacted to what I perceived as a threat."

I scoffed. "I'm flattered, Councilman, but I think we both know who held the upper hand that night."

His fingers drummed on the desk. "Perhaps we got off on the wrong foot. I'd like to extend an olive branch, if you'll allow it."

My spine stiffened. This guy was about as trustworthy as a demon with a contract. I plastered on a smile. "How generous of you."

"I know." Councilman Voss nodded. "In fact, I have a proposition that might interest you."

Agatha's claws dug into my ankle. I bit back a yelp. A proposition? From this guy? I'd rather make out with a troll. Still, curiosity gnawed at me like a gluttonous pixie.

"I'm listening," I said, keeping my intonation level.

He leaned forward. "I've heard whispers of your... unique

talents, Ms. Holland. Your gift for spell creation is quite impressive."

"Yeah. So?" I said. Trusting Voss was like trusting a snake not to strike.

He clucked his tongue. "I've heard about your little entanglement with Brad. Terrible complications for someone of your position."

My reply was ice-cold. "That's none of your concern."

Heat crept up my neck. How dare he bring up Brad? I wanted to turn him into a toad and watch him hop away.

"Ah, but it could be," Councilman Voss said, leaning back against the edge of his desk. "I might have a way around the Covenant of Veiled Boundaries."

My heart skipped a beat. "How?" The question was out before I could stop it.

Damn it. I'd taken the bait like a rookie witch. But the possibility of being with Brad without sneaking around was almost too good to be true. And that's precisely why I shouldn't trust it.

He smiled again, all teeth. "Join my team. Help me, and Brad can be yours, no more skulking in shadows."

"Help you with what, exactly?" I countered, trying to mask the high pitch of my voice. "Your vague offers are about as comforting as a curse."

"Details, details," Voss waved his hand dismissively. "We can iron those out once we're on the same page." His eyes were like chips of ice. "There are... benefits to being on my team."

"Uh-huh. And what about the Council Hall renovation?"

"Merely taking an interest in your work," he said, drumming his fingers on the mahogany surface of his massive desk. "Tell me, how is the progress coming along?"

"Fine," I answered curtly, feeling Agatha's tail brush against my ankle in an obvious signal of caution.

"Any unexpected discoveries? It's an old building. Full of history. Secrets, even."

"No, nothing."

Councilman Voss knew something, and whatever it was had its claws in deep.

"And knowledge can be as much a burden as a tool," he said, and though his drawl remained smooth, I sensed the underlying edge of steel. "And some tools can cut the hand that controls them."

"Is that another threat, Councilman?" I challenged; my tone as sharp as shards of glass.

"Merely a friendly warning." He shrugged. "After all, we wouldn't want anything unfortunate to happen, would we?"

"Of course not. I'll be sure to keep that in mind."

His gaze lingered on me a moment longer before he dismissed us with a wave. As Agatha and I left his office, my body started to relax.

"Watch your back, Sage," Agatha whispered. "Voss is playing a dangerous game."

"I know," I replied.

The Echoing Locket, Brad, the Council Hall—they were all connected somehow, and Alden Voss was right in the middle of it. Whatever was going on, I needed to find out before it found me.

CHAPTER
FIVE

I stood at the edge of my porch, the night wind ruffling the branches of the nearby trees. The sudden *need* was magnetic, irresistible—a yearning that eclipsed reason and obligation with its intensity. Brad was just across the way, separated by shadows and the lure of forbidden desire. I could feel him, as if our bond sent out invisible tendrils, seeking each other in the night.

"Unbelievable" I clenched my fists, the internal battle raging within me.

If we were caught, the consequences would be dire: expulsion from the Council's inner circle, a broken reputation. And yet, the thought of his touch caused a rebellion in my heart.

The night breeze carried Brad's drawl to my ears. "Hey."

He was leaning against the trunk of an old oak tree, hands in pockets, looking as casual as if the world wasn't about to implode around us.

"Hey yourself." My feet moved of their own accord, luring me to him like a magnet. I couldn't resist the electric hum of our bond, even though I knew better. "We shouldn't be doing this."

"I know." His grin was infectious, bright even in the darkness.

"I should go." I tried to sound firm, but my feet didn't move. The way he looked at me, like I personally hung every star just for him, made my knees weak.

He stepped closer, pine and earth mingling in the shrinking space between us. "Ah, but what's life without a little risk?"

I let out a heavy sigh. "Life is...safer. Especially with the High Witch watching my every move."

"Tell me something." His gaze sought mine, probing for an answer we both already knew. "Can you feel me even when I'm out of sight?"

"Always," I admitted. The admission hung in the air, a truth as real and powerful as the magic thrumming through my body. "It's like an invisible string ties us together."

He moved even nearer until only just a breath separated us. "Bound by something deeper than spells or destiny. Maybe it's because we're two of a kind, Sage. Misfits in a world of dusty, old rules."

"Or maybe it's because you've got a piece of my heart," I whispered.

A slow smile spread across his face. "Could be. Though I bet it has more to do with that potent seventh-level magic you wield. Forever weaving connections that shouldn't be possible."

"I think it's about you and me, not my powers," I replied, unable to suppress a smile.

"Let's make the most of tonight, then. Before reality rips us apart again." Brad's blue eyes were alight with moonglow.

"Brad..." I said, the warning clear in my tone.

But then all the reasons this was reckless and foolish dissolved, until nothing existed but the two of us.

He gathered me in his arms. His lips found mine, and I softened in his embrace, my hands tangling in his hair, holding him closer still. For a blissful moment, nothing else mattered. Not the rules we broke, nor the consequences we would face. There was only this, only him. This was reckless, dangerous, and absolutely intoxicating. I'd never felt more alive.

My skin tingled where Brad touched me, sparks of magic dancing between us. This connection, this strong attraction—it was unlike anything I'd ever experienced. Maybe this was why the High Witch feared us together. We were a force of nature, unpredictable and untamed.

When we finally broke apart, panting, he rested his forehead against mine.

"How can something so right be so wrong?" I whispered.

Brad let out a shaky laugh. "The High Witch would say it threatens the natural order she's desperate to maintain."

I wanted to scream. Natural order? More like Ingrid's twisted version of control. She'd rather see us miserable than risk her precious status quo.

I rolled my eyes. Ingrid and her precious order. As if love could be contained by rules and regulations.

"Remind me again, since when do we care about her order?" I said bitterly.

Brad's jaw tensed. "We may not have a choice. If we get caught again, there will be hell to pay."

Ingrid's wrath was no joke. I'd seen what happened to those who crossed her. But the alternative, giving up Brad, felt like ripping out a piece of my soul.

I winced, remembering the High Witch's cold violet stare, her clipped tone when she'd forbidden me from seeing Brad. The memory of Ingrid's fury still haunted me, her threat sharp as knives. She'd made it abundantly clear that if I defied her again, the punishment would be severe.

"I can't lose you," I said, hating the tremor in my voice.

My throat tightened. The thought of being separated from Brad made my chest ache, like someone had reached in and squeezed my heart.

I'd lost so much already. My parents, my childhood innocence. Brad was my anchor in this hurricane of magic and politics. Without him, I'd drift away, lost in the currents of power and expectation.

Brad gently tilted my chin up. "Hey. Look at me. I'm not going anywhere."

I searched his face. "You can't promise that. Not if she—"

"Shh. Don't go borrowing trouble." He drew me close again.

I buried my face in his chest, breathing in his scent. I really wanted to believe him, to lose myself in this moment. But the rational part of my brain wouldn't shut up, spouting worst-case scenarios like a demented spider weaving webs.

"Let's not think about the High Witch right now," Brad whispered, his fingers tracing the blue highlights in my hair. "We have this moment, Sage. Just this one."

My heartbeat slowed. Brad's touch sent a fiery fervor throughout my body, a harsh parallelism to the constant dread that had been gnawing at my insides. For once, I wanted to silence the nagging voice in my head, the one that kept reminding me of the consequences we'd face if caught.

I nodded against him, knowing he was right. We couldn't let fear steal away the precious time we had together. I wanted to be present with him, even if it was fleeting.

"Show me something new," I murmured, craving the distraction of our magic.

He led me through the fence and into his backyard where we had more privacy.

"All right," he replied, an incandescence lighting up in his face.

Releasing me, Brad stepped back and extended his hand. He focused, and the wind around us began to shimmer. Wooden beams sprung from the ground, weaving into an intricate lattice above us, blooming with lush ivy and fragrant jasmine.

My breath caught in my throat. Brad's magic never ceased to amaze me, with its raw power tempered by an artist's touch. It was moments like these that made me fall for him all over again.

"Now you, beautiful," he said, his tone affectionate.

I reached out, allowing my own power to surge forth. The flowers on the lattice burst into a kaleidoscope of colors, each hue more vivid than the last. Our combined magic swayed together, an opus of structure and beauty, his architecture and my embellishments.

"Perfect," he said.

I smiled, caught up in the wonder of what we could create together. Our gazes fastened, and in that instant, it was just Brad and me, surrounded by the magic only we could make.

He gathered me into his arms again, and I went willingly. Eagerly. Our lips met in a kiss that sent sparks flying—literally. Tiny bursts of light popped around us, a manifestation of the power coursing through our joined bodies. It was passionate and consuming, a physical reverberation of the attraction we shared.

My mind went blank, every worry and fear evaporating. In that moment, I didn't care about the High Witch, the rules, or the consequences. All that mattered was Brad, his arms around me, his lips on mine.

"Brad…" I whispered, trailing off. I clung to him, feeling both complete and utterly undone.

My heart trembled like a caged bird. This was wrong, so wrong, but it felt electric. The High Witch's warnings echoed in my head, but Brad's touch silenced them all.

"Sage," he replied, his voice rough with emotion.

Brad's fingers traced along my jawline, and I leaned into his touch, loving the warmth of his skin against mine.

"Why does it feel so good to be bad?" I pressed closer to him.

He chuckled, low and deep. "Because forbidden love is sexy."

A thrill blasted through me, equal parts excitement and fear. I was playing with fire, and I knew it. But oh, how I loved the burn.

"Fair point." I grinned, my heart sprinting. "But the High Witch—"

"Isn't here," Brad finished, his expression gleaming with mischief. "And what she doesn't know won't hurt her."

I bit my lip, torn between desire and duty. The sensible me knew we were playing with fire, but the rebellious streak that had gotten me into trouble so many times before was all too eager to throw caution to the wind.

My parents' faces flashed in my mind. What would they think of me now? But then Brad's spicy cologne surrounded me, and all thoughts of disappointment vanished.

"You're a bad influence, Bradley Adams," I teased, poking him in the chest.

He caught my hand, bringing it to his lips. "You love it."

My breath hitched. "Maybe I do."

We stood there, frozen in a moment of tension and possibility. The air sputtered with barely restrained magic. I could feel the power humming beneath my skin, begging to be released.

My fingers tingled, itching to cast a spell. Any spell. To channel this wild force flowing through me into something tangible.

"So," Brad said, breaking the silence. "What now?"

I smiled, an idea forming. "Now? We make some magic of our own."

A dog barked, and we froze. Panic surged through me like ice water.

Reality came crashing back, harsh and unforgiving. My heart pounded so hard I was sure Brad could hear it. We'd been careless. Reckless, even. How could I have forgotten where we were?

Images of Ingrid's disappointed face, of being stripped of my powers, flared to life in my head. *Stupid, stupid, stupid!*

"Someone's coming," I hissed.

"Go!" Brad urged, pushing me towards the hidden exit we'd used for months between our houses.

"Be careful," I pleaded, catching his hand for one last squeeze before slipping away into the shadows.

"Always am," he shot back with a wink that didn't quite reach his worried eyes.

As I darted through the shadows, guilt and fear battled for dominance in my chest. I'd risked everything for a few stolen moments. But even as dread sank low in my stomach, I couldn't bring myself to regret it. Not yet, anyway.

We'd been so close to getting caught. Again. Too close. As I made my way back home, the fear of discovery shadowed me every step of the way.

My skin prickled with each rustle of leaves, each distant conversation. I imagined Ingrid's spies everywhere, watching, judging. But beneath the fear, a small part of me was thrilled at the danger. At the secret I now carried.

My blood surged through my veins, a panicky tempo that matched the quickening of my footsteps. The darkness seemed to close in around me, thick and oppressive, as if it could swallow me whole. I felt it, the strain of a thousand eyes that were not there, watching, waiting for me to slip up.

My hands shook with the residual adrenaline, the tremors betraying my outward composure. I whispered incantations, spells to cloak my presence, to muffle the sound of my galloping heartbeat. But no magic could ease the gnawing fear that twisted in my gut.

As the recognizable silhouette of my home came into view, relief zipped through me in an icy wave. The light-blue paint and white trim of the house stood out against the unlit street, a beacon of safety. I slipped through the front door, leaning back against it once I was inside, allowing myself a moment to catch my breath.

Upstairs, in my room, the anxiety finally began to ebb from my shoulders. I sank onto the bed, the mattress dipping beneath me. Brad's touch still lingered on my skin, a phantom caress that caused a fluttering feeling in my stomach. The whiff of magical flowers, which we had conjured together in those stolen moments, hung in the air, sweet and heady.

I closed my eyes, letting the memories of our reunion crash over me. The way he had adoringly looked at me with such intensity, it was as if he could see straight into my soul. The way our combined powers had twirled around us in a concerto of light and sensation, evidence of what we could be together.

And with every beat of my heart, the reality of our situation descended heavier upon me. Our love was a forbidden one, a flame that could be extinguished by the Covenant of Veiled Boundaries at any moment. What would we have to sacrifice for this relationship? For a chance to be together without constantly looking over our shoulders?

Then I drifted off to sleep, dreams of forbidden kisses and the foreboding of a future filled with danger and desire cradling me into slumber.

CHAPTER
SIX

The morning sun radiated a soft, golden brilliance over Emberwick Crossing, dappling the streets with patches of light and shadow. A gentle breeze carried the fragrance of blooming flowers, and the distant chatter of sparrows perched on top of the Magical Archives Building—a grand edifice that towered above the quaint shops lining the main thoroughfare. Its spires reached for the sky like fingers of an ancient spell, grasping at the invisible magic that swirled in the air.

My stomach churned as I thought about Freya's betrayal. Some friend she'd turned out to be. I'd trusted her and look where that had gotten me. Now I had to tiptoe around my own feelings like they were landmines.

"Can you believe Freya just ratted us out like that?" I said, my voice faint enough so only Evie could hear. "Brad and I were careful. But now the High Witch is pissed that I disobeyed her, all because she couldn't keep her nose out of our business."

Evie pushed a stray lock of jet-black hair from her forehead and sighed. "I know it's tough, Sage. But Freya's always been a stickler for the rules. Maybe she thought she was doing the right thing...even if it was the wrong thing for you."

I scowled, my frustration boiling. "Well, her 'right thing' has made everything harder. Brad and I can't even look at each other without fear of being watched now." My gaze drifted to the ground, the angst of secrecy pushing down on me.

The thought of Brad made my chest ache. His crooked smile, the way his eyes crinkled when he laughed. Now I had to pretend those memories didn't exist.

Stupid rules. Stupid laws. Who was the High Witch to dictate who I could love? Oh, yeah. My boss.

Evie tilted her chin up, her expression brimming with empathy. "Hey. Try not to worry so much."

Nodding, I mustered a faint smile. It wasn't much, but having Evie by my side made my troubles seem a little more bearable.

As we entered the Magical Archives Building, the atmosphere shifted dramatically. The antique charm of the outer façade gave way to an interior that buzzed with arcane power. Warlock guards adorned in ceremonial robes stood vigilant beside sleek metallic detectors. Luminous runes pulsed along the walls, emitting an iridescent net of sensing spells designed to ward off any unwelcome intruders.

We approached the front desk.

"State your business," Mr. Thatcher commanded in a stern voice.

Mr. Thatcher, the archivist, was a peculiar sight. His wiry frame was consumed by an oversized tweed suit that seemed from another era, his spectacles resting precariously on the bridge of his nose. With a bald head that shone under the overhead lights and a beard that appeared to be home to wayward paper clips, he peered at us over the rims of his glasses with an air of suspicion.

Great. Just what we needed—a human lie detector with a penchant for office supplies. I swallowed hard; my throat suddenly dry as sandpaper.

"We need access to the historical accounts from ten years ago, please," I said, trying to sound confident even with the fluster of nerves in my stomach.

"Accessing restricted files is not a matter to be taken lightly," Mr. Thatcher replied, his inflection slow and deliberate. "May I inquire as to why such sensitive information is required by two junior witch members of our community?"

My palms grew clammy. This guy could give Ingrid a run for her money in the *intimidating authority figure* department.

"Research," Evie interjected smoothly. "For a very important project directly from the High Witch herself."

"Is that so?" The archivist stroked his beard, a skeptical glint in his eye. "And I suppose you have the necessary clearances? The paperwork? The approval codes?"

Crap. I hadn't thought this far ahead. My thoughts sprinted, grasping for any plausible excuse. Why hadn't I listened to Agatha and come up with a better plan?

"Of course," I lied through my teeth, hoping he wouldn't press further.

Evie shot me a quick glance, her expression unreadable.

"Very well," he drawled, turning to his archaic computer. "But don't think for a moment you can pull the wool over my eyes."

My heart pounded like a jackhammer. If he saw through our ruse, we'd be toast faster than you could say "abracadabra." What were we going to do now?

"Actually, we're waiting for the final authorization," Evie said before I could dig us into a deeper hole. "It should be here shortly." She gave him a dazzling smile that even Ingrid would have been hard-pressed to resist.

"Very well. I shall await your documents," Mr. Thatcher replied, barely concealing his doubt.

"Thank you, Mr. Thatcher," I said, though my insides churned like a witch's brew.

As soon as his attention returned to the piles of paperwork on his desk, Evie leaned closer and whispered, "Ready for some fun?"

"Always," I murmured back, my expression betraying a hint of excitement amidst the anxiety.

"Follow my lead," Evie whispered, a wicked glint in her eye that usually meant trouble. She fumbled in her pocket, nearly dropping the small vial twice before finally extracting it with a triumphant "*Aha!*"

Uncorking it with her teeth with a slight grimace, Evie began to chant under her breath. The incantation came out muffled and garbled, like she was trying to speak with a mouthful of marbles.

Suddenly, a comically large puff of neon pink smoke exploded outward with a *POOF*, enveloping Mr. Thatcher's head entirely. As it cleared, revealing his now cotton-candy colored hair, dozens of tiny, glittering butterflies materialized, each one sporting a miniature top hat and monocle.

Oh, sweet cauldron of chaos. This was not part of the plan. My stomach did a somersault as I watched the scene unfold, torn between horror and a twisted sense of amusement.

Mr. Thatcher's eyes bulged to cartoon proportions. He let out a high-pitched shriek that could've shattered glass and began a frantic, flailing dance. Arms windmilling, he swatted at the dapper insects, spinning in circles and tripping over his own feet.

I bit my lip to stifle a laugh. Poor guy looked like a deranged ballerina in a butterfly mosh pit. *Concentrate, Sage. This disaster's your ticket out of here.*

One particularly bold butterfly landed on his nose. Mr. Thatcher went cross-eyed trying to focus on it before letting out a massive sneeze that flung him tumbling backward into a conveniently placed mud puddle with a spectacular *SPLASH*.

As he sat there covered in muck, hair still pink and surrounded by fancy butterflies, Mr. Thatcher let out a defeated sigh. A lone butterfly fluttered down, landing on his head.

Evie snorted, trying and failing to hold back her laughter. "Oops," she managed between giggles. "I, uh, may have overshot that one a smidge. Must have mixed up my potions."

"Get these—these things away from me!" Mr. Thatcher spluttered, his usual composure crumbling like an ancient ruin.

"Right away, sir!" Evie scrambled to help him, all the while giving me the subtlest of nods.

This was my chance. I slipped away, blood pumping with each step taken down the corridor towards the restricted area. The floorboards lurched beneath me in spite of my best efforts to tread lightly. Every whisper of sound made my skin prickle. Was it just echoes or someone coming?

My heart hammered against my ribs like it was trying to escape. *Calm down, you idiot.* Getting caught now would be worse than Agatha's hairball incidents.

The dimly lit hallway stretched endlessly before me, shadows clinging to the edges like specters. Finally, I reached the imposing iron door, its surface etched with runes older than time itself. Swallowing hard, I extended my trembling hand and uttered the incantation to break the seal.

Nothing happened.

"Holly hellfire." I frowned, feeling panic rise like a tide. I tried again, pouring more power into the spell until my fingers sparked with blue magic.

Still, the door remained unyielding and shut.

"Come on, Sage. You can do this."

My palms were slick with sweat. If I couldn't crack this door, I'd never let it down. Evie's butterfly fiasco would be for nothing. No pressure or anything.

Gathering all my courage and magical prowess, I chanted a new spell for the third time, envisioning the door unlocking, the barrier dissipating—

With a muffled groan, the heavy iron yielded, swinging open to reveal the forbidden knowledge within. My breath caught in my throat. I was in.

Inside, the restricted room was a treasure trove of shadow and silence. Shelves lined with ancient tomes towered over me, their spines cracked and worn. Scrolls lay haphazardly strewn across tables, and artifacts with auras black as pitch sat encased in glass. The stale air smelled of dust and mysteries, the kind that could turn your life upside down—or end it.

I went straight for the manuscripts, scanning titles etched in languages I barely recognized. The fear of being discovered pulsed through me, but I shoved it aside. This was about my parents. About the truth.

"Come on, where are you?" My fingers traced over leather bindings and brittle paper, my gaze darting back and forth, searching desperately. Then, I found it—a stack of aged parchments tucked behind a row of ominous-looking grimoires. Their seals were grand, embossed with the insignia of the magical community's elite, and faded ink crawled across the surface like spindly legs.

"This might be it." My hand shook. I unfolded the top document, revealing the elegant script of officialdom—and a few ominous bloodstains smeared along the edges. Someone had tried hard to keep this hidden.

While I read the text, the words blurred, each sentence a punch to the gut. Corruption, blackmail, assassinations—all of it leading back to an order signed by a name I knew all too well. My throat tightened, anger boiling within me.

Why? Why did they have to die?

"Because they knew," I whispered, the realization cold and heavy in my chest. "They knew too much."

The sound of footfalls snapped me out of my grief-stricken trance. Frantic, I stuffed the documents into my bag and extinguished the orb of light hovering above me. I ducked behind a towering bookshelf.

The door creaked open.

"Everything looks clear here," a guard said, his declaration resounding in the stillness.

"Check again," another insisted. "You know the High Witch."

"Right."

My heart was thundering in my ears, pounding so hard I feared they'd hear it, or I'd break a rib. They were close now, their shadows slithering across the floor just inches away.

Inhale. Exhale. Don't make a sound. Don't—

"Hey!" one guard called out suddenly. "Did you see this?" He held up something small and shiny—my locket had fallen off when I pulled out the documents.

"Probably some archivist's trinket," the other guard guessed, disinterested. "Put it in the Lost and Found, and let's move on."

"Sure thing."

The guards left the room.

The stiffness in my body dissipated when I heard them receding. When silence returned, I allowed myself one more shaky breath. Then I slipped out from my hiding place. Holly hell. I'd lost my locket. I'd have to retrieve it from the Lost and Found...but how without giving away that I'd been in the forbidden, restricted area?

I wasn't sure, but I had to try.

With the damning evidence secure, I slipped out the door, unnoticed, unseen. The locket wasn't just any trinket—it was my connection to Mom and Dad. Losing it felt like losing them all over again.

My stomach churned. What if I never found it? The thought of their faces fading from my memory made my chest tighten. I had to get it back, no matter the cost.

The hallway stretched before me, empty and imposing. I had to get to the lost and found, but how?

A shadow moved at the far end of the corridor. I froze.

"Sage?" Brad appeared with a confused look on his handsome face. "What are you doing here?"

Crap. I forced a smile. "Brad! Hey, I was just... uh..."

Of course it had to be Brad. The universe clearly had it out for me today.

He raised an eyebrow. "Sneaking around in the restricted area?"

"No! Well, maybe. Look, I lost something important."

Brad's eyes narrowed. "In the restricted section?"

My throat tightened. "No. I can explain."

Except I couldn't. Not without digging myself into an even deeper hole. Why couldn't I have Evie's potion skills right now? Turning those guards into cute, forgetful puppies sounded pretty appealing.

"Can you?" He crossed his arms. "Because last I checked that area was off-limits to everyone but the High Witch."

I bit my lip. "It's complicated."

"It always is with you." Brad sighed. "What did you lose?"

"My locket. The one from my parents."

His expression softened. "Sage..."

A pang of guilt hit me. Brad knew how much that locket meant to me. He'd been there when I got it, after all. Now I was dragging him into my mess.

"I know, I know. It was stupid. But I need it back. The

problem is, they might realize I was in the restricted room if I go to the Lost and Found to claim it."

Brad ran a hand through his hair. "Yeah, that might be an issue."

"Then what do I do?" My voice cracked.

He hesitated, then said, "I might have an idea. But you're not gonna like it."

My heart leapt. Brad's ideas were usually either brilliant or disastrous. Given my luck today, I was betting on the latter. Still, I was desperate enough to try anything.

"Spill it, Brad. What's this brilliant plan of yours?"

He grimaced. "We stage a break-in."

My jaw dropped. "Are you insane?"

"Hear me out. We create a distraction, sneak into the lost and found, and grab your locket. They'll never know it was you."

I paced. "That's not terrible. Two distractions in one day? First Evie and now you."

He shoved his hands into his jean's pockets. "Gee, thanks for the vote of confidence."

I frowned. "But won't they suspect us? We're not exactly criminal masterminds."

Brad grinned. "Speak for yourself. I've got a few tricks up my sleeve."

"Hey! I'll have you know I once convinced Professor Elderwood his office was haunted."

I rolled my eyes. "That's because you hid in his filing cabinet and made spooky noises."

"And it worked, didn't it?"

I blew out a long breath. This was risky, but what choice did

I have? That locket was all I had left of my parents. "Fine. What's the plan?"

Brad's face lit up. "First, we need a diversion. Something big enough to draw everyone's attention."

"Like what? Setting off magical fireworks in the courtyard?"

"Too obvious. We need something subtler. We're trying to avoid suspicion, not cause more trouble."

I tapped my chin, an idea sparking. "What if we enchant all the books in the library to fly around?"

Brad smiled. "That's brilliant! Disorder without destruction."

"Plus, it'll keep the librarians busy for hours."

We high-fived, grinning like idiots. I groaned. This plan might be getting worse by the second.

"Okay, let's go."

Brad winked. "We got this."

My stomach trembled. I wasn't sure if it was nerves or Brad's stupid charm.

We crept through the corridor, our feet echoing in the cavernous halls. Brad led us down another narrow corridor I'd never noticed before.

We rounded a corner and froze. A burly guard stood outside the lost and found, looking bored out of his mind.

"Crap," I hissed. "Now what?"

Brad nudged me. "Distract him."

"Me? Why me?"

"Because you're cute and he's straight."

I glared at him. "Fine. But you owe me."

Taking a deep breath, I sauntered up to the guard, channeling my inner femme fatale. "Excuse me, sir? I seem to be lost."

The guard's eyes snapped to me, suddenly alert. "This area's off-limits, miss."

I twirled a lock of hair around my finger. "Oh, I know. But I was wondering if you could help me find the, um, bathroom?"

His brow furrowed. "It's back by the front entrance."

"Really? That's not what I heard." I leaned in close, lowering my voice. "I was told there are some very...interesting books over here."

The guard's face flushed. From the corner of my eye, I saw Brad slip into the Lost and Found.

"I-I'm not sure what you mean," the guard stammered.

I batted my eyelashes. "Oh, you know. The kind of books that make even experienced warlocks blush."

The guard jerked at his collar. "Miss, I think you should leave."

"Really? I mean, we're just getting to know each other..."

Brad appeared beside me, grinning. "There you are! I've been looking all over for you."

I feigned surprise. "Oh! I must have gotten turned around. Silly me."

We hurried away, leaving the flustered guard behind. Once we were out of earshot, we burst into laughter.

"Did you see his face?" I giggled.

Brad held up my locket, triumphant. "Mission accomplished."

My heart soared. I snatched the locket, clutching it to my chest. The familiar weight of it settled around my neck, a piece of me restored.

"Thank you," I whispered.

Brad's cocky grin softened. "Anytime, Sage. I'll see you around."

He took off and I sighed. The dangerous truth of my parents' death was mine now, and nothing would stop me from exposing it. Not even the High Witch herself.

Shimmering magic appeared beside me and Evie materialized in an impressive show of magic.

"Don't leave without me," she said with a grin.

"Let's do it, then."

Evie and I pushed open the heavy wooden doors of the Magical Archives Building, stepping out into the bright sunshine of Emberwick Crossing. The air felt lighter, but an uneasy feeling still pressed on my chest. Birds chirped in the trees lining the cobblestone streets, their songs almost mocking the turmoil inside me.

"That was intense." Evie's gaze scanned my face, as if searching for any sign of what I'd found.

"Yeah," I said, kicking a loose pebble down the sidewalk. "I found something, Evie. About my parents."

"Tell me everything," she urged, hooking her arm through mine as we walked past the quaint shops and cafes.

"Documents. Old, faded parchments with official seals—and blood stains." I shuddered. "They were involved in uncovering some serious corruption within the magical community's leadership. And it got them killed."

"Corruption? Like what?" Evie's hazel stare widened, reflecting both curiosity and concern.

"Bribery, blackmail, maybe even murder. They knew too much about the start of the supernatural uprising years ago, and someone ordered their deaths to keep it all under wraps." My fingers clenched into fists at my sides. "Why didn't the High Witch tell me? Why didn't anyone tell me?"

"Maybe they were trying to protect you," Evie said softly. "But now you know, and we can do something about it."

"Yeah, but where do we start?" I asked, feeling over-whelmed.

"I'm not sure," she replied.

"Hey, guys." Freya Weissdorn stood there, nervously fidgeting with the hem of her preppy blazer. Her blue stare darted between us, lined with regret.

"Freya," I said, my tone flat. Memories of her betrayal flooded back, how she'd reported Brad and me to Ingrid, tearing apart our relationship.

"Can we talk?" she asked.

"Talk?" Evie snapped, crossing her arms over her chest. "After what you did?"

"Please," Freya implored. "I'm really sorry. I thought I was doing the right thing, following orders. I didn't realize how much it would hurt you."

Evie scoffed. "You ruined lives because you couldn't think for yourself."

"Evie, take down a notch." I laid a hand on her arm. Then I turned to Freya. "Why now? Why apologize now?"

"Because I see the damage I've done," she said, her voice breaking. "And I hate myself for it. I miss our friendship, Sage."

"It's not that simple," I replied, struggling to keep my emotions in check. "You can't just undo what's been done."

"I know," she whispered, tears welling up in her eyes. "But I want to try. I want to make things right."

"Making things right involves more than just words," Evie retorted. "Actions speak louder."

"Let me prove it," Freya pleaded. "Give me a chance."

"How?" I asked, genuinely curious but still wary.

"By helping you," she said, wringing her hands. "With whatever you're dealing with. Please, let me help."

"She might be useful," Evie grudgingly admitted, though her glare remained icy.

"Fine." I sighed. "But one misstep, and we're done. Understand?"

"Understood." Freya nodded vigorously, relief washing over her features.

"Good," Evie said sharply. "But don't think for a second that you've earned our trust."

Freya nodded, her head lowering and her gaze dropping to the ground. Before I could say anything else, something caught my eye across the street.

"It's Councilman Voss," I said, more to myself than anyone else.

He stood tall and imposing, draped in ebony robes. His chiseled face was a mask of calm, yet his blue gaze bore into me with an intensity that made my body tremble. He was known for his impeccable fashion, but today, there was something sinister about the way his robes billowed out in the breeze.

"What's he doing here?" Freya asked.

"Nothing good," I guessed. "There are rumors of his involvement with the supernatural uprising."

"Are you sure?" Evie asked.

I nodded. "Yes."

When I moved toward him, I glared at the man, and every

muscle in my body tensed. And as soon as I reached the other side of the street, he vanished, like smoke dissipating into thin air.

"Where did he go?" Evie's eyes darted around in confusion.

"Just disappeared," I said, trying to suppress the mounting dread in my chest.

"That's not possible," Freya murmured, her hands trembling.

"With him, anything is possible," I replied, staring at the empty spot where he had stood moments before.

"Do you think he knows?" Evie asked quietly.

"About what we found? Maybe," I said, unable to halt the unsettling feeling gnawing at me. "We need to be careful. Very careful. Let's get out of here."

"Right behind you," Evie responded, her usual confidence faltering just a bit.

As we walked away from the Archives, the sun continued to shine brightly, but the road ahead felt shadowed by uncertainty. Yet, amidst the lingering dread, a small glimmer of hope glistened. Perhaps we could uncover the truth and set things right.

CHAPTER
SEVEN

We were hanging out in the living room of my house. I sank into one of the velour armchairs, its fabric a deep teal that played off the brown tones of the hardwood floor. Agatha lounged on the windowsill, her yellow stare tracking Brad as he flopped onto the couch.

The chair hugged me like an old friend, but my stomach twisted. Brad's presence always did that to me, a combo of attraction and nerves that left me feeling like I'd chugged one of Evie's experimental potions.

"Your digs always feel like a hug, Sage." Brad yawned, stretching out his long legs and crossing them at the ankles. His spiky brown hair was a deliberate mess, and his blue eyes were gleaming with mischief that matched his grin.

I shrugged with a smile, tucking a strand of my hair behind my ear. "I could do with fewer hugs from the upholstery though."

Honestly, I could use more hugs, period. But admitting that felt like inviting trouble. Or worse, pity.

"Speak for yourself, Sage." Evie reclined on the love seat, her tone light and airy. She had a pixie-like quality to her, with short, choppy blonde hair and eyes that shone like sunshine on rippling water. Her laughter was infectious. "This is the most action I've gotten in weeks."

Agatha snorted, a sound that was distinctly human and utterly incongruous coming from a feline. "Young witch, your taste in friends is as questionable as your taste in décor."

My chest puffed with a hint of pride. Agatha's barbs were how she showed affection. Usually.

"Hey now, Aggie," I protested, using the nickname that I knew got under her fur. "You adore my taste because it's as eclectic as your sass."

"Is that what they're calling hot messes these days?" Agatha huffed.

"Hot mess or not, these magical treats are really good." Brad reached for a crystal bowl stuffed with shimmering confections. Each piece looked like a tiny, edible star, winking at us. "What flavor is this again?"

"Stardust and midnight blueberry," I said, picking up one myself.

The treat dissolved on my tongue; a burst of sweetness followed by a cool tang that left trails of warmth down my throat. I savored the flavor, letting it distract me from the constant undercurrent of tension. Between Brad, the High Witch's expectations, and the looming supernatural threats, sometimes I wished I could just dissolve like these treats.

Evie watched us with an amused glint in her eye before snagging her own piece. "Who needs a boyfriend when you've got treats like these?" she joked, her tone light with humor rather than lament.

"Or a girlfriend," Brad added, raising an eyebrow in my direction. "Right, Sage?"

My heart skipped and jumped. Did he have to look at me like that? It made staying professional about a thousand times harder.

"Brad, if the High Witch heard you, we'd be turned into lawn ornaments." I rolled my eyes. "And you know the Covenant of Veiled Boundaries has us blanching the line between 'will they, won't they' until the end of time."

"Ah, to be young and cursed with dramatic, forbidden love," Agatha drawled, leaping gracefully down from the windowsill to inspect the snacks.

I sighed. "Could be worse. We could be starring in our own supernatural soap opera."

As if my life wasn't dramatic enough already. Between mentors, magic, and mayhem, some days I felt like I was living in a badly written TV show.

"Isn't that exactly what we're doing now?" Evie popped another magical berry into her mouth.

My lips curved upward. "But at least we have good company for the season finale."

And wasn't that the truth? Despite everything, I wouldn't

trade this motley crew for anything. Even if they did drive me up the wall sometimes.

Brad leaned forward, resting his elbows on his knees. "I think we've got to talk about Councilman Voss. I heard he's rallying more nutjobs for this supernatural uprising war."

My stomach twisted like a pretzel. Voss. That name alone made my skin crawl faster than Agatha could lick an empty tuna can.

Evie nodded. "Voss and his groupies are a real buzzkill. If they get their way, Emberwick Crossing won't be the same chill spot we know and love."

My cat hissed with a flick of her tail. "That man is colder than a witch's teat in a brass bra."

"Agatha, when you were human, did bras even exist?" I teased, struggling to contain my laughter.

Agatha rolled her eyes, her whiskers twitching in amusement. "Shut it, young witch."

"Right, sorry," I said, though I wasn't really. "Okay, so we all agree that Councilman Voss is bad news. If he kicks off this war, it'll tear our community apart."

The importance of our situation pressed down on me like a mountain of grimoires. I couldn't shake the image of Emberwick Crossing torn apart, magic versus mortals. My parents would've known what to do. But they weren't here, and it was up to me to step up.

"Let's brainstorm some epic ways to foil his plan," Brad suggested.

"An impromptu musical number at his next rally, perhaps?" Evie grinned, earning a snort from me.

"Because nothing says, 'stop the uprising' like a flash mob." I laughed. "Okay, so what about a love potion? Make him fall for a siren or something." I looked at my friends, tapping a finger against my chin.

Evie deadpanned. "Sure, because that worked out so well for everyone in mythology."

"Guys, come on." I groaned, throwing my hands up in exasperation. "Let's think of something that won't backfire horribly."

My thoughts whirled like a tornado in a trailer park. We needed a plan, something clever, something unexpected. But every idea felt as useful as a chocolate teapot.

"Maybe we don't need spectacle," Brad said thoughtfully. "We could just...expose him. You know, reveal his plans to the community."

"Expose him with what? A magical PowerPoint presentation?" I shook my head. "We don't have any proof."

Brad sat up. "Better than a PowerPoint. We've got Sage, decorator extraordinaire and spell inventor. What if we design a trap he can't resist walking into? Like when we bested that shadow demon thing."

A burst of excitement swelled in my chest. This was it—a chance to use my unique skills for something bigger than feng shui and color schemes. I could almost hear my parents cheering me on.

I pursed my lips. "Interior design magic meets espionage. Huh. I can dig it."

"Only if it involves zero singing," Agatha added sternly.

I nodded, already imagining how we could use my skills to turn the tide on Voss. "But first, recon. I'll grab my crystal ball—"

"Wait," Brad interrupted, a grin spreading across his face. "Did we just agree on a plan without any sarcasm or detours?"

"Miracles do happen," Evie said, raising her hands skyward.

The living room, with its mismatched throw pillows and a coffee table strewn with half-eaten magical confections, was momentarily still as I pushed myself off the plush armchair. "Mark the date. Now, let's get to work before we jinx ourselves."

As I moved to fetch my crystal ball, I felt a surge of both fortitude and anxiety buzzing through me like caffeinated bees. This was it, our chance to make a difference, to protect our home. And maybe prove that I was worthy of my parents' legacy.

"Gotta see what Councilman Pyro is up to," I said, invoking our pet name for Voss with a smirk.

The warlock gave me major creeper vibes, but we needed intel. No pain, no gain, right?

"Be careful, Sage." Evie's stare was framed with concern, her brow furrowing beneath her midnight black bangs.

"Always am." I winked at her, though my heart hammered against my ribcage.

I slipped out of the room, the soft soles of my boots making no sound on the hardwood floor. The crystal ball was seated on its ornate pedestal in my bedroom, snug amongst various trinkets and talismans that reflected the moonlight filtering through the window. With both hands, I lifted the orb—cool and smooth to the touch—and felt the hum of dormant magic waiting to be awakened.

Back in the living room, I set the ball down before me, easing into a cross-legged position on the floor. My friends watched with anticipation and gravity etched on their faces.

I exhaled slowly, letting my fingers hover above the crystal's surface before I said the incantation, "Reveal to us that which is hidden, show us the unseen."

The orb sparked to life, a blur of colors churning within its depths. The room fell away, and there he was—Councilman Alden Voss, tall and imposing even within the confines of the crystal's vision. His coal-black robes swept the ground as he paced, his followers clustered around him. He said something, and they all nodded in agreement, their expressions eager and twisted with the same fervor that lit Voss' face—a chilling audaciousness to see their uprising come to fruition.

Goosebumps prickled my skin. Voss and his groupies looked about as friendly as a pack of hungry wolves. What were they plotting? Whatever it was, I had a feeling it'd be about as fun as a root canal.

"Check it out, guys." I was transfixed by the scene unfolding within the orb.

"Who is that with him?" Brad leaned in closer, squinting at the female figure standing just behind Voss.

"Looks like he's not alone," I noted, my voice low.

The woman beside him was draped in shadows, her features obscured, yet the way she tilted her head towards him suggested an intimacy that went beyond mere conspiracy.

My brain went into overdrive. Who was this chick? Voss's evil queen or just a pawn in his war? Either way, I suspected that she was a key player in this game.

"New girlfriend or partner in crime?" Evie tilted her head, her tone held curiosity.

Agatha's tail was flicking back and forth. "Either way, it looks like more trouble."

I was eyeing the mysterious woman. Who was she? How did she fit into this war? A romantic entanglement could complicate things, or it could be leverage if we figured out who she was.

"Should we be worried that Dark Lord Pyro has a new sidekick?" Brad joked, but his shoulders slumped.

"Only if she's as fond of fire as he is," I said.

My thoughts sprinted like a hamster on a wheel. If Miss Mystery was half as tyrannical as Voss, we'd be in for one hell of a fight. But maybe we could use her to our advantage. The enemy of my enemy and all that jazz.

"Let's hope she's just a fling," Evie said.

What devious plans did Councilman Voss have, and how far would he go to see them realized?

I squinted at the hazy figures in my crystal ball, trying to make out the details like I was deciphering an abstract painting. Councilman Voss's voice rang out clearly though, his usual smug tone unmistakable.

Great, another cryptic vision. Just what I needed to spice up my Tuesday night. At least Voss' ego was coming through loud and clear, as subtle as a unicorn at a rodeo.

Councilman Voss cleared his throat. "The Echoing Locket is the key to winning this war. Its power is substantial. With it, we could—"

The shadowed woman cut him off. "Shh! These walls have ears, Alden. And some of those ears might belong to snoops we are not aware of." She glanced around furtively.

Voss scoffed. "Oh please, Eden. No one's powerful enough to scry on me without my knowledge."

I raised my eyebrows. Wanna bet, Councilman Cockypants?

My heart thumped against my ribs like a caged bird. If this jerk only knew how wrong he was. But hey, his overconfidence was my gain. *Keep talking, you pompous windbag.*

"The Schism left our world fractured. The Locket could restore the natural order... or give its wielder unrivaled power," Voss said.

"And you think you're the man for the job?" the woman asked skeptically. "Wasn't it your ancestor who caused the Schism in the first place with his lust for power?"

"Sins of the father," Voss said dismissively. "I'm my own man."

Uh huh. And I'm the freakin' Tooth Fairy.

I sighed. "Two power-hungry crazies trying to get their crusty hands on ultimate power. We gotta find that locket ASAP," I said, my fingers drumming on the crystal ball like raindrops on a tin roof. "Before Voss finds it."

My stomach churned like a washing machine on spin cycle. This was bad. Really bad. The kind of bad that made facing down a horde of zombies look like a walk in the park.

"Great. So now we're on a treasure hunt?" Evie blew a strand of hair out of her face.

"More like a prevent-the-apocalypse kind of hunt," I quipped, unable to suppress the sarcasm even as a wave of responsibility crashed over me. "We've got to get to that locket before he does."

Brad leaned forward, his brow furrowed. "Hold up, Sage. We don't even know what this Echoing Locket does."

"Duh, it's got 'vast power.' Weren't you listening?" Agatha's tail swished impatiently. "I say we swipe it and pawn it off. Mama needs a new scratching post."

I shot her a look. "Not helping, Agatha." Sometimes I wondered if Agatha's transformation into a cat had scrambled her priorities along with her DNA. "Focus, kitty. World-ending crisis here."

Evie twirled a strand of her cotton candy hair. "Maybe we should, like, tell the High Witch? This seems majorly above our pay grade."

My stomach clenched like a fist. The thought of running to Ingrid made me feel like a little kid tattling to mommy. "No way. She'd just shut us out. We need to handle this ourselves."

Ingrid might be powerful, but her trust issues were about as deep as the Mariana Trench.

"Sage..." Brad's tone was gentle, but I could hear the exasperation underneath. "This isn't some homework assignment. We're talking about potentially devastating consequences."

I stood up, pacing the room like a caged animal. "You think I don't know that? That's exactly why we can't sit on our butts and do nothing."

My palms were sweaty, knees weak, arms heavy. Okay, maybe I'd been listening to too much Eminem lately, but the sentiment still stood. We had to act, and fast.

Evie raised her hand timidly. "Um, quick question. What's the Great Magical Schism?"

I paused, the realization hitting me like a ton of bricks. "Um, I don't actually know."

Well, that was embarrassing. Some savior of the magical world I was turning out to be. Couldn't even explain the big bad history we were supposed to be preventing from happening.

Brad pinched the bridge of his nose. "Fantastic. So, we're chasing after an artifact we know nothing about, to prevent a schism we can't explain. Solid plan, guys."

"Look," I said, my voice rising. "All I know is Voss wants it, which means its bad news. We have to at least try to find it first."

Agatha yawned dramatically. "Well, count me out. I've got important cat business to attend to. Like napping."

I glared at her. "Some familiar you are."

I had the urge to cast a spell, maybe turn my cat into a slightly more helpful creature. Like a goldfish. Or a potted plant.

Agatha huffed. "Hey, I didn't ask for this gig, Sage. Or to be reincarnated into a cat."

Now I felt bad for being irritated with her. Poor Agatha, stuck in feline form like a genie trapped in a furry lamp. At least she got to keep her snark.

Evie stood up. "I'm in, Sage. We can at least do some research, right?"

I felt a surge of gratitude, like a balmy ray of sunshine breaking through dark clouds. "Thanks, Evie. Brad?"

He sighed, running a hand through his hair. "Fine. But if things get too dicey, we bail."

I nodded, relief flooding over me. "We've got a magical community to save."

"True. And what's the worst that could happen?" Brad asked.

"End of the world. NBD," I shot back.

Joking about the apocalypse felt like whistling past a graveyard, but humor was my shield against the fear gnawing at my insides.

"Okay, team, let's strategize," Evie said, her tone all business now. "Brad, you're the muscle and tech guy. Sage obviously brings the magical firepower. And Agatha...well, she's Agatha."

Agatha ignored my best friend, licking her paw with feigned disinterest.

"Muscle, tech, and firepower," I echoed. "Sounds like we're ready for an epic quest—or a very strange rock band."

A nervous laugh inched up in my throat. We were about as prepared for this as a snowman for summer vacation.

"Let's not forget your snark, Sage. It's definitely your most powerful weapon," Evie teased, her grin infectious despite the gravity of the situation.

"Snark, sass, and spell craft. Got it." My palms were sweaty. I wiped them on my jeans, trying to shake off the jitters. This wasn't just another magical mishap we could laugh off over coffee later. "Guys, this is serious," I said after a moment, the humor fading. "Think about it. Voss could use it to control or destroy. We can't let that happen."

"Then we won't," Brad stated firmly, his usual levity gone. "We stick together. We always have."

Evie bumped her fist against mine. "Team Weird saves the day, right?"

"Team Weird for the win," I agreed.

My throat tightened. I wanted to believe it, but doubt crept in like shadows at twilight. Were we really ready for this?

"All right, it's getting late," Brad said with a glance at his watch. "We should probably call it a night and start fresh in the morning."

Evie stood up and stretched. "Agreed. Besides, my brain's fried. Can't plot world saving strategies on a tired mind."

Evie hugged me quickly. "Goodnight, Sage. We've got this. Sleep well, dream of magical victories."

"Thanks, Evie. You, too."

"Night." Brad moved towards the door and then paused, turning back with a crooked grin. "Don't do anything I wouldn't do, Sage."

My heart did a little flip-flop, like a fish out of water. A flock of butterflies took flight in my stomach, flapping their gossamer wings. Brad's smiles always had that effect, even after all these years. The urge to reach out, to pull him close and never let go, crashed over me like a tidal wave.

Then I clenched my fists, fingernails digging into my palms. I pushed the feeling down, reminding myself that we were strictly in the friend zone now.

Ugh, thanks a lot, High Witch. Buzzkill.

I plastered on a grin. "Considering your threshold for *wouldn't do*, that leaves our options wide open, don't ya think?"

He winked at me. "Guess you'll have to wait and see." Brad stepped out into the crisp night air, the door clicking shut behind him with an air of finality.

I released a breath I didn't realize I'd been holding. One of these days, that warlock was going to be the death of me, I swear. But what a way to go.

Sighing, I turned to Agatha, who was now sprawled across the armrest of the couch. "You think we're up for this, cat?"

"Meow," she replied nonchalantly.

"Your confidence is not reassuring." My joke dripped with sarcasm, though fondness for my familiar warmed my heart.

I flopped down onto the couch, letting the silence envelop me. The Echoing Locket—a relic capable of unraveling the very fabric of our world if it fell into the wrong hands.

My thoughts churned like a cauldron of anxiety soup. This

wasn't just another magical mishap we could laugh off later. This hefty responsibility pushed down on me, heavy as a troll's backside. I couldn't help feeling that we were way out of our league, like a bunch of kids playing dress-up in their parents' ceremonial robes.

"Let's hope finding the locket isn't just a wild goose chase or a wild warlock chase," I said.

Sighing, I glanced at the shimmering crystals hanging by my window, catching the moonlight and throwing rainbow specks of light across the room.

"Team Weird," I murmured into the quiet. "We've faced weirder."

But had we really? My thoughts sifted through our past adventures, each one seeming like child's play compared to this. The locket could literally tear reality apart. And the fate of the magical world was hanging in the balance. I rubbed my temples, wishing I could summon some courage from thin air like one of my spells.

I shuffled through the dusty relics of my attic, the musty air thick with the redolence of forgotten years. I was looking for old photo albums of my parents when I found a discovery.

Within the faded picture albums and moth-eaten garments was an old music box that could've been mistaken for mundane by any non-practitioner's eyes. But as I lifted the lid, a soft glow bathed my face and ethereal chimes floated in the silence. A parchment curled out like a tongue, inscribed with words that made my ears start ringing: "Seek the forgotten beneath the hallowed halls, where knowledge hides and magic calls."

This wasn't just another dusty trinket from Mom and Dad's collection. No, this was a clue, a breadcrumb leading to something big. I could feel it in my bones, that eminent tingle of magic and mystery.

"Brad! Evie! You need to see this!" I called, clutching the music box as if it were as fragile as the truth it held.

Moments later, Brad burst through the attic door, his spiky hair a disheveled crown. "Sage, what's got you in such a—"

"Shh, look!" I cut him off, unveiling the glowing music box.

"Wow, I didn't take you for a collector of... antique nightlights," Brad said, but his jest died in his throat after he read the message.

Evie peered over his shoulder, her blonde hair framing her concentrated expression. "So, the Echoing Locket is beneath the local library? This is big."

With a nod, I closed the lid, extinguishing the light but not the burn of anticipation. Together, we descended from my attic, and then left the house and headed towards Emberwick Crossing's oldest library.

The library materialized before us, a grand structure of weathered stone and stained glass that refracted the dying sunlight into a rainbow hue of pretty colors. My friends and I walked up to its towering arched doorway, exchanging tense glances. Then we crossed the threshold.

The Echoing Locket—a mythical artifact I'd only read about in dusty tomes. If it were real, if we could find it. The possibilities made my palms sweat.

"Remember, stay sharp," I said.

A chill ran down my spine as we entered. The air felt different here, saturated with a sorcery that made the hairs on my arms stand up. This wasn't just any library; it was alive with rare magic.

"Whoa, did you see that?" Brad pointed at a shelf sliding across the floor, mutely reshaping the intricate aisles.

"Books aren't just for reading here," Evie said, her expression flecked with awe. "They're alive."

"Let's keep moving," I urged.

With each step, the library revealed its mysteries. Shelves twisted into new configurations, ensnaring us in a maze of leather-bound enigmas. It felt like the books themselves were watching, their spines rustling with the magic of a thousand spells yet cast.

I wanted to linger and to read every tome, to absorb their knowledge. But we had a mission. The locket. That's why we were here.

Evie paused; head tilted. "Does anyone else hear that?"

The faint murmur of voices floated on the air, speaking languages I'd never heard before.

"We're here for the archive, not a history lesson," I reminded them, though my heart thrummed with curiosity.

"Right, because breaking into a library afterhours is just another Tuesday for us," Brad joked, but even his laughter couldn't mask the undercurrent of tension.

"Over here!" I spotted an ornate door half covered by a sliding bookcase.

We rushed over, and as I reached for the handle, the ground beneath us trembled.

"Careful, Sage!" Evie warned.

I turned the handle, and the door swung open, revealing

dimness, obscurity beyond. We stepped inside, the door shutting behind us with a definitive thud.

Brad's hand found mine in the dark. His touch was warm, grounding.

"Let's find what's waiting for us," I replied, sounding steady despite the eerie chill of the room.

We had hardly taken a step forward when a spectral figure wafted into existence before us. Draped in tattered robes that flapped as if caught in a breeze, the spirit librarian glowed with a pale, otherworldly light.

"Seekers of knowledge," she intoned, her voice echoing off the stone walls like a dirge, "answer my riddles three, and the path shall be laid bare."

"Shit. Ghostly gatekeepers now? What's next, a dragon guarding treasure?" Brad said, then he stepped forward, his blue eyes alight with the challenge.

"Speak your riddle, spirit," I demanded, meeting her translucent gaze.

"Very well," she said, her accent a whisper of wind through autumn leaves. "I have cities, but no houses. Forests, but no trees. Rivers without water. What am I?"

"A map!" Evie exclaimed almost instantly, her expression bright with triumph.

"Correct," the librarian said, nodding.

A section of the wall slid away, revealing another passage.

"Lead on, Sage," Brad said.

We entered the newly revealed corridor. While we traversed the twisting halls, Brad's hand found mine again, sending a zing up my arm. But this wasn't the time or place for romantic feelings. We had to keep our attention on our goal.

"Another riddle?" I prodded when we met an impasse.

"Without fingers, I point, without arms, I strike, without feet, I run. What am I?" The librarian spirit's riddle came like a gust.

"A clock," I answered after a heartbeat's pause.

Magic thrummed in the air as another barrier dissolved, opening the way forward.

"Nice one," Brad said.

"Keep it together, you two," Evie chastised gently, though her lips quirked in a half smile. "We're not done yet."

Our expedition took us deeper until we reached a chamber where reality seemed to fray at the edges. Objects floated mid-air, books flapped around like birds, papers fluttered upwards like leaves in reverse. This place under the local library was crazy intense!

My stomach lurched as the room spun. So much for my usual grace under pressure. I'd take a horde of angry pixies over this fun house any day.

"Watch out!" I cried as a chair zoomed past us, narrowly missing Brad's head.

"Gravity's gone haywire," he said, gripping a floating shelf to anchor himself.

"Look!" Evie pointed at symbols etched on a series of plat-forms hovering in the air. "We need to press those in the right order!"

Great. A magical puzzle in zero G. Just what we needed to make this day even more interesting.

"Easy for you to say," I retorted, leaping onto a platform that promptly flipped, tossing me into the air—or was it the ground now?

My thoughts were in disarray as I flailed, desperately trying to regain control. Next time, I should bring a personal gravity spell.

"Got it!" Brad called out, pressing the last symbol just as I managed to right myself. The door ahead clicked open.

"Next room, quickly!" I urged, relieved to feel solid ground beneath my feet once more.

The next chamber was dimly lit, dominated by an enormous mirror that stretched from floor to ceiling. Our reflections stared back at us, but they twisted, morphing into grotesque carica- tures that embodied our deepest fears.

This was bad. Really bad. I'd seen enough horror movies to know where this was going.

"Brad, don't look!" I warned.

Then his reflection contorted into a monstrous version of himself, his features sharp and cruel.

My breath caught in my throat. That wasn't Brad. It couldn't be. I knew him better than that...didn't I?

"Evie, your potion knowledge!" I shouted over the rising cacophony of our doppelgängers' taunts.

"Yeah!" Evie fumbled in her bag, plucking out a vial. She hurled it at the mirror, and the glass shimmered, the nightmare images dissolving into smoke.

"Is it over?" Evie's body trembled.

"Let's not wait to find out," Brad replied, ushering us forward as the door on the opposite side slowly slid open.

We spilled into the hallway. My hands shook as we moved on. Whatever was behind that door, I hoped it didn't involve any more mirrors. Or chairs with a vendetta against gravity.

The hallway led to a dead end, but not just any dead end.

The wall before us was alive with moving symbols and glowing runes—an elaborate magical lock that seemed to shimmer and shift under our gaze.

"Okay," I said, stepping closer. "This lock needs our combined magical signatures."

Brad nodded. "I'll start with the foundation rune."

"Evie, you're up for the intuition sigils." I pointed to the swirling designs that moved like quicksilver.

"Got it, Sage." Evie had her hands poised and she concentrated on the patterns.

We each reached out, channeling our magic into the lock. The symbols began to resonate with a quiet hum that grew louder, vibrating through the stone floor and into our bones.

"Is it working?" Evie asked, her voice imbued with hope.

"Keep going!" I urged.

The air around us hummed with energy as our powers intertwined. The intricate patterns on the lock aligned perfectly with our efforts. With a thunderous click, the lock disengaged, and the wall slid away, revealing an ancient vault bathed in a golden light.

"Whoa..." My mouth dropped open.

"Look at all this..." Evie trailed off.

Shelves lined with dusty tomes, artifacts encrusted with jewels, and relics that sighed of millennia past surrounded us. We were in the heart of Emberwick Crossing's magical history.

So much power, so much history. Mom and Dad would've loved this place.

Brad scanned the room, his brow furrowed. "Where's the Echoing Locket?"

"Let's find anything that could be a clue," I suggested,

catching a glint of metal. I reached for an ornate scroll case; its surface etched with the same kind of symbols that had adorned the lock. "Here." I was quickly unraveling the parchment within.

This could be it. The key to everything we'd been searching for.

It wasn't the locket. It was a map, ancient and cryptic, depicting landmarks and inscriptions that made little sense at first glance.

Disappointment punched me in the gut. But wait...

"Look, this symbol here," Brad pointed. "Isn't that—"

"Nightfall Tower," I finished for him, my throat tight. "It's suggesting the locket is hidden in Ingrid Nightspire's personal quarters."

The High Witch. My mentor. The woman I looked up to. Could she really be involved in this?

"Are you serious?" Evie gasped. "That's not good."

"Understatement of the century," I said. "Ingrid's quarters are off-limits to everyone. And she's no ordinary witch, she's—"

"The High Witch," Brad interjected. "Sage, this is insane."

We were way out of our depth here. But giving up wasn't an option.

"Insane or not, it's our only lead." I rolled up the map. "We have to get into Nightfall Tower."

Evie sighed. "From gravity-defying rooms to breaking into a High Witch's private quarters. What could possibly go wrong?"

We were about to cross a line from which we couldn't uncross. But sometimes, to do what was right, you had to do what's wrong first.

"Everything?" I marched ahead, tucking the map securely into my bag. "But we don't have a choice. We need that locket."

CHAPTER
NINE

I rapped on the heavy oak door, my heart beating a frantic rhythm against my ribcage. My palms were sweaty, and I wiped them on my jeans. This was it. The moment of truth. No turning back now.

Agatha, an obsidian shadow at my heels, yawned. "This better be worth it, young witch. I missed second breakfast for this."

Confronting the High Witch about the Echoing Locket would be tense and awkward.

"Shush," I hissed.

The door opened, revealing the High Witch's study—a room

that breathed antiquity, its walls lined with shelves groaning under the weight of leather-bound grimoires. The air was thick with the musk of old parchment and the tang of spell ink.

Ingrid Nightspire, her silvery hair flowing like quicksilver down her back, peered at me over half-moon spectacles. "Sage Holland," she said, her accent bearing the power of authority. "To what do I owe this unexpected visit?"

"High Witch, I need to speak with you about something... sensitive." My throat tightened, and I stepped into the sanctum of Emberwick Crossing's most powerful sorceress.

Ingrid gestured to a pair of high-backed chairs before her desk. As I sat, the magical sorcery in the room prickled my skin, reacting to my nervousness—or was it hers?

"Out with it then," Ingrid prompted, leaning back in her chair, her stare sharp as daggers.

I took a deep breath, steeling myself. This was the moment I'd rehearsed a hundred times in my head. *Don't screw it up, Sage.*

"It's about the Echoing Locket," I said, my tone careful, measured.

Agatha curled around my ankles, her attention fixed on Ingrid, who stiffened noticeably.

"Is that so?" The High Witch's tone was icy, betraying a hint of surprise.

"Agatha and I believe it's in your quarters." My accusation hung between us, a spark ready to ignite.

"Be cautious, Sage," Agatha warned, tail flicking. "You're treading on cursed ground."

Ingrid's violet eyes narrowed, a thunderstorm brewing

within them. "And what precisely has led you to this conclusion?" She leaned forward, hands folded neatly on the desk.

My adrenaline was surging. This was it. The point of no return. I swallowed hard, my mouth dry as sandpaper.

"A map," I blurted, ignoring Agatha's warning hiss. "It led me to you."

"Preposterous!" Ingrid snapped, the air sizzling with her rising ire. Around us, the magical current intensified, papers fluttering and floating.

"Then there's my parents," I pushed on, undeterred. "They knew about the corruption, the lies festering within our leadership. They were silenced because of it."

"Watch it, kid," Agatha growled under her breath. "Don't poke the sleeping basilisk."

"Silenced?" Ingrid repeated, her voice a dangerous whisper. "You dare suggest—"

"I dare," I interjected, emboldened by the truth burning in my chest. "And the locket—they were going to use it to expose everything, weren't they?"

"Enough!" Ingrid stood abruptly, her chair clattering backwards. "You think you understand the credence of these accusations?"

Magical power crackled like static, lifting strands of my blue highlighted hair.

"Better than you think," I shot back, standing to meet her towering presence. "I'm not blind to the shadows creeping through Emberwick Crossing. And neither are you."

"Your youthful audacity—" Ingrid said, but I cut her off.

"Isn't it time we stop hiding behind veils and secrets? If

we're to protect this community, the truth needs to come out." My voice wavered but didn't break.

"Perhaps," Ingrid conceded after a tense pause, her gaze softening just a fraction. "But at what cost, Sage? At what cost?"

The silence stretched, a chasm between Ingrid and me. I watched as the High Witch's hard, violet stare narrowed, her resolve wavering like a candle flame in a draft.

Ingrid, the unshakeable pillar of our magical community, actually looked... uncertain? It was like seeing a crack in a marble statue. I didn't know whether to be intrigued or terrified.

"Fine," she relented, her voice sounding heavy with an emotion I couldn't quite place. "The Echoing Locket is indeed more than just an artifact. It...it belonged to my older sister. Archmage Zephyria."

"Your sister?" I echoed, disbelief coloring my tone. It was odd to think of Ingrid having family, being anything other than the High Witch.

My mind reeled. Ingrid with a sister? Next thing you know, we'd discover she had a secret boy band obsession or collected rubber ducks. The image of stern, imposing Ingrid surrounded by squeaky yellow bath toys almost made me snort.

"Family heirloom, huh?" Agatha asked.

Ingrid shot a glare at Agatha, but the cat merely yawned, her fangs glinting briefly before she licked a paw nonchalantly.

I bit back a grin. Leave it to Agatha to cut through the tension with her sardonic charm. Sometimes I wondered if her feline form was less a curse and more a perfect match for her personality.

Ingrid's lips tightened into a thin line. "It's more than a mere heirloom, Agatha. The Echoing Locket holds memories."

My eyebrows shot up. "Memories?"

Memories in a locket? It sounded like something out of a fairytale, but then again, my life was hardly normal. Still, the gravity in Ingrid's voice made me uneasy.

"Yes." Ingrid's fingers traced an invisible pattern on her desk. "Zephyria imbued it with her most powerful spells. It's a repository of knowledge that could reshape our magical world."

A chill crawled up my spine. "And now it's missing?"

"Worse." Ingrid's eyes met mine, sharp as broken glass. "It's been stolen."

My stomach dropped. Stolen magical artifacts were never good news. I'd seen enough movies to know where this was heading, and it wasn't to a whimsical musical number.

Agatha's tail swished. "Let me guess. You want us to play fetch?"

I shot my familiar a look. "Not helping."

"Actually," Ingrid said, her body stiff, "that's precisely what I need."

My mouth went dry.

Great. Just great. I was barely able to keep my house clean with magic, and now Ingrid wanted me to track down some world-altering magical locket? I half expected her to tell me the fate of the universe depended on it. *No pressure or anything.*

"Sage," Ingrid leaned forward, her perfume—sandalwood and sage—tickling my nose. "You're the only one I trust with this. Your unique abilities, your connection to—" She stopped abruptly, pain flashing across her face.

"To what?" I pressed.

My pulse quickened. There it was again, that flicker of vulnerability. What wasn't she telling me? And why did I suddenly feel like I was standing on the edge of a very deep, very dark rabbit hole? And she was about to push me in?

Ingrid's jaw clenched. "To me. To this magical community."

Yet her hesitation nagged at me. There was more she wasn't saying. I narrowed my eyes. Ingrid was many things, but a bad liar wasn't one of them. Whatever she was hiding, it was big. And probably dangerous.

"Why me?" I asked. "Why not the Council?"

Ingrid's laugh was bitter. "The Council? They'd sooner use the Locket's power for themselves than return it."

"And you wouldn't?" Agatha muttered.

Ingrid ignored her. "Sage, please. Will you help me recover it?"

I swallowed hard. This was bigger than anything I'd faced before. Bigger than me.

Panic burned in my chest. I was just an interior designer who could barely keep her plants alive, not some magical Indiana Jones.

I looked at Ingrid.

My resolve hardened. Whatever this was, whatever secrets Ingrid was keeping, I couldn't turn my back on her. Not when she looked at me like that.

"Is this why my parents were killed?" I pressed, feeling the sting of betrayal. "Because of some family squabble over jewelry?"

The accusation left my mouth before I could stop it, sharp and rude. I kind of wanted to take it back, but a larger part of me needed to know. The wound of my parents' death had never truly healed, and now it felt like salt was being poured directly into it.

"It is not just jewelry!" Ingrid snapped, her composure cracking. "It is power—the kind that can upend Councils or expose deep-seated corruption. Your parents were... perceptive." Ingrid sighed, her shoulders slumping as if the admission weighed on her. "The locket would have given credence to their claims. They could have dismantled everything we've built."

"Built or buried?" Agatha said with a hiss. "You're one to talk about integrity, Nightspire."

"Enough, Agatha," I said without heat.

"Your parents' deaths were not my doing," Ingrid said. "But yes, they were silenced by those who feared exposure."

"And all this time, you let me believe—"

"Believe what?" Ingrid challenged, her gaze searching mine. "That our world is pure? That our leaders are infallible? Sage, we are at war. Your parents became casualties in a battle for the soul of Emberwick Crossing. In the supernatural uprising."

My parents had been soldiers then, fighting with truth as their weapon. And now, it was my turn to arm myself with the legacy they left behind.

Before the gravity of Ingrid's claim could fully sink in, a piercing alarm sliced through our tense standoff. Red lights flashed across the opulent walls of the study, painting us all in a sinister glow.

"Damn it," I grumbled. "Yikes, that's the Council Chamber's alarm."

"Voss," Ingrid hissed, her violet gaze flaring with an inner light. "It has to be."

The door burst inward, wooden splinters flying like lethal rain as a group of robed figures surged into the room. Their

411

hands glowed with preternatural force—crimson, emerald, and sapphire arcs of raw, elemental fury.

"Agatha!" I shouted, ducking a bolt of hissing green sorcery that seared the air where my head had been a second earlier.

"Way ahead of you, young witch," Agatha's voice held glee rather than fear, her shadowy form expanding and undulating around the attackers. Spectral tendrils lashed out, snaring ankles and wrists, yanking them off balance with feline precision.

"Get the locket!" one of the invaders bellowed, his face hidden beneath a hood.

Except the Echoing Locket wasn't here. And if Councilman Voss was looking for it, then he didn't have. But then who did?

"Over my dead body," Ingrid declared, her fingers weaving intricate patterns through the air. Threads of silver light formed a protective barrier around us, but it wouldn't hold for long against such numbers.

I didn't waste time with prepared spells. Improvisation was more my style. Summoning my own power, I crafted a vortex of swirling air, picking up books, papers, and small artifacts from around the room, turning them into a makeshift maelstrom of debris.

"Nice trick." Agatha dissolved into shadows to avoid a fiery comet that incinerated the very spot she'd occupied moments before.

"Thanks, I just made it up," I said through gritted teeth, concentrating on sustaining the commotion around us.

The attackers were relentless, though, their magic tearing through the study with destructive force, incinerating priceless tomes and shattering ancient vases.

"Attention on Voss!" Ingrid commanded. "He'll be here soon to claim what he believes is his."

"Great," I replied, sarcasm edging out panic. "So, Voss obviously doesn't know the locket was stolen then."

"I suppose not. Greedy bastard," Ingrid said, a wry smile flickering on her lips for a split second before vanishing in the grim set of her jaw. "We must protect ourselves at all costs."

"Protect and expose," I corrected, sending out a wave of concussive force that knocked back several of the hooded figures. "My parents died for this. We're not just going to hide in the shadows like cowards."

"Then we stand and fight," Ingrid agreed, steel in her tone.

As the battle persisted, I grimaced at the feeling of betrayal that gnawed at me. Ingrid had kept so much from me, yet now we fought side by side. The Echoing Locket wasn't just a symbol of my parents' sacrifice, it was the key to vindicating them and revealing the rot that festered within our ranks, but who had it? Voss wanted it and he was going to be pissed off when he realized it wasn't here in Ingrid's study.

"Let's make sure my parents didn't die in vain," I whispered, readying myself for the next onslaught.

My stomach clenched. Mom and Dad's faces flashed in my mind, their proud smiles twisting into disappointment. No. I couldn't let them down. Not now, not ever.

I gritted my teeth and threw up a shield just as a fireball hurtled toward us. The heat seared my skin, but I held firm.

"Voss, you coward!" I yelled. "Face us yourself instead of hiding behind your lackeys!"

A deep chuckle resonated through the building. Councilman Voss stepped forward, flames expanding in his palms. "Oh, little witch. So naive, so...expendable."

The word hit like a sucker punch. I'd show him *expendable*. I'd show them all. My fingers tingled with pent up magic, begging for release. My insides trembled. I glanced at Ingrid, whose face was set in grim resolve.

"Expendable? I'll show you expendable," I snarled, hurling a blast of concussive force at Voss.

He deflected it with a wave of his hand. "Is that the best Holland's brat can do?"

My jaw clenched. I was so sick of being underestimated, of being seen as just some kid playing dress-up in my parents' legacy.

Before I could retort, a familiar voice rang out. "She's not alone, asshole!"

Brad materialized beside me, the air shimmering around him. Evie appeared moments later, her hands glowing with potion-fueled witchery.

"Cavalry's here! We got your back, Sage." Evie thrust a fist into the air. "Team Sage!"

Voss's eyes narrowed. "More children playing war. How quaint."

My friends. My team. My family. A surge of fierce protectiveness crashed over me. I'd be damned if I let Voss hurt them.

"Less talk, more action," Agatha hissed from the shadows.

I nodded, my hands crackling with enchantments. "You heard the cat. Let's end this."

The room exploded into anarchy. Voss' soldiers circled us, their hoods concealing twisted faces. I ducked under a punch, retaliating with a spell that hurled my attacker flying. The stench of ozone saturated the air and magic fought against magic.

"Sage, duck!" Brad yelled.

I dropped to the floor as a chunk of ceiling sailed over my head, crushing two of Voss' men. Brad grinned, his hands outstretched.

"Show off," I said, but couldn't help smiling.

Evie's laughter rang out when she lobbed a potion at a group of soldiers. There was a pop, and suddenly a cluster of confused rabbits sat where the men had been.

"Really, Evie?" I called out.

She shrugged. "What? They're easier to deal with this way!"

I rolled my eyes and turned back to the fight.

The mayhem of the room made it difficult to see, but I could make out Ingrid's fierce determination as she battled against Voss.

Ingrid and Voss stood in the center, their hands glowing with power as they clashed in a fierce battle. The flashes of light illuminated the hooded figure in front of me, their features hidden. Her spells, a bright blue color, crashed against his sinister strength. The air around them vibrated with power, casting a haze over the room.

As I began to approach them, a hooded figure stepped in my way, his face obscured by the darkness of his cloak. His expressions shone with malice, and in his hand, he held a twisted and jagged wand.

"Going somewhere?" the goon growled, lunging at me.

I sidestepped, grabbing his arm and using his momentum to

throw him into a bookshelf. He crashed through it with a satisfying crunch.

"Yeah," I panted. "To kick your boss' ass."

I charged toward Voss, my blood pounding in my ears. The air sizzled with magic, thick and oppressive. Voss' eyes bore into mine, a sneer twisting his lips.

"Come to join the grown-ups' fight, little girl?" Voss taunted.

I stood tall, ready to unleash a spell. "Funny, I only see one child here."

Councilman Voss' face contorted with rage. He hurled a fireball at me, but I was ready. I dove to the side, feeling the heat singe my hair. When I rolled to my feet, I caught sight of Brad grappling with two of Voss' goons.

"Brad, behind you!" I shouted.

He spun, narrowly avoiding a dagger to the back. With a grunt, he slammed his attacker into the wall.

"Thanks, Sage!" he called back. "Watch your own ass, will you?"

A shadow darted past my feet. Agatha hissed in my ear, "Stop daydreaming and focus, you lovesick fool!"

Right. Focus. I turned back to Voss, who was still trading spells with Ingrid. My mentor's face was a mask of concentration, but I could see the strain in her eyes.

"Hey, Voss!" I yelled. "Bet you can't hit me!"

It was a childish taunt, but it worked. Voss' attention wavered for a split second. Ingrid seized the opportunity, landing a brutal hex that sent him staggering.

I didn't waste a moment. Channeling my power, I conjured

a spell I'd been working on for months. The air around Voss began to shimmer and twist.

My heart pounded as I watched my creation come to life. Months of late nights and singed eyebrows were about to pay off.

Please work, please work...

"What..." he frowned, but it was too late.

The spell took hold, warping the space around him. Voss' own flames rebounded, singeing his expensive robes. He howled in exasperation, trying to break free.

A fierce grin spread across my face. *Take that, you arrogant jerk. Maybe next time you'll think twice before underestimating a novice witch.*

"Not so expendable now, am I?" I spat.

Voss' expression blazed with hatred. With a roar, he unleashed a torrent of fire that shattered my spell. The backlash knocked me off my feet, my head slamming against the floor. Stars exploded in my vision.

Crap. I'd forgotten how much raw power he had. My teeth rattled from the impact, and for a moment, I couldn't tell which way was up.

"Sage!" I heard Evie's panicked voice.

I blinked, trying to clear my head. Voss loomed over me, flames dancing in his palms. "I'll teach you to meddle in affairs beyond your understanding," he snarled.

Oh, real original. Did he practice that line in the mirror? I almost wanted to roll my eyes, but the sight of those flames made my stomach lurch.

My muscles screamed as I tried to move. Too slow. Voss' hand descended, wreathed in fire...

A blur of fur and shadow slammed into Voss' face. Agatha yowled, claws raking across his face. He stumbled back, cursing.

"Nobody barbecues my witch but me," Agatha growled.

I scrambled to my feet, ignoring the throbbing in my skull. Around us, the tide of battle had shifted. The Councilman's men were falling back, overwhelmed by our combined assault. Voss' gaze darted around the room, assessing the situation. His face twisted into a snarl of frustration.

My legs felt like jelly, but a spark of hope flared in my chest. We might actually pull this off.

"This isn't over," he hissed. With a wave of his hand, he vanished in a column of flame.

His remaining soldiers followed suit, disappearing in puffs of smoke. The sudden silence was deafening.

I stood there, panting, adrenaline still coursing through my veins. My knees felt weak, and I had to resist the urge to collapse right there on the floor.

The room spun, and I tasted copper in my mouth. That last spell had taken more out of me than I'd realized. But we'd done it. We'd actually driven Voss back. A hysterical laugh bubbled up in my throat, but I swallowed it down. No time to lose it now.

"Well," Evie said, brushing dust off her clothes. "That was fun."

CHAPTER
TEN

The dust settled like a thin, gray shroud over Ingrid's office, muting the echoes of the battle that had just torn through it. Shelves lay toppled, books sprawled open with their pages crushed, and the air was thick with the acrid stench of spent magic. Amidst the wreckage, I found myself standing, chest heaving, my hands trembling with an adrenaline hangover.

My stomach roiled as I surveyed the chaos. This was my fault. If I'd been faster, smarter, maybe we could've stopped Voss before he tore through here like a tornado on steroids. But no, I'd fumbled, and now look at this mess.

My friends and Agatha had left to go downstairs and give their statements to the authorities.

"Damnation, Sage." Ingrid's influence punctured sharply through the haze, her gaze scanning the ruin. "Voss tried to outplay us."

I followed her gaze to the empty pedestal where the Echoing Locket used to rest—an absence that clawed at my insides.

"At least he doesn't have it," I said.

She gave me a clipped nod, her slender fingers tight around her wand. "But you shall find it for me."

My jaw dropped. Me? Find a magical artifact that even Ingrid couldn't keep safe? Yeah, right. And pigs might sprout wings and do the cha-cha.

"But why me?" I stammered, struggling to keep my voice steady.

"Your parents may not have wielded magic, but they gave you something more potent—resolve," Ingrid remarked, coolly assessing the damage around us.

A lump formed in my throat at the mention of my parents. Would they be proud of me now, standing in this disaster zone? Or disappointed that I'd let things get this far?

"Resolve won't track down dangerous stolen artifacts."

The High Witch sighed, a rare flash of weariness passing over her face, "But you are a creator. You craft new spells as easily as breathing. My family's locket...I need someone to find it who understands the intricacies of magic."

Creator? More like chaos-bringer. My spells had a nasty habit of going sideways when I least expected it. But Ingrid's faith in me, misplaced as it might be, triggered a warm sensation through my chest.

"Understands, maybe. But controlling it?" I shook my head, bits of plaster falling from my hair. "That's a different story."

Ingrid frowned, stepping carefully over a shattered vase. "Control comes from confidence, Sage. Your natural flair for magic, it's unrefined, but it's there. And it is the crucible that will forge your strength."

Crucible, schmucible. I'd rather face a pack of ravenous werewolves than go toe-to-toe with Voss again. But something in Ingrid's expression, a mix of hope and desperation, made me bite back my protests.

"But let's not forget the part where Voss, the Council's golden boy, has gone rogue."

"Former golden boy," she corrected with a thin smile. "The authorities will have to hunt him down."

I sighed, rolling my shoulders to release some tension. "They'll have a hard time outwitting the warlock with a penchant for fire and theatrics with an army of loyal allies."

And here I was with my ragtag group of misfits, expected to outmaneuver him. Talk about bringing a spoon to a gunfight.

"Begin at dawn. Time is of the essence."

"Isn't it always?" I spat, watching her regal figure move amidst the wreckage.

"Now, go home and get cleaned up," the High Witch ordered. "And get some rest. Your mission to retrieve my locket starts tomorrow, young lady."

I wasn't some errand girl she could boss around. But as I opened my mouth to argue, exhaustion hit me like a tidal wave. Maybe a shower and a nap weren't such bad ideas after all.

An hour later, I made it home. Dragging my feet across the threshold, I felt every bruise and scratch from the battle in Ingrid's office with an acute sting. The quiet was startling compared to the din of spells and curses that had filled my ears mere hours ago.

"Welcome back, young witch," Agatha greeted, her feline form slipping out from a shadow in the corner. "You look like you've been through hell and back. Worse than me."

My muscles ached, and my head throbbed. I swear I could still smell the acrid stench of Voss' fire magic clinging to my clothes.

"Holy hell." I groaned, collapsing onto the couch. "That's putting it mildly."

Agatha leaped onto my lap. "The Echoing Locket...any idea who could have taken it if not Voss?"

"None." My fingers plucked at the frayed edges of a throw pillow, my thoughts whirling. "It has to be someone with access to Ingrid's sanctum. Someone we wouldn't expect."

The list of suspects grew longer by the second. Each name brought a new wave of unease, settling like lead in my stomach.

"An inside job," Agatha mused, her yellow eyes narrowing. "Ingrid won't rest until she finds it. That locket isn't just powerful, it's personal."

"Yeah, I know." I sighed, recalling the reverence with which Ingrid spoke of her sister, Zephyria. "It's as much about family legacy as it is about magical security."

"And it was nice that Evie and Brad showed up to help us battle Voss earlier. I'm glad everyone is okay," Agatha said.

"Me too." My heart ached at the thought of Brad—my rock,

my best friend, the one whose hand I longed to hold without fear of reprimand. Brad and I were a ticking time bomb, ready to blow up at any moment under the scrutiny of Ingrid and the Council.

The memory of his worried expression during the battle made my chest tighten. I pushed the feeling down, burying it beneath layers of duty and responsibility.

"Can we talk about something else?" I asked, desperate for distraction. "Like how Voss managed to fool everyone? How he led the supernatural uprising right under our noses?"

"Ah, yes. The Council's prodigal son turned traitor." Agatha sneered. "His fall from grace will cause distress throughout Emberwick Crossing."

"He wasn't working alone. There's a whole conspiracy we're missing."

Who else might be involved? How deep did this betrayal run?

Agatha's tail flicked in agitation. "With Voss on the run, it's only a matter of time before his cronies start scurrying out of the woodwork. We need to be ready."

"Ready to face friends who might be foes, and foes who might be allies," I added, the gravity of the situation settling deep in my bones. "Emberwick Crossing will never be the same after this."

"Change is often necessary for growth," Agatha observed sagely. "And you, Sage Holland, will be at the heart of it."

"Goody for me," I said dryly, standing up with Agatha still perched on my shoulder.

She yawned, jumping down and sauntering towards the kitchen. "Now, let's eat. I'm famished, and you need your strength. Tomorrow, we hunt for a locket and unmask a conspiracy."

"Sounds like a typical Thursday," I joked weakly.

As I followed Agatha to the kitchen, my head buzzed with unanswered questions and half-formed plans.

I rummaged through the fridge, grabbing some leftover Chinese takeout. "Chicken lo mein, dinner of champions," I quipped, shoveling a forkful into my mouth.

Agatha eyed me critically. "Nutritious. I'm sure that'll fuel that big brain of yours for the coming battle of wits and magic."

"Hey, don't knock it till you've tried it. Besides, I need comfort food right now. Plotting against powerful magical foes is stressful business."

"Fair point," Agatha conceded, hopping up on the counter. "So, what's our first move, Sherlock? Please tell me it involves me getting to scratch someone's eyes out."

I snorted. "As much as I appreciate your bloodthirsty enthusiasm, I think we need to play this smart. Gather intel first, then go in claws blazing."

"You're no fun," Agatha pouted. "But I suppose you're right. Where do we start digging up dirt on our suspect list?"

"I say we hit up Eden," I suggested, polishing off the last of the lo mein. "That gossipy aide seems to have her nose in everyone's business. If anyone knows something about this locket situation, it'll be her."

"Ooh, I like the way you think," Agatha purred approvingly. "A little subtle interrogation over tea and crumpets. The trick will be getting her to spill without letting on what we're really after."

"Well then, it's a good thing subtlety is my middle name," I said with a wink.

Agatha rolled her eyes. "I thought it was Danger. Or was it Reckless Overconfidence?"

"Ha ha," I deadpanned. "Seriously though, this is our chance to prove ourselves. To show everyone that we're more than just the quirky witch and her snarky cat sidekick."

"Excuse you. I am nobody's sidekick," Agatha huffed indignantly. "But I take your meaning. It's time to step up and show these magical bigwigs what we're made of."

I nodded. "No, now it's time to eat."

Once we'd finished, I cleaned up the kitchen while Agatha went to take a nap.

Stepping out into the cool night air, I found Brad waiting for me in my backyard, his silhouette outlined by the soft glow of the porch light. He turned at the sound of the door closing behind me, his blue eyes searching mine.

"Hey," he said gently.

"Hey."

My stomach twisted into knots. Brad's presence always did this to me—a fusion of contentment, lust, and desire. And right now, I wanted to run to him and away from him all at once.

The tension from earlier had yet to dissipate, and now, cloaked in shadows and secrecy, it ratcheted higher.

He took a cautious step closer. "You, okay?"

"Define 'okay,'" I huffed, hugging myself against the chill. "I feel like I'm standing in quicksand, Brad. Everything's shifting beneath me."

My admission clung to the air, leaden with voiceless fears. Part of me wished I could take them back, stuff them down where they belonged. But another part of me relished the honesty, the uninhibited vulnerability.

He nodded, reaching out to push a loose strand of hair from my face. "We'll figure this out, Sage. We always do."

His touch set off electricity through me, a harsh reminder of everything we couldn't have. I bit my lip, fighting the urge to lean into his hand.

"Even when we're not supposed to be together?" I couldn't keep the bitterness from seeping into my question.

"Especially then. The Covenant of Veiled Boundaries can't dictate how we feel. It can only tell us what we're allowed to show."

"Which is nothing," I whispered.

A lump formed in my throat. Nothing. That's what we were reduced to—stolen moments and whispered promises. It wasn't enough. It would never be enough.

"Listen to me. What we have—it's real. And no law, no matter how ancient, is going to change that."

"Real and impossible," I mumbled.

My chest ached with the suckage of it all. Real, impossible, and utterly maddening. How were we supposed to navigate this minefield of emotions and rules?

"But since when has impossible stopped either of us? You're the most resourceful person I know."

"Resourceful enough to find a stolen magical locket and expose a conspiracy, but not enough to keep the guy I—" I caught myself, the confession dangling precariously on my lips.

I'd almost said it. Those three little words that would change everything...or maybe nothing at all.

"Keep the guy you what?" Brad moved closer.

"Never mind." I shook my head. "It's all too complicated."

Complicated didn't begin to cover it. This was a tangled mess of feelings, duty, and magic that even my best spells couldn't unravel.

His smile held a sad edge. "Complication doesn't mean defeat. We can be strong for each other, even if we can't be together."

"It's the wanting more and knowing I shouldn't."

Wanting more felt like a betrayal of the Covenant, of my mentor, of everything I'd worked for. But denying it felt like a betrayal of myself.

"Wanting more is human, Sage. And so is fighting for it." Brad stepped back, giving me space yet somehow remaining my anchor. "No matter what happens, I'm here for you. You know that, right?"

"Knowing it is the easy part." I managed to smile. "Believing it when everything else is falling apart—that's the tough one."

"Then let's start by believing in each other," he said, and there was a promise in his voice that felt as solid as the earth beneath our feet.

Brad leaned in, his breath cool on my cheek. Before I could react, his lips met mine in a passionate kiss. For a moment, I melted into him, feeling the tenderness, the connection. Then reality crashed over me like a bucket of ice water. I jerked away abruptly, my hand flying to my mouth.

Oh, gods, what was I doing? This was exactly what we'd promised not to do. My heart pounded, with lingering desire and rising panic.

"Brad, we can't," I choked out, fighting back tears. "This... us... it's getting too dangerous."

His face clouded with hurt. "Sage, I care about you so much."

His declaration and devotion twisted like a knife in my gut. I cared too, more than he knew. But caring wasn't enough, not with the stakes so high.

I shook my head, steeling myself. "No, we can't. The Covenant of Veiled Boundaries isn't just some rule we can bend. It's magical law, Brad. Ancient and binding. And Ingrid wouldn't hesitate to—"

"To what? We're both consenting adults, Sage."

I paced, swallowing hard "You don't understand. As a civilian, you're not protected. If Ingrid catches us again..."

Images flashed through my mind: Brad stripped of his magic, exiled from our world. All because of me. My throat tightened.

Brad reached for me, but I stepped back. "Then we keep it secret. We've done that before."

"And look where that got us," I said. "I can't risk you losing your magical builder license, Brad. I won't. We can't...it's over. I'm sorry."

The words felt like ash in my mouth. Every fiber of my being screamed to take them back, to throw caution to the wind and choose love. But I couldn't. Not when the cost was Brad's entire future.

Brad's jaw clenched, his expression flashing with both hurt and frustration. "So that's it? You're just going to throw away everything we have?"

I wrapped my arms around myself, trying to hold it together. "Brad, please. Don't make this harder than it already is."

"Harder?" He let out a bitter laugh. "Sage, you're the one making this impossible. We can be careful. We can—"

"No," I cut him off, my tone sharp. "We can't. Don't you get it? Every stolen moment, every secret touch... it's like playing with fire. And sooner or later, we're going to get burned."

My stomach twisted into knots. Brad's optimism was like a knife to the gut, reminding me of everything we could never have. I wanted to scream, to shake him until he understood the impossibility of it all.

Brad stepped closer, his sexy smell making my head spin. "I'm willing to take that risk."

I backed away, bumping into the wall of my house. "Well, I'm not. Not with your future on the line."

Tears stung my eyes. I couldn't let him see how much this was killing me. If he knew, he'd never let go.

"That's my choice to make," he argued, frustration coloring his tone.

"Is it?" I shot back. "Because last time I checked, I'm the one with the power to strip you of everything you've worked for. One slip-up, one moment of weakness, and poof—your magic, your career—gone."

Brad's face fell, the reality of our situation finally sinking in. "There has to be another way," he said.

I shook my head, blinking back tears. "There isn't. Not as long as the Covenant stands."

"Then we fight it," Brad said. "We go to the Council, we—"

"Stop," I pleaded, my resolve crumbling. "Just...stop. It's over, Brad. It has to be."

I could hear my own heart hammering in my chest, feel unshed tears burning behind my eyes.

Brad's shoulders slumped. "I love you, Sage," he said softly, his voice breaking.

Those four words shattered what was left of my composure. All the air left my lungs, and for a moment, I forgot how to breathe.

A sob escaped my lips before I could stop it. "I know," I said. "That's why I have to let you go."

FAMILIAR DESTINY

MAGGIE SHAW

FAMILIAR DESTINY

CHAPTER
ONE

I woke up with a start, breathing fast. Sweat slicked my skin, and my heart hammered against my ribcage like it wanted out. The nightmare clung to me like a relentless echo of the past—my parents' faces twisted in horror, their voices cut short by an unseen force that had snatched them from this world five years ago. The images haunted me, blurring the lines between dream and memory, leaving a bitter taste of unresolved anguish.

Jeez, brain. Way to start the day with a bang. Or more like a whimper. At least my subconscious was consistent, serving up the same horror show on repeat.

"Bad one, huh?" Agatha asked, slinking into my bedroom. The early morning light seeping in through the blinds streaked her black fur with bands of gold. Her green eyes held a depth that seemed almost human, and she jumped up onto the bed.

"Yeah, really bad," I said, raking a hand through my hair. "Holy hell..."

"Language, young witch. And...I'm sorry about your parents."

Agatha was more than my feline familiar, she was a confidant, a fragment of sanity in my chaotic world. I reached out to scratch behind her ears, and she leaned into the touch, purring her approval.

"Right, the Echoing Locket." I slid my legs over the edge of the bed.

The power of the amulet was not lost on me, and if it fell into the wrong hands...well, we'd all be up the proverbial creek without a paddle.

A knock at the door jolted me from my thoughts, and I padded across the room, still wrestling with the tendrils of sleep. I swung the door open to find my best friend, Evie, a coffee in each hand, her hazel eyes bright.

Ah, Evie. My personal caffeine fairy. If friendship had a smell, it'd be freshly brewed coffee at stupid o'clock in the morning.

"Morning, sunshine," she greeted, pushing one of the cups into my hands. "Figured you'd need this."

The aroma of freshly brewed coffee was enough to chase away the last remnants of the nightmare.

"Thanks." I took a grateful sip. The warm liquid thawed the

coldness from the nightmare, grounding me back to reality. "Let me go change. Be right back."

I headed back to my bedroom, the wood floor cool beneath my feet. The mirror above my dresser reflected a disheveled version of me, with tangled hair and dark circles under my eyes from the remnants of sleep. I peeled off my sweat-soaked nightgown, tossing it into the laundry basket with a sigh.

Great. I looked like a zombie extra from a B-grade horror flick. Maybe I could market this as a new trend. *Nightmare Chic*. It'd be all the rage at the Institute for the Arcane Arts.

Opening the closet, I pulled out a pair of well-worn jeans and slipped them on. I paired them with a cute floral blouse that added a touch of brightness to my otherwise gloomy mood. My favorite ankle boots, scuffed but stylish, completed the outfit. I ran a brush through my hair, taming the wild strands into something more presentable, and then went into the bathroom and splashed my face with cold water to erase the last traces of the nightmare.

Feeling more like myself, I returned to the living room where Evie was waiting. She was flipping through a magazine on the coffee table, her own cup of coffee half empty.

"Ready to face the day?" she asked, looking up with a smile.

"Ready as I'll ever be." I took another sip of my coffee, feeling the warmth seep into my bones.

Evie drank her mocha latte. "I came by because I think we should start looking for the Echoing Locket. If we don't find that thing before someone uses it for nefarious purposes, Ingrid will have our heads."

I nodded. "That locket was Ingrid's pride and joy, a piece of history. The Archmage Zephyria's work, no less. We need to get to Ingrid's office. See what we can scrounge up."

"Let's do it, bestie." Evie nodded.

"Try not to bring the building down, young witch," Agatha said.

"Wouldn't dream of it, but you're coming with us." I finished my coffee and slipped on my jacket.

We stepped out into the brisk morning air, a trio bound by friendship, purpose, and the pursuit of a dangerous truth. Emberwick Crossing was waking up around us.

"Off to Ingrid's office, then?" Agatha leaped onto my shoulder, her claws gently grazing my jacket.

"Yep," I said.

My friends and I made our way up the hill towards the Institute for the Arcane Arts. The towering castle-like structure emerged against the blue morning sky, its Gothic spires piercing the clouds.

"I miss school." Evie was eyeing the grand wrought-iron gates that creaked open at our approach.

"Welcome back to college." I smiled.

We navigated through the stone corridors and spiraling staircases until we reached Ingrid's office. The door was ajar, which was unusual for someone like the High Witch, who prized privacy like a dragon hoards gold.

"Looks like the High Witch isn't here." I pushed the door open with a tentative hand.

"Or maybe she's invisible and watching us." Agatha deadpanned, jumping down off my shoulder to prowl the room.

Still feeling a little sleepy, I yawned before turning to Evie. "Let's see if there's anything weird."

Evie nodded, and we began to scour the room, looking for clues that would help us find the Echoing Locket. Everything appeared untouched. Too untouched, like a staged scene right out of a play. I moved to Ingrid's ornate desk, running my fingers over the polished surface. The neatly stacked papers and pristine quill seemed out of place for someone as busy as the High Witch. I carefully opened the top drawer, revealing an array of precisely organized scrolls and sealed letters. Each item was in perfect order, not a single piece out of alignment.

Evie rifled through the bookshelf on the opposite wall. She pulled out volumes at random, flipping through pages and checking for any hidden compartments. Her frustration grew evident as each book revealed nothing but dust and ink.

Agatha, prowling the floor with feline grace, stopped at the base of a tall cabinet. She sniffed around its edges before looking up at me with a curious glint in her eyes. "Something's off here." She meowed, her tail whooshing with impatience.

I joined her, opening the cabinet to find rows of potion bottles and labeled jars, all meticulously arranged. I carefully examined the contents and everything seemed ordinary. Closing the cabinet, I turned to Evie, who was now inspecting the large, imposing portrait of Ingrid that hung above the desk.

"Anything?" I asked, feeling a sense of urgency rise within me.

Evie shook her head, her hazel eyes reflecting our shared frustration. "This place is too perfect. It's like she knew we'd come snooping."

I approached Ingrid's personal datebook, prominently displayed on a pedestal. The book was locked, and a quick spell from Evie's hand opened it. I flipped through the pages and dates, then I noticed something odd—a torn page, seemingly ripped out in haste. It was the only imperfection in an otherwise flawless room.

I stepped away from the pedestal, showing the ripped edges to Evie. "Found something. Whatever was on this page, Ingrid didn't want anyone to see it."

Evie nodded, a grim look on her face. "I heard Freya works here part-time as healer. She might know something."

"Good call." I glanced at Agatha. "You coming?"

"If I must." My cat lifted her head from where she sniffed at the bookshelf.

We found Freya in the infirmary. She had a compassionate countenance that made people want to tell her their life story.

"Freya, hey," I greeted. "Have you noticed anything strange around Ingrid's office lately? There is a missing item, and we're trying to track down what might've happened to it."

"Not really. Only the usual enchantments." Freya's brow furrowed. "There was an odd energy the other night, though. Felt like dark magic static in the air."

Damn. Because regular magic wasn't complicated enough, now we had to deal with its evil twin.

"Static could mean a lot of things, but dark magic? That only means one thing—badness." Evie frowned, exchanging a glance with me.

Freya shrugged. "It's hard to say more without knowing the exact nature of it."

"Thanks, Freya," I said.

We left her to her duties.

"An 'odd energy' could mean someone was messing with the locket," I said.

"Or trying on new perfumes." Agatha snickered. "That office always smells like a potion gone wrong."

"Helpful as ever." I rolled my eyes.

"Let's go back and—" Evie stopped mid-sentence.

Professor Elderwood emerged from a nearby classroom, his auburn hair a disheveled halo around his head.

"Professor Elderwood, do you have a sec?" I called out.

"Ah, Miss Holland, what can I do for you?" He lifted a hand, adjusting his glasses in a distracted manner.

"Did you notice anything unusual around Ingrid's office recently?"

He scratched his cheek. "Um, yes... dark energies were amiss." He sighed. "Your parents, bless their souls, they knew how to read the signs. Used to frequent an old bookshop for rare magical texts. Might hold some clues to this darker energy."

My chest tightened at the mention of my parents. Their absence felt like a perpetual stubbed toe on my heart.

"In Emberwick Crossing?" Evie slanted her head.

"Yes, indeedy! Mystic Tomes, it's called. Now run by a peculiar little man, but don't let appearances deceive you... because...because..." Professor Elderwood said, his voice trailing off. "Now I can't remember. Anyway, you should check there, kids."

"Thank you, Professor," I said.

"Anytime, anytime...and do visit the bookshop." Professor Elderwood was wandering off in his own world again.

"Looks like we've got our next stop," Evie said.

"Let's just hope this isn't another wild broom chase," Agatha muttered.

I laughed.

"Better than a snipe hunt," Agatha said, sashaying ahead of us.

We made our way out of the Institute for the Arcane Arts with a new lead and walked back into town.

The door of Mystic Tomes creaked ominously when we stepped into the brightly lit bookshop. The perfume of aged paper mixed with the subtle tang of magic filled the air, a cocktail for the senses that made my skin tingle with anticipation. Rows upon rows of ancient tomes and leather-bound volumes lined the shelves. Dust motes danced in the sunlight streaming through the large, arched windows, creating an almost ethereal glow.

My eyes were drawn to the far corner where a small reading nook was located, complete with overstuffed armchairs and a cold fireplace. The walls were adorned with intricate tapestries depicting scenes from magical history, and every available surface was cluttered with stacks of books.

The shop's owner stood behind the counter, his long, white beard flowing down to his chest and his brown eyes bright. He gave us a nod, then went back to sorting through a new shipment.

We moved further into the bookshop, each step on the groaning wooden floorboards seeming to echo throughout the building. I half expected the floor to give way and dump us into some magical basement filled with talking books and snarky bookworms.

"Feels like stepping into a forgotten world," Evie whispered, her gaze sweeping over the spines of countless books.

"Or a dust mite's paradise." Agatha was perched on my

shoulder, her eyes glinting in the brilliant morning light filtering through the stained-glass windows.

I grinned at her dry humor.

We moved deeper into the warren of bookshelves, each one packed with volumes. I felt a buzz under my skin, a tingling sensation tickling my fingertips every time they brushed against the leather-bound spines.

Great. I liked that my magic was acting up like an overexcited puppy in a park full of squirrels. This was going to be fun.

"Whoa! Do you guys feel that?" My voice was hushed.

"Feel what? The overwhelming urge to sneeze?" Agatha glanced around with a hunter's focus.

"Your intuition kicking in, Sage?" Evie's hazel eyes met mine.

"Something's calling out to me." I frowned, following the feeling until my hand landed on an out-of-place grimoire, its cover less dusty than the others.

Typical. Of all the books in this magical library, I just had to pick the one that screamed "danger" louder than a banshee at a rock concert.

"Odd duck out, huh?" Evie leaned closer.

I pulled the book from its slot. It fell open to a page marked by a cryptic note, symbols floating and glowing before our eyes —clear signs of powerful magic at play.

Nothing said *relaxing day out* quite like stumbling upon ancient, potentially world-ending magic. Mom and Dad would be so proud.

"The Archmage Zephyria." I instantly recognized the sigils associated with the legendary witch who vanished without a trace. "Could this be connected to the Echoing Locket?"

"Did you say The Archmage? Oh, no, young witch, this is like finding a needle in a haystack...if the needle was also trying to poke your eyes out," Agatha said, her whiskers twitching.

Leave it to Agatha to sum up our predicament with a dash of sarcasm and a pinch of impending doom. I couldn't decide whether to laugh or start planning my will.

"Looks like more than just bedtime stories for dark witches." Evie moved closer, leaning in to study the fragmented messages.

I bit my lip, trying to process the gravity of our discovery. We were just two witches and a witchy cat, stumbling upon what could be the magical equivalent of a ticking time bomb. And to think, I'd woken up this morning worried about whether I'd remembered to water my plants.

"Let's take this with us. We need time to decode it." I tucked the note into my pocket after purchasing the grimoire

I noticed the shopkeeper eyeing us with an unreadable expression. "Careful, witches," he warned in a gravelly voice.

"Careful is my middle name," I replied.

"More like Reckless," Agatha murmured.

I grinned. "Let's not argue semantics now, Agatha."

We stepped outside the bookshop and froze.

"Think you're going somewhere?" a masked figure snarled, emerging from the shadows with three others clad in dark clothing, bearing the emblem of the supernatural uprising.

"Evie, get ready," I whispered, my heart pounding in my chest.

"Shadow playtime!" Agatha hissed, slinking off my shoulder and melding into the shadows around the building.

Overhead, the sun rose higher in the sky as it neared afternoon.

"Let's have some fun." Evie smirked, rolling her shoulders.

"Bring it on." I backed up, conjuring a shield of whirling scripts and glyphs around us.

"Look at the little witches and their parlor tricks," one of the attackers mocked, lunging forward with a blade shimmering with dark energy.

"Watch it, that's not child's play. Well, not really. "Evie retorted, dodging and weaving through the assault, her potions at the ready.

I cast a spell that solidified the air around one assailant, trapping him in place.

"Nice trick, young witch." Agatha purred from the shadows, her own magic entwining with the enemies feet, causing them to stumble.

"Keep them busy!" I shouted, throwing another spell that burst into blinding light, disorienting the attackers.

"Okay!" Evie called out, her concoctions turning one assailant into a harmless, if rather large, fluffy bunny.

"Should've brought more than knives to a magic fight," I taunted, feeling adrenaline surge through me as we fought tooth and nail against the mysterious aggressors.

"Remember, Sage, no collective triumph," Agatha reminded me, a wry edge to her voice despite the chaos.

"Wouldn't dream of it," I promised, as we each held our ground.

The air fizzed with magical electricity. I deflected another attack, my shield of glyphs shimmering with each impact. One of the masked figures lunged at me, dark magic swirling around their fists.

"Sage, watch out!" Evie yelled.

I ducked, the attacker's fist sailing over my head. "Thanks for the heads up!"

"Anytime, bestie." Evie grinned, hurling a potion that exploded into a cloud of rainbow smoke.

Two assailants stumbled out, coughing and disoriented. One had sprouted donkey ears, and the other now sported a peacock tail.

I grinned. "Cute look. Really brings out your eyes...I mean masks."

"Enough games!" the leader snarled, conjuring a whip of crackling power.

I raised my hands, ready to counter, when Agatha's voice purred from the shadows. "Allow me, Sage."

A tendril of darkness shot out from Agatha, wrapping around the whip and yanking it from the attacker's grasp.

"Oops. Butter paws." Agatha snickered.

The leader growled in frustration. "Take them down!"

The four assailants charged, magic pulsing from their hands. I braced myself, drawing on my power to craft a new spell.

"Hey, uglies!" Evie shouted, lobbing another potion. "Catch!"

The vial shattered at their feet, releasing a swarm of glowing butterflies. The delicate insects swarmed the attackers, their wings leaving trails of sparkling dust.

"Aw, how sweet," I teased. "They like you."

One of the masked figures sneezed violently, stumbling backward. "What is this stuff?"

Evie smirked. "Just a little pixie dust. Side effects may

include sneezing, itching, and sudden urges to frolic in meadows."

I seized the opportunity, weaving a complex pattern in the air. The ground beneath the attackers' feet softened, transforming into sticky taffy.

"What the hell?" one yelped, struggling to lift their feet.

"Sage, you genius!" Evie cackled. "Now that's what I call a sticky situation!"

I grinned but my victory was short-lived. The leader raised his hands, dark energy sizzling and sparking between his palms. "Enough of this nonsense!" he roared.

A wave of black magic exploded outward, shattering my taffy trap and sending us flying backward. I hit the ground hard, the breath knocked from my lungs.

"Sage!" Evie called out, scrambling to her feet.

I pushed myself up, wincing. "I'm okay. Where's Agatha?"

A low growl answered my question. Agatha materialized from the shadows, fur standing on end. "Right here, Sage. And not amused."

The leader of the masked group stalked forward, dark energy swirling around them like a malevolent aura. "You've been a thorn in our side for too long. It's time to end this."

I stood my ground, magic tingling at my fingertips. "Bring it on, ugly."

The leader's hands shot forward, tendrils of darkness lashing out like venomous snakes. I threw up a hasty shield, the impact making my teeth rattle.

Evie darted to the side, fumbling with her potions. "I'm running low here, guys!"

"Then make it count!" I shouted, reinforcing my shield while another barrage of dark magic slammed into it.

Agatha's voice echoed from my side. "Perhaps it's time for a change of tactics, kittens."

Before I could ask what she meant, Agatha burst from the darkness, growing to the size of a panther. She pounced on one of the masked figures, her shadowy form passing right through him.

The attacker screamed, his body convulsing as Agatha's magic coursed through him. The man collapsed, twitching.

"Holy crap, Agatha!" Evie exclaimed. "Since when could you do that?"

Agatha's disembodied voice chuckled. "A lady never reveals all her secrets, honey."

The remaining attackers hesitated, clearly unnerved by Agatha's display. I seized the moment, channeling my power into a new spell.

"Hey, mask squad!" I called out. "Ever wonder what it's like to be a pinball?"

I clapped my hands together, and suddenly the air around us solidified into shimmering, translucent walls. The attackers found themselves trapped in a giant, magical pinball machine.

"Evie, now!" I yelled.

My best friend grinned, pulling out her last potion. "Time for the grand finale!"

She hurled the vial into the center of my magical construct. It exploded in a burst of swirling, kaleidoscopic energy. The masked figures were sent ricocheting off the walls, bouncing wildly when my magic and Evie's potion combined into a dizzying light show.

"Woo! High score!" Evie cheered.

I maintained the spell, sweat beading on my forehead. I kept the magical pinball machine running. "Agatha, a little help here?"

"With pleasure, young witch."

Shadows coalesced around the bouncing attackers, forming into ghostly hands that grabbed and spun them, adding to their disorientation.

The leader, however, wasn't going down without a fight. They managed to steady themselves mid-bounce, dark magic crackling around them.

"Enough!" they roared, releasing a pulse of energy that shattered my spell.

The magical walls dissipated, and our opponents tumbled to the ground, groaning and disoriented. All except the leader, who stood tall, radiating fury.

"You think this is a game?" he snarled. "You have no idea what forces you're dealing with!"

I stepped forward, magic swirling around my hands. "Why don't you enlighten us then? Who are you working for?"

The leader laughed, a cold, mirthless sound. "You'll find out soon enough. This was just a taste of what's to come."

The mages raised their hands, sinister power gathering between their palms. I braced myself for another attack, but instead, the energy exploded outward in a blinding flash. When the spots cleared from my vision, the masked figures were gone.

"Well, that was dramatic." Evie sighed, brushing dust off her clothes.

I nodded, the adrenaline slowly fading. "Yeah, but they got away. And we're no closer to figuring out what's going on."

Agatha materialized beside me, back in her normal cat form. "Don't be so sure, young witch. I managed to snag a little souvenir."

She dropped something at my feet—a small, silver pin bearing the emblem of the supernatural uprising.

I picked it up, turning it over in my hand. "Nice work, Agatha."

"Always happy to help. Now, I believe I was promised tuna for my efforts?"

Evie laughed. "Guys, what do we do now? Those creeps know where to find us."

I pocketed the pin, my mind racing. "We need to tell the High Witch."

"And tell Brad," Evie added. "He needs to know what's going on."

I nodded, trying to ignore the flutter in my chest at the mention of Brad's name. "Right. Let's get outta here before they want a rematch."

The afternoon air had a chill to it, biting at my exposed skin. Agatha, Evie and I trudged down the streets that led back to mine and Agatha's place. Agatha sauntered beside me, while Evie's boots clicked loudly against the stone.

"Trouble has a scent, and I smell it on you three."

I turned, finding Councilman Alden Voss materializing from the trees, his presence like a dark cloud descending upon us. He stood tall, his tailored suit impeccable despite the late hour, eyes sharp and beady under the elegant sweep of his dark hair streaked with silver.

Fantastic. The universe decided we hadn't suffered enough for one day. It had to throw Mr. Perfect-Hair-Even-in-a-Hurricane at us too.

"It is time that you stay out of matters that don't concern you, Ms. Holland." The Councilman's voice dripped with condescension. "The locket is not your concern."

I crossed my arms and glared at the enemy. "Geeze, if it isn't Mr. Sunshine himself. And here I thought we'd get home without any more drama."

My sass-o-meter was cranked up to eleven. Probably not the smartest move when facing a powerful warlock, but hey, go big or go home, right?

"Your levity is misplaced," Councilman Voss said coldly. "The path you're on is fraught with peril. It would be...unfortunate, should you continue to interfere."

"Is that a threat, Councilman?" Evie huffed, stepping forward with a hint of a threat in her voice.

You tell him, Evie. I'd hug her if I wasn't worried about ruining her intimidating stance. But, hey, no pressure or anything. Just the fate of the magical world potentially hanging in the balance. You know, typical witchtastic stuff.

"Consider it sage advice." His lips curled into an oily smirk.

"Ooh, Sage advice. Get it?" Agatha laughed dryly. "Because our Sage always needs guidance from the likes of you, Councilman."

I could always count on Agatha to throw a verbal grenade into tense situations. It was like having a sarcastic, furry bodyguard.

I lifted my chin. "I appreciate your concern, but I can handle myself."

The words came out strongly, but inside I felt like a wobbly Jenga tower. One wrong move, and I'd crumble. But if there was one thing I'd learned, it's that sometimes you gotta bluff your way through life's poker game.

Fake it 'til you make it. I hoped my bravado wasn't as transparent as it felt.

"Very well." Councilman Voss gave a curt nod, his blue stare and hard and ominous. "But remember, some secrets are best left buried—with those who guard them."

I rolled my eyes. I swear, these Council types must have a guidebook for ominous one-liners.

I clenched my fists, feeling the magic surge through me. "Buried secrets? That's rich coming from you, Councilman. I bet you've got enough skeletons in your closet to start a dance troupe."

Magic tingled in my fingertips, a reminder of the power I held. It was both thrilling and terrifying, like riding a roller coaster blindfolded.

Councilman Voss' nostrils flared, a crack in his polished facade. "You're treading on thin ice, Ms. Holland."

"Good thing I'm a pro at ice skating," I shot back, adrenaline making me bolder.

Where was this sass coming from? It was like my mouth had a mind of its own, spitting out quips faster than I could think them up. Part of me wanted to high-five myself, while another part was screaming to shut up before I dug my grave deeper.

Evie snorted, her hand on my shoulder. "Careful, Sage. His ego might melt that ice."

Agatha stretched lazily, her tail swishing. "Yes, I'd say his ego's big enough to sink the Titanic, but that'd be an insult to icebergs everywhere."

"Such insolence," Councilman Voss hissed, his composure slipping. "You have no idea what forces you're meddling with."

I scoffed. Please. I've dealt with worse things in the Institute's cafeteria. But a nagging voice in the back of my head wondered if I was in over my head this time.

I rolled my eyes. "Oh, please. Spare us the cryptic villain monologue. We've all seen this movie before."

"Yeah," Evie chimed in. "Next, you'll be twirling your mustache and tying someone to train tracks."

Councilman Voss' face darkened. "You find this amusing? Your ignorance is truly staggering."

More like willful defiance. But with each passing moment, I felt the gravity of the situation sinking in. This wasn't just another Council squabble. Something bigger was brewing, and I was stirring the pot.

I stepped back. "Nah. What's staggering is how you manage to fit that massive ego through doorways."

The Councilman's hands began to glow with an ominous orange fire. "Perhaps a demonstration of the stakes is in order."

Oh, crap. This was escalating faster than a magical duel at the Academy. My heart pounded, but I forced my face to remain neutral. No way was I giving him the satisfaction of seeing me sweat.

Evie tensed beside me. "Whoa there, Sparky. Let's not do anything hasty."

I raised an eyebrow at Councilman Voss. "Resorting to violence already? And here I thought we were having such a lovely chat."

Councilman Voss snarled. "Your flippancy will be your downfall."

Evie crossed her arms. "And your condescension will be yours. We're not backing down."

"Yeah," Agatha added. "So why don't you take your fancy suit and inflated sense of self-importance elsewhere?"

Councilman Voss's lip curled. "You're making a grave mistake, children."

I shrugged. "Wouldn't be the first time. But at least my mistakes don't involve bad hair dye and megalomania."

My heart thumped wildly, a mix of adrenaline and defiance coursing through me. Part of me knew I should probably shut up, but the words tumbled out anyway. Voss's condescension always brought out my snarkiest side.

The Councilman's face flushed an impressive shade of crimson. "You insolent little bitch—"

"Now, now," Agatha interrupted. "No need for name-calling. Though if we're going there, I've got a few choice ones for you, Councilman."

Councilman Voss took a deep breath, visibly trying to regain his composure. "This petty banter changes nothing. The locket is beyond your comprehension."

I snorted. "Right. Because only the almighty Voss can possibly understand its immense power. Give me a break."

I wanted to believe I could handle it, but doubt gnawed at the edges of my confidence. What if Voss was right?

Councilman Voss sneered. "Your mockery only proves my point. You're children playing with forces beyond your control."

Evie stepped forward, her voice steely. "And you're an adult throwing a temper tantrum because we won't play by your rules."

Councilman Voss' hands clenched at his sides. "You will regret this defiance. You foolish children have no idea what's coming. The Archmage will—" He cut himself off abruptly, but the damage was done.

We all froze, the cheeky atmosphere evaporating in an instant.

"Archmage Zephyria?" I repeated, my voice barely above a whisper. "As in, the same The Archmage who vanished after the Great Magical Schism?"

My mind reeled, struggling to process this info. The Archmage was supposed to be a myth, a boogeyman to scare young witches. If she were really alive and real and involved in this mess, we were in way, way over our heads.

Councilman Voss' face had gone pale. "I've said nothing."

Agatha's fur stood on end. "Oh, you've said plenty, Councilman. Seems like the cat's out of the bag...and this cat wants answers."

"Spill it, Voss," Evie demanded, all traces of humor gone from her voice. "What's Archmage, the High Witch's sister, got to do with any of this?"

The Councilman's jaw clenched. "This conversation is over."

I stepped forward, my heart pounding. "Like hell it is. You can't drop a bomb like that and just walk away."

Panic clawed at my throat. We needed answers, and Voss was our only lead. I couldn't let him slip away, not when we were so close to uncovering the truth.

"Watch me." Councilman Voss huffed, raising his hands.

A gust of wind whipped around us, and before we could react, the Councilman vanished in a swirl of leaves and magic.

"Well, shit," I muttered, staring at the spot where he'd been.

Frustration and fear battled for dominance in my chest. We'd pushed too hard, and now Voss was in the wind with all his secrets. I felt like we'd just lost our only chance at understanding what we were up against.

Evie turned to me, her face grim. "Sage, what do we do now?"

I took a deep breath. "We find out everything we can about Archmage and her connection to the locket. And we do it fast."

"Before Voss and his cronies can stop us." Evie squeezed my shoulder. "Hey, we've got this. Team Badass Witches, remember?"

I couldn't help smiling. "Yeah, Team Badass Witches. With one token warlock—Brad."

Evie cleared her throat. "We should probably get moving. Who knows how long before Voss sends reinforcements?"

"Right." I nodded, squaring my shoulders. "Let's bounce before things get even messier."

Agatha sighed. "Well, he was about as subtle as a unicorn at a horse race. I'd have to be an idiot not to pick up on that thinly veiled threat."

Unfortunately for him, subtlety and I were only nodding acquaintances.

The locket, the secrets, the veiled threats—it was like trying to solve a jigsaw puzzle in the dark while wearing oven mitts.

Agatha strolled ahead on the sidewalk. "Well, that was fun. Nothing like a cryptic warning from a power-hungry warlock to really spice up an evening stroll."

I snorted and started walking again. "Yeah, because our lives weren't exciting enough already. We should send him a thank you note for livening things up."

"Ooh, can I dictate it?" Evie clapped her hands and kept pace beside me. "Dear Councilman Voss, thanks for the ominous warning. We were worried we might have a peaceful afternoon for once. Kisses, your favorite troublemakers."

I cracked a smile. Leave it to Agatha and Evie to find humor in the face of danger. It was probably why we got along so well. That and Agatha's inexplicable ability to always know where I'd hidden the good snacks.

Evie sighed, her earlier bravado fading into weariness. "We should get moving. I don't fancy another run-in with any more Council members or their lackeys."

I nodded. "I've had my fill of cryptic warnings for one day. Let's go home and figure out our next move."

The tension in my shoulders eased a bit at the thought of retreating to familiar territory. Home meant safety, a place where we could regroup and strategize without looking over our shoulders every two seconds. Plus, I was dying for a cup of chamomile tea and maybe some of those cookies Evie pretended not to like but always managed to sneak when she thought I wasn't looking.

Evie frowned, tucking a lock of her jet-black hair behind her ear. "His threats barely masked his own fear. What do you think he's so desperate to hide?"

"Well, we already know he's involved with the supernatural uprising, and possibly he's connected to that locket," I replied.

"Careful, young witch," Agatha warned, her yellow eyes

462

gleaming. "You're playing with fire, and not just because Councilman Voss loves his little pyrotechnics."

I shrugged. "Then let's not get burned. He doesn't scare me...well, maybe a little. We need to find out what they're planning. If the Echoing Locket is involved, we could be facing something big—something that could change everything for the magical community."

"Or end it," Evie said gravely. "The stakes are sky-high, Sage."

A small voice in the back of my head whispered that maybe we should be more scared. After all, we were up against powerful forces with unknown motives, but fear wouldn't solve anything. Action would.

"I know. We've got each other's backs, remember?"

"Of course, yeah." Evie smiled, though worry shadowed her features.

I wished I could erase that worry from her face. Evie had always been the cautious one, the voice of reason to balance out my impulsiveness.

"Let's just hope our backs are fireproof," Agatha said, already moving ahead. "Come on, witches. We've got work to do."

I thrust a fist in the air and made a joke. "Watch out, magical world. The troublemakers are on the case, and we aren't about to let a little thing like mortal peril stop us."

This was bigger than anything we'd faced before, but it was also a chance to prove ourselves, to make a difference. And if we happened to uncover some juicy magical secrets along the way? Well, that was just a bonus.

We reached my home just as the afternoon sunlight beamed

down on us, splashing the sky with yellows and oranges. My house, a cozy cottage with an overgrown garden, felt like a vacay after the day's chaos. After everything that had happened, I craved the comfort of my own space like a warm hug.

"Welcome to the witches' den," I announced, pushing open the door. "Let's crack this code."

I took the note from my pocket and set the grimoire it came in on the coffee table. The cryptic note was spread out on the surface, its symbols seemingly mocking us with their secrets. Agatha hopped onto the table and hissed. Evie turned on the bright overhead lights, and I opened the curtains to let the sunshine into the room.

The symbols on the paper seemed to dance under the light, taunting me with their hidden meaning. A mix of excitement and dread churned in my gut. Whatever this message held, it was big. Like, change-our-lives-forever big.

"All right, let's put my family's translation spell to the test," I said, reaching for my late grandmother's grimoire. The ancient leather-bound book was stiff as I flipped through the pages, finding the incantation passed down through generations.

Gram's presence seemed to linger in every word, guiding me. I took a deep breath, steadying myself for whatever we were about to uncover.

"Here it is," I said, feeling the spark of magic tingling at my fingertips. "Linguae antiquitatis, revelare veritatem."

The room thrummed with energy. The symbols on the paper began to shimmer and twist, rearranging themselves into words I could understand. "Holy crap." I blinked, my eyes widening. "It says...'Archmage lives.'"

My heart skipped a beat. Archmage? The boogeyman of the magical world was real and alive? That was next-level bonkers.

"Like, literally?" Evie peered over my shoulder.

"Looks like it. And if she's alive..." I swallowed hard, unsure how to process the bombshell we'd just uncovered.

A chill ran through me as the implications hit. If Archmage was out there, everything we thought we knew about our world could be a lie. Talk about an existential crisis.

"Then all our worst nightmares are having a party," Agatha finished flatly.

Evie grimaced. "Just when you thought things couldn't get more warped."

"Okay, I think it's time to scry." I stood up, moving to set up the crystal ball that had been passed down my family line for who knew how long. The orb was etched with delicate patterns, each swirl and line holding the weight of my ancestors' gaze.

This wasn't just any scrying session, we were potentially peeking into the darkest corners of our world. But someone had to do it, right? Might as well be the girl with a knack for stumbling into trouble.

"Be careful, Sage. Scrying can attract unwanted attention," Agatha warned.

I swallowed hard, trying to ignore the swarm of butterflies in my stomach. Agatha's warning echoed my own fears, but I couldn't let that stop me. We needed answers, and I was determined to find them.

"Relax. We're just going to take a little peek," I reassured her, though my heart thumped hard.

Nervously, I focused on the crystal ball, letting my magic flow freely. The mist within churned then cleared, revealing an image of Archmage Zephyria. She stood in a dark room adorned with occult symbols, speaking to a shadowy figure.

My breath caught in my throat. Archmage was alive and right in front of us. Part of me wanted to look away, to pretend I hadn't seen her, but I forced myself to keep watching, knowing that ignorance wouldn't protect us.

"Be extra cautious." Archmage's voice came through, cold and calculated. "The Echoing Locket is key to our uprising. We must not falter now."

"Who's she talking to?" Evie whispered.

"Can't see their face. But whoever they are, they're part of the supernatural uprising movement," I replied.

A coldness ran through me. I realized the enormity of what we were witnessing. This wasn't just some small-time magical mischief, this was a full-blown conspiracy that could change everything.

"Probably another Council member," Agatha said, her tone dripping with disdain. "Birds of a feather plot tyranny together."

"Shh, I'm trying to listen," I said.

"Ensure the preparations are complete now that I have the locket back from my sister," Archmage continued. "And remember, discretion is paramount. We cannot afford another setback."

"Setback? I wonder what happened?" Evie murmured.

"Could be thanks to us," I said with a smirk.

A spark of pride flickered in my chest. Maybe we weren't just bumbling around in the dark after all. Maybe we were actually making a difference, even if we didn't realize it.

"Or someone else is working against them," Agatha said.

Brad? Was he working alone on this?

"Either way, we know what we're up against now," I said, pulling away from the crystal ball. "Archmage is alive, and she's planning something big. Really big...with the locket."

"Then we're all screwed," Evie said, setting her jaw.

"You can say that again," Agatha said. "The game is afoot. And we'll need every ounce of magic and wit to stay one step ahead."

I felt a fire kindled in my chest. A burning desire to uncover the truth and protect the only world I'd ever loved.

We'd gone looking for answers and found a whole new set of questions instead. But at least now we had a direction, a purpose.

THREE

I had just finished aligning the living room chakras with a new spell when the knock came. There was no mistaking that rhythm—it had the same cadence as my heartbeat whenever I thought of finding the Echoing Locket. A little rush of excitement fluttered in my chest as I opened the door to find Brad standing there looking like an Abercrombie model who'd lost his way and ended up in our quaint magical suburb.

My breath caught in my throat. Damn, why did he have to show up now looking like a snack?

Just when I thought I'd mastered the art of magical feng shui, here came Brad to shake up my carefully arranged chi. It

469

was like the universe had a twisted sense of humor. But I couldn't deny the spark of joy his presence ignited.

"Hey, stranger," I said, leaning against the door frame. My gaze swept over him—spiky dark brown hair that looked like it had been styled by a tempest, those sexy blue eyes, and casual clothes that somehow accentuated his well-built frame. He wore a simple white tee that hugged his biceps in all the right ways and jeans that were lovingly frayed at the edges. "Lost your way to the gym?" I teased.

I bit my lip, trying to keep my cool. It was like he'd stepped out of my daydreams, all rugged charm and effortless sex appeal. The Covenant of Veiled Boundaries could go stuff itself for all I cared in that moment. I inwardly groaned. Maybe next I could ask him to flex, just to really drive home how not affected I am.

The Covenant, aka the ultimate relationship cockblock of the magical world. They probably had a secret division dedicated to ruining moments like these. I could almost picture their slogan: *Keeping hot warlocks and witches apart since forever.*

He flashed me that lopsided grin, the one that always made me feel like we were two steps away from trouble. "Nah, just taking the scenic route to see you."

My heart did a little somersault. How did he always manage to say the right thing? It was infuriating and intoxicating all at once.

"Enter at your own risk." I smiled, stepping aside to let him in.

Hells bells, did he have to look so damn good? The Witch's Council would have a field day if they knew what kind of impure thoughts were swirling in my head about the boy next door.

"Nice place you got here." Brad whistled appreciatively as he strolled into the living room in my magically enhanced abode. "New spell work?"

Pride swelled in my chest. I'd poured my heart into this space, infusing every corner with a piece of myself. It was more than just décor, it was an extension of my magic, my soul. But at least someone appreciated my magical OCD. I was a regular mystical Martha Stewart.

"Perks of being an interior designer with a knack for enchantments." I gave him a nonchalant shrug while closing the door behind him.

It had been a month since he'd dropped the L-bomb, and I'd thrown it right back like a hot potato. I'd told him I had to let him go, but it hurt. Easier said than done.

A month. Four weeks of pretending I didn't miss him, of telling myself I made the right choice. And here he was, looking like a walking reminder of everything I'd given up. The universe really had a sick sense of humor. Or maybe it was just testing my resolve. Either way, I was pretty sure I was failing spectacularly.

"How've you been?" He was leaning against my bookshelf lined with ancient tomes and modern spell books alike.

Such a loaded question. I missed him so much my heart ached. Memories flooded back—passionate kisses, late-night dates that turned into make out sessions. But those days were gone, crushed under the burden of duty and ancient laws. I swallowed hard, pushing down the lump in my throat.

"Um." I pushed a blue-streaked lock of hair behind my ear. "Still looking for the Echoing Locket."

Brad nodded, his expression turning serious. "Which is why

I'm here. I want to help if I can. You know, keep it out of the wrong hands?"

His offer to help sent a spark of affection through me, quickly doused by the cold reality of our situation. The Covenant of Veiled Boundaries loomed between us like an invisible wall.

"Brad, you know we can't be more than friends—" I said.

He cut me off, "Hey, I get it. Star-crossed lovers, different magical backgrounds, blah, blah, blah." His voice was gentle but firm. "But this isn't about us, Sage. It's bigger than some high school romance rekindled. We've got skills that complement each other, and you know it."

His words hit home. We did make a great team. But working together would be like dangling a cookie in front of a starving person—pure torture.

"High school romance, huh?" I smirked, rolling my eyes. "Is that what we're calling it now?"

"Call it whatever you want, but we were high school sweethearts," he said, stepping closer. Close enough for me to catch a whiff of his cologne—sandalwood, musk, and something uniquely Brad and extra yummy. It took every ounce of willpower not to lean in closer. I was playing with fire and I knew it. "But you can't deny we make a pretty damn good team."

I wanted to reach out, to touch him, but I clenched my fists instead. The fate of Emberwick Crossing was at stake.

I sighed with mock seriousness, tapping my chin. "Okay, partner. Let's find that locket. But remember, we're strictly in the friend zone. The High Witch would have our heads otherwise."

"Scout's honor," he replied, holding up three fingers and winking.

"Did you ever even go to Scouts?" I laughed, shaking my head.

He grinned. "Details, details."

"Purely platonic," I reiterated, my voice wavering. "We're in this for the greater good, not for...whatever we had."

Brad nodded, his lips quirking into a half-smile. "Platonic partners in supernatural crime-fighting."

Though my resolve wavered when he flashed that boyish grin that always melted my defenses.

I swallowed hard. "All right then. Now, about that lead—"

"Wait," Brad interrupted, stepping closer. "Before we dive into all that, I just want to say...I missed you, Sage. A lot."

My heart somersaulted in my chest. "I missed you too, Brad. More than you know."

He closed the distance between us in two strides, his eyes searching mine. "Sage," he whispered, his breath warm on my cheek.

Then his lips were on mine, and the world fell away. The kiss was electric, fierce and passionate. It ignited something primal within me, a hunger I'd tried to bury. His hands found my waist, pulling me closer, and I melted into him. I ran my fingers through his hair, relishing its softness. Brad's stubble scratched my chin, sending tingles across my skin. He tasted like mint and possibility, familiar yet thrilling. It felt like coming home after a long journey, only to realize the place I'd left was where I belonged all along.

We broke apart, both breathless. Brad rested his forehead against mine, his chest rising and falling rapidly.

"Wow," I murmured, my lips still tingling.

Brad chuckled softly. "Yeah, wow."

Reality came crashing back. I stepped away, wrapping my arms around myself. "Brad, we can't—"

"I know," he said, his voice husky. "But damn, I needed that."

"Me too," I admitted, my chest tight with regret and longing. "But it can't happen again. You know the rules."

Brad ran a hand through his hair, messing it up in that adorable way I loved. "Screw the rules, Sage. This feels right."

I shook my head even as every fiber of my wanted to kiss him again. "The High Witch would never allow it. We'd be risking everything."

"Maybe it's worth the risk," Brad said, his tone serious. He took my hand, his thumb tracing circles on my palm. "Don't you ever wonder what we could be if we gave us a real shot?"

I bit my lip, fighting the urge to throw caution to the wind. "Of course, I do. But we have responsibilities, Brad. The supernatural uprising, the fate of the magical community, the law forbidding us to be together...it's bigger than the both of us."

Brad's shoulders slumped. "You're right, as always." He managed a weak smile. "Doesn't make it any easier, though."

I squeezed his hand. "I know. But hey, at least we get to work together, right? Platonic partners and all that."

"Yeah," Brad said, brightening a little. "So, about that lead..."

"Right, the lead," I said, trying to regain my composure. "What did you find?"

"It was in an old journal, buried under a pile of forgotten lore in the library's hidden chamber that once belonged to the apprentice of Archmage, who we know mysteriously vanished into Emberwick Crossing's underbelly."

I kept stealing glances at him. The way his brow furrowed in concentration, the slight quirk of his lips when he was thinking...it was all so achingly him.

"Go on," I urged.

Brad paced. "The apprentice wrote about an older district that even the locals avoided. A place where our infamous Archmage dabbled in dark magic and plotted for power."

"Sounds charming. And you think that's where we'll find the Echoing Locket?"

"Maybe. It's our best shot," he replied. "We should definitely check it out. But, uh, maybe we should bring back-up this time? After what happened last month with that rogue pixie swarm..."

I laughed, the tension between us easing. "Don't tell me you're still sore about that."

Brad rubbed his arm, wincing dramatically. "Hey, those little guys pack a punch! I had welts for days."

"Poor baby," I teased. "Next time, I'll be sure to kiss it better."

The words slipped out before I could stop them. Brad's gaze snapped to mine, and the air between us charged once more.

"Sage," he said, his voice low and rough.

I held up a hand. "I know, I know. Just kidding. Platonic, remember?"

Brad nodded but his gaze lingered on my lips. "Right. Platonic."

We stood there for a moment.

Finally, I cleared my throat. "So, um, about that back-up. I was thinking we could go it alone this time."

"Good idea," Brad agreed. "But Evie's potions have saved our butts more times than I can count."

I grinned. "True. Remember that time she turned that angry troll into a fluffy hamster?"

Brad laughed, the sound warming me from the inside out. "How could I forget? The look on its face was priceless."

But reality had a way of intruding. My familiar, Agatha, sauntered into the room, fixing us with a knowing stare. "Well, well," she drawled. "Isn't this cozy? Should I come back later, or are you two done swooning over each other?"

I felt my cheeks heat up. "We weren't...I mean... we're just—"

"Discussing strategy," Brad finished smoothly.

Agatha's tail swished skeptically. "Uh-huh. And I suppose that 'strategy' involved swapping saliva?"

"Agatha!" I hissed, mortified.

Brad coughed, avoiding my gaze. "Are you ready to take a little carpet ride?"

"Are we talking about that ratty old thing your dad calls *transportation*?" I teased.

"Hey, it gets the job done," Brad defended with a chuckle. "Just hold on tight."

I grinned, grabbing my coat. We stepped out the door, leaving behind the warmth of my living room and the lingering heat of our forbidden kiss.

Brad turned back to me on the porch, his expression soft. "For what it's worth, I don't regret it. Any of it."

My heart swelled. "Me either," I whispered.

The abandoned district of the manufacturing area of Emberwick Crossing swallowed us whole, a desolate expanse of decay where magic hung heavy in the air like a suffocating mist. Once resplendent structures now stood as crumbling sentinels to a bygone era, their facades marred by the relentless passage of time and dark spells. A pervasive sense of foreboding crept over me as we navigated the twisted streets, strewn with debris from failed enchantments and littered with the remnants of protective hexes.

"Can you feel that?" I murmured, my senses prickling.

"Like static on my skin," Brad replied, scanning our surroundings with cautious intensity.

We landed on a patch of weeds and overgrown grass and stepped off. The carpet curled up and zoomed away.

Brad frowned. "Damn. Now we need to find another way home," he grumbled.

We picked our way through the ruins. Suddenly guardians—nightmarish creatures twisted by dark magic, appeared.

"Holy hell," I said, staring at the first ghastly figure.

A wolf with scales shimmering in the dim light prowled forward, its red eyes seething with hatred. The second creature, more humanoid in shape, dragged its elongated limbs across the pavement, claws scraping, its body slick with an oil that sizzled upon contact with the ground.

"These creatures... I've heard about them," Brad said, his voice tense as he eyed the monstrous forms. "They are loyal servants to Archmage. But now, they've been corrupted by her dark magic."

I glanced at him. "What does that mean for us?"

"It means they'll stop at nothing to protect their master's secrets," Brad replied grimly.

"Watch out for that icky stuff," I warned, pointing at the corrosive liquid pooling around our feet.

"Got it." Brad nodded, positioning himself back-to-back with me.

The third monstrosity loomed larger than the others, like a golem made of stone and mud, constantly shifting shape as if deciding which form would best spell our doom.

"Party crashers are the worst," Brad said, readjusting his stance.

I extended my hands, drawing upon my magic. "You take Tall, Dark, and Ugly. I've got Scales and Oily."

"Copy that."

The battle was swift and brutal. We moved in unison, spells and counterspells weaving an intricate tapestry of survival. With every incantation, I poured my will into subduing these abominations of nature, while Brad summoned barriers and constructs to deflect our assailants' vicious attacks. I felt a rush of adrenaline coursing through me.

"Sage," Brad called out as we fought, "Don't hold back!"

"Like I ever do!" Smirking, I dodged another swipe from the wolf-creature's razor-sharp talons. "Let's wrap this up. I've got a date with destiny, and she hates being kept waiting."

"Destiny's got nothing on you, babe," Brad replied, admiration in his tone.

With our combined strength and cunning, we killed the three creatures. I panted when the last of them lay defeated at our feet.

"Come on, let's find Archmage or the locket before more party favors show up uninvited," I urged.

With a nod, Brad followed me deeper into the heart of the gloomy manufacturing district. I felt a magical sensation leading past buildings and abandoned cars.

Ah, the joys of a magical scavenger hunt in the creepiest part of town. Nothing says *fun date night* like dodging tetanus-ridden debris and hoping we didn't stumble upon any wayward ghosts with unfinished business. At least Brad's company made the whole ordeal slightly less terrifying. His presence was like a walking, talking security blanket—if security blankets could cast spells and had great hair.

I felt it the strongest outside a creepy laboratory.

Why couldn't it be a nice, cozy bakery or a cheerful flower shop? But no, apparently sinister secrets and world-altering magic preferred the ambiance of mad scientist lairs.

We stood before the ancient door, marked with glowing runes. Its power pulsed like a heartbeat against the silence of the area.

The door's pulsing magic reminded me of those novelty t-shirts with built-in LED lights, except this one probably came with a side of potential doom. I wondered if Archmage had a flair for the dramatic or if ominous, glowing entrances were just standard issue for powerful magic users. Maybe I should consider adding some pizzazz to my own front door.

"Hmmm..." I observed, eyeing the door's ornate carvings. "Ready to crack this cryptic code?"

I tried to sound confident. In reality, my insides were doing an interpretive dance routine

"You can do this, Sage." Brad gestured at the door.

Brad's unwavering faith in my abilities was touching, really. It was also mildly terrifying. What if I messed up? What if, instead of unlocking the door, I accidentally summoned a horde of paper clips with a vendetta against humanity?

I reached out tentatively, hands hovering over the runes. Their eerie light cast ghostly shadows on our faces—our final barrier to Archmage's secrets.

I took a deep breath, then exhaled, tracing the patterns with my fingertips. The faint brilliance brightened at my touch, bending to the will of my magic.

I began the magical equivalent of picking a lock with a strand of spaghetti. The runes responded to my touch, their glow intensifying like I'd just flipped the switch on the world's fanciest night light. I silently prayed that this wasn't some elaborate magical prank show, and that the door wouldn't suddenly burst open to reveal a laughing Archmage and a camera crew. Although, given the state of my hair after trekking through that hell hole, I definitely wasn't ready for my close-up.

"Got it," I murmured.

Then the door swung open, revealing a half-lit lit staircase that spiraled downward like a descent into the abyss itself...or Hell.

With a nod at Brad, I took the lead.

"Watch your step," I said, half to myself and half to Brad.

The air grew colder, the kind of cold that seeped into your bones. Flickering torches placed on the walls cast long, moving shadows along the corridor. The stone steps were worn and uneven.

"Feels like we're walking into a trap," Brad whispered, his voice reverberating in the confined stairwell.

"Doesn't it always?"

My heart thundered in my chest, but I kept going. This locket was important to protecting the magic of my hometown—the very same magic Archmage sought to control.

The staircase ended, opening into a vast underground chamber. It was like stepping into a mausoleum of magical sciences.

The room was an alchemist's fever dream, cluttered with tables holding bubbling potions and strange herbs that even I couldn't name. Animal cages—some occupied, some disturbingly empty—lined the walls. The place smelled like enigma magic, dust, and decay, a redolence so potent it was almost a taste on the tongue.

"Creepy doesn't begin to cover it," I said, scanning the eerie lab equipment.

At the center of the room stood a large, ornate pedestal, and upon it, an open book glistening in an eerie glow. Its pages seemed to turn off their own volition, as if inviting us to look closer.

"Is that what I think it is?" Brad asked.

We both knew it could only be one thing—Archmage's personal grimoire.

"Yup. A dark witch's grimoire." I approached the pedestal cautiously, stretching out a hand to let the tips of my fingers brush against the parchment. The moment my skin made contact, the pages fluttered like the wings of a trapped bird, then stilled to reveal Archmage's plan. It detailed the use of the

Echoing Locket to amplify her own dark magic, to bend the wills of others like twigs before her mighty intention.

My body trembled. "Check it out—looks like Archmage has big plans."

Brad shook his head. "What a damn control freak."

"We have to stop this, Brad. No matter what."

Reading the intricate diagrams and notes spilled across the grimoire's pages, detailing the twisted creation of those creatures we'd narrowly escaped. My breath caught. I read something unexpected—my parents' names etched in the margins. A revelation that struck like a bolt of lightning. My stomach lurched. I knew my parents had opposed the plans for the supernatural uprising, and that their defiance was met with silence...permanent silence.

The truth hit me like a sucker punch to the gut.

All this time, I'd been living in a fog of uncertainty, grasping at straws to understand why they were taken from me. Now, the pieces were falling into place, forming a picture so horrifying I almost wished I could un-see it. My parents, the pillars of my world, had been silenced not by chance, but by malevolent design. The weight of this knowledge pressed down on me, threatening to crush my spirit.

"Dammit," I whispered. "It's true the supernatural uprising movement murdered them...possibly on Archmage's orders."

My mind reeled, struggling to process this earth-shattering revelation. How many nights had I spent wondering, hoping that their death was just a tragic accident? Now, knowing the truth, I felt a surge of emotions—grief, anger, and a fierce determination that burned through my veins like liquid fire. They died fighting for what was right, and I'd be damned if I let their sacrifice be in vain.

Brad laid a hand on my shoulder. "We'll make this right, Sage. For them."

I wanted to believe him, to cling to the hope in his words. But a nagging voice in the back of my mind whispered doubts. How could we, two young magic users barely out of school, hope to stand against a force powerful enough to orchestrate my parents' demise?

Before we could even consider our next move, a hidden door slid open on the far side of the lab. The Archmage Zephyria Nightspire appeared the embodiment of dread authority. She was draped in dark clothing embroidered with ancient runes that thrummed with latent power. Her raven hair was woven into braids so intricate they were artworks unto themselves, her eyes cold, dark pools were filled with malevolent intelligence. The smile that curled her lips was chilling.

My heart hammered against my ribcage and matched the panic rising in my throat. This was the woman responsible for so much pain, so much loss. I wanted to scream, to lash out with every ounce of magic I possessed. But fear held me in place, my limbs frozen as if caught in a binding spell.

"Looks like we've got company," Brad said.

How could he sound so collected when we were face-to-face with the architect of our nightmares? I envied his composure, wishing I could borrow just a fraction of it.

"Hello, there." Archmage's voice slithered through the air, smooth and cold, every word calculated. "You've come far, but this is where your journey ends. The Echoing Locket will ensure my rule, and no one will stand in my way."

Her words sent ice through my veins. The Echoing Locket —that damned magical artifact that had caused so much strife. Panic flared within me, hot and wild, but before it could translate into action, the dark witch lifted her hand. Magic crackled from her fingertips, weaving into a spell that swept over us like an unstoppable tide.

I was desperately trying to conjure a counter-spell, anything to shield us from her magic. But it was like trying to stop a tidal wave with a paper fan. I felt helpless, my own magical abilities seeming laughably inadequate in the face of such raw power.

"Brad!" I reached for him, but it was too late.

Blinding light enveloped us, disorienting and pulling us away from that underground tomb of secrets. When my vision cleared, we were teleported back to Emberwick Crossing, standing dazed in the streets.

The sudden shift left me reeling, my senses struggling to adjust. One moment, we were face-to-face with our nemesis, and the next, we were back on home turf. It felt like a cop-out, like we'd been dismissed as mere annoyances rather than genuine threats. The thought stung my pride and fueled my determination.

"Damn, she's powerful," Brad muttered, his gaze sweeping our surroundings.

"Powerful, extra crazy, and scared," I corrected, my obstinacy hardening like set concrete. "We may be back where we started, but we have more information now. We know her plans, and we know she's afraid of us."

"Right. Yeah." Brad nodded. "And if Archmage thinks a fancy teleport spell is going to stop us, she's dead wrong."

The fear and doubt that had paralyzed me earlier began to

recede, replaced by a steely resolve. Archmage might have the upper hand for now, but we had something she didn't—the truth. And armed with that truth, I was ready to fight tooth and nail to honor my parents' memory and protect the world they died trying to save.

B rad, Agatha, and I walked through the corridors of the
Institute for the Arcane Arts towards the High Witch's
office with a secret that could shake the magical world
to its core. The air was heavy with the fragrance of ancient
books and wax mingling with the faint tang of magic, the kind of
smell that stuck to your clothes.

It was supposed to be a quick in-and-out deal: share what
we knew about Archmage and bolt before anyone could say
"spell cast."

As we walked toward Ingrid's office, my heart pounded with
the knowledge of what we had recently uncovered—Archmage's

whereabouts and her leadership in the supernatural uprising movement.

Brad and Agatha flanked me, their expressions as tense as mine. The corridors echoed with our footsteps, the overhead light blinking on the stone walls. As we neared the Council meeting room, voices drifted towards us, growing louder with each step. My pulse accelerated, realizing we were about to overhear something we weren't meant to.

This could be our chance to gather crucial intel, but the risk of getting caught made my palms sweat.

"Hold on," I whispered, raising my hand.

With a swift incantation, I cast a hasty invisibility spell, the familiar tingle of magic washing over us. Brad and Agatha shimmered and vanished from sight, and I felt myself fade into the background.

The rush of power that came with casting always gave me a thrill, but this time it was tempered by the gravity of our situation. I couldn't help but wonder if my parents would be proud of me now, using my magic for something so important. Or would they be worried sick about the danger I was putting myself in?

We edged closer to the door, careful not to make a sound. Through the slight crack, we could see Ingrid and Councilman Voss deep in conversation. The walls were dressed in tapestries and portraits. Behind a pillar, we found our hiding spot.

I felt like a kid again, playing hide-and-seek, except the stakes were infinitely higher. One wrong move, one misplaced breath, and we'd be busted.

Ingrid was all regal grace with her white hair flowing like a banner, standing apart with an aura that demanded respect. She didn't just wear power, she embodied it like she was born to hold the world on her shoulders.

Councilman Voss, on the other hand, was cut from a different cloth. Blue eyes sharp as ice chips, dark hair streaked with silver and slicked back with precision. He was a picture of control, his tailored suit like modern armor. But it was his smile that got me—the kind that never reached his eyes, a perfect facade covering something much darker.

I'd always admired Ingrid's strength, but seeing her now, I felt a twinge of something new. Was it fear? Disappointment? The woman I'd looked up to suddenly seemed like a stranger. And Voss? Well, he'd always given me the creeps, but now his every gesture seemed loaded with sinister intent.

The High Witch's voice was hushed. "Your carelessness could have cost us everything, Voss."

I leaned in closer, desperate not to miss a word.

"Please," Councilman Voss replied, his tone steaming with condescension. "You worry too much. The plans are perfection."

Were they talking about the uprising?

"Plans that seem to change with the wind or on Archmage's sudden whims." Ingrid grunted, her formality not quite masking her irritation.

Holly hellstorm. Did she just mention her sister? My mentor in league with...Archmage? Or was there too much wax build-up in my ears?

The shock hit me like a bucket of ice water. Ingrid, the High Witch, the woman I'd trusted and admired, was involved with Archmage. How long had this been going on? What did it mean for the magical community? For me?

"Change is the nature of our art, High Witch." Councilman Voss tilted his head in mock reverence.

I glanced at where I knew Brad and Agatha were beside me, wishing I could see their reactions. Were they as floored as I was? As scared? Agatha hopped up onto my shoulder, her front paws resting on my collarbone.

That's when I remembered the crystal ball nestled in my backpack, a tool to capture moments just like this. I eased the orb out, letting it hover before me, hidden by my cloaking magic. A few hushed words later, and the ball sparked to life, swirling with bluish energy, ready to record the venomous conversation before us.

Holy hell, this was it. The moment of truth. My heart pounded so hard I was sure Brad and Agatha could hear it. I'd dreamed of uncovering some big conspiracy, but now that I was here, eavesdropping on Ingrid and Councilman Voss, I wished I could just go back to my house and curl up with a good spell book. I knew I couldn't. I had to do this for the magical community, for my parents' memory. They'd always taught me to stand up for what was right, even when it was scary. And boy, was this scary.

The crystal ball hummed softly, capturing every word. I held my breath, straining to hear more.

Ingrid's voice dripped with disdain. "Your arrogance will be our undoing, Voss. We must tread carefully."

"Careful? Ha!" Councilman Voss scoffed. "We have the now have enough supporters eating out of our hands. Your sister's plan is flawless."

This was getting weirder by the second.

"Flawless?" Ingrid hissed. "Need I remind you of the Holland girl? She's far too inquisitive for her own good."

My stomach dropped. They were talking about *me*.

Brad's hand found mine, squeezing gently. I could feel the tension radiating off him.

Poor Brad, he'd only come along to help me with speaking with the high witch. Now here we were, uncovering a huge magical conspiracy. I owed him big time after this. Maybe I'd enchant his drafting table to automatically sharpen his pencils or something.

Councilman Voss waved dismissively. "That little witch? Please. She's barely out of the Academy. What threat could she possibly pose?"

Ouch. Talk about a blow to the ego. I might not be some centuries-old warlock, but I had skills. I thought about my magic, about the spells I'd created and the power I wielded.

"You underestimate her," Ingrid growled. "She has a knack for sniffing out trouble. We need to keep her distracted."

I bit my lip, fighting the urge to gasp. My own mentor, the woman I'd looked up to for years, was plotting against me. The betrayal stung like a slap to the face. All those late nights helping Ingrid with her paperwork, all the times I'd rushed across town to fetch her a specific magical ingredient, and this is how she repays me? Now I felt like an idiot for even trusting her.

"And how do you propose we do that?" Councilman Voss drawled.

Ingrid's lips curled into a cruel smile. "We use her weakness. The boy."

Brad stiffened beside me.

Oh no. No, no, no. They couldn't mean Brad. My grip on his hand tightened.

"Ah, yes. The architect," Councilman Voss mused. "What was his name again? Brad?"

"Bradley Adams," Ingrid confirmed. "We'll use him as leverage. Keep Sage in line. I tried to separate them by invoking The Covenant of Veiled Boundaries, a primeval law that strictly forbids any romantic entanglements between members of the Council's inner circle, like Sage, and civilians, like Brad."

My blood ran cold. I wanted to scream, to rush in and confront them, but Brad's grip on my hand tightened, anchoring me in place.

So that's why Ingrid had been so insistent on keeping Brad and me apart. It wasn't about some ancient law or protecting the integrity of the magical community. It was all part of her scheme. The realization made me feel sick.

Agatha's tail swished angrily. "I always knew that old bat was a bitch," she hissed in my ear.

I had to stifle a snort. Leave it to Agatha to sum up the situation so eloquently. Her blunt honesty was exactly what I needed right now, keeping me from spiraling into panic.

Councilman Voss rocked on his heels, looking smug. "And what of your sister, Archmage? Is she prepared for the next phase?"

Ingrid's face hardened. "Archmage is...unpredictable, but she's committed to the cause. The supernatural uprising will proceed as planned."

"Good." Councilman Voss nodded. "And the Echoing Locket?"

"Safe," Ingrid assured him. "Archmage has hidden where no one will think to look."

My thoughts reeled. I had already guessed that the Echoing Locket, the mysterious amulet Archmage had created, was in her possession. But where she kept it, I had no clue.

Councilman Voss nodded. "Excellent. Soon, Emberwick Crossing will be ours. And after that—"

"Then the entire magical world," Ingrid finished, a wicked gleam in her expression.

My stomach roiled, and I felt sick. This was worse than I could have imagined. Not only was Ingrid involved, but she was at the heart of it all. My mentor, my friend...

My heart clenched as I processed the enormity of their plan. I glanced at Brad, his jaw set in a hard line, anger radiating off him in waves. Agatha, resting on my shoulder, rubbed her furry cheek against mine.

Ingrid cleared her throat. "Speaking of leverage, I've been meaning to ask. How did you manage to dispose of Sage's parents so cleanly? Wasn't it you who orchestrated that little... accident?"

I froze, every muscle in my body tensing. Unbelievable!. My breath caught in my throat, and a cold dread washed over me. This couldn't be happening. I'd always suspected foul play, but hearing it confirmed so casually was like another punch to the gut.

Brad's grip on my hand tightened to the point of pain, but I barely noticed.

The pain in my hand was nothing compared to the ache in my chest. My parents, gone because of these monsters. I wanted to scream, to unleash every ounce of magic I possessed and tear this room apart. But I couldn't. Not yet. We needed more information, and losing control now would only put us in danger. I bit my lip hard, tasting blood, using the sharp pain to ground myself.

Councilman Voss chuckled, a sound that sent ice through me. "Oh, yes, it was. One of my finer moments, I must say. Those pesky Hollands were getting far too close to uncovering our plans. It was a simple matter to tamper with their car's brakes. A shame, really. They were quite talented. But your sister ordered their demise, and who am I to argue?"

The world tilted on its axis. I stumbled, and Brad caught me, steadying me with an arm around my waist. My blood boiled at Voss' casual cruelty. This man, this murderer, had been walking free all this time. How many Council meetings had I attended, unknowingly sharing space with my parents' killer? The urge to vomit was overwhelming. I swallowed hard, forcing back the bile rising in my throat.

But oh, how I longed to wipe that smug smile off Voss' face with a well-placed hex.

"You bastard," I whispered, the words lost in the invisibility spell.

Agatha hissed, her fur standing on end. "I'll claw his eyes out," she snarled softly.

No insult could encompass the depth of my hatred for this man. I wanted to scream. Revenge would come, but not at the cost of exposing ourselves prematurely.

Ingrid's lips curled in distaste. "Must you be so crass about it, Voss? It was a necessary evil, nothing more."

My jaw clenched so hard I thought my teeth might crack. There was nothing necessary about murdering my parents.

They were good people, kind people. And I hated these power-hungry sociopaths. The injustice of it all threatened to overwhelm me.

Councilman Voss smirked. "Come now, Ingrid. We're all friends here. No need for false modesty. You were the one who suggested we target them in the first place."

I swayed. Even Agatha and Brad's comforting presence couldn't quell the storm of emotions raging inside me. Grief, rage, and a bone-deep weariness warred for dominance.

Each new revelation was like a dagger to my heart. How could I have been so blind? I'd trusted her, respected her. Now, I wanted nothing more than to see her fall from her lofty perch.

The High Witch's face hardened. "On Archmage's orders. Let's not forget who truly pulls the strings here."

The pieces clicked into place with sickening clarity. Archmage. The true mastermind behind it all. The one who had sentenced my parents to death. The scope of her evil was staggering. How many other families had she torn apart in her quest for power?

Brad whispered, "Sage, we need to get out of here."

He was right, of course. Yet I shook my head minutely. We couldn't leave. Not yet. Not when we were finally getting answers. Knowledge was power, after all. And we'd need every scrap of power we could get if we hoped to bring down Archmage and her twisted cabal.

Councilman Voss waved a hand dismissively. "Yes, yes, all hail the great Archmage. But let's not sell ourselves short, High Witch. We're hardly powerless pawns in this battle for supremacy."

Ingrid's nostrils flared. "Watch yourself, Voss. Archmage

doesn't suffer fools or traitors lightly." The High Witch's face flushed with anger. "I serve Archmage faithfully. Unlike some, I know my place in the hierarchy."

Councilman Voss laughed, the sound grating on my nerves. "Oh, spare me the sanctimonious act. We both know you're itching to step out of your sister's shadow. Why else would you be so eager to keep that little protégé of yours under your thumb?"

Ingrid's eyes narrowed. "Sage is none of your concern, Voss. I'll handle her as I see fit."

"Handle me?" I mouthed, indignation rising in my chest.

Brad squeezed my hand in warning, but I barely noticed. My heart and mind were distraught over everything I'd heard. My parents' murderer, standing mere feet away. The conspiracy larger and more insidious than I'd ever imagined.

Holy hell, these two were like snakes in the grass, all hisses and hidden fangs. And Voss? His interest in my abilities was even more unsettling.

Councilman Voss stroked his chin thoughtfully. "You know, I've always wondered. Why did Archmage spare the girl? Surely it would have been simpler to eliminate the entire Holland family."

Ingrid's lip curled. "Archmage has her reasons. It's not our place to question them."

"Perhaps..." Voss shrugged. "Or perhaps she saw potential in young Sage. Unrestrained, untapped talent that could be molded to our purposes."

Ingrid scoffed. "Don't be ridiculous. Sage is hardly some secret weapon. She's a mediocre witch at best, useful only as a distraction and occasional errand girl."

Her dismissive words stung more than I cared to admit. After everything I'd done to prove myself, to make her proud...

Brad's arm tightened around me. Agatha pressed against my neck, her tail twitching in agitation.

Councilman Voss raised an eyebrow. "You underestimate her, Ingrid. I've seen her work. The girl has a skill for creative spellcasting that could prove quite useful in the right hands."

Ingrid waved a hand dismissively. "Parlor tricks and frivolous charms. Hardly the stuff of legend."

"But with proper guidance...well, let's just say I see potential where you see only mediocrity."

Ingrid's eyes flashed dangerously. "Are you questioning my judgment, Voss?"

He held up his hands in a placating gesture. "Not at all. I'm merely suggesting that we keep our options open. After all, one can never have too many allies in a revolution, and you just seem overly fond of the girl."

Ingrid's lips thinned. "Sage's loyalty is not in question. I've made certain of that."

"Have you now?" Councilman Voss' tone was sickeningly smug. "And how, pray tell, did you manage that?"

A cruel smile played at the corners of Ingrid's mouth. "By giving her exactly what she wanted, of course. A chance to prove herself. To be part of something greater...and I'm like a mother figure to her now."

My stomach churned. Were all those late nights, the extra assignments, the constant push to improve nothing more than manipulation?

Councilman Voss snickered. "Ah, yes. The old 'carrot and

stick' approach. And I suppose young Bradley is the stick in this scenario?"

Ingrid's smile widened. "Precisely. Sage is so desperate for approval, so eager to please. It's almost too easy. Dangle the promise of advancement before her, threaten to take away the boy she loves...she'll do anything I ask."

Rage boiled within me, hot and fierce. How dare she! How dare she twist my feelings, my ambitions, into something so perverse!

Brad's grip on my hand was almost painful now, but I welcomed the anchor. Without it, I might have done something foolish, like dropping the invisibility spell and confronting them then and there.

Councilman Voss clapped his hands together. "Well, well. It seems you have everything well in hand, Ingrid. I must say, I'm impressed. Perhaps Archmage was right to put her faith in you after all."

Ingrid preened at the praise, but her eyes remained cold. "Your approval means little to me, Voss. I serve Archmage and the cause. Nothing more."

I'd come here seeking help and I'd found only betrayal. My mentor, the woman I'd trusted and admired, revealed as a manipulative monster. And looming over it all, the shadowy figure of Archmage, the puppet master of this whole twisted plot.

We couldn't stay here much longer. We had to get out, to process what we'd learned, to figure out our next move. They thought me weak, easily manipulated. The supernatural uprising jerks had no idea of the strength within me, the power I'd kept hidden all these years. Well, they were about to learn. I would bring their whole corrupt system crashing down around their ears.

For my parents. For Brad. For myself.

Let them underestimate me. Let them think me a lovesick girl, desperate for approval. I would use their arrogance against them, turn their own tricks back on them. The betrayal stung, a gaping wound in my chest. Beneath the pain, a fire was kindling. Ingrid, my mentor, the woman I'd trusted, was working with Archmage and Voss to overthrow everything. And they were using Brad against me.

And now, armed with the truth and the evidence captured in my crystal ball, I was more dangerous than they could imagine. Once the dust settled, they would rue the day they ever crossed Sage Holland.

Agatha's tail brushed against my leg, and I glanced down to see her looking up at me with fierce love.

Brad leaned close, his breath cool against my ear. "We need to get out of here now," he whispered urgently.

I nodded, my heart hammering in my chest. But as I turned to leave, my elbow knocked against a nearby shelf. A small figurine toppled to the floor with a resounding crack.

Ingrid and Councilman Voss whirled around, their faces masks of suspicion.

"What was that?" Councilman Voss demanded, rising from his seat.

Ingrid's hand glowed with black energy. "We're not alone."

Panic surged through me. I frantically reinforced the cloaking spell, praying it would hold.

"Show yourself!" Ingrid commanded, her voice booming with authority.

I held my breath, willing us to stay invisible, intangible, undetectable.

Councilman Voss stalked towards our hiding spot behind the pillar, his nostrils flaring. "I smell cat."

Agatha bristled. "How dare he!" she hissed indignantly.

"Shh!" I pleaded silently, my hand clamped over her furry mouth.

Ingrid's hard gaze swept the room. "Whoever you are, know this—your meddling ends now. The uprising cannot be stopped."

Brad tugged on my arm, gesturing towards the door. I nodded, and we began to inch our way out, Agatha tucked safely in my arms.

Just as we reached the threshold, Councilman Voss' hand shot out, inches from Brad's face. "Wait," he said, his voice low and dangerous. "I sense magic. A spell."

My heart nearly stopped. Had he detected us?

Ingrid joined him, her fingers tracing intricate patterns in the air. "Yes. Faint, but there. A cloaking spell, perhaps?"

I silently cursed myself. Of course, they'd be able to sense magic. How could I have been so careless?

"Reveal yourself," Ingrid commanded. "Or face the consequences."

I felt my cloaking spell begin to waver under the force of her will. Anxiety clawed at my throat.

Brad squeezed my hand. I knew what he was asking. Should we run?

But before I could decide, Agatha took matters into her own paws. With a yowl that would wake the dead, she leapt from my arms and darted between Ingrid and Councilman Voss' legs.

"What in the name of—" Councilman Voss spluttered, stumbling backwards.

Ingrid's concentration broke, her spell fizzling out. "That blasted cat!" she snarled.

In the chaos, Brad and I slipped out the door. We sprinted down the corridor, not daring to look back.

"Smart cat," Brad said and panted.

I nodded, too breathless to speak. We ducked into an alcove, pressing ourselves against the wall as footsteps thundered past.

"Find that cat!" Ingrid's voice echoed through the halls. "And search every inch of this building. Someone was listening, and I want to know who!"

When the coast was clear, Brad turned to me, his face pale. "Sage," he whispered, "what are we going to do?"

I clutched the crystal ball to my chest, its surface still swirling with captured secrets. "We're going to stop them," I said, my voice steadier than I felt. "We have to."

Brad nodded, his jaw set. "Then let's get kick some ass"

I managed a weak smile. "That's the plan."

Agatha appeared, bolting past us, and we followed, running hard out of the castle and away from our enemies.

I wasn't going down without a fight. And with my friends by my side, I felt invincible. Their reign of terror was about to meet its match in one seriously pissed-off interior designer with a prowess for creative spellcasting.

CHAPTER
FIVE

T he brightly lit room was filled with shadows, the only sources of light coming from overhead chandeliers. The walls were adorned with intricate tapestries depicting mythical creatures and symbols, creating an aura of magic and mystery.

This place gave me the creeps. It reminded me of those stuffy old libraries where you're afraid to breathe too loud. I half expected some cranky librarian to shush us any second.

In the center of the room stood a large wooden table, surrounded by three imposing figures. Brad and I could see the Council sitting at the front of the room on a raised platform, their faces stern and stoic, their bodies adorned in flowing robes that seemed to shimmer with magic. Their eyes flickered with concern and inquisitiveness.

These folks looked like they'd stepped right out of a fantasy novel, all regal and mysterious. I wondered if they practiced those stern expressions in the mirror every morning.

The air was clotted with friction, causing the hairs on the back of my neck to stand on end. Whispers echoed off the stone walls like scurrying insects, adding to the eerie atmosphere.

Holy hell, this was intense. I felt like I was in some kind of magical courtroom drama.

"All right, let's present our case and hope they understand," I said to Brad, who gave my hand a squeeze.

His touch steadied me, reminding me why we were here. We had to expose the truth, no matter how scary it felt. I took a deep breath, channeling my inner confident witch.

I faced the three Council members. The first, High Chancellor Sorin, had piercing green eyes and a crown of silver hair that framed his severe expression. Beside him, Magister Eldric, a broad-shouldered man with a beard as dark as night, exuded a quiet intensity. The last, Lady Morgana, was younger, with fiery red hair and a gaze that seemed to see right through me.

"Members of the Council," I said, my voice carrying across the hushed room. "We've got a serious dumpster fire on our hands." I lifted the crystal ball. "And you're gonna want to see this."

Okay, maybe not the most elegant way to start, but at least I had their attention. I could practically feel their curiosity radiating off them like heat from a bonfire.

Brad nodded at me and then addressed the Council with his

usual empathetic tone, "With respect, this evidence cannot be ignored."

I triggered the crystal ball recording, an orb of memories and truth, and it sprang to life, projecting the holographic images of Councilman Voss and Ingrid caught in candid treachery. They spoke of leading the supernatural uprising, their words weaving a tapestry of betrayal that hung heavy in the chamber.

Watching the High Witch and Councilman Voss' faces in the crystal ball made my stomach churn. These were people we'd trusted, leaders of our community. And here they were, plotting to destroy everything we held dear.

I leaned forward, my hands gripping the edge of the table. "Since the Archmage's disappearance, this uprising has been fermenting in the shadows, plotting to establish a regime where freedom is but a myth." I swept my arm across the room, gesturing to each Council member. "It's not just about power, it's about control, choking the life out of our world's diversity and magic."

The Council members shifted uneasily in their seats, exchanging worried glances.

I hoped my words hit home. This wasn't just some petty disagreement, it was the future of our entire magical society at stake.

"And you have evidence of this and a betrayal?" asked High Chancellor Sorin, his voice sharp with disbelief. "The Council's role as the governing body of the magical society has never faced such a dire threat. We've maintained balance for centuries, but this insurrection could topple everything we stand for."

"Be mindful though," I said quickly, "the crystal ball can

only replay events its witnessed once. After that, the memory fades—like a really expensive Snapchat."

Magister Eldric's fist slammed onto the table. "Bring in Councilman Voss and High Witch Ingrid."

The guards marched from the room, and we waited in tense silence. Minutes ticked by, each second stretching out unbearably. Brad and I exchanged worried glances as the tension in the room grew thicker.

Finally, the sound of hurried footsteps echoed down the corridor. The guards returned, their expressions grim and troubled.

"They're not here," one guard reported, a hint of urgency in his voice. "We've searched the entire building and sent word to check their homes. It's as if they've vanished."

The revelation sent a ripple of shock through the room. It was as if the earth had swallowed them whole, leaving behind only the echo of their conspiracy. A collective gasp rippled through the council members, their faces mirroring the growing concern.

My heart sank. Of course they'd vanished. Why would anything in my life ever be simple? I should've known better than to hope for an easy resolution.

"Vanished?" I could feel Brad's hand tighten around mine. "That sucks."

"Highly," Brad agreed, eyebrows knitting together.

The Council members exchanged worried glances, the severity of the situation sinking in.

Magister Eldric turned back to us, his expression hardening. "We need to act swiftly. This insurrection must be stopped before it can gain more power."

This was really happening. The supernatural uprising we'd been dreading was finally here, and it felt like a punch to the gut. I'd always known Ingrid and Voss were shady, but this? This was next-level villainy.

"Impossible," declared High Chancellor Sorin, his disbelief mirroring our own shock. "They were under constant surveillance."

Yeah, right. As if constant surveillance had ever stopped anyone determined enough. These weren't amateurs we were dealing with, they were powerful, cunning, and apparently way better at keeping secrets than we'd given them credit for.

"Unless," I said slowly, piecing it together, "they somehow knew they'd were about to be exposed and bolted. This whole thing reeks worse than month-old gym socks."

The pieces were falling into place in my mind, each revelation more unsettling than the last. How long had they been planning this? Had we really been that blind, or were they just that good at deception?

"I wholeheartedly agree, Miss Holland," Magister Eldric said stiffly. "Councilman Voss' cunning is matched only by his ambition for power. And Ingrid... her visions have always hinted at darker aspirations."

No kidding. Voss had always given me the creeps, but Ingrid? She was supposed to be one of us. The betrayal stung, leaving a bitter taste in my mouth. I wondered if there was still some good in her, buried beneath all that ambition.

"Whatever their reasons," Brad said, his voice a calm counterpoint to the rising panic, "we must act swiftly. This is bigger than any one of us."

Brad's steadiness grounded me, reminding me why I'd

fallen for him in the first place. But our forbidden romance seemed trivial now, compared to the looming threat.

As the reality of the situation seeped into the room like a cold draft, the Council members, High Chancellor Sorin, Magister Eldric, and Lady Morgana, exchanged grave looks, and I felt the urgency pressing down upon us all.

I thought of my parents, wondering what they would do in this situation. Would they be proud of me, standing here among the most powerful witches and warlocks in Emberwick Crossing? Or would they be terrified for my safety? The ache of their absence hit me anew, and I wished more than ever for their guidance.

Giving up wasn't an option. We had to fight, had to find a way to stop this insurrection before it destroyed everything.

"Is there anything more?" Lady Morgana said.

I shifted under Brad's supportive gaze and took a deep breath. "Actually, there is one more thing. It's about the Covenant of Veiled Boundaries."

My palms were sweaty, and my heart thundered in my chest. This was it—the moment I'd been dreading and anticipating for weeks. The Council's faces swam before me, a sea of stern expressions and raised eyebrows. I swallowed hard, trying to quell the nervous energy bubbling up inside me. What if they laughed? What if they dismissed me outright? No. I had to do this. For Brad. For us. For every witch and warlock who'd ever fallen for someone they weren't supposed to.

The Council members leaned forward, their expressions sharp. This archaic rule had long been a thorn in my side, and now it was time to challenge it.

My hands clenched at my sides. "Look, this law—it's

ancient, and it's unfair. It keeps people like me from being with...well, people like Brad." I gestured towards him.

I could feel Brad's presence beside me, solid and reassuring. His warmth gave me strength even as doubt gnawed at my insides. The Council's piercing gazes made me want to shrink away, to dissolve into the floor. But I stood my ground. I had to. This wasn't just about me and Brad anymore. It was about challenging an outdated system, about pushing for change in a world that desperately needed it.

High Chancellor Sorin's posture stiffened. "I understand that, Miss Holland, and the Covenant serves to prevent distractions and conflicts of interest within our ranks."

Of course, they'd fall back on the old excuses. But I wasn't about to let them off that easily. I took a deep breath, steeling myself for what came next. The words I'd rehearsed a hundred times in my head threatened to jumble together, but I forced them out anyway.

I stood before the Council table. "But that's just it! Who says love is a distraction? Dammit, I'd argue it makes us stronger! And if we're facing an uprising, don't you think we need all the strength we can get?" My voice sounded high and shrill.

I winced inwardly but kept my chin up. No backing down now. I'd come too far, risked too much. The memory of all those stolen moments with Brad, all the times we'd had to hide our feelings, fueled my determination. We deserved better. We all did.

Brad stepped up beside me. "Council members, our friendship has only ever inspired our dedication to protect this community and we're in love. At least, I know I am."

My breath caught in my throat. Brad's words sent a rush of warmth through me, momentarily drowning out my anxiety. He loved me. He'd said it out loud, in front of everyone. I wanted to turn to him, to throw my arms around him and never let go, but I couldn't. Not yet.

Magister Eldric stroked his beard thoughtfully. "We must consider the implications. The Covenant was established for a reason."

I bit back a frustrated groan. Always with the implications, the reasons, the excuses. Couldn't they see that the world was changing? That we needed to change with it? I took another deep breath, trying to channel my frustration into something more productive. I couldn't lose my cool now, not when we were so close.

I leaned forward, sensing their hesitation. "Times change. And so should we. If we cling to outdated traditions, how are we any better than those who seek to overthrow us?"

There was a moment of silence, heavy with contemplation. I held my breath, searching their faces for any sign of agreement. The silence stretched on, each second feeling like an eternity. My legs trembled beneath me, but I refused to show weakness. Not now. Not when everything was on the line.

Lady Morgana's shoulders relaxed. "Perhaps it is time we reevaluate some of our more antiquated regulations."

A glimmer of hope sparked in my chest. Were they actually considering it? I wanted to cheer, to jump up and down, but I forced myself to remain still. The suspense was killing me, making my skin prickle with nervous energy.

After what felt like an eternity but was probably only a few minutes, the Council members exchanged glances.

High Chancellor Sorin's chin lifted. "The law shall be revoked. Your relationship with Mr. Adams will no longer be governed by the Covenant of Veiled Boundaries."

Relief washed over me like a cleansing rain. "Thank you."

Brad took my hand and squeezed.

I couldn't believe it. We'd done it. Actually done it. The urge to pinch myself was almost overwhelming. This had to be a dream, right? But no, Brad's hand in mine was real, solid, anchoring me to this moment. We were free. Finally, truly free to be together. The implications of what we'd just accomplished hit me all at once, leaving me dizzy with joy and disbelief.

~

WE THANKED the Council members and then burst out of the Council chambers, giddy with victory. Brad's hand found mine, our fingers intertwining as we strolled through the sunny streets of Emberwick Crossing towards our homes. My heart raced from the electricity of his touch.

Holy crap, we did it. The Council had actually listened to us! I couldn't believe it. After all those nights of worrying and planning, it felt surreal to walk hand-in-hand with Brad in broad daylight. No more hiding, no more stolen glances. My chest swelled with a mix of relief and excitement. I wanted to skip down the street, to shout from the rooftops that Brad was mine. But I settled for squeezing his hand tighter, relishing the warmth of his skin against mine.

I thought of my parents, wondering if they'd be proud of the witch I'd become. Would they approve of the risks I'd taken for love? Of the stand I was about to take against dark forces threatening our world? I hoped so.

At my doorstep, I pushed it open, noticing the unusual quiet. The silence was eerie. No snarky comments, no judgmental meows. And I was glad, since I had other plans that didn't involve a sarcastic feline audience.

"Agatha must be out terrorizing the local bird population again," I said, stepping inside.

Brad chuckled, following me in. "Or plotting world domination. You never know with that cat."

The house felt different without Agatha's judgy stares, but I couldn't complain. Alone time with Brad? Holy hell, yes please.

We'd been alone before, sure, but this was different. No more looking over our shoulders, no more guilt. Just us, finally free to be together. I struggled to keep my cool, to not jump into his arms right then and there.

"Can you believe it?" Brad's voice was low, filled with wonder. "We actually did it. The Council denounced the Covenant." His arms snaked around my waist, pulling me close.

I leaned back, savoring his warmth. "Mmm hmm. No more sneaking around. No more pretending."

Gods, his arms felt good. Strong, secure. I'd dreamed of this moment for so long, imagined it a thousand different ways.

"No more pretending," he echoed, his breath tickling my ear.

We were free. Actually, truly free to be together.

I turned in his arms, drinking in the sight of him. Spiky hair I'd always wanted to run my fingers through. That crooked smile that made my knees weak.

How many times had I stopped myself from touching him

like this? From really looking at him, memorizing every detail? Too many to count. But now? Now I could stare all I wanted. Touch all I wanted. The realization hit me like a tidal wave of happiness.

"Brad," I whispered, "I love you. Have since we were kids, flinging spells in the backyard and dreaming of being great witches."

The words tumbled out before I could stop them, not that I wanted to. They'd been bottled up for so long, aching to be said. And now that they were out there, hanging in the air between us, I felt lighter. Freer. Like I could finally breathe after holding my breath for months.

Brad's lips crashed into mine, longing poured into a single, electrifying kiss. My fingers tangled in his hair. His hands roamed my back, leaving trails of fire in their wake. Each kiss deepened as we fondled and caressed, lost in the moment we'd both craved for so long.

Hellfire, the man could kiss. It was like every cheesy romance novel come to life, but better. Because this was real. This was us. No more fantasizing about what it would be like. No more stolen pecks in dark corners. This was Brad, here, now, kissing me like his life depended on it. And I was right there with him, pouring months of pent-up love and desire into every touch.

I melted into his embrace, enjoying the delicious heat of his body against mine. His touch made my skin come alive, igniting a passion I'd never felt before. The smell of his cologne, sandalwood and citrus, filled my senses and made my head spin.

"Sage," Brad whispered, his voice husky with desire. "Damn, you're a good kisser."

I pulled back, drinking in the sight of his flushed cheeks and swollen lips. "You are too, Bradley. , we are finally free to be a couple now. We should have spoken to the Council sooner. Why did we wait so long?"

The question nagged at me. All that time wasted, tiptoeing around our feelings. But then again, maybe we needed that time. To grow, to be sure. To make this moment all the sweeter.

He chuckled, the sound sending pleasant vibrations through my body. "Because we're both idiots?"

Idiot or not, he was my idiot now. And I wouldn't have it any other way.

"Speak for yourself," I teased, leaning in for another kiss.

This time, it was slower, more deliberate. Brad's lips moved against mine with a tenderness that made my heart ache. His hands cupped my face, thumbs caressing my cheeks as if I were something precious. I sighed contentedly, pressing myself closer to him. My hands slid down his chest, feeling the rapid beat of his heart beneath my palm. It matched the frantic rhythm of my own, a surge of desire and affection. Brad's kisses trailed along my jaw, then down my neck. I tilted my head, giving him better access as I gasped at the sensation.

"Brad," I breathed, my fingers digging into his shoulders.

He nipped at my collarbone, then soothed the spot with his tongue. "You're so beautiful, Sage. So perfect."

I pulled his face back to mine, capturing his lips in another fiery kiss, our tongues exploring and tasting. I reveled in the way he tasted like mint ice cream. My hands slid under his shirt, caressing the defined muscles of his back. Brad groaned, the sound sending a vibration of lusty desire through me. His own hands slipped beneath my top, his calloused fingers leaving goosebumps on my exposed skin.

We broke apart, both panting heavily. Brad rested his forehead against mine, his breath warm on my face. "I love you, Sage," he said softly, his gaze intense and full of emotion. "I've loved you for years, and I can't stop saying it. I love you."

My heart soared at his words. I cupped his cheek, my thumb brushing over his lips. "I love you too. More than I can say."

His answering smile was radiant, lighting up his entire face. He pulled me close again, this kiss softer but no less passionate. It was a promise, a declaration, a beginning. When we finally parted, I couldn't stop smiling. Brad's hair was mussed from my fingers, his lips swollen from our kisses. He still looked utterly kissable, and I had to resist the urge to pull him back in for more making out.

"So," Brad said, a glint in his eye. "What happens now?"

I grinned, running my hands down his arms. "Well, Mr. Magical Architect, I think we have some exploring to do."

The thrill of possibility zipped through me. After all the rules and restrictions, we were finally free to be together.

The Covenant of Veiled Boundaries had loomed over us for so long, casting shadows on our relationship. But now? Now we could step into the light as a couple without fear of repercussions.

"Is that so?" He raised an eyebrow, his hands settling on my hips.

"Mmm hmm," I hummed, pressing a quick kiss to the corner of his mouth. "And I can't wait to start."

"Gods, Sage," he murmured against my lips. "I never thought—"

"Me neither," I cut in, grinning even wider.

He laughed, the sound sending butterflies dancing in my stomach. "Just two rebels with a supernatural uprising cause."

"Two rebels in love," I corrected, pulling him in for another kiss.

Love. The word tasted like honey on my tongue. It was a balm to all the fears and doubts that had plagued us. We still had a world of trouble ahead, but right now, in this moment, everything felt possible.

"You're incredible, you know that? Brilliant, beautiful, and brave as hell."

I felt my cheeks flush at his words. "Flatterer," I teased.

I wondered if he knew just how much his words meant to me, how they bolstered my confidence when I needed it most.

"It's not flattery if it's true. You stood up to the Council, Sage. You changed centuries of magical law. All because you believed in us."

"We did it together," I reminded him. "You and me against the world now."

Brad's smile widened. "I like the sound of that."

His words echoed my thoughts, and I felt a surge of determination. We were a team now, officially and irrevocably.

As we stood there wrapped in each other's arms, I knew I loved Brad so much that I'd never let anyone stand in our way of being together again. Now, I just had a supernatural apocalypse to stop.

I was Sage Holland—spell creator extraordinaire, with a talent for crystal ball scrying and a flair for magical interior design. I'd faced loss, loneliness, and an outdated magical bureaucracy. A supernatural uprising? Bring it on.

CHAPTER
SIX

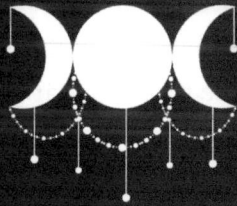

This derelict area of Emberwick Crossing was rundown and dilapidated, with broken windows and graffiti covering the walls. The abandoned buildings and overgrown foliage covered everything in thick vines and weeds. The afternoon sun beat down on the cracked pavement. Dark and foreboding shadows lined the alleys, as if warning us of the danger ahead. In the distance, a large, looming structure stood tall—the abandoned lab of the dark witch, the Archmage.

I led twenty-three members of the magical community, including Agatha, Evie and my boyfriend Brad. Holly hell, I loved calling him my boyfriend. But right now, I needed to focus. We were here to confront the Archmage once and for all.

"I hope this surprise assault on the Archmage works," I said, a charged magical current running through my veins.

Brad squeezed my hand, his blue eyes steadfast. "We trust you, Sage. If anyone can pull off an unprecedented attack, it's you."

Evie tossed her black hair over her shoulder, giving me a grin. "And if things go belly up, I've got potions that'll turn the lot of us into squirrels. Quick getaway."

Agatha sat atop my shoulder, her yellow eyes glinting. "Charming optimism, Evie. But let's not hedge our bets on turning tail."

As we neared the lab, a chill crept over my skin. Guarding the entrance stood six stone gargoyles, their eyes glowing with a sinister red light. I felt the thrum of dark magic in the air.

I tilted my head, my gaze zeroing in on the crystals dangling from necklaces around their stony necks. "Those necklaces. They're the source of their animation."

"Distraction then destruction." Evie reached inside her pouch strapped to her belt and then uncorked a vial filled with shimmering liquid and tossed it at the feet of the nearest gargoyle. As it erupted into a cloud of glittering mist, the creature's head swung around, momentarily transfixed.

The other magical residents stood back and watched.

Brad rubbed his hands together, calling forth his magic. "Time to loosen those necklaces." His hands glowed with an amber hue as his magic worked through the stone structure.

"Go!" I urged.

Brad sprang forward, manipulating the stone with deft

precision. The gargoyle's grip on its crystal necklace slackened. I darted between claws and snapping jaws, everything narrowing to the pulse of the crystal in my grasp. With a surge of willpower, I channeled my energy into my palm. The crystal cracked, its light extinguished.

I darted between stone claws and snapping jaws, the world narrowing to the pulse of the crystal in my grasp. With a surge of will, I channeled my energy into the palm of my hand, and the crystal cracked, its light extinguished.

"Left flank, Sage! Don't dilly-dally!" Agatha said.

I nodded, pivoting just in time to see Brad shatter another crystal. "Cover me!" I called out as I lunged for another gargoyle.

Evie retaliated by throwing another vial at a different guardian. The liquid exploded into a dazzling haze that swirled around the creature's head like confetti gone wrong at a parade. "That's it! Keep 'em disoriented!"

Agatha melded into shadow, darting between our adversaries like a phantom. She emerged behind one gargoyle and swatted at its necklace with her paw, causing it to swing precariously.

"Sage! A little help here?" Brad's voice was strained as he wrestled with a particularly stubborn guardian.

I waved my hand in intricate patterns while murmuring an incantation under my breath. A burst of energy shot forth and struck the necklace on Brad's foe. It shattered into fragments that scattered like fallen stars.

"Another one down!" Brad hollered.

One of the gargoyles lunged at Evie. She barely had time to react before it closed in on her but managed to pull out another vial and smashed it on its foot. The liquid glowed bright green and sprouted vines that wrapped around its limbs.

"Don't you just love nature's fury?" Evie winked as she dodged its snapping jaws.

Brad summoned more magic, molding stone beneath his fingers like clay until yet another crystal came loose and clattered to the ground. "That makes four, if anyone's keeping score!"

"Did you think this was some kind of game?" Agatha quipped while batting away at another necklace with surprising agility for a cat.

"Always so serious," Evie remarked, distracted by yet another blast from her pouch as she tossed it toward an encroaching gargoyle.

Ducking under a massive stone claw, I grabbed hold of one more necklace and poured all my energy into breaking it apart. My strength melded with the crystal until it cracked and dimmed. "That's five!"

The remaining gargoyle roared in defiance but was quickly subdued by our combined efforts—a final vial from Evie erupted in its face while Brad manipulated its joints until it could no longer move freely. And their threat was reduced to mere sculptures once again.

"Nice work." Brad panted heavily.

Evie punched him lightly on the shoulder. "I'd say we make quite the team—when we're not bickering over potion ingredients."

"I'd prefer less excitement next time." Agatha reappeared from her shadow form beside me and licked her paw nonchalantly.

"Let's keep moving," I said, adrenaline singing in my veins. "The Archmage won't wait for us to catch our breath."

Pushing forward, we moved further into the abandoned section of the city, the sun high in the cloudless blue sky.

We advanced through the overgrown foliage towards The Archmage's lab, each step resounding with a sense of foreboding. As we neared, the trees, their branches seemed to turn against us, twisting into monstrous shapes, and deadly vines reaching out like serpents poised to strike. The foliage attacked our group.

The sight of nature turning against us made my hands clench. I'd always found solace in the forest, but now it felt like a disloyalty. The Archmage's influence had corrupted even the most innocent of things. Anger flashed through me.

"Figures she'd animate the greenery," I said

I watched as the twenty residents who had volunteered to help us take down The Archmage, Councilman Voss, and the High Witch, used their magic and staffs, to fight the foliage with various incantations. The sound of spells clashing against nature gone wild filled the air.

I felt a twinge of pride for our makeshift army. These were ordinary witches and warlocks, stepping up to face extraordinary danger. Their bravery bolstered my own resolve.

Evie threw a shimmering concoction that turned the thorns sprouting from a vine into harmless dandelion fluff before they could impale anyone. "Careful!"

Agatha's form melded into my shadow. "Watch it, young witch! Your left!"

I whipped around, casting a shield just in time to deflect a swinging branch. Brad was beside me, and his hands shaped invisible blocks of force, constructing barriers to protect our group.

My heart hammered. I realized how close that branch had come. Agatha's warning had saved me from a nasty blow.

My muscles strained. "Keep pushing through!"

We carved a path toward the lab, the sound of battle outside receding as we entered the darkened threshold. Inside, the air was stagnant and leaden with the noxious smell of old magic and dust.

The sudden quiet was unnerving. The lab's interior felt like a tomb, preserved in time since The Archmage's disappearance. I had the bad feeling that we were disturbing something that should have remained buried. But we had no choice. The fate of our community hung in the balance.

Agatha's tail twitched. "Trap ahead."

I took the lead down the hall that opened into a large chamber. "Everyone, stay alert."

My breath caught as I spotted it—a room clouded with swirling, noxious gas.

I'd heard whispers of The Archmage's experiments, but seeing the evidence firsthand was chilling. How many innocent magical beings had suffered for her twisted ambitions?

Evie peered over my shoulder. "The Archmage's been busy. I heard she's studied ancient alchemical texts. This brew targets magical beings specifically. Nasty stuff."

I grimaced. "This is annoying."

Brad's face etched with concern. "Can you clear it?"

I focused on the currents around us. "Air manipulation. Brad, we'll need your shields too."

This was what I'd trained for—creating new spells on the fly, adapting to impossible situations.

Brad stepped forward. "Right behind you."

Agatha leapt gracefully onto my shoulder, digging her claws in slightly for purchase. "Don't get any ideas about making this a permanent arrangement."

I smirked. "Wouldn't dream of it." My expression turned serious. "Ready?"

Evie gripped my free hand. "Let's do it."

Brad took my other, and together we formed an unbreakable chain. As our hands connected, I felt a surge of energy. It wasn't just magic, it was trust, friendship, and shared purpose.

Momentarily, my doubts faded away. We might be outnumbered and outgunned, but we had something The Archmage and her cohorts could never understand—genuine friendships forged through loyalty and love.

I closed my eyes, calling upon my power over the elements. Air swirled at my command, rushing to create a sphere of breathable space amidst the poison. Simultaneously, Brad's magic surged, reinforcing the bubble with a lattice of protective energy.

"Move," I instructed, and we stepped forward into the haze.

"Feels like walking through a swamp." Evie coughed, the pressure of the gas pressing against our makeshift barrier.

"Keep going," Brad urged, his voice steady even as his brow furrowed in concentration.

We shuffled through the toxic cloud, every step a testament to our will and combined strength. Finally, we emerged on the other side, gasping for the cleaner air of the following chamber.

"Nice work." Brad exhaled, releasing my hand. "But don't relax yet. The Archmage isn't one for easy paths."

"Who needs easy when you've got ingenuity and good company?" I quipped, trying to lighten the mood as I brushed off Agatha from my shoulder.

"Speak for yourself," Agatha grumbled, but there was a hint of relief in her tone.

The next room was dimly lit, shadows dancing across the walls, creating an eerie atmosphere. It didn't take long to realize this wasn't just poor lighting, illusions flickered in and out of existence, disorienting and surreal.

Brad was squinting as he tried to discern reality from mirage. "The Archmage has harnessed ancient illusion spells. From forgotten realms, no less. This is a devious nightmare."

With a deep breath, I drew on my magic to see beyond the deception. Hidden within the deception, a pattern emerged. A sequence of symbols acting as breadcrumbs through the illusions.

"Agatha, your instincts are sharp, even sharper than her illusions. And Brad, use that analytical mind of yours. Evie, stay close. We need to decode these symbols," I instructed, pointing towards the shifting images.

Evie nodded, her gaze sharpening. "Between the four of us, we've got this."

Brad identified the first symbol, and we followed the pattern he traced with his finger.

"Next one's there." I stepped carefully to align with the symbol that pulsed faintly under my gaze.

"Got another one." Evie pointed.

"Two more to go, young witch." Agatha rubbed her cheek against my chin.

Methodically, we decoded the sequence until we reached the far side of the room, untouched by the illusions' dizzying effects.

I blew out a breath, a smile on my lips. "Now let's find The Archmage and the Echoing Locket."

The door to The Archmage's lab creaked open, revealing a scene that was both fascinating and sinister. Shelves lined with spell components and ancient tomes surrounded us, but it was the woman at the center of the room who commanded our attention. The Archmage Nightspire stood before an altar, the Echoing Locket clasped tightly in her pale hand, its surface pulsing with captured spells.

"Archmage!" I called out, my voice steady despite the unease knotting my stomach. "This ends now."

"Ah, Sage Holland," she replied, her tone smooth as ice, "do you really believe you can stop me?"

I could feel the energy coursing through me, the air around me thrumming. "Actually, yes. We're not playing by your rules anymore."

Brad stepped forward. "You're outnumbered, and we're not backing down."

"Outnumbered, perhaps," Archmage said coolly. "But outmatched? Hardly."

Evie's hand found mine, squeezing it briefly before she flung a vial to the ground. A thick purple fog rolled across the floor, obscuring our vision, but more importantly, disrupting The Archmage's concentration.

The evil witch narrowed her gaze and extended her free

hand. Crackling energy surged from her fingertips, aiming to dispel the fog. "Pathetic tricks," she muttered.

"Shadow bind," Agatha hissed, leaping from my shoulder.

The room dimmed further as tendrils of darkness coiled around The Archmage, eliciting a snarl of frustration from her. She twirled with surprising agility, manipulating the shadows to constrict and then snap back at Agatha.

"Enough!" She flicked her wrist sharply. Agatha yelped and retreated but remained vigilant.

"Try this on for size!" Brad shouted, his hands moving swiftly as he conjured a lattice of glowing runes around The Archmage, each one designed to disarm and disorient.

She glared at Brad without losing focus on dissolving his runes with delicate precision. "Runes?" She smirked. "Child's play."

I focused all my power, feeling the elemental magic at my fingertips responding to my will. With a flick of my hand, I sent a gust of wind toward the locket, attempting to wrench it from The Archmage's grasp.

"Persistent, aren't you?" Her voice wavered slightly as she reinforced her grip on the locket with an incantation. Lightning flickered around her as she struggled to maintain control.

"Sonofabitch," I muttered. She was tougher than we anticipated.

Brad slammed his foot into the ground, and stone spikes erupted beneath The Archmage's feet. She jumped nimbly aside but stumbled as one caught her ankle.

"I don't need spells to deal with amateurs!" Her voice broke into a shout.

Evie's fingers danced in complex motions as she prepared another elixir. "Sage! Now!"

Drawing upon my magical energy, I thrust both hands forward and unleashed a torrent of magic aimed directly at The Archmage's defenses.

She winced but held firm against our combined assault. "You think, you can beat me?" The icy composure in her voice cracked.

"We think we already have," Brad replied calmly.

The Archmage managed to maintain her grip, but her voice had lost some of its composure. "But I've planned for every contingency."

"Did you plan for this?" I said, weaving together a new spell —the product of countless sleepless nights. It was untested, but I trusted my instincts.

Forming a complex pattern with my hands, I channeled pure creative energy into the air.

A radiant lattice of spell work coiled around The Archmage, tightening like an ethereal serpent. She gasped, a flicker of fear rippling across her otherwise impassive face, as the lattice started to unravel her defenses piece by piece.

"Impossible!" she hissed through clenched teeth.

"Hate to break it to you," I said, feeling a surge of confidence. "But this spell rewrites your contingencies."

The dark witch struggled against the luminescent bonds, her movements becoming frantic. As the magic took hold, the ground beneath us thrummed with power. Her expression morphed from disbelief to sheer rage.

"I will not be undone by the likes of you," The Archmage spat.

"Funny," Brad said, stepping closer. "Looks like you already are."

I had to hand it to Brad—his one-liners were on point tonight. Maybe I should start taking notes.

The Archmage's final barrier cracked audibly before shattering completely under the weight of my spell. Her defiance faded into frantic desperation as she tried to summon more energy but found none left to conjure.

"You've underestimated us," I said quietly.

My friends and I were like the magical Avengers minus the cool outfits and billion-dollar budget.

Her response was a guttural growl of frustration, but for the first time since this all began, it sounded more like surrender than defiance.

Agatha purred from the shadows. "Let's wrap this up. My dinnertime is sacred, and I hate being late."

Ah, Agatha. Always keeping our priorities straight. Who needed to save the world when there was a can of tuna waiting at home?

"Always about your stomach, eh, Agatha?" Evie said, lobbing another potion that exploded into a dazzling display of light and sound, momentarily stunning The Archmage.

With a cruel smile, the evil witch vanished into thin air, taking the Echoing Locket with her. Her laughter echoed from the walls, mocking us even in her retreat.

JUST WHEN I thought we had her. Typical villain move, always ruining a perfectly good climax with their disappearing acts.

I frowned. "Damn it! She got away."

The air sizzled with dark energy, and Councilman Voss teleported before us, his face twisted in fury.

"Meddling children," he spat, his voice dripping with condescension. "Do you have any idea what you've done?" Voss roared, raising his hand to unleash a torrent of magical energy.

"Shield up!" Brad yelled, throwing up a barrier just in time to absorb the brunt of the attack.

"Evie, I need those potions *now*! Agatha, shadows—blind him if you can!" I called out, drawing on every ounce of strength left in me.

Nothing like a little teamwork to really bring out the best in people. Or cats, in Agatha's case.

"You're being bossy, young witch." Agatha darted through the room like a wraith, her shadowy form a blur.

"Here, catch!" Evie tossed a handful of vials that exploded around Councilman Voss, releasing clouds of smoke and bursts of light that caused him to stagger.

"Let's see how you like being trapped," Brad growled, and he constructed an intricate maze of magical walls around Voss.

Brad's architectural skills never ceased to amaze me.

"Your tricks won't hold me forever!" Councilman Voss bellowed, struggling against the constraints.

With a determined expression, Brad manipulated the stone beneath Voss' feet. Cracks began to form rapidly before spiraling into a jagged pit that consumed Voss up to his waist. Brad didn't relent. My boyfriend condensed the stone around Councilman Voss like a vise, crushing and suffocating the warlock's fire spells until his cries turned into weak gasps. Blood gurgled up and out of his mouth.

"Is this the part where you beg for mercy?" Agatha circled the trapped Councilman, her yellow stare keen.

Voss coughed, his voice little more than a whisper now. "No...but, Sage, I must confess something."

"Confess what?" I watched him struggle for each shallow breath.

"It was me..." He drew in a ragged gulp of air. "I killed your parents...because of Ingrid." His blue eyes, ice-cold and remorseless even now, met mine.

I stared at Voss, my mind reeling from his confession. The world seemed to tilt on its axis, and I struggled to breathe. "You...what?" My voice came out as a strangled whisper.

Voss coughed, blood splattering his chin. "Ingrid...I loved her. I did it for her, even though I knew she never loved me back. Your parents...they were in the way."

Rage surged through me, hot and violent. "You monster!" I lunged forward, but Brad caught me, holding me back.

"Let me go!" I thrashed against his grip. "I'll kill him myself!"

"Sage, don't," Brad said, his voice pained. "He's not worth it."

Agatha prowled closer to Voss, her tail lashing. "Well, well. The truth comes out at last. How deliciously tragic."

Evie knelt beside me, her face a mask of concern. "Sage, I'm so sorry, but at least you know the full truth now."

Councilman Voss wheezed, his breaths growing more labored. "Ingrid...I did it...all for her."

"You took everything from me," I snarled, tears streaming down my face. "And for what? A woman who never loved you back?"

"Love makes fools of us all," Voss gasped, a bitter smile twisting his bloodied lips.

I wrenched free from Brad's grasp, stumbling towards Voss. "Tell me why. Why them? Why not just...just..."

"Your father...was going to expose Ingrid's plans," Voss rasped. "Your mother...collateral damage."

I sobbed, my voice rising hysterically. "She was a person! They both were!"

Agatha's fur bristled. "Young witch, step back. Let the bastard die in peace."

I whirled on her. "He doesn't deserve peace!"

"No," Voss agreed, his voice fading. "I don't. But I'm sorry. For what it's worth."

I laughed bitterly. "It's worth nothing."

The Councilman's gaze grew distant, unfocused. "Tell Ingrid...I always loved her. Even now."

With a final, rattling breath, Councilman Alden Voss slumped in his stone prison. The light faded from his gaze, leaving behind empty, glassy orbs staring at nothing.

I stumbled back, my legs giving out. Brad caught me, lowering us both to the ground.

"He's gone." Evie checked Voss's pulse. "His life is over."

But it wasn't over. Not for me. The truth of my parents' deaths, hidden for so long, now lay exposed like a raw nerve. I curled into Brad's chest, sobs wracking my body.

"Shh, I've got you," Brad murmured, stroking my hair. "Let it out, Sage. I'm here."

Evie knelt beside us, wrapping her arms around us both. "We're all here, Sage. You're not alone."

Agatha padded over. "Well, this is a fine mess. What now, young witch?"

I lifted my head, wiping my tears. "Now? We find Ingrid. And we make her pay."

Brad tensed. "Sage, revenge won't bring them back."

"I know that," I snapped, then softened. "I'm sorry."

Evie squeezed my hand. "And we'll get justice for their deaths."

Agatha snorted. "How heartwarming. Now, can we please get out of this dreary lab? The stench of death is ruining my appetite."

Through the sniffles and tears, I found myself laughing. It was a broken, hysterical sound, but it was something. "Only you could think about food at a time like this," I said, shaking my head.

Agatha preened. "What can I say? I'm a cat of simple pleasures."

Brad helped me to my feet, his arm steady around my waist. "Come on. Let's get out of here."

As we made our way out of The Archmage's lab, leaving Voss's body behind, Ingrid was still out there, and now I knew the truth about her involvement in my parents' deaths.

Agatha trotted ahead, her tail held high. "Now, about that food..."

I rolled my eyes, grateful for the distraction. "You're incorrigible."

"I prefer 'charmingly persistent'." Agatha lifted her chin.

Outside, the enchanted foliage writhed and twisted around the magical residents fighting valiantly.

I closed my eyes for a moment, reaching deep within. "Folium cessare!" I chanted, my hands weaving a new pattern in the air. A pulse of clear energy radiated from me, calming the violent greenery until it lay dormant at our feet.

"The Archmage has fled, but this isn't over!" I declared, turning to face the crowd.

Their cheers and applause warmed me, but the ache in my heart remained.

Everyone left the lab and headed back towards our homes.

"I can't believe it," I murmured as we walked. "All this time...Voss was their killer..."

"So, what's the plan?" Evie asked, her voice tentative.

I squared my shoulders. "We find Ingrid and her psychopathic, crazy sister."

Agatha looked up at me. "Sage, are you sure that's wise? Those two are dangerous."

"I know," I said, my voice hardening. "But so am I."

Agatha chuckled darkly. "Now that's what I like to hear. A little revenge never hurt anyone."

"Except, you know, the person we're taking revenge on," Evie pointed out.

I shook my head. "This isn't about revenge. It's about justice. For my parents and for anyone else Ingrid and The Archmage have hurt."

Brad sighed but nodded. "All right. But we do this smart. No rushing in half-cocked."

"Okay, yeah," I said, then smiled.

As we made our way back to my house, I felt a strange mix of emotions swirling inside me. Grief, anger, determination, and underneath it all, a fierce love for the makeshift family surrounding me.

"Thank you," I said softly. "All of you. I couldn't do this without you."

Evie squeezed my arm. "That's what friends are for, bestie."

Brad kissed the top of my head. "You're my everything, Sage. And I won't let you do this alone."

Agatha predictably ruined the moment. "Yes, yes, we're all very devoted. Now, about that meal..."

I laughed. "Fine, you glutton feline. We'll stop for takeout on the way home."

As we walked, I felt a transformation within me. Something had changed today beyond just learning the truth about my parents. I'd always known I was strong, but now...now I felt dangerous.

Ingrid had no idea what was coming for her. And neither did The Archmage.

For the first time since this whole mess started, I felt a glimmer of hope. We were going to take them down, and we were going to do it soon.

Well the three of us, plus one very demanding cat.

"If you don't feed me soon, I may have to resort to cannibalism," Agatha announced dramatically.

I rolled my eyes. "You're a cat. Technically, that would be humanibalism."

"Whatever." Agatha sniffed.

We rounded the corner and the sight of our favorite takeout

place came into view. For a weird moment everything felt normal again.

But I knew better. Nothing would ever be normal again. And strangely, I was okay with that.

Because normal had never included justice for my parents. And now, finally, I had a chance to get it.

Watch out, Ingrid. I'm coming for you.

CHAPTER
SEVEN

T he forest had swallowed the evening sun, casting
elongated shadows on the pine needles strewn
ground. It was the perfect hideout—an old ruin, its
stones cracked and covered in ivy. The air buzzed with magic,
thick and potent.

With me were Evie, Freya, Professor Rowan Elderwood,
and Brad for the final showdown with Ingrid and her sister, The
Archmage.

This was it. The moment for which we'd been preparing.
My palms were slick with sweat, and my heart pounded in my
chest. But I couldn't let fear take over. Not now. I had to be

strong, for my parents, for my friends, for all of Emberwick Crossing. The fate of our magical community rested on what happened here tonight.

I tucked a blue-streaked lock behind my ear. "Freya, Rowan, thanks for joining our little army."

Freya adjusted her preppy outfit. "Glad to help if I can. I don't have any battle skills, but I can tend to anyone wounded."

Professor Elderwood just nodded, his gray eyes inspecting the tree line as if deciphering an invisible code.

Freya's healing abilities could be crucial, and Rowan's wind manipulation might give us an edge. But a nagging voice in the back of my mind wondered if it would be enough. We were up against two of the most powerful witches in Emberwick Crossing. The odds weren't exactly in our favor.

An eerie chill crept over us as we approached the ancient redwood, a gnarled giant that seemed to pulse with dark power. The tree was adorned with intricate carvings of arcane symbols and mystical spells, each one seeming to vibrate with energy.

Standing next to the tree were The Archmage and Ingrid Nightspire, their presence adding to the ominous atmosphere. As the wind whipped through the forest, The Archmage's long, black hair swirled around her like a nest of serpents.

These were the witches responsible for so much pain and suffering. The ones who'd orchestrated my parents' death. Anger bubbled up inside me, hot and fierce. I wanted to lash out, to unleash every spell I knew upon them. But I held back. Losing control now would be disastrous.

"Ah, Sage Holland and her little band of rebels have arrived," The Archmage said, her tone smooth, cold.

Ingrid smirked beside her. "And you've brought friends."

Their arrogance made my blood boil. Did they really think we were just some ragtag group of misfits?

But what if we'd overlooked something? What if their powers were stronger than we'd anticipated?

"Good grief, you're annoying," I said, clenching my jaw.

"Your bravado is misplaced." Ingrid scoffed with flippant indifference, eyeing us like we were nothing more than gnats.

Her dismissive attitude only fueled my resolve. I'd show her just how misplaced her own confidence was!

"Hello, Ingrid." Brad stepped forward with a confidence that made my heart skip.

With Brad beside me, it gave me a burst of courage. We'd been through so much together, and his love meant everything to me. But a flicker of fear pinched my chest. What if something happened to him? To any of us? The thought of losing someone I cared about was almost paralyzing.

I lifted my chin. "You won't get away with whatever twisted plan you've got."

THE ARCHMAGE LAUGHED, a sound devoid of any genuine amusement. "My twisted plans are simple. With the Echoing Locket, I will bend every magical being to my will. Then I shall become the ultimate authority in Emberwick Crossing. "

"Over my dead body," I said.

"Very well," Ingrid said, almost bored.

The battle erupted with a roar. Spells and curses collided in mid-air, bursts of multicolored energy crackling like fireworks. The ground trembled beneath us, the atmosphere charged with magic.

Brad stood beside me, his hands shaping the air as he conjured barriers out of thin air. "Sage, focus on countering! I'll handle defense!"

Freya was a whirlwind of motion, darting between us and healing wounds as quickly as they formed.

Ingrid smirked from the shadows, her hands weaving complex sigils to summon a horde of shadow beasts.

A ball of dark energy hurtled toward Evie and Freya, only to be deflected by one of Brad's barriers.

Ingrid, her eyes glowing with malevolence, hurled fireballs at the tree line, setting the forest ablaze as the sun dipped below the horizon.

Evie grinned, her fingers twitching. "Time to cuteify some baddies!" She flicked her wrist, transforming an attacking shadow beast conjured by The Archmage into a bewildered, fluffy dog.

Professor Elderwood stood a few paces away, wind swirling around him as if he were the calm within the storm. "Your tactics are futile," he declared, hurling gusts at The Archmage.

The dark witch laughed, flicking a hand to dispel his wind effortlessly. "You call that a spell? Pathetic." She raised her hands, and dark tendrils snaked from her fingers towards the professor.

Holy hell, this was not going according to plan. I'd hoped for a dramatic showdown, but this felt more like a magical food fight gone wrong.

Cackling wickedly, Ingrid summoned thorny vines from the forest floor, ensnaring unwary combatants as the last rays of sunlight faded.

I groaned. Now we had evil plants to deal with. As if

battling two power-hungry witches wasn't enough of a green thumb challenge.

Professor Rowan's expression hardened as he foresaw the attack just in time to counter with his own elemental magic. "You'll never take Emberwick Crossing!"

I had to admire the professor's gusto.

Drawing on every fiber of my being, a powerful binding spell shimmered around The Archmage momentarily before she shattered it with a mere flick of her wrist.

Damn!

Ingrid laughed coldly, summoning more shadowy creatures with each movement of her hand.

"Is that all you've got?" The Archmage jeered.

Brad's voice was urgent beside me. "We need to combine our strengths! Now!"

My boyfriend, ever the problem-solver. If only we could build a magical fortress to keep these villains out.

With a sinister grin, Ingrid conjured a swarm of shadowy bats, sending them to harass us.

Oh joy, flying rodents of doom.

Freya ducked as a bat swooped over her head, stepping closer to me. "Sage, try your spell creation—something new."

Something new? Sure, let me just pull a never-before-seen spell out of my witchy hat. No pressure.

Evie threw another potion. "And make it sparkle!"

I rolled my eyes. Leave it to Evie to request glitter in the middle of a magical showdown.

Freya's hands glowed with protective energy as she shielded our group from incoming attacks.

My thoughts raced through options. Then it hit me—an

amalgamation spell combining our unique powers might do the trick. Chanting an incantation under my breath, symbols were drawn in the air.

Ingrid's eyes blazed with malice as she hurled bolts of dark energy at our defensive line.

Brad's architecture manipulation melded seamlessly with my creation power. A glowing pattern emerged between us—a swirling vortex pulling in unrestrained magical energy from everyone involved.

Evie sang between potion throws, her movements fluid and unpredictable as she dodged enemy spells.

"Keep it steady!" Professor Elderwood ordered and paused his attacks long enough to lend wind energy to the vortex.

Focusing intently, my hands wove intricate patterns to maintain the spell's stability.

The Archmage's smug expression faltered for a fraction of a second before she unleashed another barrage of dark magic at us. The vortex absorbed it like fuel for our combined spell.

"Now!" We released the energy we had harnessed in one explosive burst aimed directly at The Archmage.

The impact knocked her back several feet, staggering but not defeated. Her eyes narrowed dangerously. The dark witch began chanting again, this time more intensely.

Freya's hands glowed with healing magic as she tended to our wounds

"Fall back!" the professor commanded.

Evie tossed a smoke bomb, creating a thick cloud of magical mist to cover our retreat.

Ingrid circled the battlefield, her eyes scanning for weaknesses in our defenses.

Agatha appeared out of nowhere—a blur of shadow and fur —and leaped at The Archmage's face, claws extended. The sudden distraction was enough for us to regroup momentarily.

Brad wiped sweat off his brow and turned to me. "This won't hold forever."

Breathlessly nodding, my eyes remained fixed on Agatha as she harassed The Archmage like an avenging feline fury. "But it bought us time."

Evie readied another smoke bomb potion. Then Evie stepped forward. "Look out!" she yelled.

A tendril of shadow whipped toward me. It splintered against my hastily conjured barrier, showering me with sparks.

"Nice try." I launched a counterattack with a flick of my wrist.

"Your efforts are futile," The Archmage taunted, her voice never losing its chilling composure. She parried my spell effortlessly, her own magic dark and suffocating.

"Brad, now!" I called.

My boyfriend sprang forward, his hands weaving a complex pattern. The earth responded, roots and vines rising to bind The Archmage's ankles.

"Pitiful." Ingrid sneered, but her eyes betrayed a flicker of concern as she watched her sister struggle against the living restraints.

"Never underestimate a builder warlock." Brad was straining while he reinforced the binding spell.

"Professor, a little help, if you please?" I asked, dodging another volley of curses from Ingrid.

"Quite right, Sage, quite right." Elderwood unleashed a fresh rush of wind that turned the dark witch's spells awry.

"Evie, Brad—cover him!" I shouted over the roar of magic clashing.

"Got it!" they both cried in unison.

Freya's healing aura pulsed around us, knitting together minor cuts and bruises.

"Freya, keep it up!" Gasping, I felt the abrasion on my arm seal under her healing power. "We can't let them break us."

"No way," Freya replied, her hands aglow with a soft, verdant light that wove between us like threads of life itself.

Professor Elderwood's wind magic whirled around us, creating a protective barrier of swirling leaves and branches.

"Evie, can you—" But I didn't have to finish the sentence.

My best friend was already lobbing another potion, this one bursting into blinding brilliance upon impact with Ingrid and The Archmage.

"Ha! Take that!" Evie cheered, her voice sounding with infectious bravado.

The witch sisters hurled dark spells at our group, their malevolent energy crackling through the twilight.

"Agatha, shadow strike now!" The command barked from my lips.

My familiar leapt from the darkness, claws extended towards our foes with supernatural precision. Agatha's shadowy form slashed across Ingrid and The Archmage, leaving them reeling and disoriented.

"Troublesome creatures," Ingrid hissed, swatting at Agatha with a spell that turned to smoke upon contact.

Agatha snorted derisively. "You haven't seen anything yet."

Brad's builder magic conjured massive roots from the forest floor, ensnaring the evil witches' feet.

Ingrid cackled maniacally, her hands glowing with dark magic as she prepared to strike again.

"Focus, everyone!" Professor Elderwood's voice was strained. The warlock maneuvered the winds in a protective circle around us.

Ingrid's dark magic crackled, threatening to break through our defenses. I gritted my teeth, searching for a solution.

"Any bright ideas, Sage?" Evie called out, fumbling with another potion vial.

I wracked my brain. "Working on it! Kinda hard to think with all this evil energy flying around."

"Perhaps a dash of chaos is in order," Agatha purred, her tail swishing mischievously.

"Pandemonium? We've got plenty already," Brad grunted, straining to maintain his root barrier.

Professor Elderwood's voice cut through the din. "Focus, Miss Holland! Your unconventional spell craft may be our only hope."

I nodded, drawing a deep breath. "Right. Unconventional. That's me in a nutshell."

"Less nutshell, more action!" Freya urged, her healing magic faltering under the onslaught.

The Archmage Nightspire's laughter echoed across the battlefield. "Your pitiful resistance only delays the inevitable!"

"Inevitable?" I scoffed. "The only thing inevitable here is your bad hair day!"

Ingrid snarled, hurling another volley of dark energy. "Insolent witch! We'll crush you and your pathetic friends!"

"Ooh, touched a nerve, did we?" Agatha taunted, melting into the shadows.

Brad's voice strained with effort. "Sage, whatever you're planning, do it fast! These roots won't hold forever!"

I closed my eyes, reaching deep within myself. The familiar tingle of magic coursed through my veins, building to a crescendo.

"Evie!" I called out, "I need your most ridiculous potion. The weirder, the better!"

My best friend's face lit up with a mischievous grin. "One bottle of pure chaos, coming right up!"

As Evie concocted her brew, I began to weave an intricate pattern in the air, my fingers trailing sparks of magic.

"What are you doing?" Freya asked, her brow furrowed in concentration as she maintained her healing aura.

"Something stupid," I admitted. "But hey, it might just work!"

Professor Elderwood's wind barrier faltered, and his voice strained, "Whatever you're planning, Miss Holland, I suggest you hurry!"

The Archmage's voice dripped with contempt. "Your pitiful tricks cannot save you now!"

"Save the villainous monologue for your memoirs, sister dear," Ingrid hissed. "Let's finish this!"

As the evil witches prepared another assault, Evie tossed me a swirling, multicolored vial. "Here's your bubbly cocktail!"

I caught the potion and wove it into my spell, feeling the conflicting energies merge and twist.

"Brace yourselves!" I shouted, unleashing the spell with a burst of wild magic.

The air crackled with energy as my unconventional creation

took form. A swirling vortex of color and light erupted between us and our foes, pulsing with chaotic power.

Ingrid recoiled, her face a mask of confusion. "What manner of trickery is this?"

The Archmage's eyes narrowed. "Whatever it is, destroy it!"

But as the dark witches launched their attacks, the vortex absorbed and twisted their magic, sending it ricocheting in unpredictable directions.

"Ha!" Agatha cackled, materializing beside me. "Now that's what I call a spell!"

Brad whooped with delight. "Sage, you're a genius!"

"An unpredictable genius," Freya added, a hint of worry in her voice.

Professor Elderwood studied the swirling magic with fascination. "Remarkable. Utterly reckless, but remarkable, nonetheless."

Evie bounced on her toes, clapping her hands. "It's like a magical disco ball of doom!"

As the vortex grew, it began to affect our surroundings. Trees bent at impossible angles, rocks floated in midair, and the very ground beneath our feet seemed to ripple and shift.

"Uh, Sage?" Brad called out, his voice tinged with concern. "You can control this thing, right?"

I bit my lip, concentrating on maintaining the spell. "Um, yeah..."

Ingrid and The Archmage struggled against the chaotic energy, their own magic turning against them in unpredictable ways.

"This is impossible!" The Archmage roared, her carefully preserved spells unraveling before her eyes.

Ingrid's precognition seemed to be going haywire, her eyes darting wildly as she saw a thousand possible futures at once. "Make it stop!"

"Sorry, no refunds on karma," I said, channeling more energy into the vortex.

Freya's healing magic pulsed erratically, causing flowers to sprout from the cracks in the ground. "Sage, I think we might be overdoing it a bit!"

"Nonsense!" Evie cackled, tossing more potions into the fray. "Let's see what happens when I add a little extra zing!"

As her concoctions mixed with the chaotic energy, the vortex began to spin faster, pulling everything towards its center.

"Miss Black!" Professor Elderwood admonished, his wind magic struggling against the pull. "This is not the time for experimentation!"

"Au contraire, Professor," Agatha purred, her shadowy form stretching and twisting in the chaos.

Brad grunted, using his construction magic to anchor us to the ground. "Maybe we should dial it back a notch?"

I shook my head, my hair whipping wildly in the magical winds. "No way!"

Indeed, Ingrid and The Archmage were being drawn inexorably towards the center of the vortex, their powers useless against its pull.

"This cannot be!" The Archmage wailed, her carefully laid plans crumbling around her.

Ingrid's voice was shrill with panic. "Sister, do something!"

As they struggled, I felt a surge of triumph. We were

winning! But then I noticed the trees around us starting to uproot, and the sky above twisting into impossible shapes.

"Uh, guys?" I called out, my confidence wavering. "I think we might have a tiny problem."

Freya's voice was strained. "Oh?"

Before I could respond, the vortex pulsed with a blinding light, and everything went silent. For a moment, the world seemed to hold its breath. The Archmage lifted the Echoing Locket around her neck and grinned at me. My blood ran cold. Muttering a spell while holding the amulet, The Archmage's magic exploded outward, and the vortex disintegrated.

"Professor, watch out!" Brad yelled.

Another surge of dark energy, blacker than the void, erupted from The Archmage's outstretched hands, aimed straight for us. Elderwood, eyes wide, stepped in front of the blast to protect us.

"Rowan, no!" Freya screamed.

The explosion rocked the forest, ancient stones tumbling from the blast. Professor Elderwood's form was engulfed in the dark maelstrom. My heart lurched. Time seemed to fracture. My heart lurched.

This couldn't be happening. Not Professor Elderwood. Now he was gone in an instant, swallowed by that inky darkness.

We were alone now, facing two of the most powerful dark witches in existence. And they'd just taken out our strongest ally without breaking a sweat.

Panic clawed at my throat, threatening to choke me. But beneath it, something else stirred. A spark of defiance, of rage. How dare they? How dare they waltz in here and destroy everything we held dear? First my parents, now Professor Elderwood. When would it end?

I felt my magic roiling inside me, responding to my turmoil. It wanted out. It wanted justice. Or was it vengeance? In that moment, I wasn't sure I cared about the difference.

The anger bubbling up inside me was unlike anything I'd ever felt before.

This wasn't me. I didn't lose control like this. Yet here I was, teetering on the edge of something dangerous and exhilarating.

"Professor!" The word tore from my throat. At his death, I felt something inside of me snap free—instinctive, unbridled magic flooding my veins.

The rush of power was intoxicating. It coursed through me like liquid fire, setting every nerve ending alight. I'd always known I was capable of powerful magic, but this? This was something else entirely. It was as if a dam had broken, releasing years of pent-up potential in one cataclysmic surge.

Evie and Brad stood frozen in shock while Freya sobbed uncontrollably, her hands covering her face.

The protective instinct that had always been a part of me roared to life, demanding action.

Ingrid's smirk faltered. "Sage thinks she can—"

"*Shut up!*" The rage in my voice startled even me.

For a brief moment, I wondered if this was how villains were born—in a moment of unchecked anger and power. But no, I reminded myself. I wasn't like them. I was fighting for something greater than myself.

Levitating off the ground, power surged through every cell, alight with seventh-level magic. An ethereal glow enveloped my body as the air crackled with raw energy, leaves and debris swirling around in a vortex of unleashed power.

The sensation of floating was surreal. I felt weightless, untethered from the physical world. Was this what true power felt like?

It was tempting, oh, so tempting, to lose myself in it completely.

Knowing I should've been terrified, an overwhelming need to end this and protect what was left of my world surged through me.

Wild and untamed magic filled every corner of my being, threatening to tear me apart from the inside. Holding on, channeling and shaping it became my focus. This gift, this curse, was ready to be put to use.

I'd always been the responsible one, the level-headed witch who thought things through. But now? Now I was chaos incarnate, a force of nature barely contained in human form.

For the first time in my life, I understood why some witches went dark. The allure of such unbridled magic was nearly impossible to resist.

"End this, Sage," Agatha said, her voice cutting through the haze of power.

Yes, end this. That's exactly what I intended to do.

My familiar had seen the rise and fall of countless witches. Was I destined to be just another cautionary tale?

For me, this wasn't about revenge or power. It was about protection, about safeguarding the future of Emberwick Crossing. I'd been given this power for a reason, and I intended to use it wisely.

I looked at The Archmage and Ingrid. Really looked at

them. They thought they were invincible, that their dark magic made them unstoppable. But I saw the truth. They were scared. Scared of change, scared of losing their grip on power. And now, they were scared of me.

And I liked it. Then I saw them for what they truly were— not all-powerful beings, but scared, desperate individuals clinging to outdated ideals. It was almost pitiful. Almost. But then I remembered all the pain they'd caused, all the lives they'd ruined, and my resolve hardened.

For my parents, for Brad, for Evie, for all of Emberwick Crossing. This was our stand.

A smile spread across my face. "The Archmage and High Witch." My voice rang clear as I addressed the two dark witches. "Your night ends here!"

The Archmage sneered and backed up. "Brave words, you little bitch."

Her insult barely registered. What mattered was the fear in her eyes, the slight tremor in her voice. She knew, just as I did, that everything was about to change.

Good. Let them be afraid. Let them feel a fraction of the terror they'd inflicted on others. I'd make them regret ever setting foot in Emberwick Crossing.

A dark part of me relished their fear. It was a heady feeling, knowing I held their fate in my hands. But I couldn't let that darkness consume me. I was better than that. I had to be.

With a cry that blended grief with fury, a torrent of pure energy erupted. Brilliant azure flames burst forth, engulfing the forest in an eerie glow. The magical inferno surged towards Ingrid and her sister, its tendrils lashing out like vengeful spirits.

The spell was unlike anything I'd ever cast before. It was

beautiful and terrifying, a manifestation of every emotion I'd bottled up over the years. Grief for my parents, anger at the injustice, hope for a better future—all of it poured into this single, devastating attack.

The Archmage sprinted behind the massive tree to hide, while Ingrid took the full force of the magic, her screams echoing through the forest.

"Brad, cover me!"

Sensing him step closer, his builder strength lent solidity to my casting.

"Anything for you," he affirmed, his confidence lending support.

Agatha jumped into the tree and sat on a branch over-looking us.

I glanced at my best friend. "Evie, your potions—"

She was already sending swirls of colored mist to augment the potency of the spell. "Go, Sage!" Evie exclaimed with tears glistening in her eyes.

Freya backed up out of harm's way.

With a final burst of energy, the spell struck true, and Ingrid's body convulsed in agony. Her piercing scream echoed through the darkness. As her lifeline to this world was severed, she collapsed to the ground in a crumpled heap, her once strong and imposing figure now reduced to a lifeless shell. Blood oozed from her wounds, staining the ground beneath her as her breaths came in ragged gasps.

The sight of Ingrid's broken body filled me with a mixture of satisfaction and horror. This was what I'd wanted, wasn't it?

But as I watched the life drain from her, I wondered if I'd crossed a line I could never uncross.

I'd taken a life. Justified or not, that was a burden I'd carry forever.

But my magic was still pulsing and darkening around us. Then, with a deafening crack, reality itself seemed to splinter. The magic whirl collapsed in on itself, taking trees and foliage with it. Instead of disappearing, it began to expand outward, warping everything it touched.

"What's happening?" Brad shouted over the roar of magic gone wild.

Agatha's voice was grim. "It appears Sage has torn a hole in the fabric of reality itself."

EIGHT

M y eyes widened. "Oops?" I frantically tried to rein in the spell, but it was like trying to catch smoke with my bare hands. "I can't control it!"

Agatha huffed from above us in the tree. "Well, this is a fine mess you've gotten us into, Sage. Any brilliant ideas for getting us out?"

As the chaos spread, I realized with growing horror that we might have just made things infinitely worse.

"Don't suppose anyone knows how to patch a hole in reality?" I asked weakly, watching as the world around us began to unravel.

Brad's jaw dropped. "Patch a hole in reality? Sure, let me just grab my cosmic sewing kit."

I shot him a hard look. "Not helping, Brad."

My warping magic continued to spread, twisting trees into impossible shapes and tearing chunks of plants from the ground. Leaves swirled in a whirl of disorderly energy, their edges glowing an eerie purple.

Evie stumbled forward, her hands raised. "Maybe we can contain it? Like, create a magical barrier?"

"Worth a shot." I nodded, focusing my energy. Except when I tried to form a shield, the wild magic latched onto my new spell, warping it into something unrecognizable. "Okay, scratch that idea. I still don't have full control over my seventh-level magic yet. Obviously."

Agatha yawned from her perch. "This is a fine mess, and I'm hungry."

I gritted my teeth. "If you've got any helpful suggestions, I'm all ears."

The cat spirit yawned again. "I'd rather watch the show, thanks. It's not every day you get to see reality unravel."

Brad pressed his palms to the ground, his face scrunched in concentration. The earth rumbled, and I thought he might be able to counteract my magic. The twisted magic only absorbed his attempts, creating a nightmarish landscape of impossible architecture.

"Well, that's unsettling." He stood, wiping sweat from his brow.

Freya pushed through the group. "We need to ground the energy. Sage, your power started this. It needs to end it too."

I blinked at her. "How exactly am I supposed to do that?"

She grabbed my hands. "Focus. Feel the magic flowing through you. It's part of you, not separate. You control it, not the other way around."

I closed my eyes, trying to concentrate with my crazy magic swirling around us. My magic vibrated within me, wild and untamed. I focused and sensed the familiar heat of my own power beneath the maelstrom.

"That's it," Freya encouraged. "Now, imagine roots growing from your feet, anchoring you to the earth."

I did as she said, picturing thick, gnarled roots spreading from my toes and burrowing deep into the soil. The image steadied me, and I felt a subtle shift in the magic's flow.

Brad grunted. "Uh, guys? Not to rush you, but we've got company."

My eyes snapped open to see mysterious figures emerging from the warped landscape. Must be The Archmage's magical tricks. The creatures were vaguely humanoid and ugly.

Evie let out a nervous laugh. "Like this situation wasn't fun enough already."

I struggled to maintain my concentration. "A little help here?"

Brad nodded, his hands glowing with power. "On it." He thrust his palms forward, and chunks of plants rose to form a protective wall around us.

Evie fumbled in her bag, pulling out a handful of vials. "Time to see if these work on whatever the heck those things are." She hurled the potions at the approaching creatures.

Where the potions struck, the creatures momentarily solidified into...rabbits?

"Seriously?" I shook my head.

Evie shrugged. "Hey, it worked. Sort of."

The rabbit like creatures twitched their noses before melting back into their previous forms. They pressed against Brad's barrier, their touch causing the thick underbrush and vines to bend and crack.

"Anytime now, Sage." Brad grunted, struggling to maintain the wall.

I redoubled my efforts, channeling my power through the imaginary roots. My ferocious magic resisted, pushing back against my attempts to control it. It was like trying to redirect a river with my bare hands.

"It's not working," I gasped, my frustration building.

Freya squeezed my hands tighter. "Don't fight it. Work with it. The magic is an extension of you, remember?"

I took a deep breath, rearranging my approach. Instead of trying to force the magic into submission, I opened myself to it. The power surged through me, no longer feeling foreign and chaotic, but subdued and alive.

"That's it!" Freya exclaimed. "Now, guide it back to where it belongs."

With newfound clarity, I could sense the tear in reality. It was like a gaping wound in the fabric of the world, exposed and painful. Slowly, carefully, I began to weave the magic back together, mending the tear strand by strand.

The murky creatures let out unearthly wails when their connection to our world was severed. They dissipated like mist in the morning sun, leaving behind only a faint chill in the air.

As the last of my magic settled, the forest around us gradually returned to normal. Twisted trees straightened, floating chunks of earth settled back into place, and the eerie purple glow faded from the leaves.

I sagged against Freya, exhaustion hitting me. "Did it work?"

She nodded, a smile on her face. "You did it, Sage. The tear is sealed."

Brad lowered his hands, the stone wall crumbling back into the earth. "Nice job, babe. Though maybe next time, let's stick to smaller spells? You know, ones that don't threaten to unravel the universe?"

I managed a weak chuckle. "Where's the fun in that?"

Evie plopped down beside me, her hair a tangled mess. "Well, that was super-duper intense. Anyone else feel like we just ran a magical marathon?"

Agatha meowed from her branch. "I found it quite entertaining. Though I do think you missed your calling as a magician, Evie. Those rabbit tricks were something else."

Evie rolled her eyes. "Oh, ha ha. Next time, you can be on creepy creature duty."

As the adrenaline faded, the reality of what had just happened began to sink in. My gaze drifted to Ingrid's still, lifeless form.

Brad followed my line of sight, his expression softening. "Hey, you okay?"

I swallowed hard. "I...I don't know. I killed someone, Brad. And then I nearly destroyed reality. That's a lot to process."

Freya placed a comforting hand on my shoulder. "What happened with Ingrid was self-defense, Sage. And as for the rest? Well, we all make mistakes. The important thing is that you fixed it."

"Yeah," Evie said. "Plus, now we know what not to do if we ever face off against another evil witch. No reality-warping spells."

Brad helped me to my feet. "Now we need to deal with her." He nodded towards The Archmage, who was still hiding behind the tree.

I nodded, trying to push aside my tumultuous emotions. There would be time to process everything later.

Agatha leapt down from her perch, landing gracefully beside us. "Well, as thrilling as this little adventure has been, I suggest we move quickly. Who knows what other nasty surprises the evil bitch might have in store for us?"

The Archmage peeked from around the tree, her cold facade cracking as she realized the magnitude of what had transpired. Her sister was dead.

When I locked eyes with the evil witch, I saw something I never expected vulnerability. For a brief second, she wasn't the all-powerful witch who'd terrorized Emberwick Crossing. She was just a woman who'd lost her sister. And I was the one responsible.

The moment of vulnerability vanished as quickly as it appeared, replaced by an icy glare. The Archmage's rage seemed to radiate from her like heat from a flame, distorting the air around us.

"You'll pay for killing my sister, you bitch!" The Archmage hissed through gritted teeth. She thrust her hand forward, sending a wave of dark energy that knocked the breath out of me.

"Evie, distract her!" I yelled.

"Got it, Sage!" Evie flung a concoction of her own creation.

A sparkling mist enveloped The Archmage, causing her to cough and sputter, her concentration broken.

Channeling my new seventh-level magic, I summoned a torrent of pure, blinding light that surged towards The Archmage, its power overwhelming her dark energy and enveloping her in a cocoon of radiant force.

The Archmage's screams echoed through the forest as the blinding light surrounded her, drowning out the sounds of the birds settling down for the night. The sheer power of my magic tore through her defenses, the dark energy around her disintegrating into nothingness. Her form flickered, struggling against the overwhelming force, but she was no match for the raw, unbridled power I now wielded.

"Sage, keep it up!" Brad shouted from behind me.

I focused every ounce of my willpower into maintaining the spell, feeling the power surge through my veins like liquid fire. The forest around us seemed to hold its breath, the trees and underbrush bathed in the ethereal glow of the magical battle.

The Archmage's figure finally collapsed, her energy spent and her body crumpling to the ground. The radiant light dissipated, leaving behind a stillness that felt almost surreal. I lowered my hands, breathing heavily.

Evie rushed to my side, her eyes wide with awe and concern. "Sage, are you okay?"

I nodded, still trying to catch my breath. "Yeah, I'm okay. Is it over?"

Brad stepped forward, his eyes locked on The Archmage's motionless form. "I think so. But we need to make sure."

We cautiously approached the witch, the air around her still crackling with residual energy. I could see the rise and fall of her chest, indicating she was still alive, but barely. Her eyes fluttered open, and for a moment, she looked up at me with a mixture of hatred and sorrow.

"You...you think you've won?" she whispered, her voice weak and rasping. "This isn't over. My plans? They will live on."

"No, they won't. Not while I'm protecting this town," I said firmly. "Brad, keep her contained."

I sensed the power thrumming within him. My boyfriend raised his hands, and the earth responded, stone shackles emerging to hold The Archmage's feet firm.

Nearby, Freya knelt beside an injured Evie, her hands glowing with a soft, healing light as she tended to her wounds with her healer magic.

"Agatha, with me," I said. "We need to get that locket from around her skinny neck."

Without hesitation, my feline familiar leaped into action. Her shadowy tendrils reached out, snaking around The Archmage, and reinforcing every restraint.

"Damn you all," she spat, struggling against the combined might of our magic. But it was no use, because this time we had her.

Cautiously approaching, I was ready to harness every ounce of my magic to finish what we'd started. I extended my hand, palm outstretched, and The Archmage's eyes widened as she felt her own power waning.

With a final push of my will, I stripped her of the Echoing Locket, severing her connection to its dark magic.

The evil witch slumped, defeated, her menace reduced to nothing more than a bitter memory. My friends rallied around me, their faces a mixture of relief and exhaustion.

"Is it over?" Evie asked, her voice both hopeful and weary.

"Almost," I replied, turning my attention to the locket now resting in my palm. The intricate silver piece seemed to pulse with malevolence, begging to be used, to corrupt.

"Destroy it, Sage," Freya urged. "It's the only way."

I knew she was right, but the locket's power called to me, promising strength beyond measure.

"Meow!" Agatha's voice cut through my hesitation. "Young witch, don't even think about it."

I met her yellow gaze, finding resolve within those wise old eyes. "I need your help, Agatha. Familiar and witch," I said.

My cat nodded, her form blurring when she tapped into her shadow magic.

"Goodbye, unholy darkness," I whispered, channeling all my magic into the locket. Agatha's power intertwined with mine, shadows and light spiraling toward the cursed object.

There was a thundering crack. The locket splintered into pieces, each shard evaporating before it could touch the ground. The forest seemed to breathe a sigh of relief, the oppressive presence of The Archmage's ambition dissipating like fog.

The sudden absence of the locket's power left me dizzy. For a moment, I couldn't quite believe it was over. All our struggles, all our fears, gone in an instant. But the cost... Professor Elderwood's face flashed in my mind, and my throat tightened.

"We did it!" Evie squealed, throwing her arms around me. "We really did it!"

"An era ends, and hope is reborn." Freya sighed.

Hope. Such a small word for such a big concept. I wondered if I was ready for it after everything we'd been through.

"Looks like we're finally free." Brad placed a gentle kiss on my forehead.

I leaned into Brad's touch, grateful for his steady presence. Then I smiled, looking at the faces of my friends.

They'd been through hell with me, stood by me when the world seemed to crumble. My chest swelled with affection and gratitude.

Heavy footfalls pounded through the forest, and we all turned to see what was headed our way.

My heart leapt into my throat. After everything, was there more danger?

"Whoa, look sharp everyone!" Brad called out, his voice a mix of warning and wonder.

A group clad in midnight robes emerged from the tree line, their cloaks embroidered with silver sigils that glinted in the fading light. They moved with purpose, an air of authority swirling around them like mist.

Who were these people? Friends or foes? After The Archmage's betrayal, I wasn't sure I could trust anyone new.

"Brad, who are they?" I asked, my hand reaching for a power I hoped I wouldn't need to summon again.

"Those are the Arbiters of Balance," he explained, his tone signaling respect and caution. "My dad mentioned them —new enforcers the Council put together after our last meeting."

"Regulators of magic, here to maintain order," Freya said, her voice laced with awe. "Good guys."

The Arbiters' leader stepped forward, his eyes fixed on The Archmage, who lay bound and powerless at our feet.

I held my breath, torn between hope and fear. Would they

understand what we'd done? Or would they see us as vigilantes, to be punished alongside The Archmage?

"The Archmage," he intoned, his voice as smooth and unyielding as obsidian. "For your crimes against the magical community, you will be taken into custody."

Whew. They weren't here for us. We'd done the right thing, and they recognized it. The knot in my chest began to loosen.

"Justice," Agatha hissed beside me, "served cold and late, but served nonetheless."

I glanced at my familiar, seeing the satisfaction in her feline eyes.

"Yes," the Arbiter agreed with a nod.

As they levitated The Archmage away, the relief flooding through me was tinged with a bittersweet ache. Professor Elderwood's sacrifice hung over us like a shadow. The Arbiters of Balance also took the bodies of the professor and the High Witch. They didn't question us or demand answers. They just left as quickly as they'd appeared.

"Poor Professor..." Evie's voice caught.

"We'll remember him always," I said.

"His memory will live on in every student he taught," Freya added softly, her compassionate gaze meeting mine.

Brad wrapped an arm around me. "Let's go home."

We walked back toward Emberwick Crossing, the town now safe from the threat that had loomed over it.

"Never easy, is it?" Agatha mused, brushing against my leg.

"Never," I replied. "But always worth it."

"I suppose. Now can we eat?" she asked.

Everyone laughed, and we continued onward, a patchwork family held together by love, loss, and the magic that bound us.

EPILOGUE

FIVE YEARS LATER

I cradled our newborn, a swaddle of joy with Brad's blue eyes and my wild hair. Five years had flown by like a leaf on the Emberwick Crossing wind, but here we were, standing at the precipice of a new era. Brad and I had gotten married last year among our friends and family. He had torn down both of our houses and rebuilt a new home on our combined properties, big enough for our new family.

Holy hell, who would've thought I'd be here? From battling

supernatural uprisings to magical interior design to changing diapers. Talk about a career change.

"Look at her." Brad leaned in close enough for his breath to warm my ear. "She's perfect, Sage."

"Absolutely adorable." I smiled at our daughter's gentle coos.

The door to the hospital room opened, and in swept Freya, Evie, and Agatha. I wondered if they'd brought any magical baby gifts. A self-rocking cradle would be nice.

Evie, with her black hair bouncing around her shoulders, moved toward the hospital bed. "Let me see the newest witch-ling of Emberwick!"

"Easy there." I laughed, adjusting the baby in my arms as Evie peered over my shoulder. "You'll have your turn, just after Freya and Agatha."

I mentally prepared a shield spell, just in case Evie's excite-ment caused any accidental potion spills. Turning my newborn into a bunny wouldn't be funny.

Freya edged in beside Evie, her gaze softening when she laid eyes on the little one. "Oh, she's got such a strong aura already."

Brad stayed by my side, his hand on my shoulder.

My cat hopped up onto the bed and inched closer. "Out of the way, you two." Agatha's yellow stare met mine, and for a moment, the world seemed to hold its breath. "Young witch," she said, her voice a purring growl, "you've done well."

Coming from Agatha, that was practically a standing ovation. I half expected her to break into a cat rendition of "Circle of Life."

Brad grinned. "Thanks, Agatha."

Evie stretched her hands out. "May I?"

"Of course." I carefully passed my daughter into her arms.

Evie cradled the baby with utmost gentleness. "Looks like she could turn any beast into a bunny with a single giggle."

Brad squeezed my shoulders. "Let's hope she only uses that power for good."

Evie flashed a mischievous grin. "Or for epic prank wars."

Everyone's laughter mingled with the baby's gurgles.

I gestured toward the window where Emberwick Crossing basked under the bright sun. "Hey, it's been five years, and just look at us now."

From supernatural showdowns to domestic bliss. If someone had told me this would be my life five years ago, I'd have checked them for a confusion curse.

Brad mimed raising a glass. "Here's to a brighter future."

Freya intertwined her fingers with Evie's. "Unity."

Evie gazed adoringly at the baby. "Hope."

I smiled warmly. "And new beginnings."

Brad leaned down to kiss our daughter's forehead.

As I watched my little family, both magical and mundane, I couldn't help but think *bring on the dirty diapers and midnight feedings*. After facing down dark witches and supernatural uprisings, how difficult could parenthood really be?

Parenthood, the ultimate boss battle. At least this time, I wouldn't need to invent a spell to change diapers...or would I?

Agatha's tail twitched. "New beginnings? More like new headaches. Just wait until she starts levitating her toys."

I giggled. "Thanks for the vote of confidence, Agatha."

"Always here to keep it real," she purred, stretching lazily across the foot of the bed.

Freya stepped closer, her hands glowing softly. "May I perform a blessing? It's a tradition among healers."

"Of course," Brad and I said in unison.

As Freya began her incantation, Evie bounced on her toes.

"Ooh, I have something too!" She rummaged in her bag, pulling out a small vial. "A protection potion. Totally baby safe, I promise."

Brad raised an eyebrow. "You sure about that? Remember the time you tried to cure my cold?"

Evie rolled her eyes. "That was one time! And the yak hair eventually fell out."

Brad frowned, running a hand through his hair as if checking it was still there.

I stifled a laugh. "It's okay, Evie. We trust you."

Ah, the joys of magical mishaps. At least yak hair was a step up from last year when Evie accidentally turned my cat into a throw pillow. Poor Agatha still refused to sit on the couch.

Freya finished her blessing, a soft golden glow surrounding the baby. "There. A little extra magical fortification."

Brad sighed. "I think we should probably start baby-proofing the house. Magical and otherwise."

I groaned. "Don't remind me. We'll need anti-levitation wards on all the furniture."

"And flame-retardant everything," Evie said helpfully.

Agatha snorted. "Don't forget soundproofing spells. Trust me, you'll need them."

Brad laughed. "Always the optimist, aren't you, Agatha?"

"Realist," she corrected, licking a paw. "Someone has to be."

Freya smiled softly. "Have you decided on a name yet?"

Brad and I exchanged glances.

"We're still debating," I admitted.

Naming a magical baby felt like trying to pick the perfect spell ingredient—one wrong choice and you might end up with an exploding cauldron instead of a love potion.

"How about Morgana?" Evie suggested. "Or Circe? Ooh, or Hecate!"

"We're not naming our daughter after ancient witches," I said firmly.

Brad nodded. "We want something more normal and modern."

"What about Aurora?" Freya suggested. "It's magical without being too on-the-nose."

I considered it. "That's not bad, actually."

"Aurora Adams," Brad tested it out. "I like it."

Evie beamed. "It's perfect! Little Aurora, the newest witch of Emberwick."

The baby—Aurora—let out a tiny sneeze. A shower of sparks erupted from her nose, briefly illuminating the room.

We all froze for a moment, then burst into laughter.

"Well," I said, "I guess that settles it. Aurora, it is."

Brad leaned in to kiss my cheek. "Our little sparkler."

Agatha's tail swished. "Great. Now we'll have to fireproof the nursery too."

Evie clapped. "Oh! I can brew a flame-resistant paint! It'll be my gift to you."

Freya shook her head, smiling. "I'll bring some healing balm, just in case."

I laughed. "What would we do without you all?"

Undoubtedly have a lot fewer magical mishaps and a lot more boring dinner parties.

"Probably have a much quieter life," Agatha mumbled.

Brad grinned. "But where's the fun in that?"

Aurora gurgled, a tiny spark dancing on her fingertip. Parenthood might just be the wildest adventure yet.

I smiled down at her. "Welcome to the family, little one. It's a bit crazy, but you'll get used to it."

"Or go mad trying." Agatha made herself comfortable beside me on the bed.

Evie waved her hands in the air. "Oh! We should have a naming ceremony! I'll bring the fireworks!"

Brad and I exchanged alarmed glances.

I gazed at Aurora, marveling at how this tiny human had already wrapped us all around her little finger. She was going to grow up surrounded by love, laughter and maybe a few magical mishaps.

Poor kid didn't stand a chance of having a normal childhood. But then again, normal was overrated.

"Maybe we'll skip the fireworks," I said hastily.

"Aww," Evie pouted. "Fine. Sparklers?"

"How about nice, safe, non-flammable balloons?" Freya suggested diplomatically.

Thankfully, Freya was the voice of reason. I made a mental note to buy her a "World's Most Sensible Witch" mug for her birthday. Maybe with a built-in spell to keep her tea at the perfect temperature.

Evie brightened. "Ooh, I can enchant them to change colors!"

I shook my head, laughing. "You're all impossible." And yes, but in the best way possible.

Brad squeezed my hand. "But you love us anyway."

His touch sent a surge of warmth through me, with a side of heart-fluttering, and the strong urge to create fireworks of our own.

"Yup, I sure do," I admitted.

Aurora yawned, her tiny fist curling around Brad's finger.

My heart melted faster than a snowman in July. How could something so small make me feel so big? Like I could conquer the world, or at least master the art of diaper changing without accidentally summoning a plague of locusts.

Freya smiled softly. "I think Aurora's ready for a nap."

"Join the club," Agatha murmured, already half asleep at the foot of the bed.

I wondered if her previous life as a witch had involved professional napping. If so, she was certainly keeping her skills sharp.

As my friends gathered around, cooing over Aurora's sleeping form, I felt a sense of peace wash over me. This was my family – quirky, magical, and absolutely perfect.

THE END

www.ingramcontent.com/pod-product-compliance
Ingram Content Group UK Ltd.
Pitfield, Milton Keynes, MK11 3LW, UK
UKHW020159100125
453025UK00024B/6

9 781763 716629